FANTAGRAPHICS BOOKS

Edited by Eric Reynolds . Designed by Jacob Covey
Production by Paul Baresh . Published by Gary Groth
Promoted by Jacq Cohen

Fantagraphics Books Inc.
7563 Lake City Way NE, Seattle, WA 98115
www.fantagraphics.com

Subscribe to NOW*: Visit www.fantagraphics.com/now for details.*

ISBN 978-1-68396-169-7
Library of Congress Control Number: 2018949686

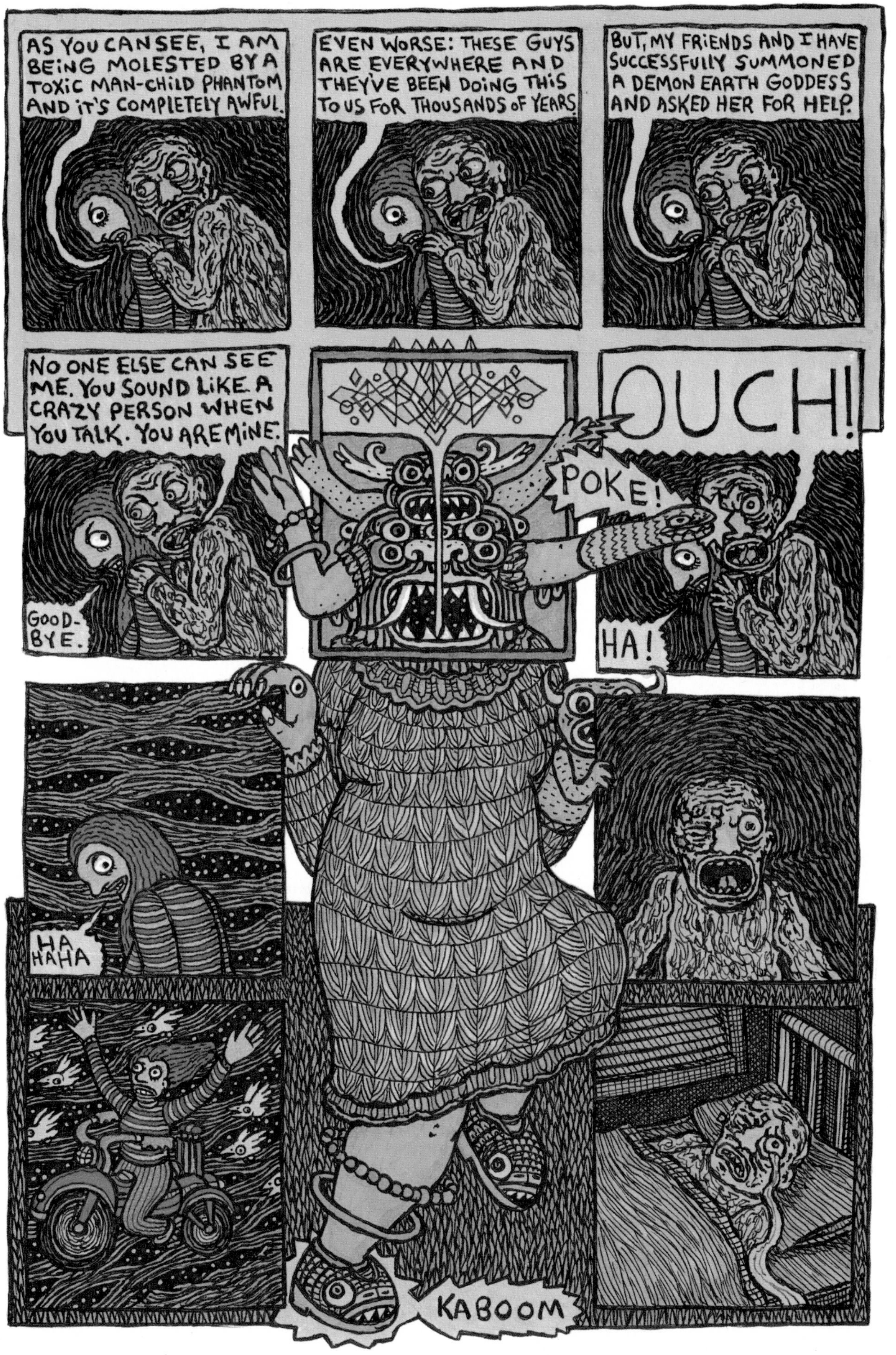
AS YOU CAN SEE, I AM BEING MOLESTED BY A TOXIC MAN-CHILD PHANTOM AND IT'S COMPLETELY AWFUL.
EVEN WORSE: THESE GUYS ARE EVERYWHERE AND THEY'VE BEEN DOING THIS TO US FOR THOUSANDS OF YEARS.
BUT, MY FRIENDS AND I HAVE SUCCESSFULLY SUMMONED A DEMON EARTH GODDESS AND ASKED HER FOR HELP.
NO ONE ELSE CAN SEE ME. YOU SOUND LIKE A CRAZY PERSON WHEN YOU TALK. YOU ARE MINE.
GOOD-BYE.
OUCH!
POKE!
HA!
HA HAHA
KABOOM

Now What?

- Since our last issue, *NOW* has not only received its first Eisner Award nomination but also lost its first Eisner Award. Though content with being nominated, we regret not winning if only for the lost opportunity to publicly thank those who have been so central to *NOW*'s existence: Gary Groth, Jacob Covey, Jacq Cohen, RJ Casey, Emily Silva, Kristy Valenti, Alessandra Sternfeld, Anna Pederson, Rhea Patton, and, of course, all of the contributors thus far.

- Ana Galvañ's story this issue was translated from Spanish by Jamie Richards.

- We want to hear from you. Send us your letters of comment, and your submissions, via fbicomix@fantagraphics.com and write "NOW" in the subject header. Just remember, please, that patience is a virtue.

Further Reading:

STÉPHANE BLANQUET: blanquet.com
DRT: kvoriouscomics.bigcartel.com
DW: instagram.com/kidclampdown
ANA GALVAÑ: anagalvan.com
MAGGIE UMBER: maggieumber.com
EROYN FRANKLIN: eroynfranklin.com
ROMAN MURADOV: bluebed.net
JOSE QUINTANAR: josejajaja.com
WALT HOLCOMBE: twitter.com/waltholcombe
WALKER TATE: varietypak.net
KEREN KATZ: kerenkatz.carbonmade.com
DARIN SHULER: darinshuler.com
JESSE REKLAW: instagram.com/jessejamesreklaw/
NICK THORBURN: howiedoo.tumblr.com

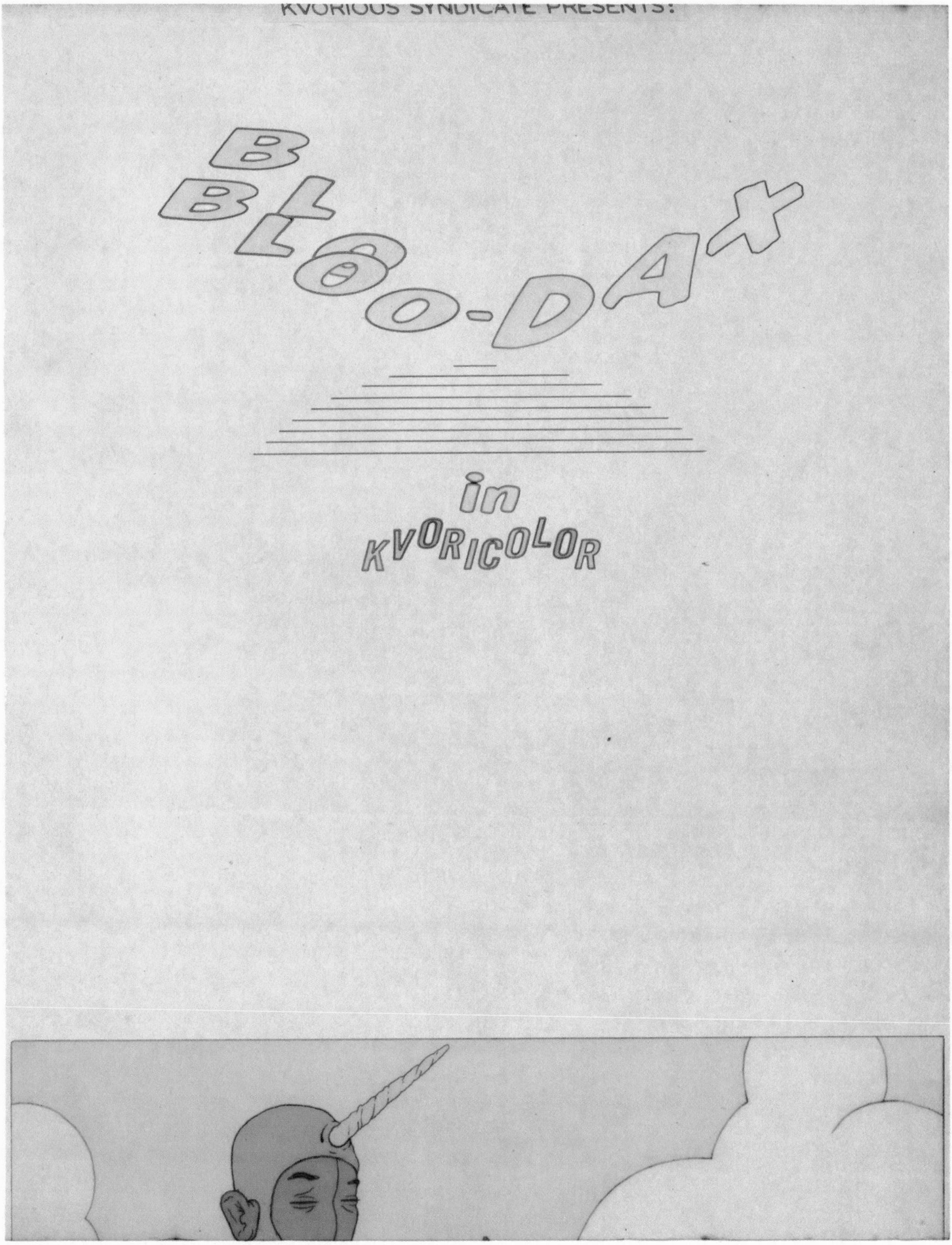

KVORIOUS SYNDICATE PRESENTS:
BLOO-DAX
in
KVORICOLOR

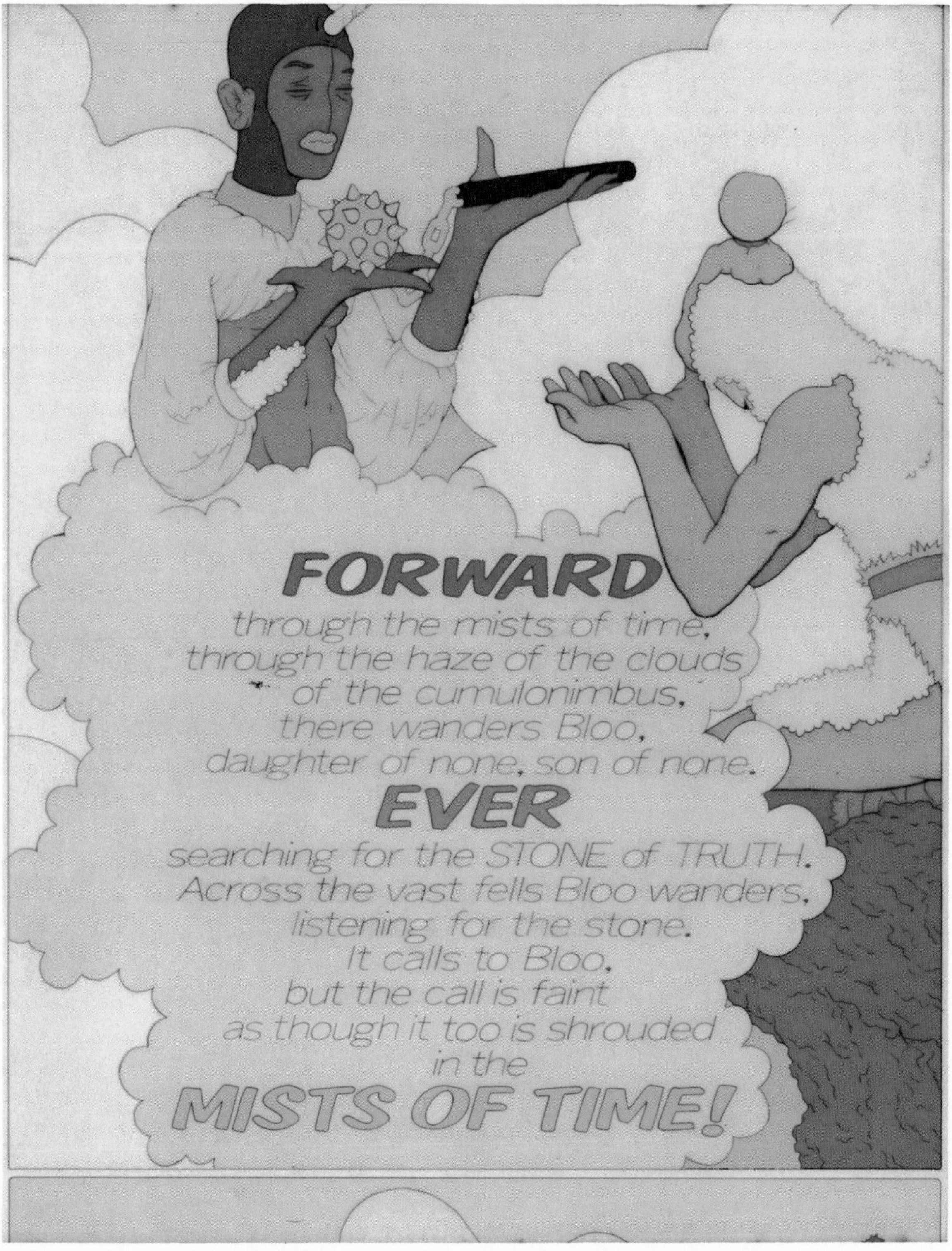
FORWARD
through the mists of time,
through the haze of the clouds
of the cumulonimbus,
there wanders Bloo,
daughter of none, son of none.
EVER
searching for the STONE of TRUTH.
Across the vast fells Bloo wanders,
listening for the stone.
It calls to Bloo,
but the call is faint
as though it too is shrouded
in the
MISTS OF TIME!

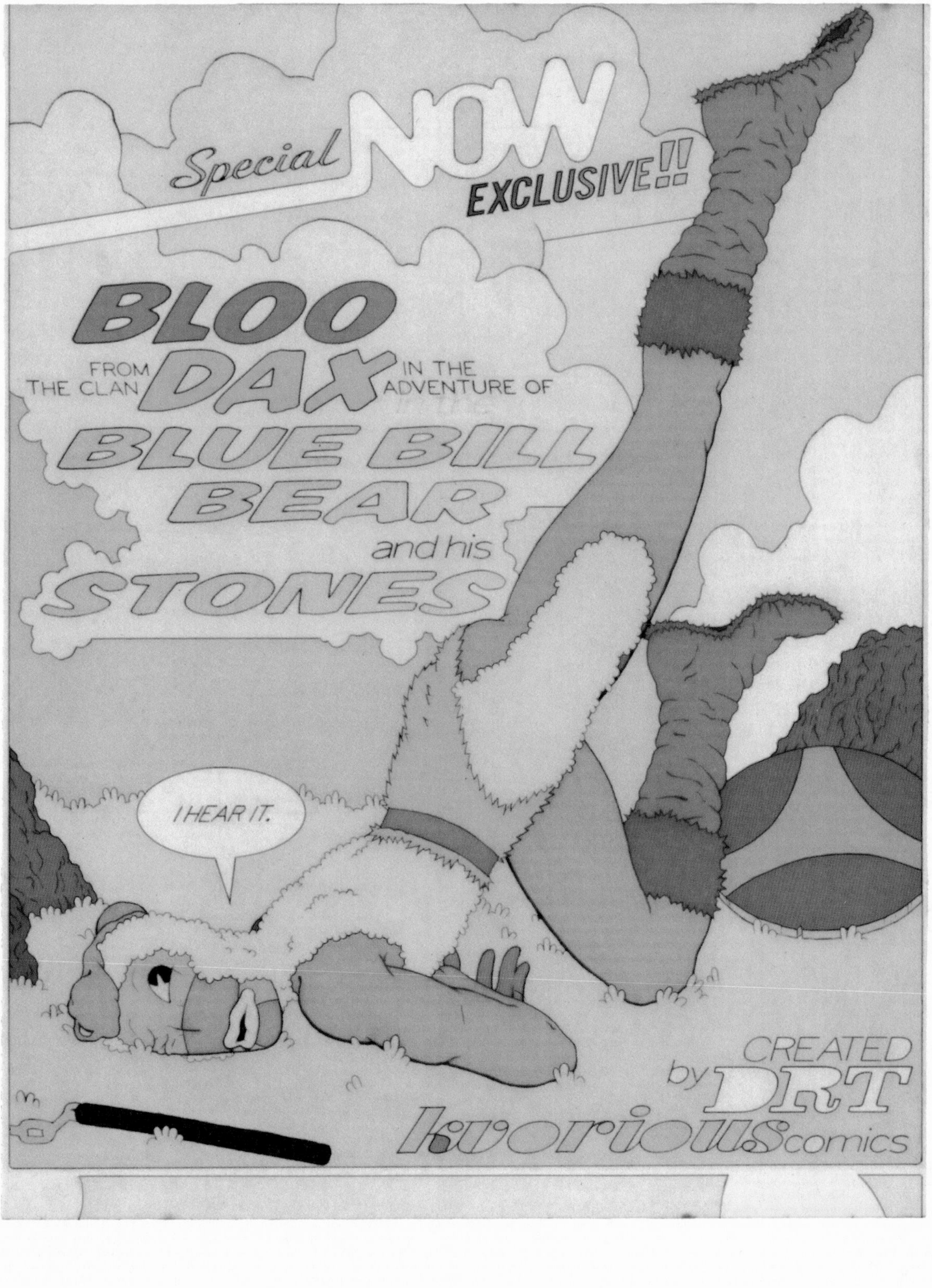
Special NOW EXCLUSIVE!!
BLOO
FROM THE CLAN
DAX
IN THE ADVENTURE OF
BLUE BILL BEAR
and his
STONES
I HEAR IT.
CREATED by DRT
kvorious comics

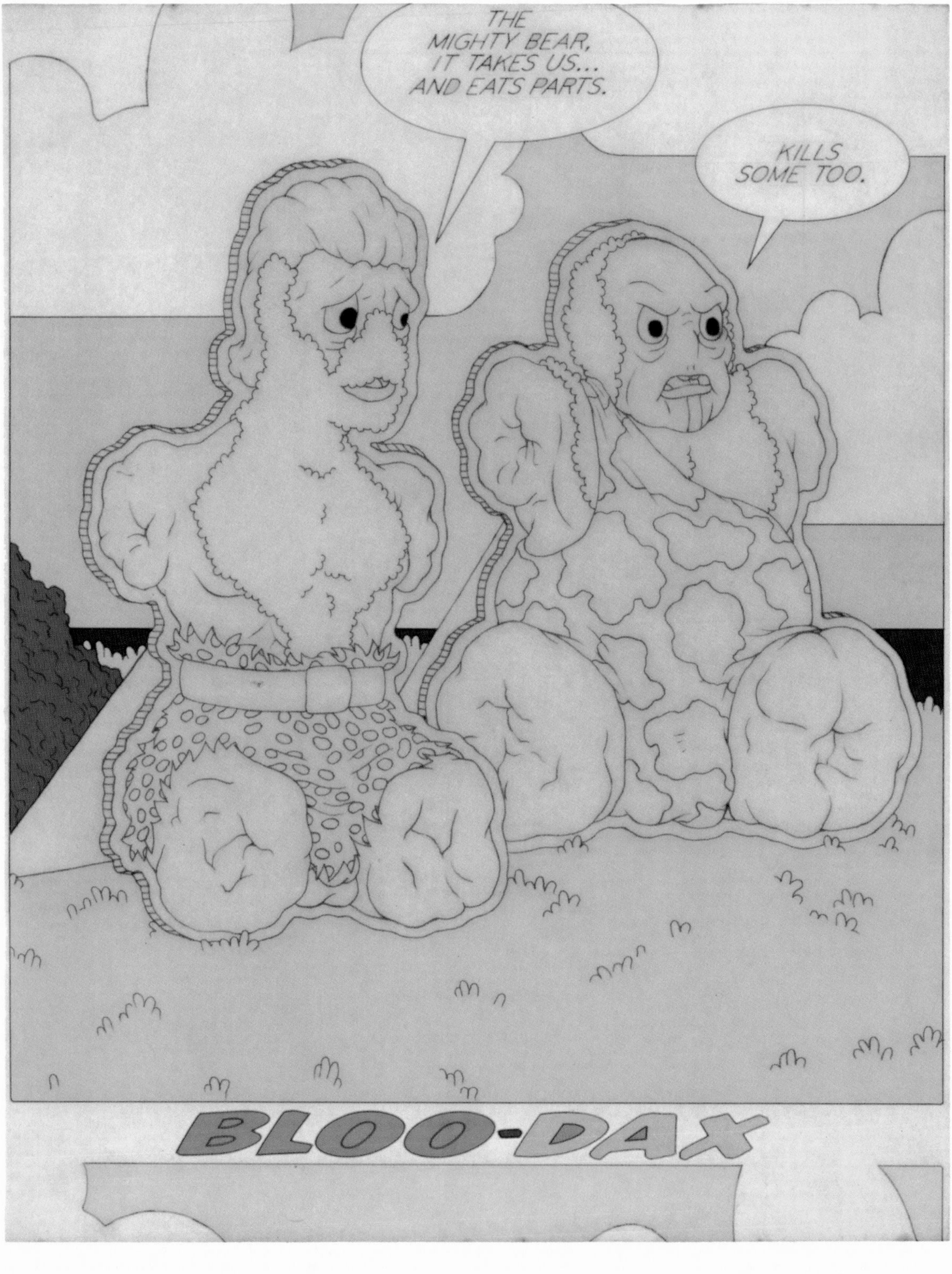
THE MIGHTY BEAR, IT TAKES US... AND EATS PARTS.
KILLS SOME TOO.
BLOO-DAX

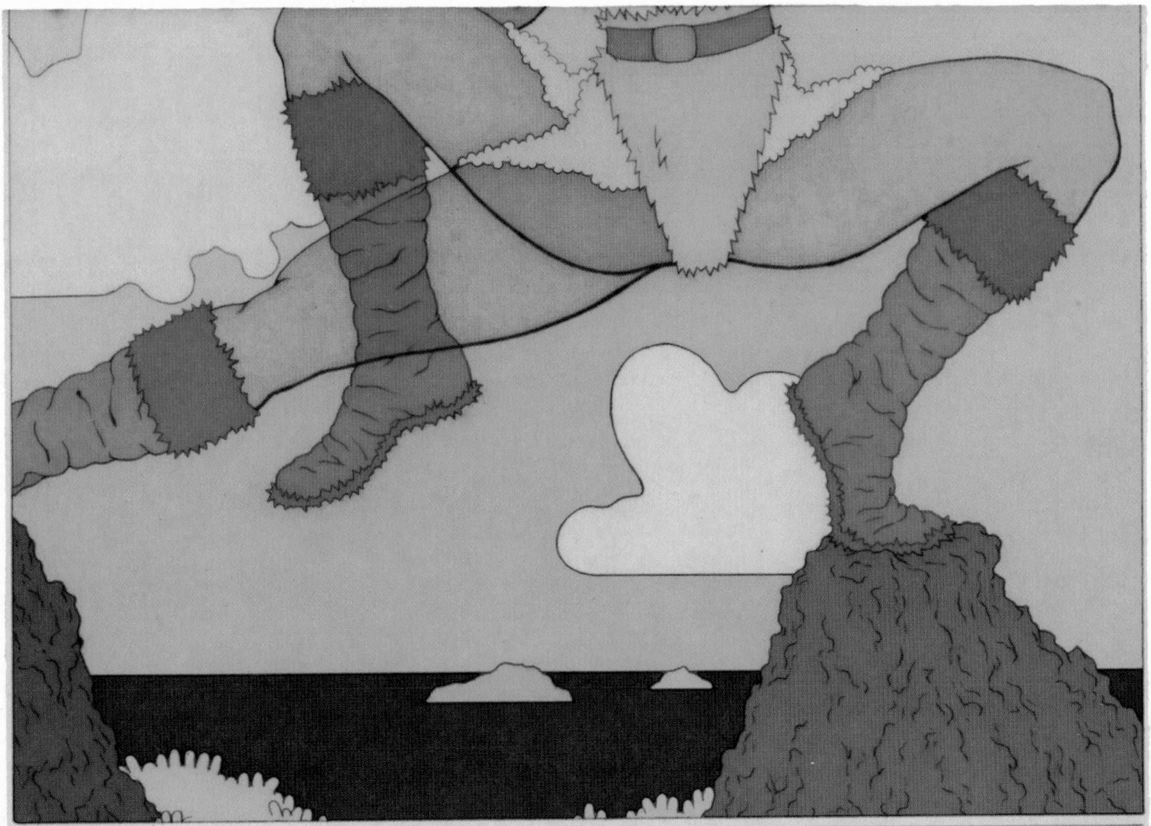

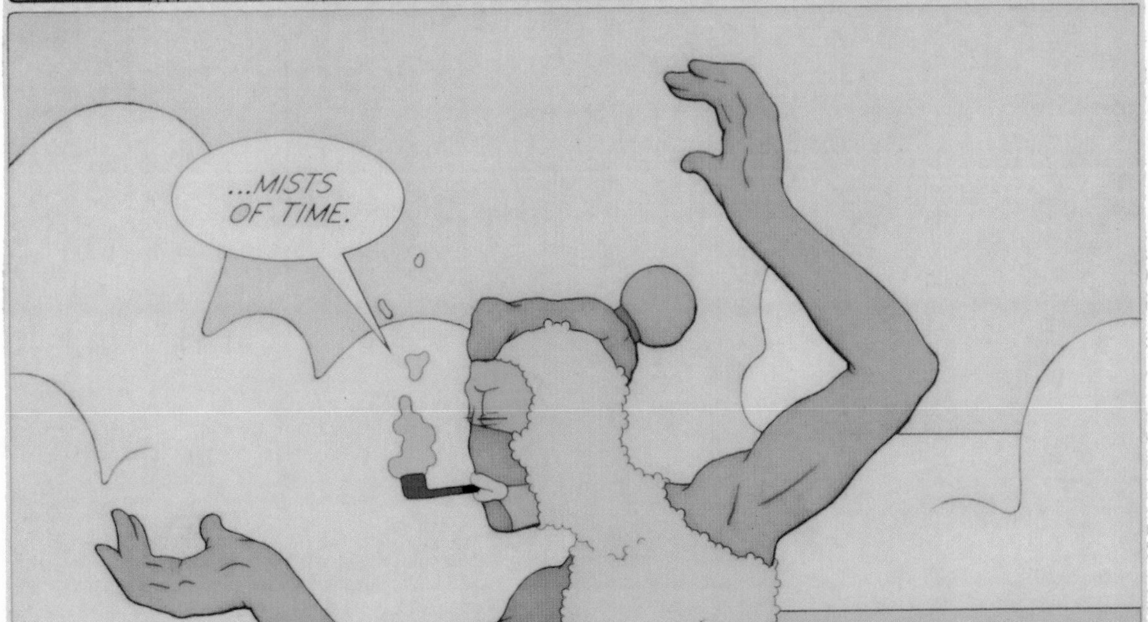
...MISTS OF TIME.

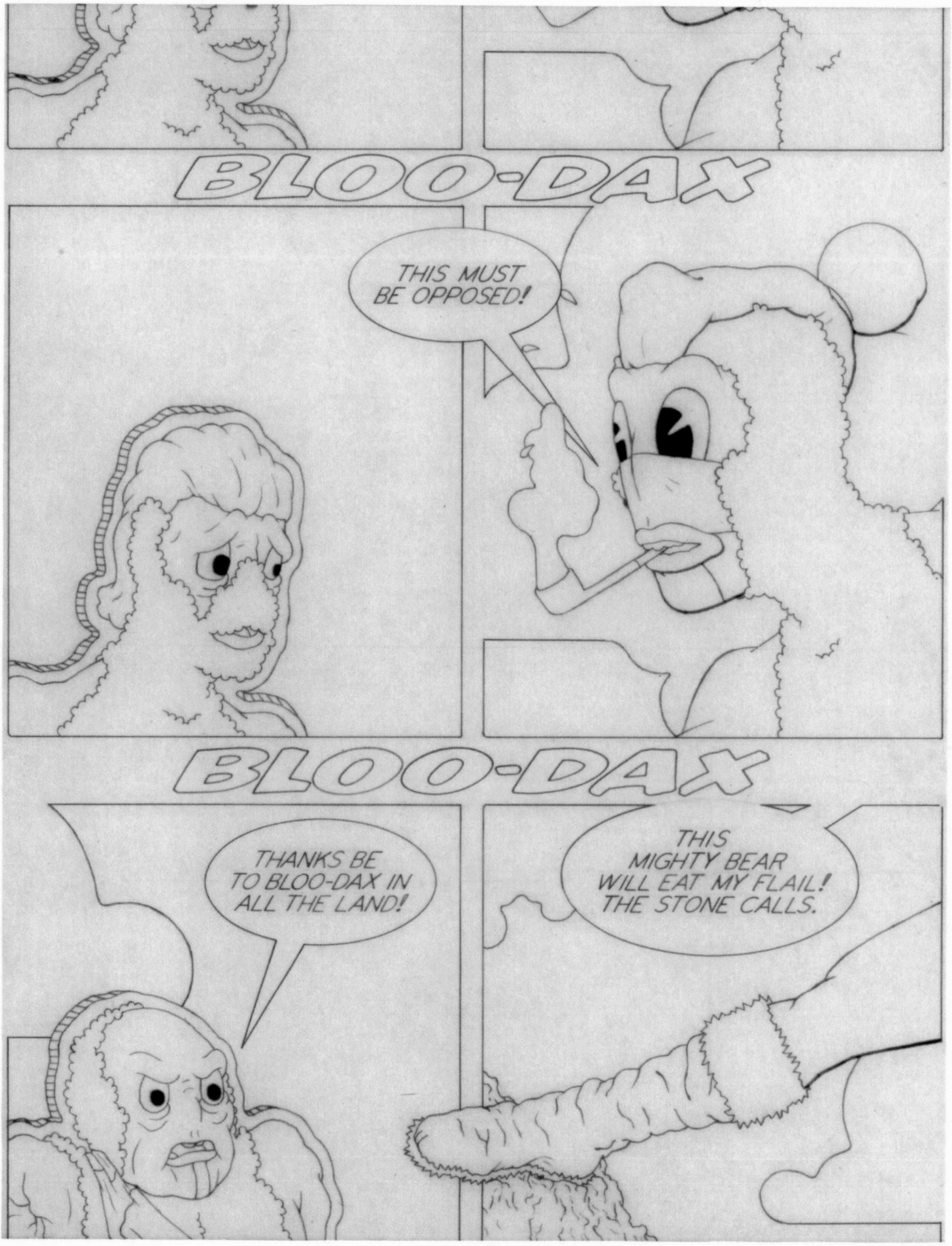
BLOO-DAX
THIS MUST BE OPPOSED!
BLOO-DAX
THANKS BE TO BLOO-DAX IN ALL THE LAND!
THIS MIGHTY BEAR WILL EAT MY FLAIL! THE STONE CALLS.

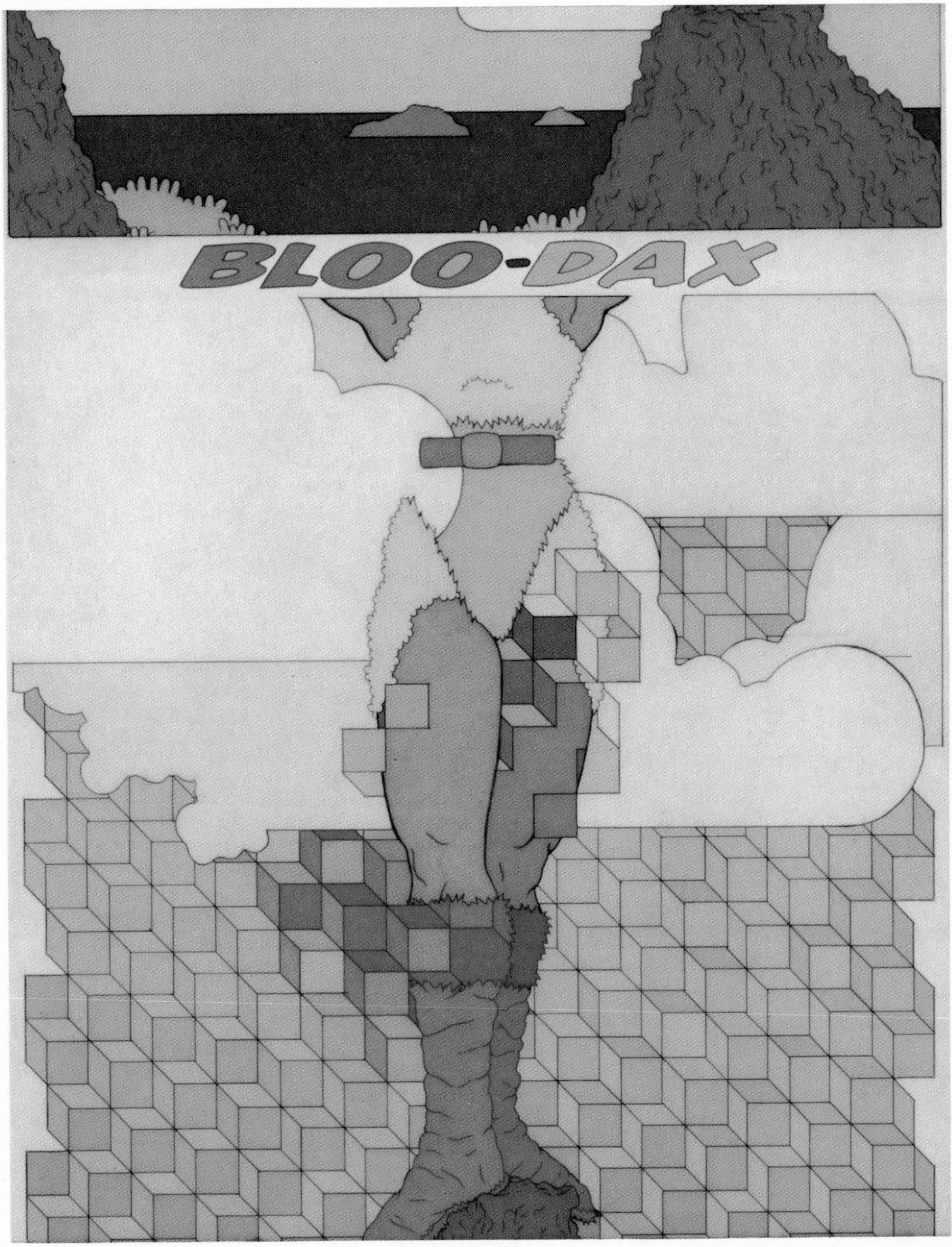
BLOO-DAX

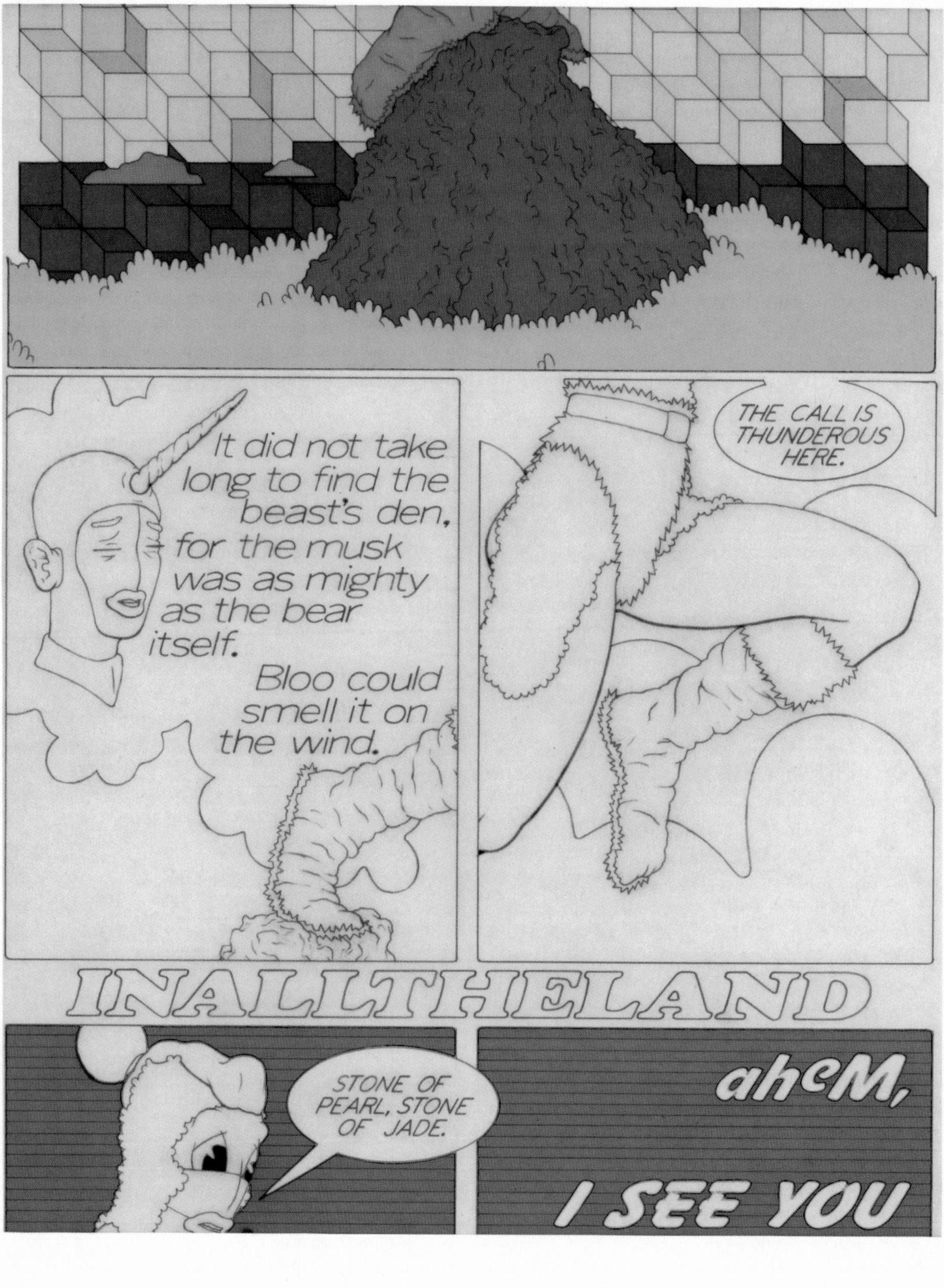
It did not take long to find the beast's den, for the musk was as mighty as the bear itself.
Bloo could smell it on the wind.
THE CALL IS THUNDEROUS HERE.
INALLTHELAND
STONE OF PEARL, STONE OF JADE.
aheM,
I SEE YOU

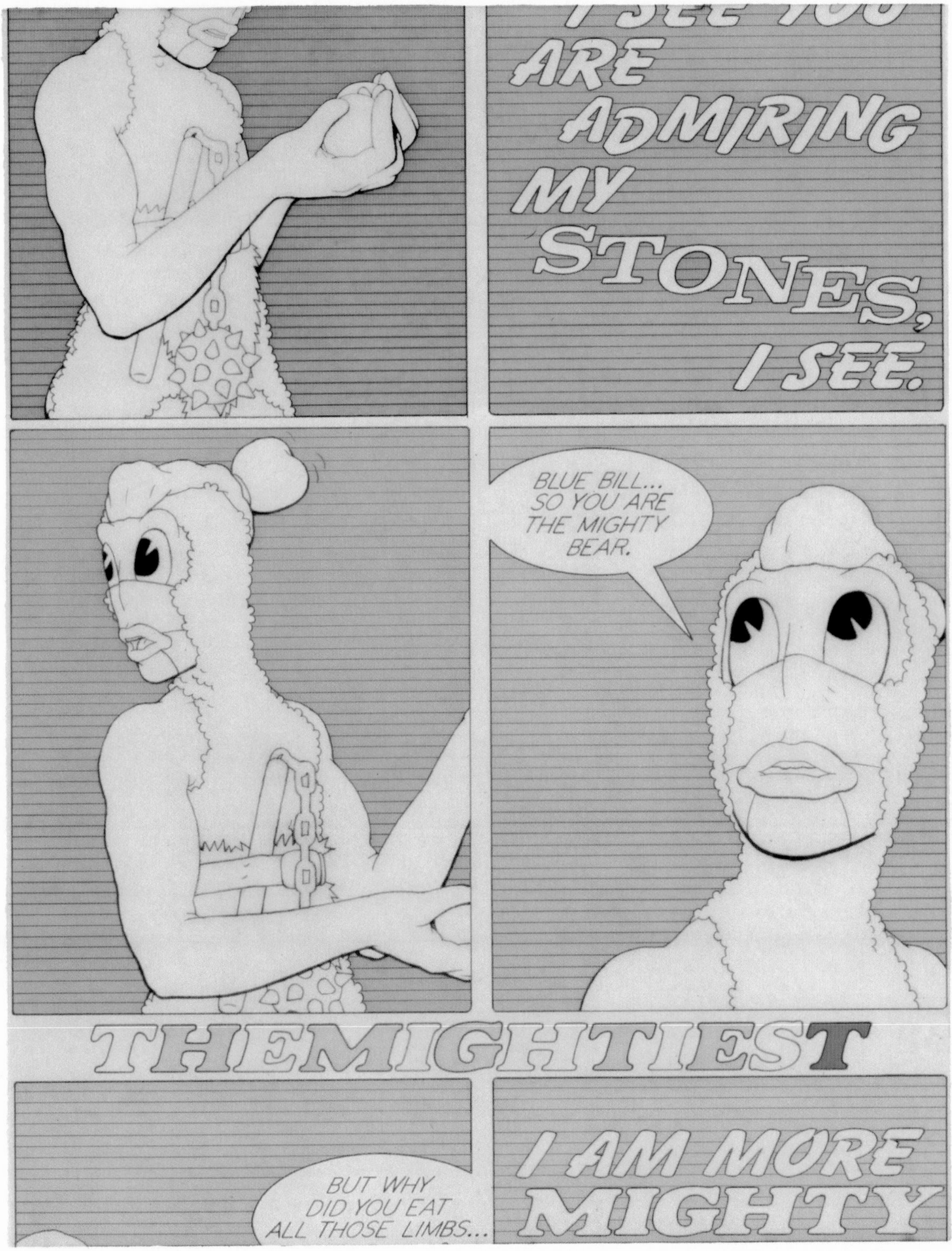
ARE ADMIRING MY STONES, I SEE.
BLUE BILL... SO YOU ARE THE MIGHTY BEAR.
THEMIGHTIEST
BUT WHY DID YOU EAT ALL THOSE LIMBS...
I AM MORE MIGHTY

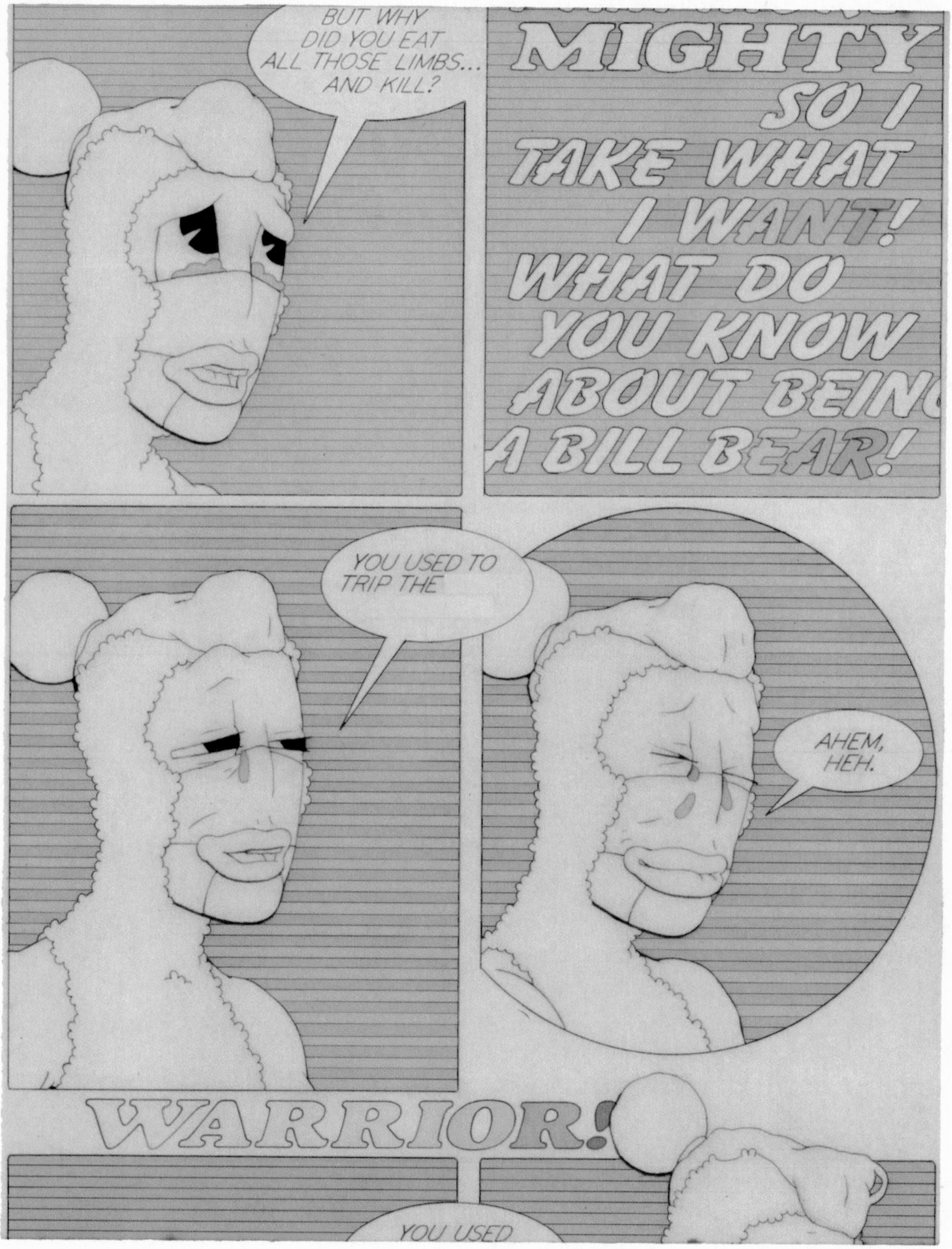
BUT WHY DID YOU EAT ALL THOSE LIMBS... AND KILL?
MIGHTY
SO I TAKE WHAT I WANT! WHAT DO YOU KNOW ABOUT BEING A BILL BEAR!
YOU USED TO TRIP THE
AHEM, HEH.
WARRIOR!
YOU USED

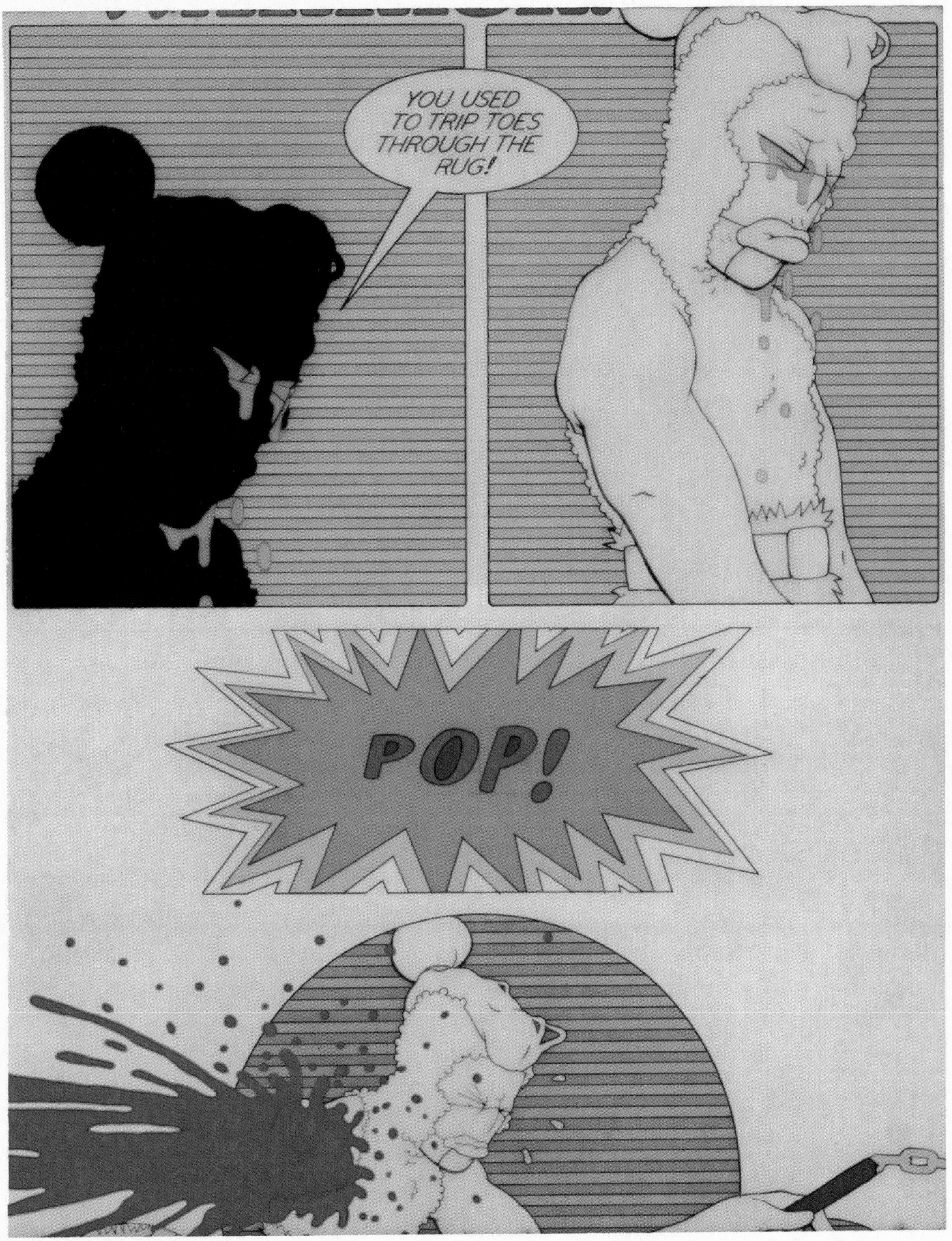
YOU USED TO TRIP TOES THROUGH THE RUG!
POP!

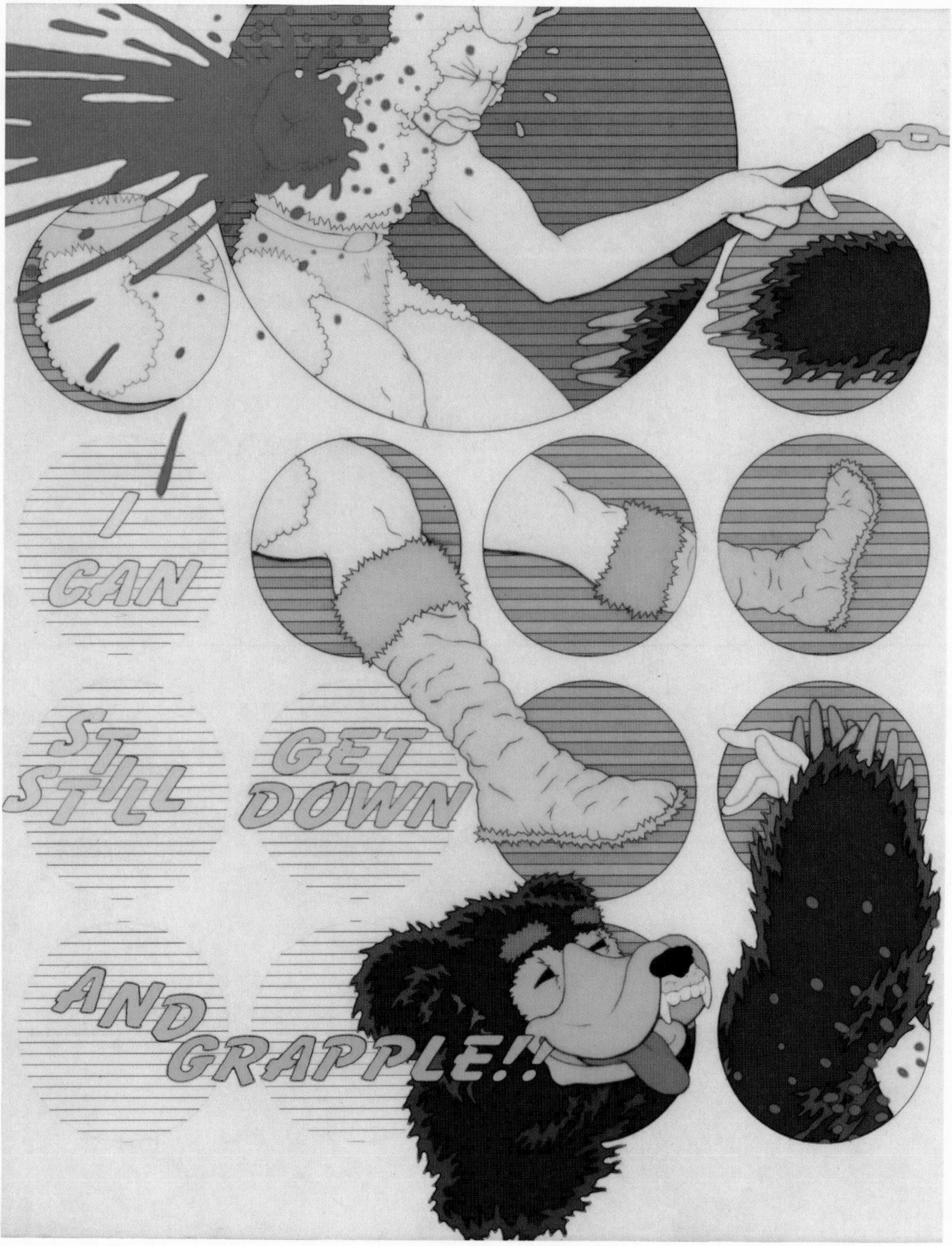
I CAN
STILL GET DOWN
AND GRAPPLE!!

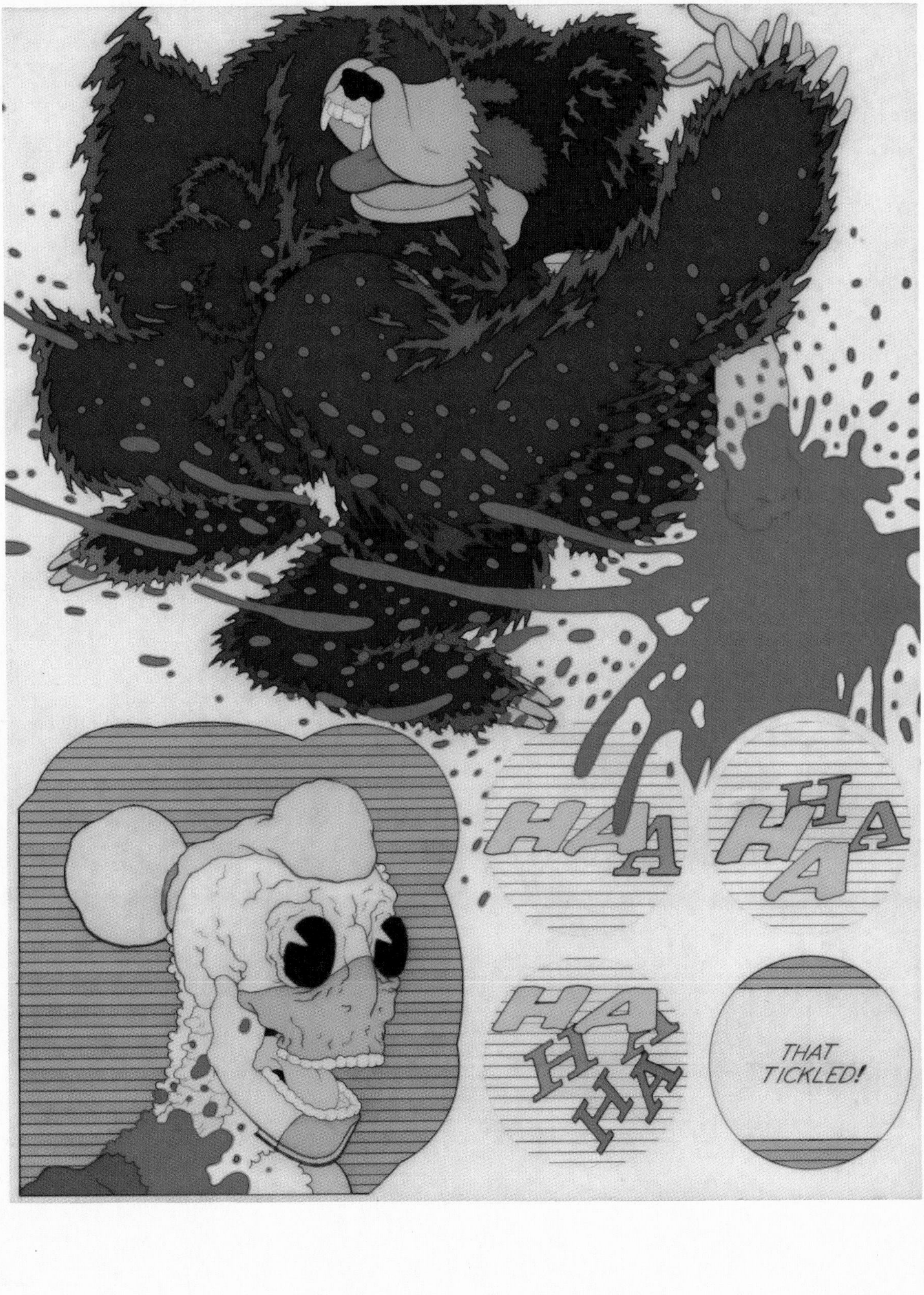
HA
HA
HA
HA
HA
HA
HA
HA
THAT TICKLED!

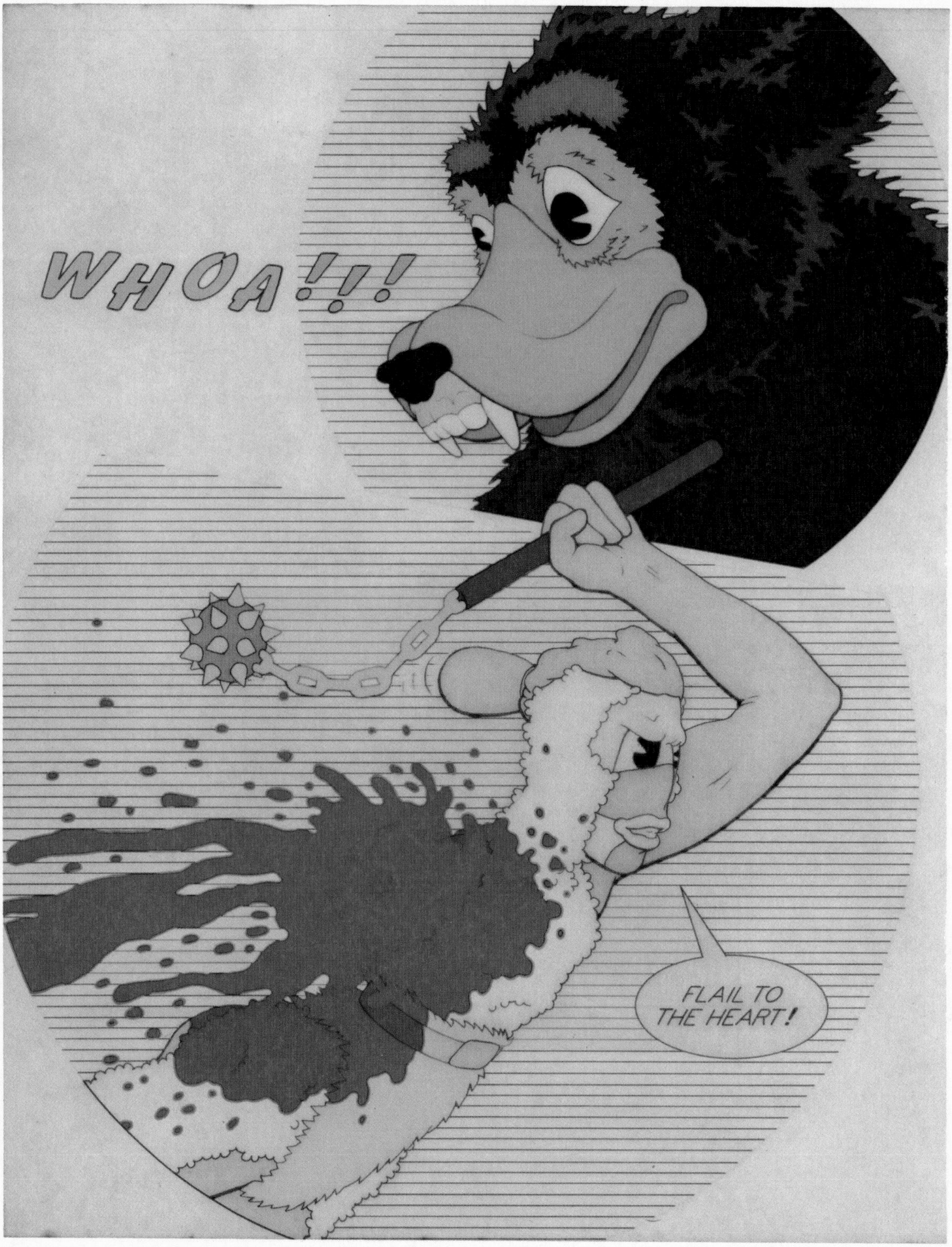
WHOA!!!
FLAIL TO THE HEART!

And so
the domination
of the mighty

BLUE BILL BEAR

ceased.
Bloo emerged from the vile den
with her booty of stones
to find it was dusky twilight.
Shaking the heart blood off of the

FLAIL OF FURY

with a mighty joggle.
Bloo contemplated the raindrops
that fell sporadically.
With the shower
there arose an impenetrable mist
masking the foul deeds
made right in this place,
and its toll on the warrior.
The cumulonimbus was erasing it
almost as though it had never been.

ALAS,

the villagers could not now be saved
from getting pulped by the
great torrent of the thunderhead.

AGAIN,

Bloo was moving through the

MISTS OF TIME,

listening.

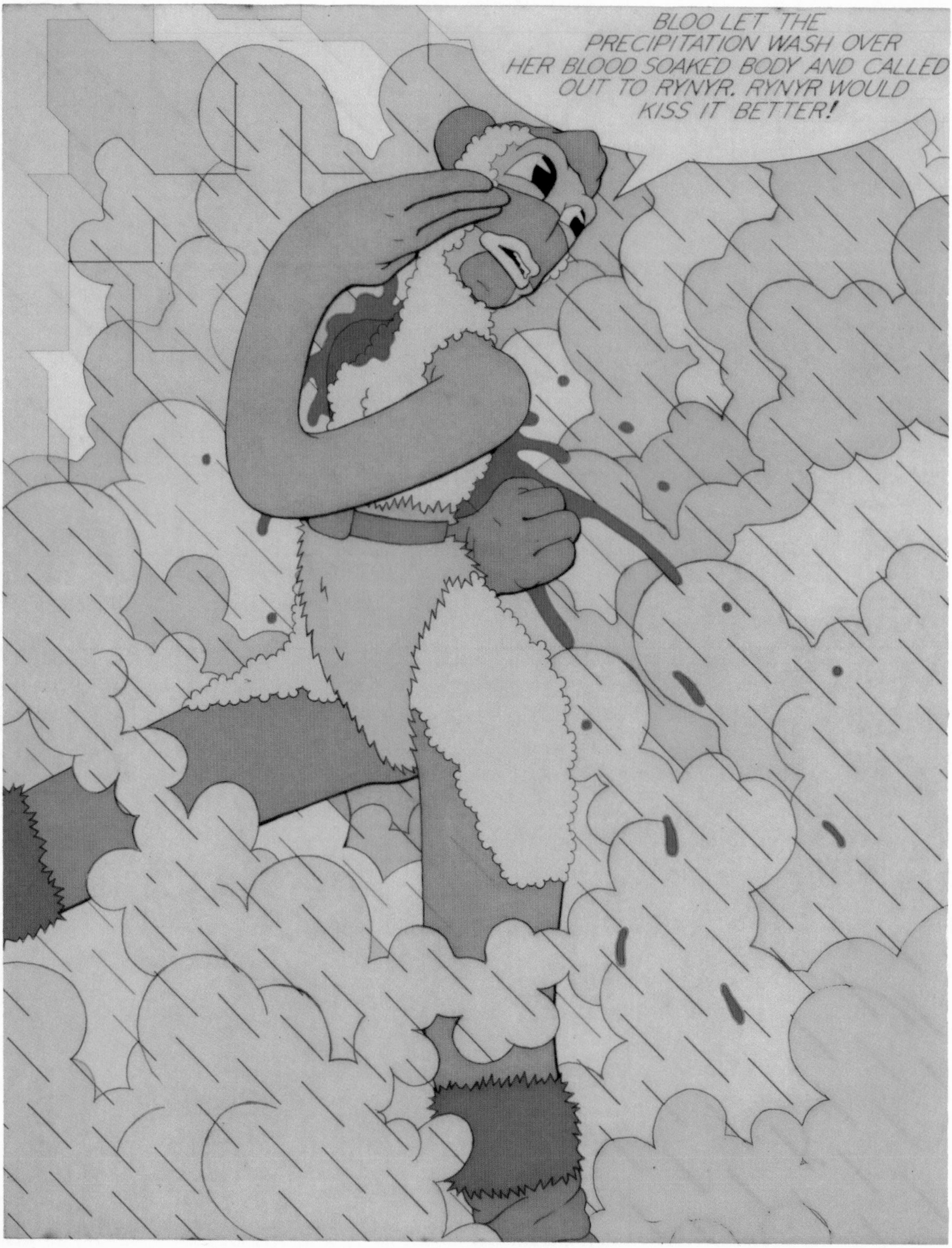
BLOO LET THE PRECIPITATION WASH OVER HER BLOOD SOAKED BODY AND CALLED OUT TO RYNYR. RYNYR WOULD KISS IT BETTER!

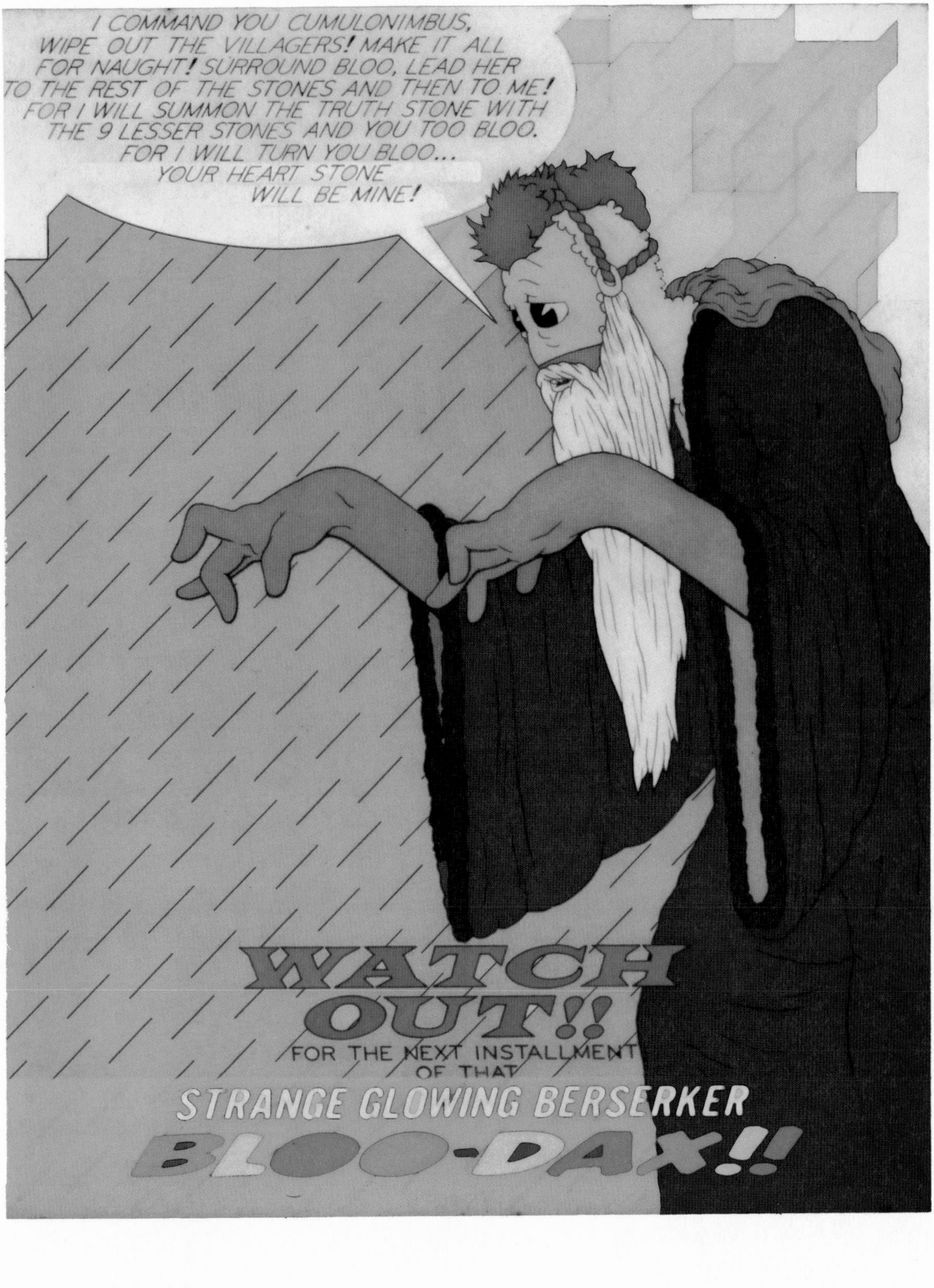
I COMMAND YOU CUMULONIMBUS, WIPE OUT THE VILLAGERS! MAKE IT ALL FOR NAUGHT! SURROUND BLOO, LEAD HER TO THE REST OF THE STONES AND THEN TO ME! FOR I WILL SUMMON THE TRUTH STONE WITH THE 9 LESSER STONES AND YOU TOO BLOO. FOR I WILL TURN YOU BLOO... YOUR HEART STONE WILL BE MINE!
WATCH OUT!!
FOR THE NEXT INSTALLMENT OF THAT
STRANGE GLOWING BERSERKER
BLOO-DAX!!

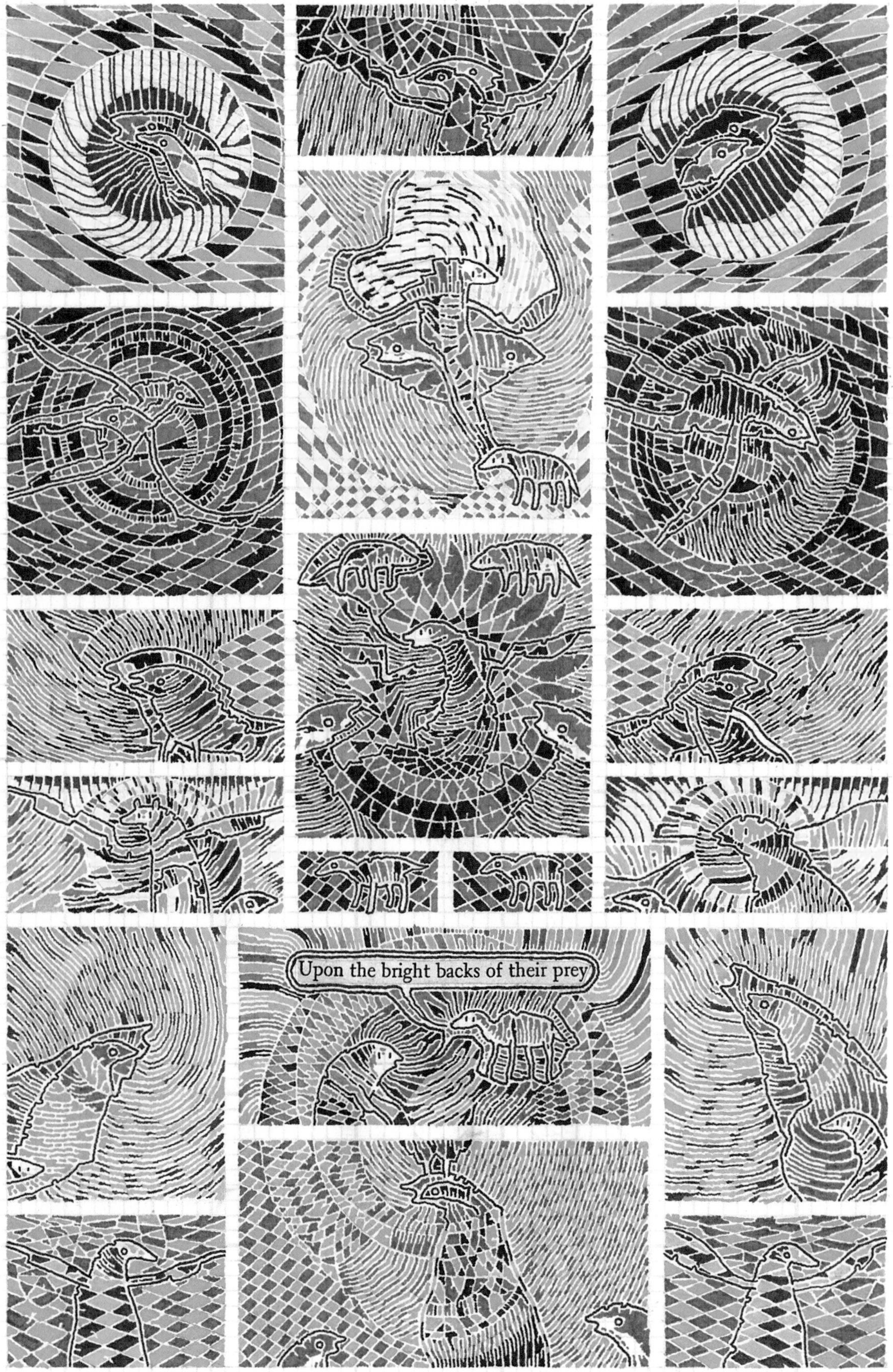
Upon the bright backs of their prey

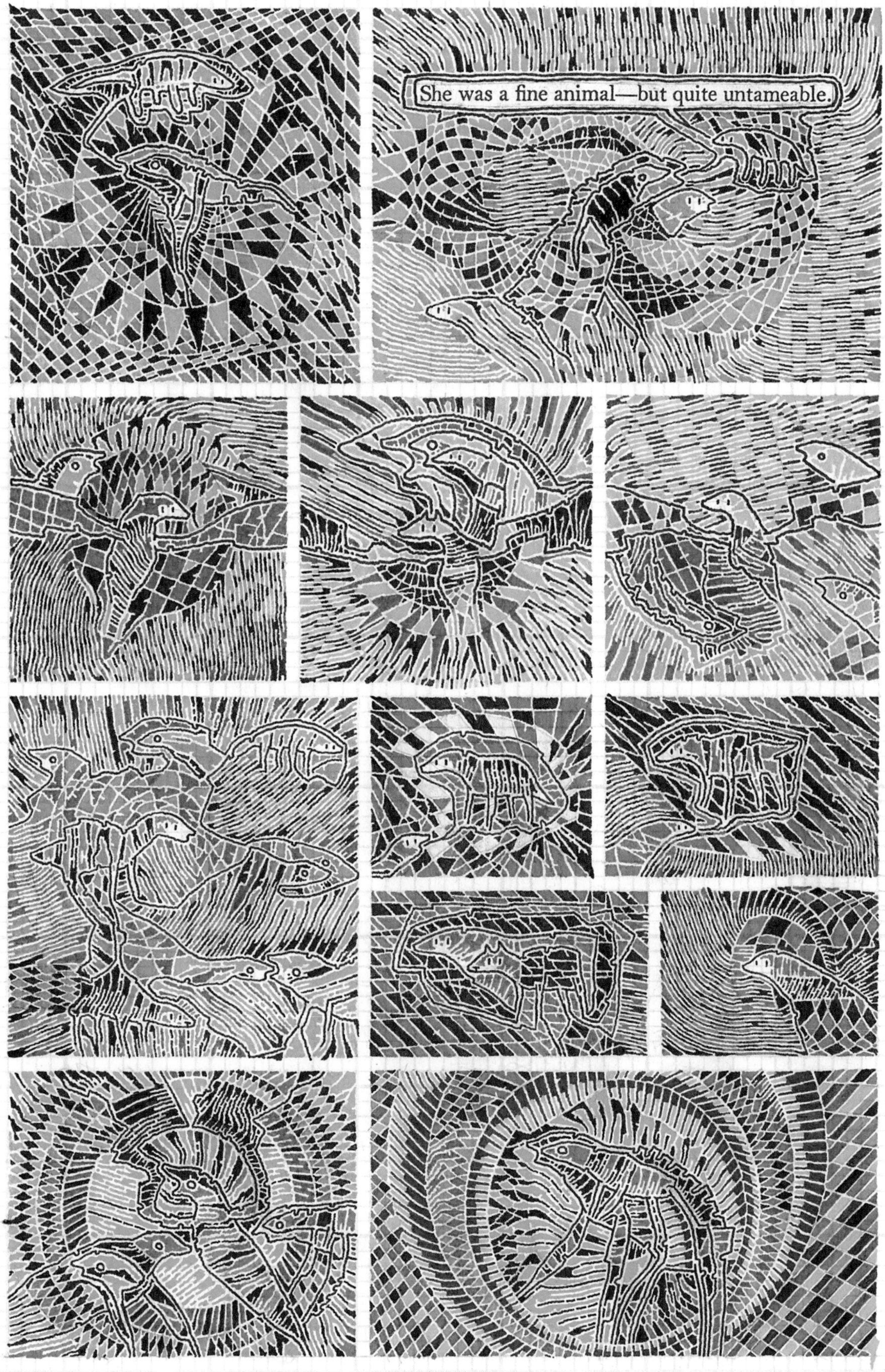
She was a fine animal—but quite untameable.

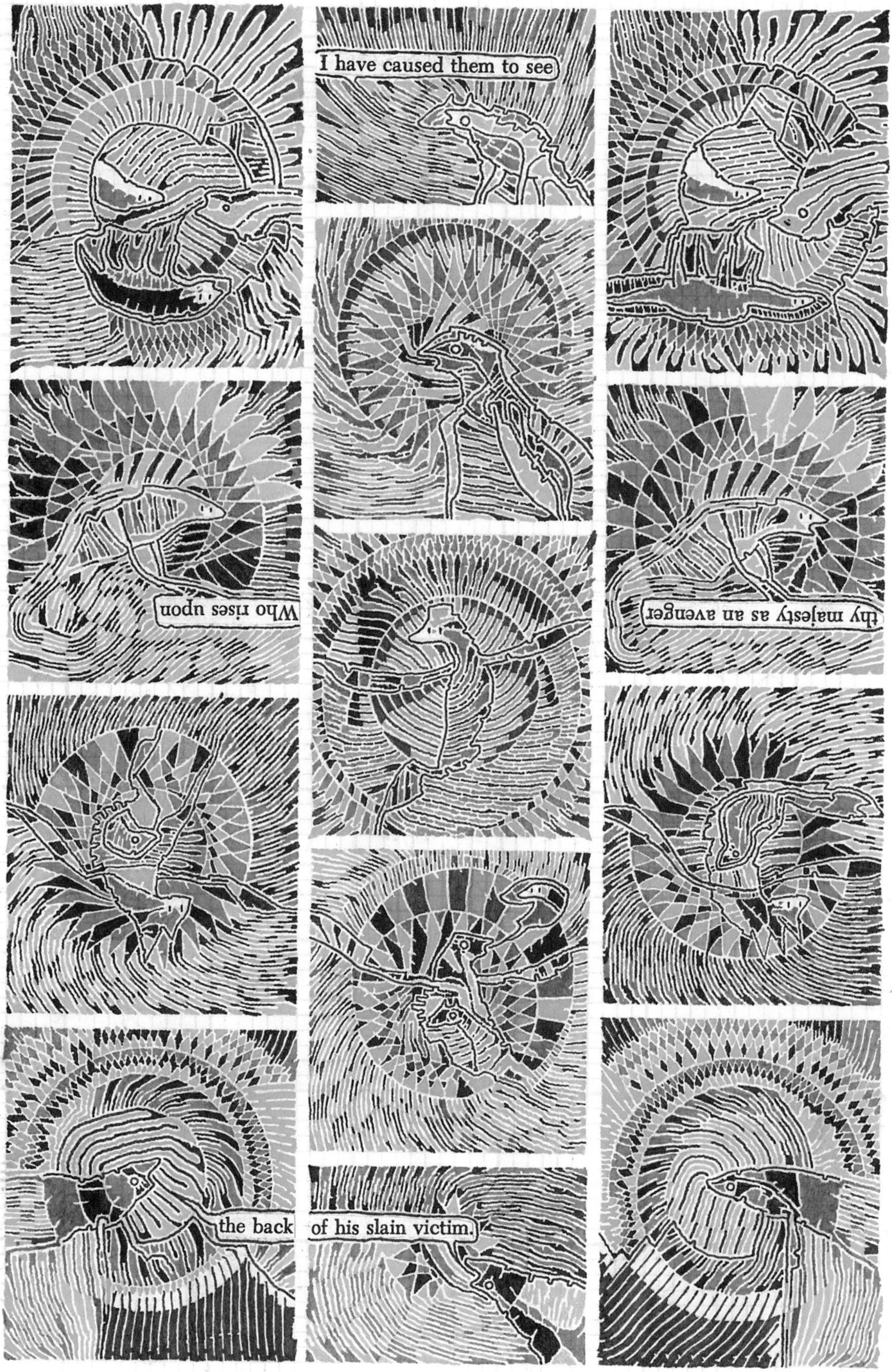
I have caused them to see
thy majesty as an avenger
Who rises upon
the back
of his slain victim.

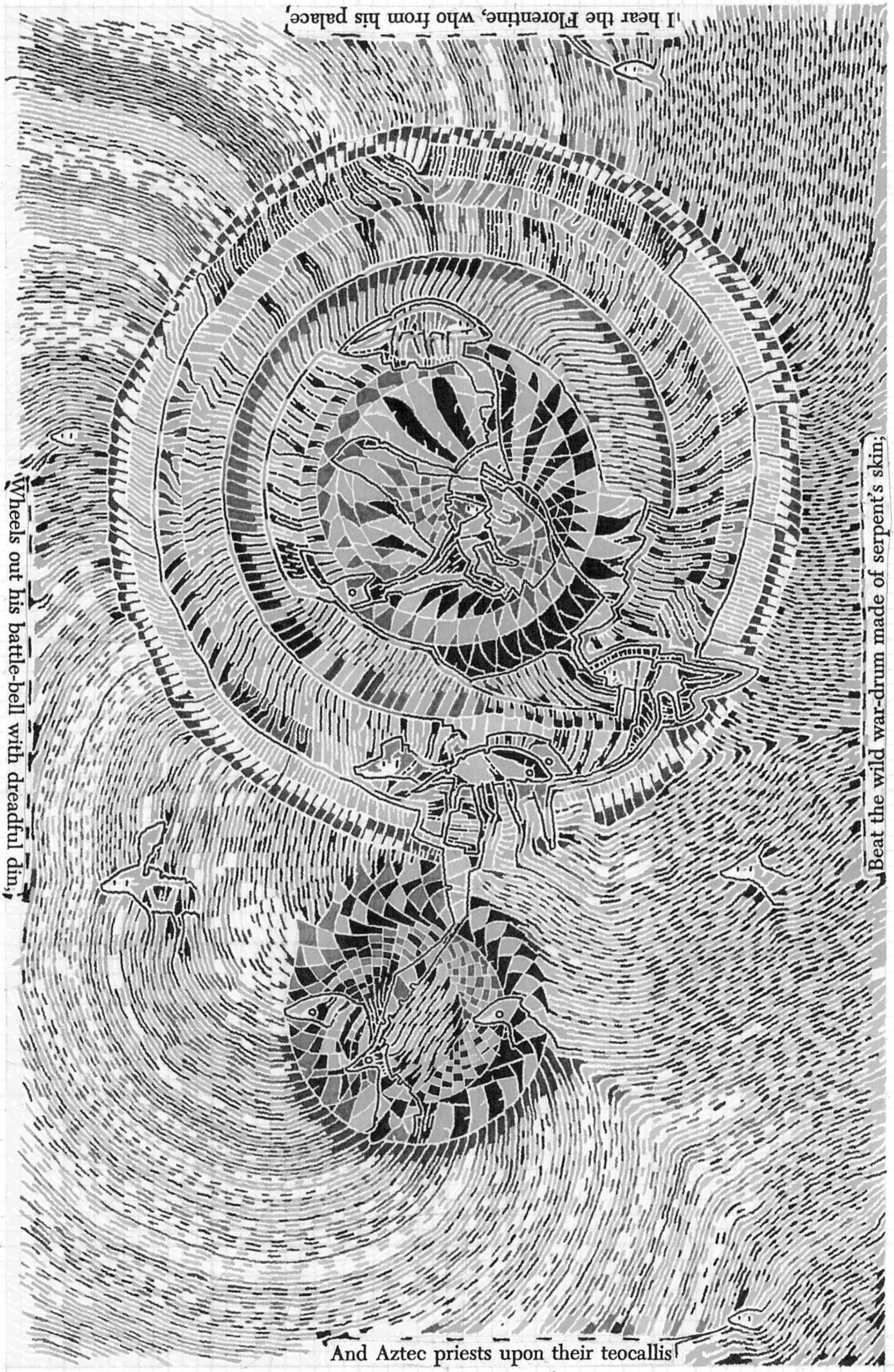
I hear the Florentine, who from his palace
Wheels out his battle-bell with dreadful din,
And Aztec priests upon their teocallis
Beat the wild war-drum made of serpent's skin;

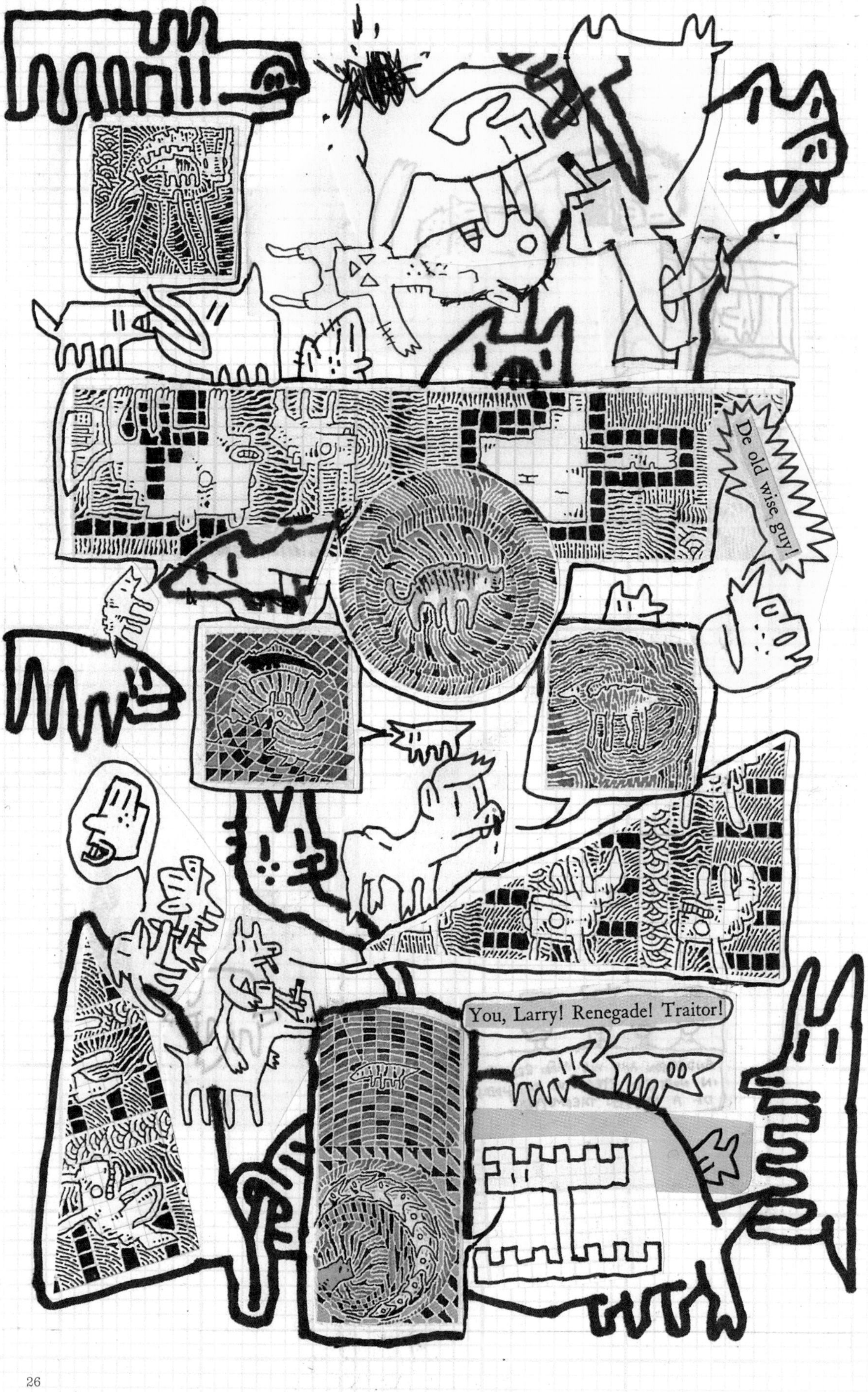
De old wise guy!
You, Larry! Renegade! Traitor!

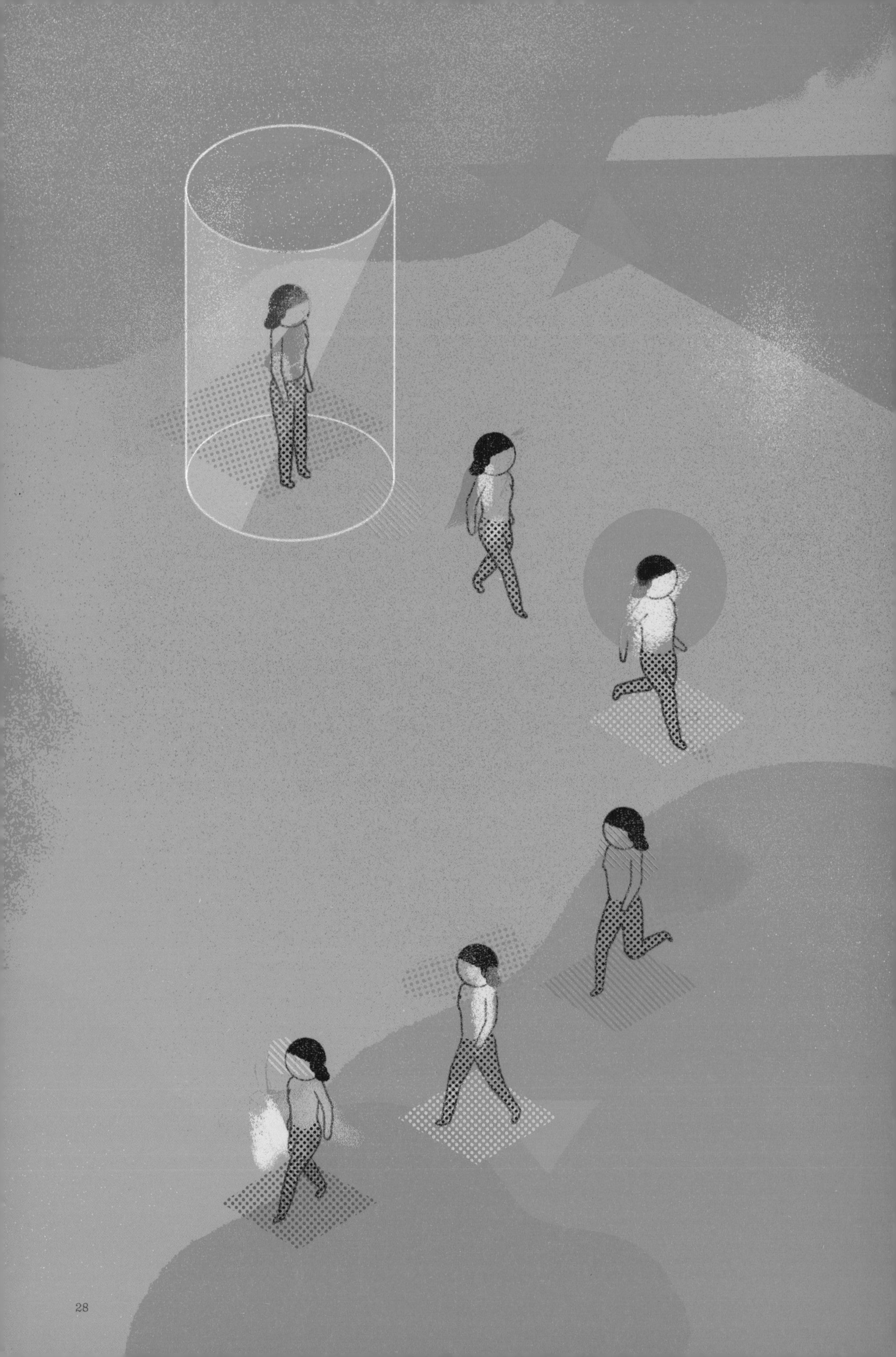

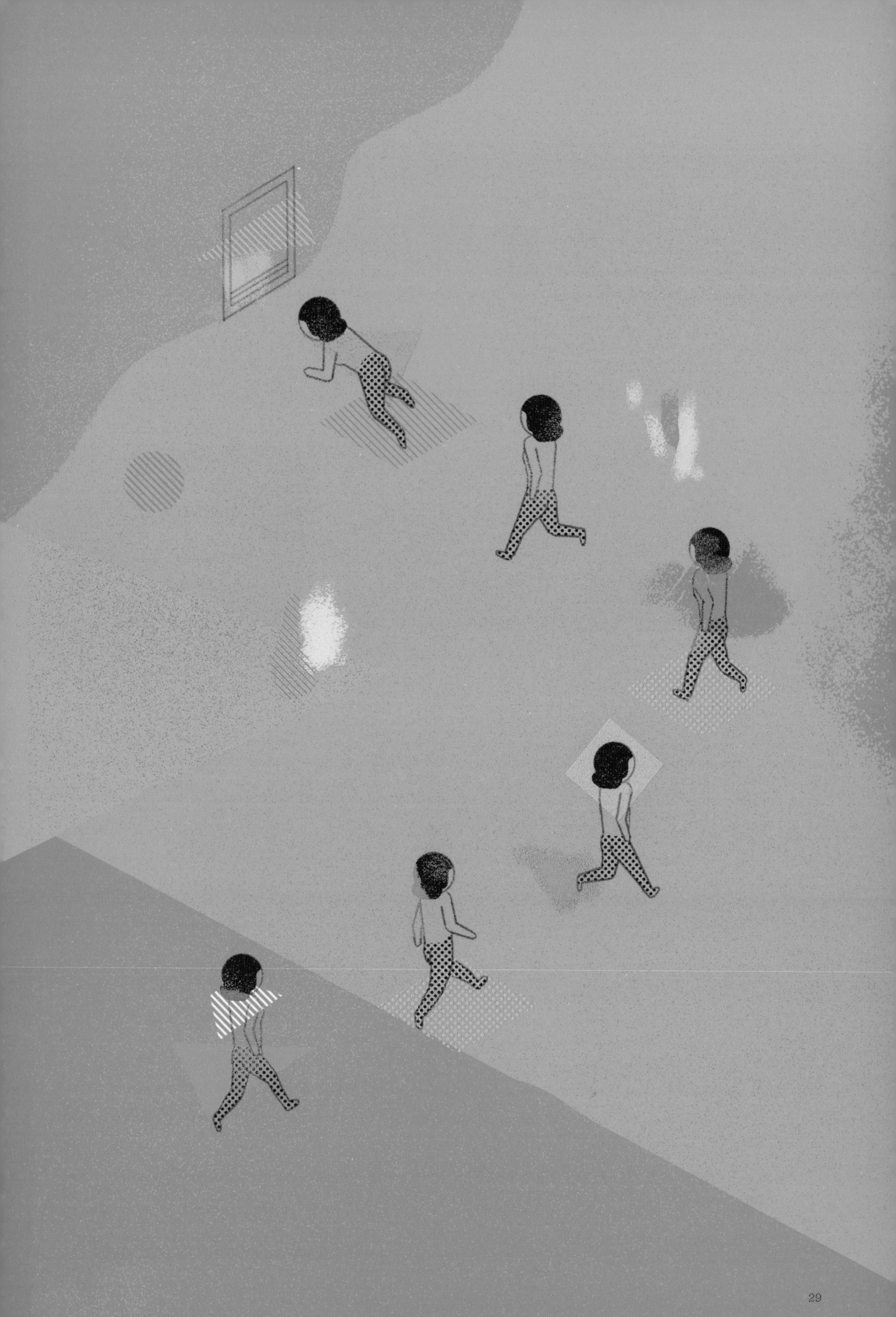

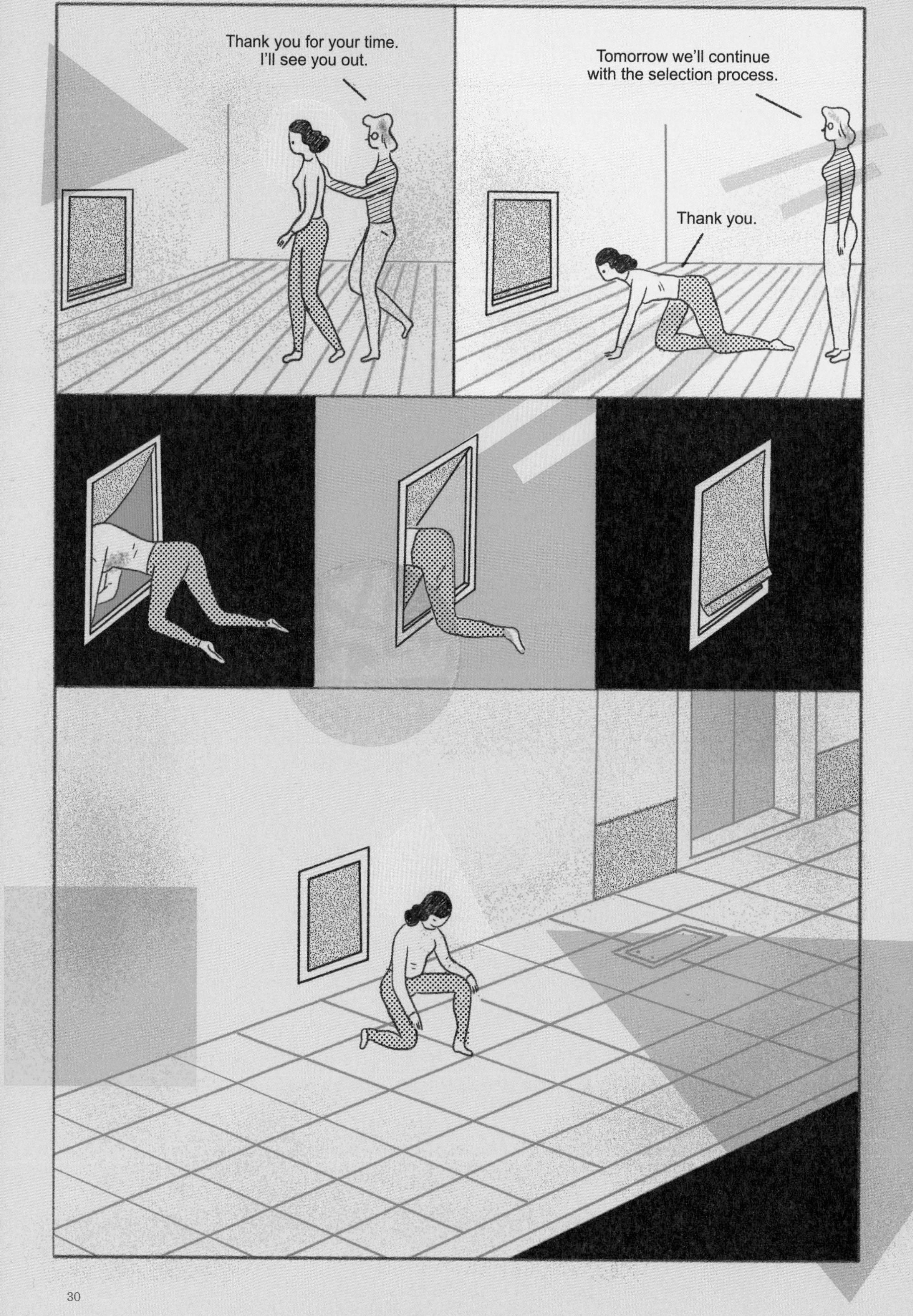
Thank you for your time.
I'll see you out.
Tomorrow we'll continue
with the selection process.
Thank you.

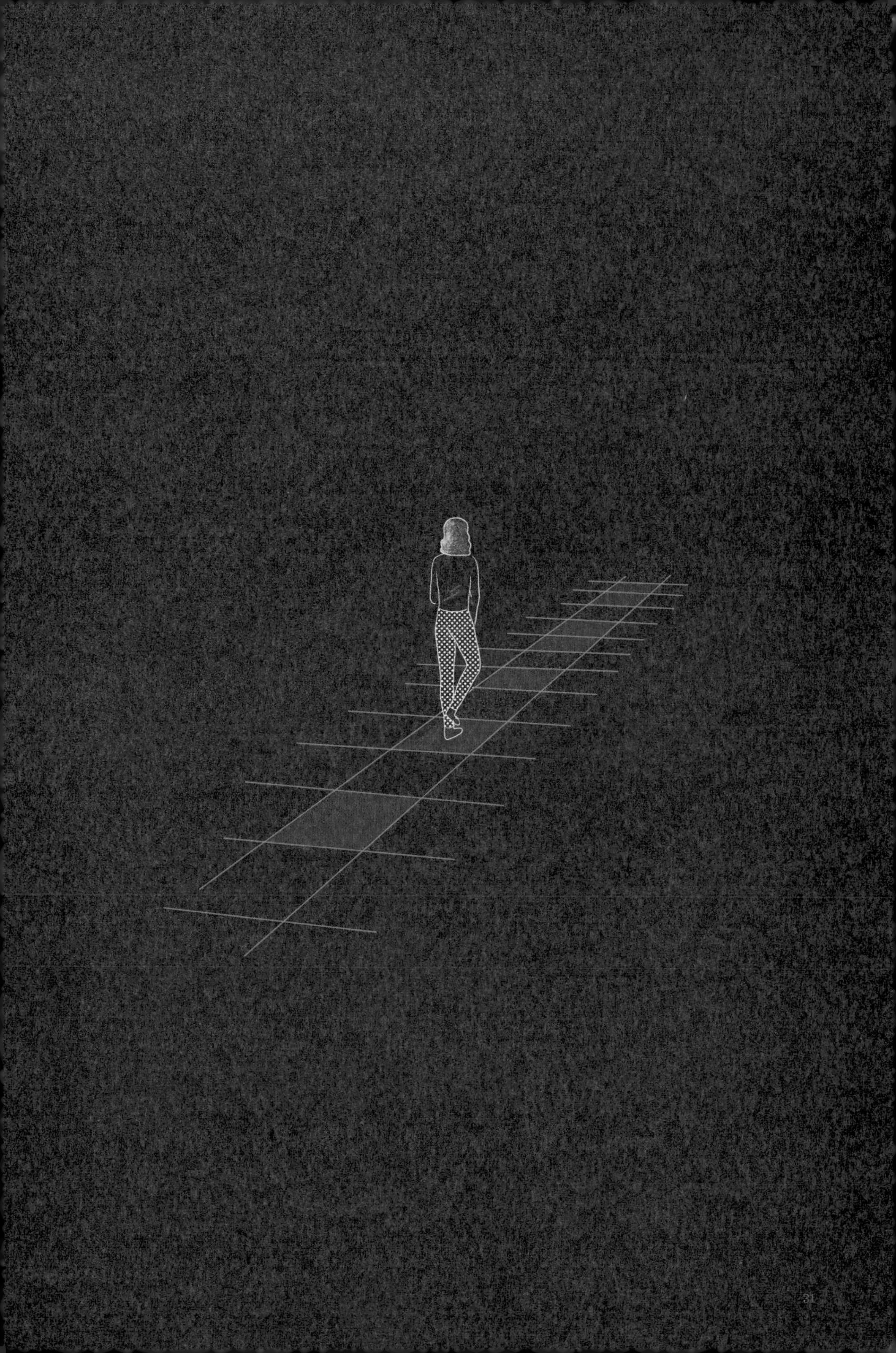

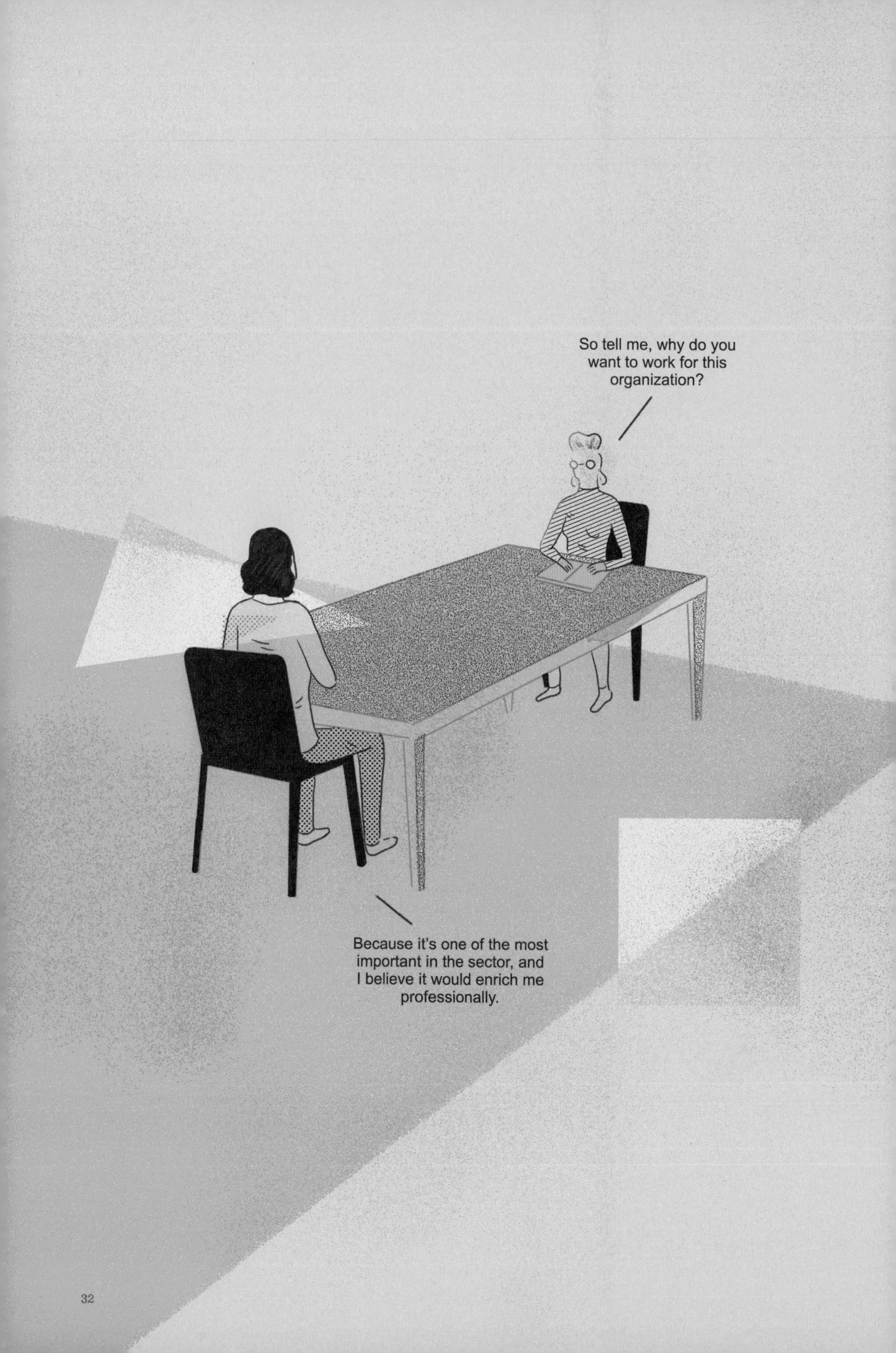
So tell me, why do you want to work for this organization?
Because it's one of the most important in the sector, and I believe it would enrich me professionally.

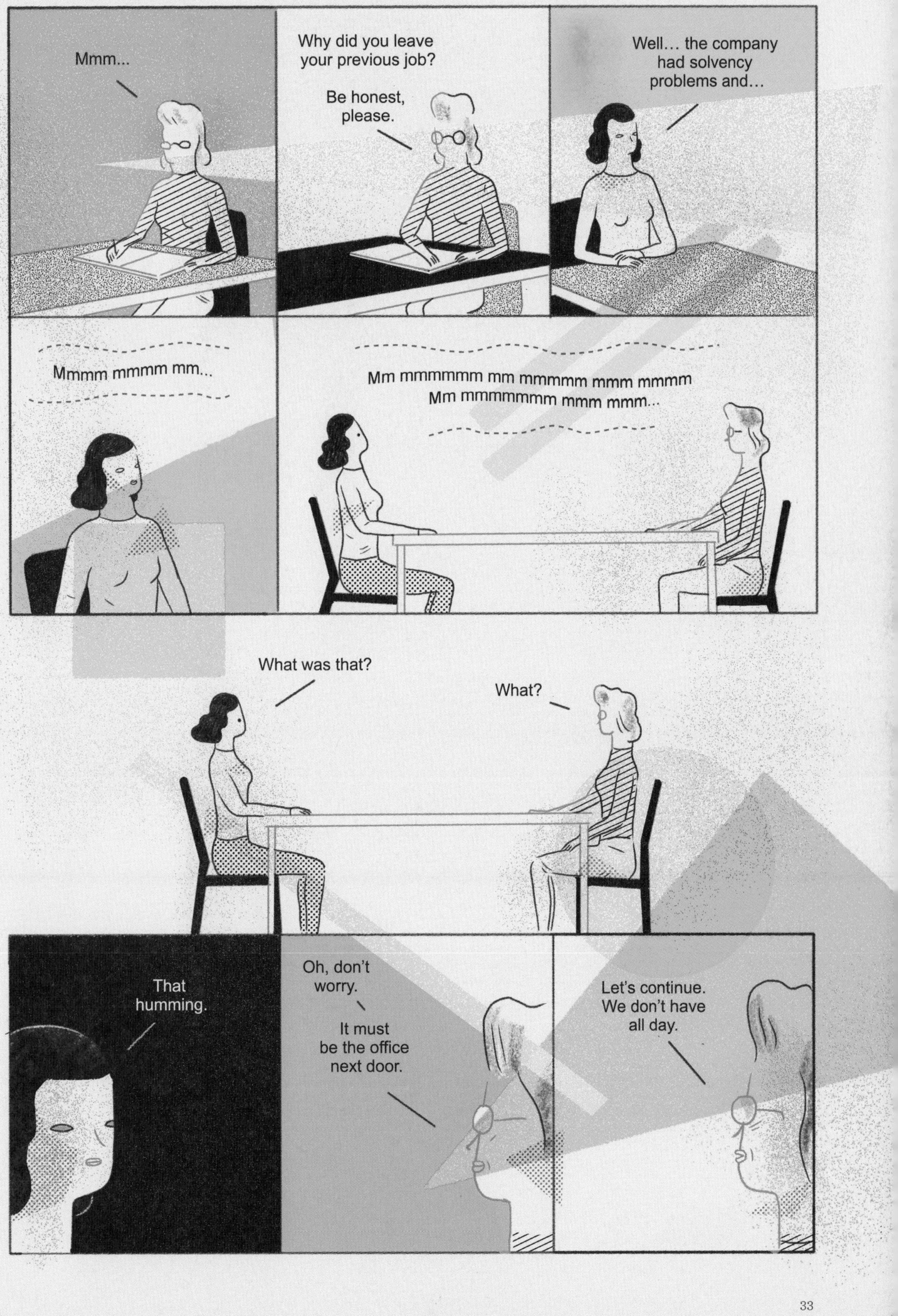

Mmm...
Why did you leave your previous job?
Be honest, please.
Well… the company had solvency problems and…
Mmmm mmmm mm...
Mm mmmmmm mm mmmmm mmm mmmm
Mm mmmmmmm mmm mmm...
What was that?
What?
That humming.
Oh, don't worry.
It must be the office next door.
Let's continue. We don't have all day.

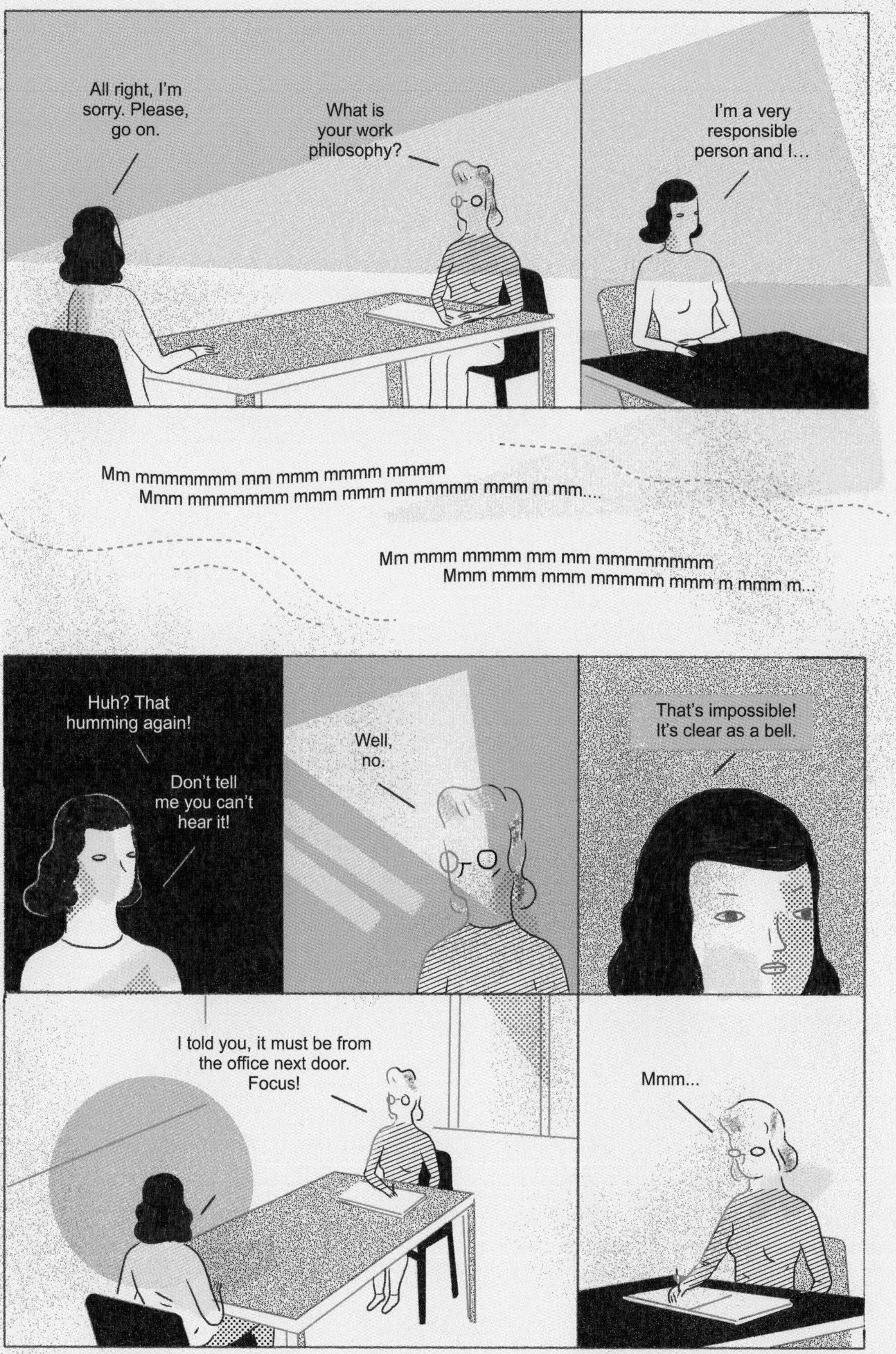
All right, I'm sorry. Please, go on.
What is your work philosophy?
I'm a very responsible person and I...
Mm mmmmmmm mm mmm mmmm mmmm
Mmm mmmmmmm mmm mmm mmmmmm mmm m mm....
Mm mmm mmmm mm mm mmmmmmmm
Mmm mmm mmm mmmmm mmm m mmm m...
Huh? That humming again!
Don't tell me you can't hear it!
Well, no.
That's impossible! It's clear as a bell.
I told you, it must be from the office next door. Focus!
Mmm...

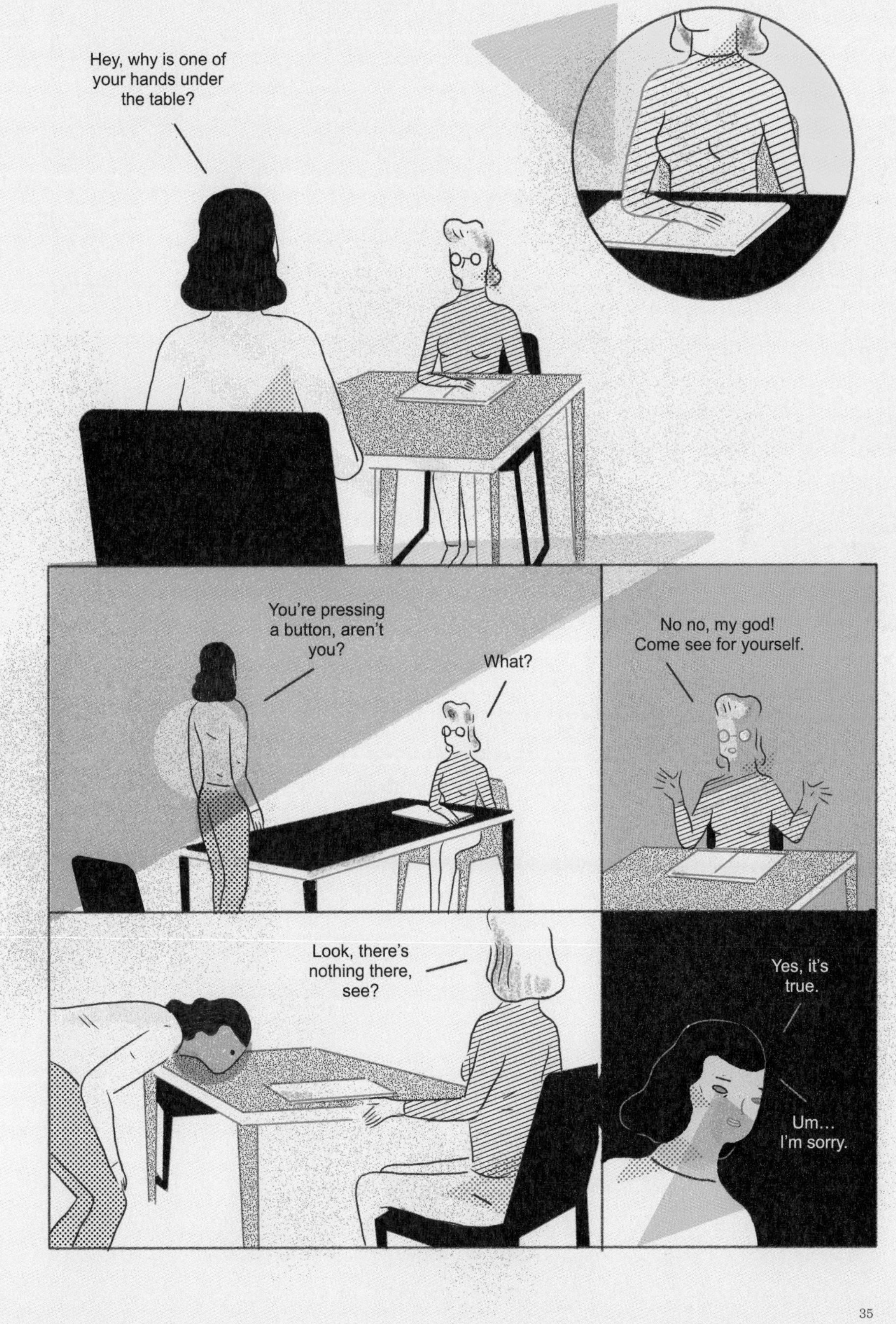

Hey, why is one of your hands under the table?
You're pressing a button, aren't you?
What?
No no, my god! Come see for yourself.
Look, there's nothing there, see?
Yes, it's true.
Um... I'm sorry.

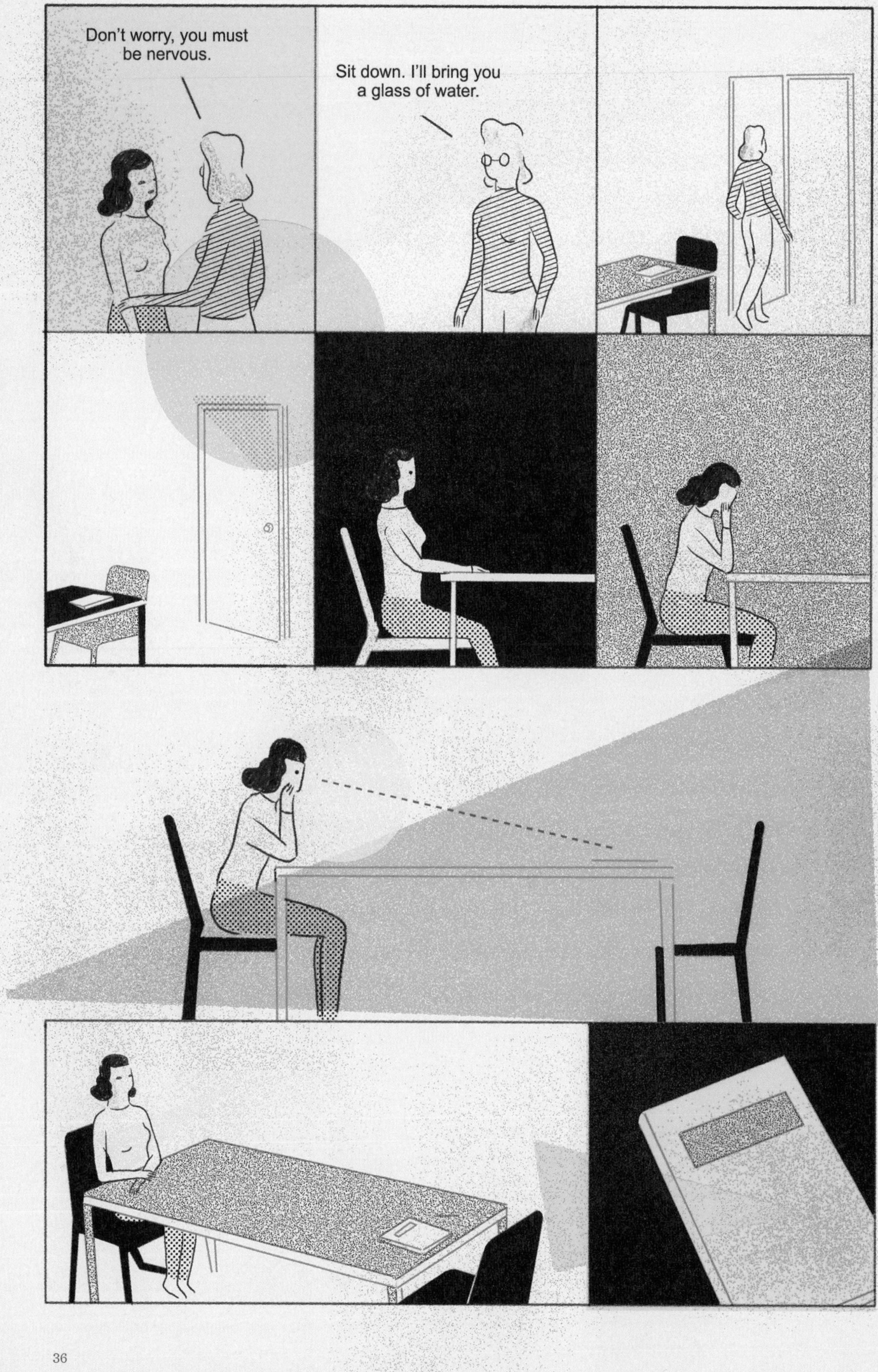
Don't worry, you must be nervous.
Sit down. I'll bring you a glass of water.

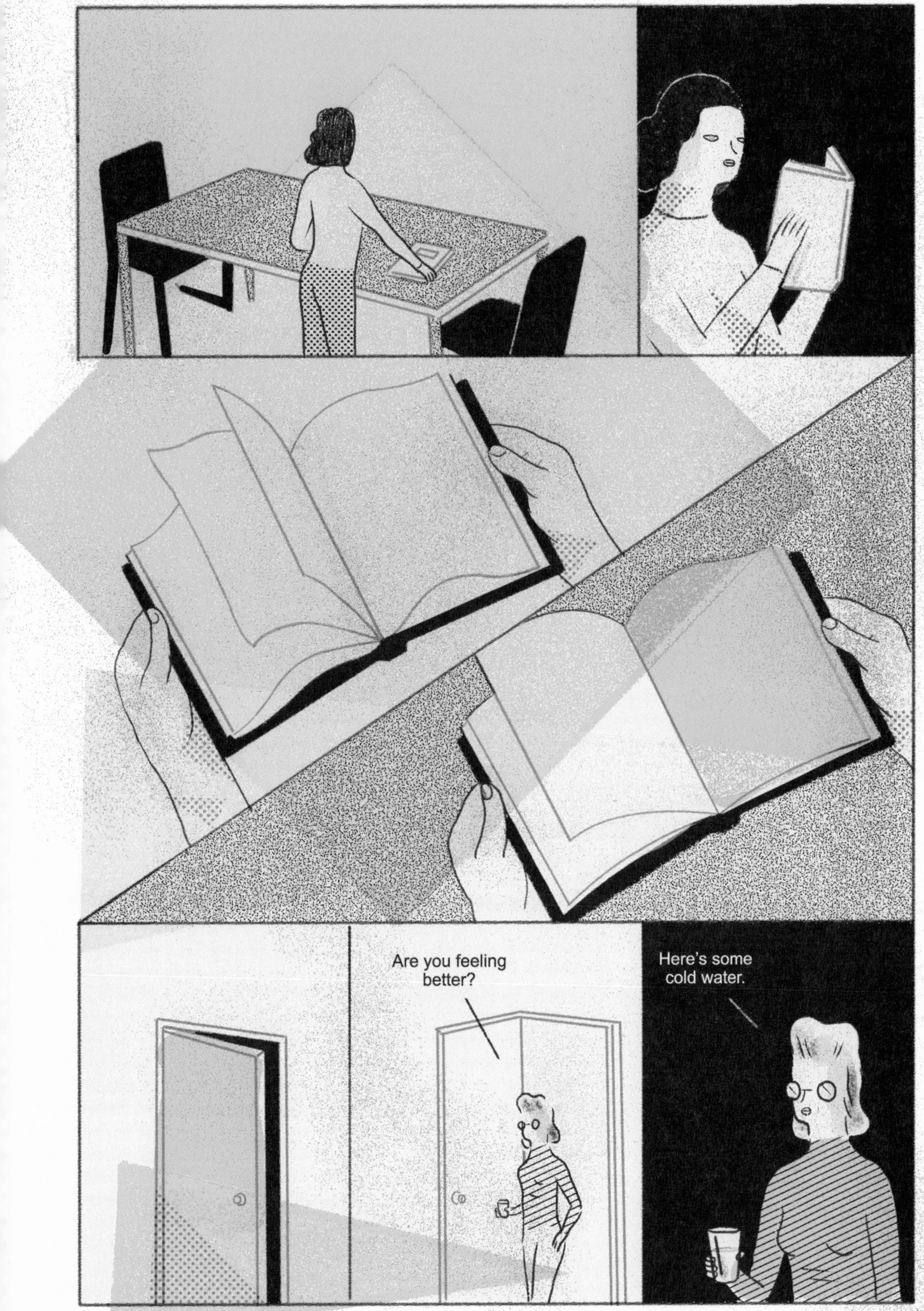
Are you feeling better?
Here's some cold water.

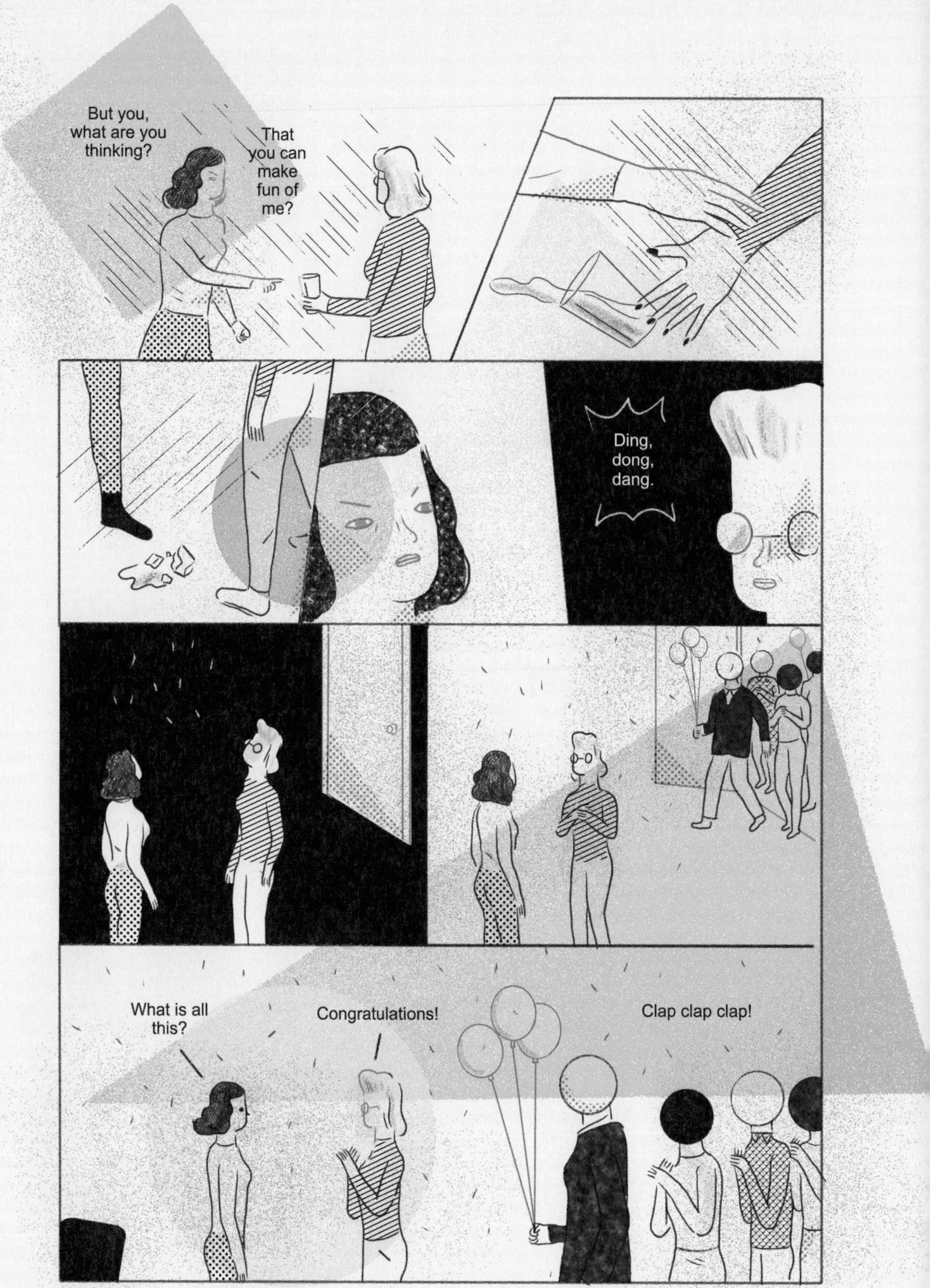
But you, what are you thinking?
That you can make fun of me?
Ding, dong, dang.
What is all this?
Congratulations!
Clap clap clap!

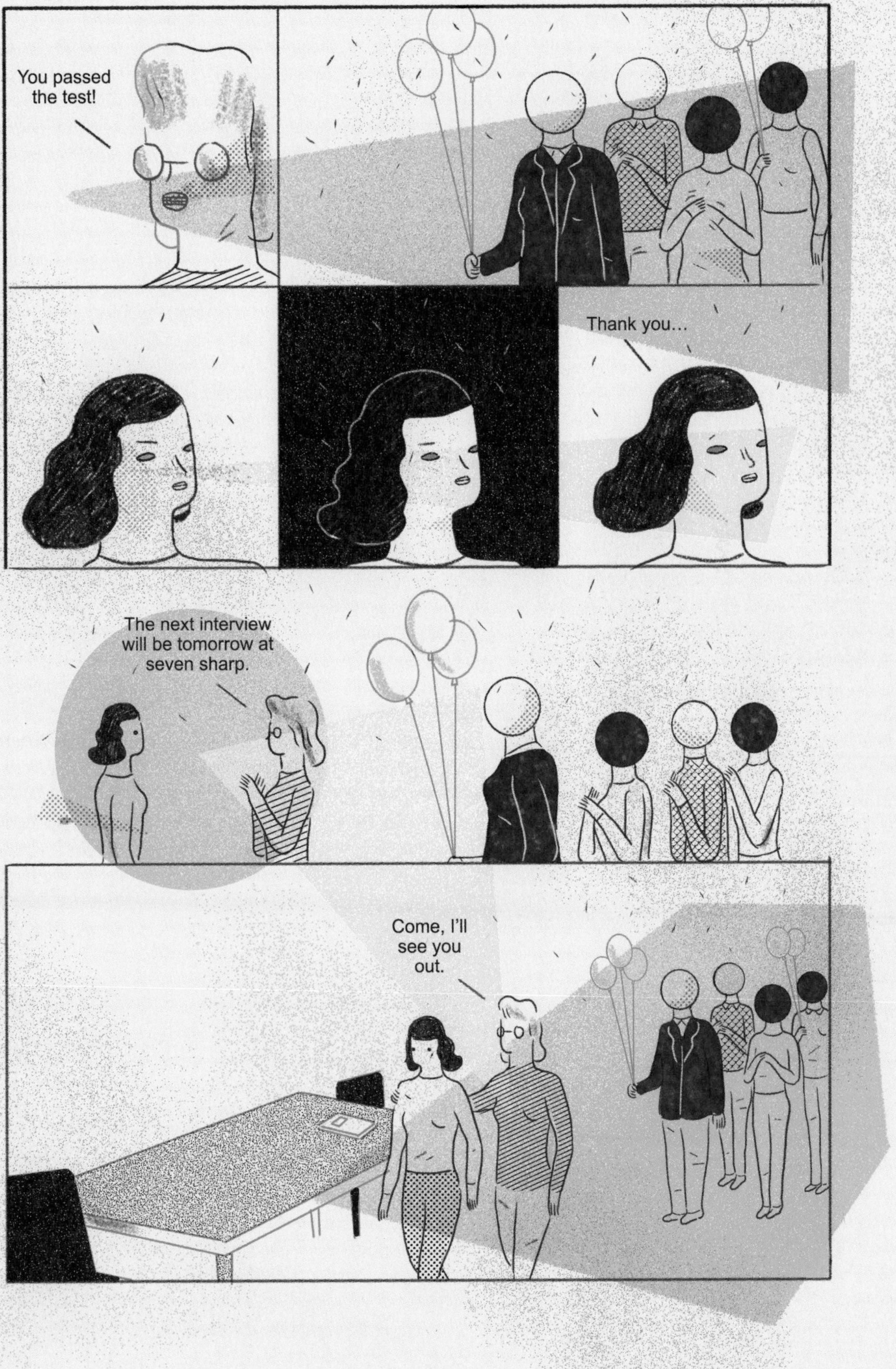
You passed the test!
Thank you...
The next interview will be tomorrow at seven sharp.
Come, I'll see you out.

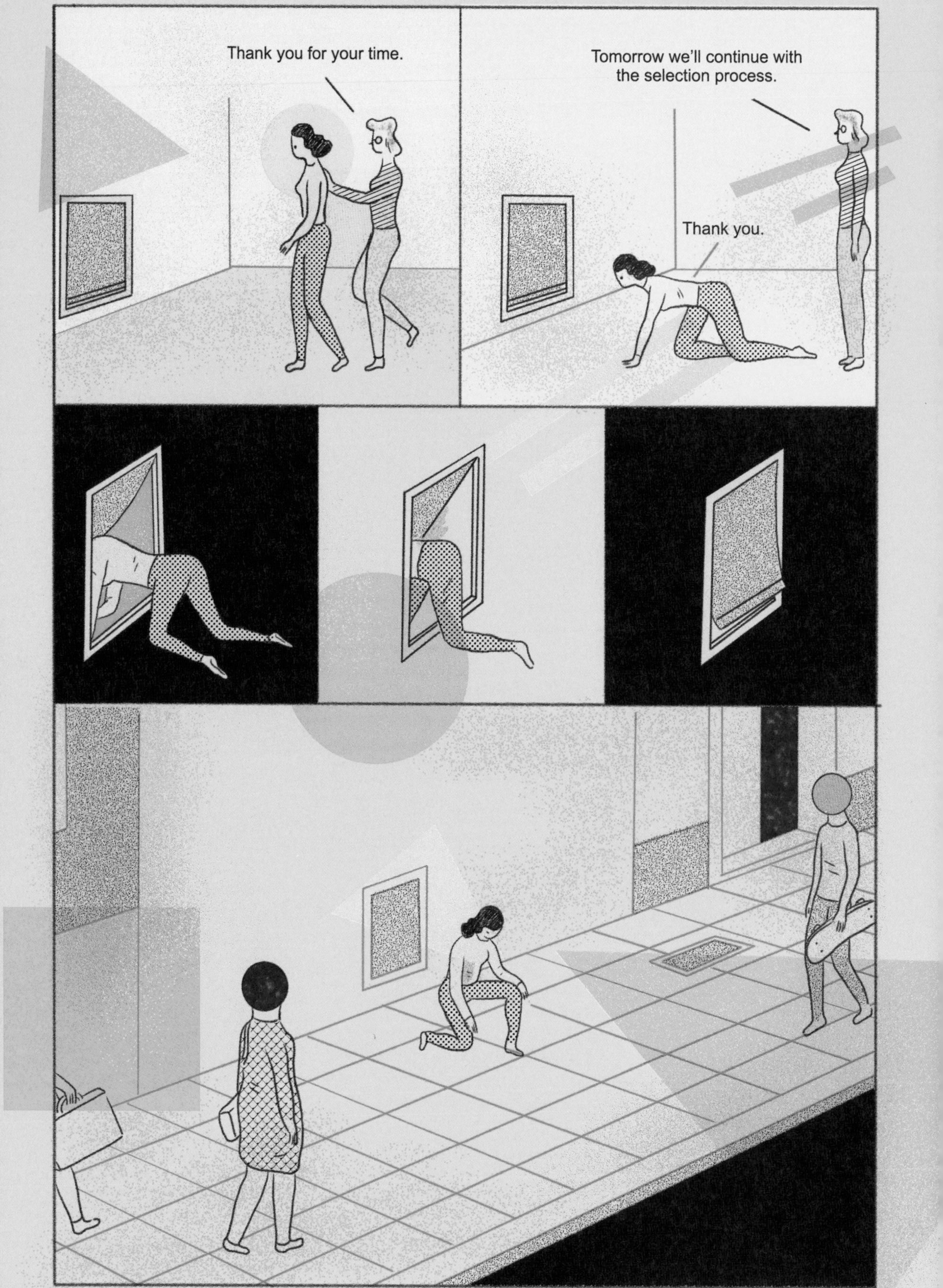
Thank you for your time.
Tomorrow we'll continue with the selection process.
Thank you.

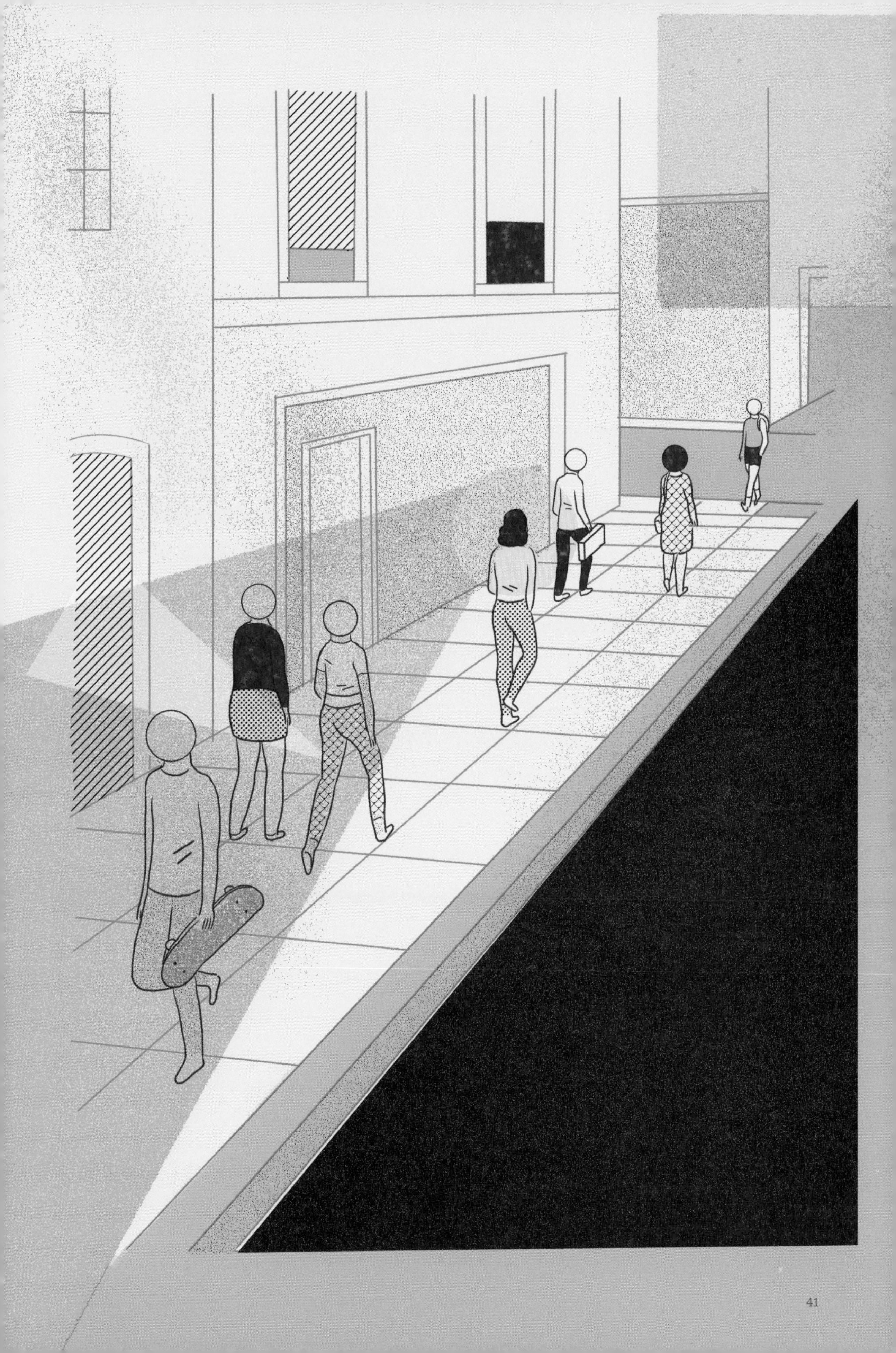

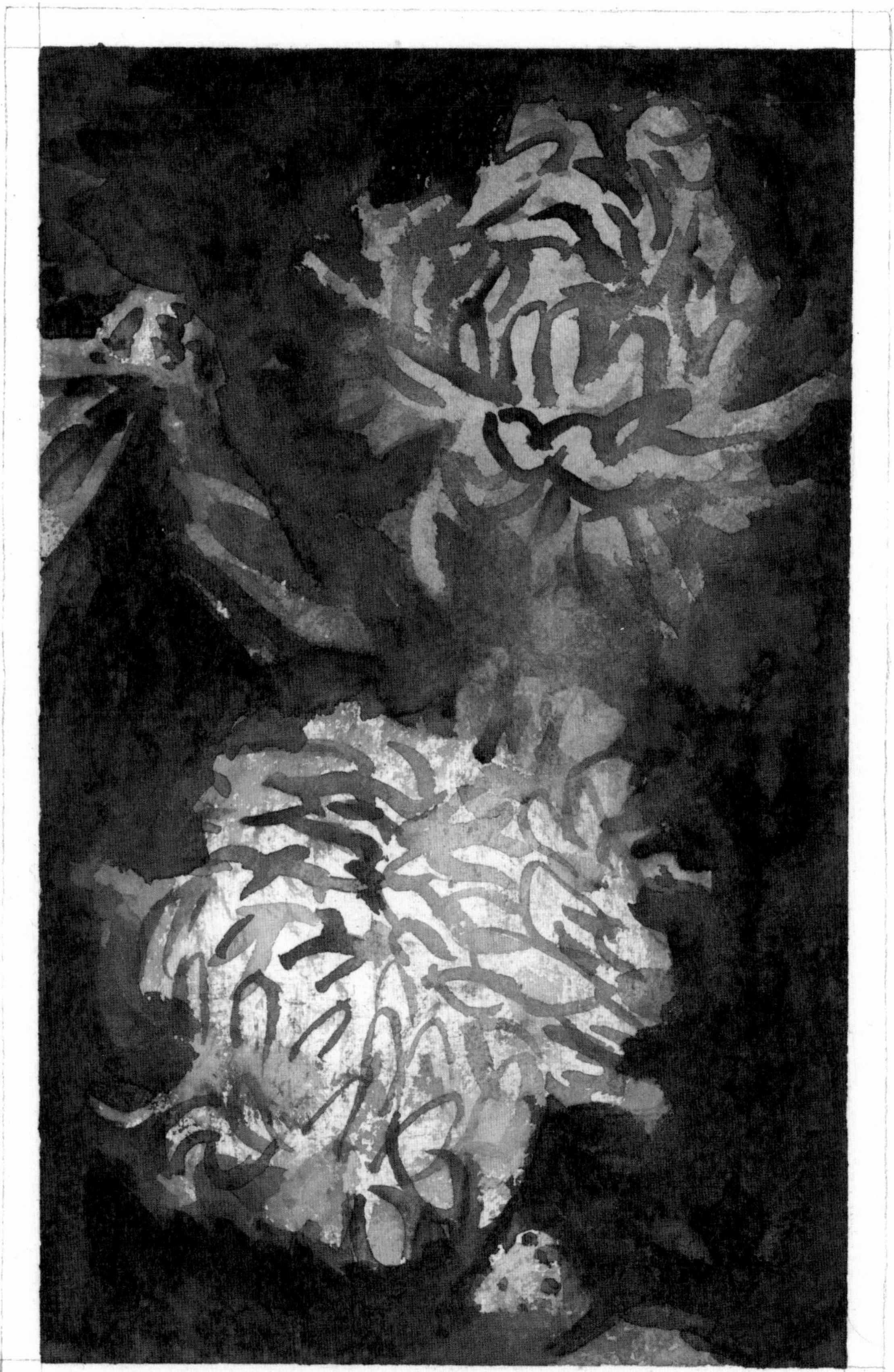

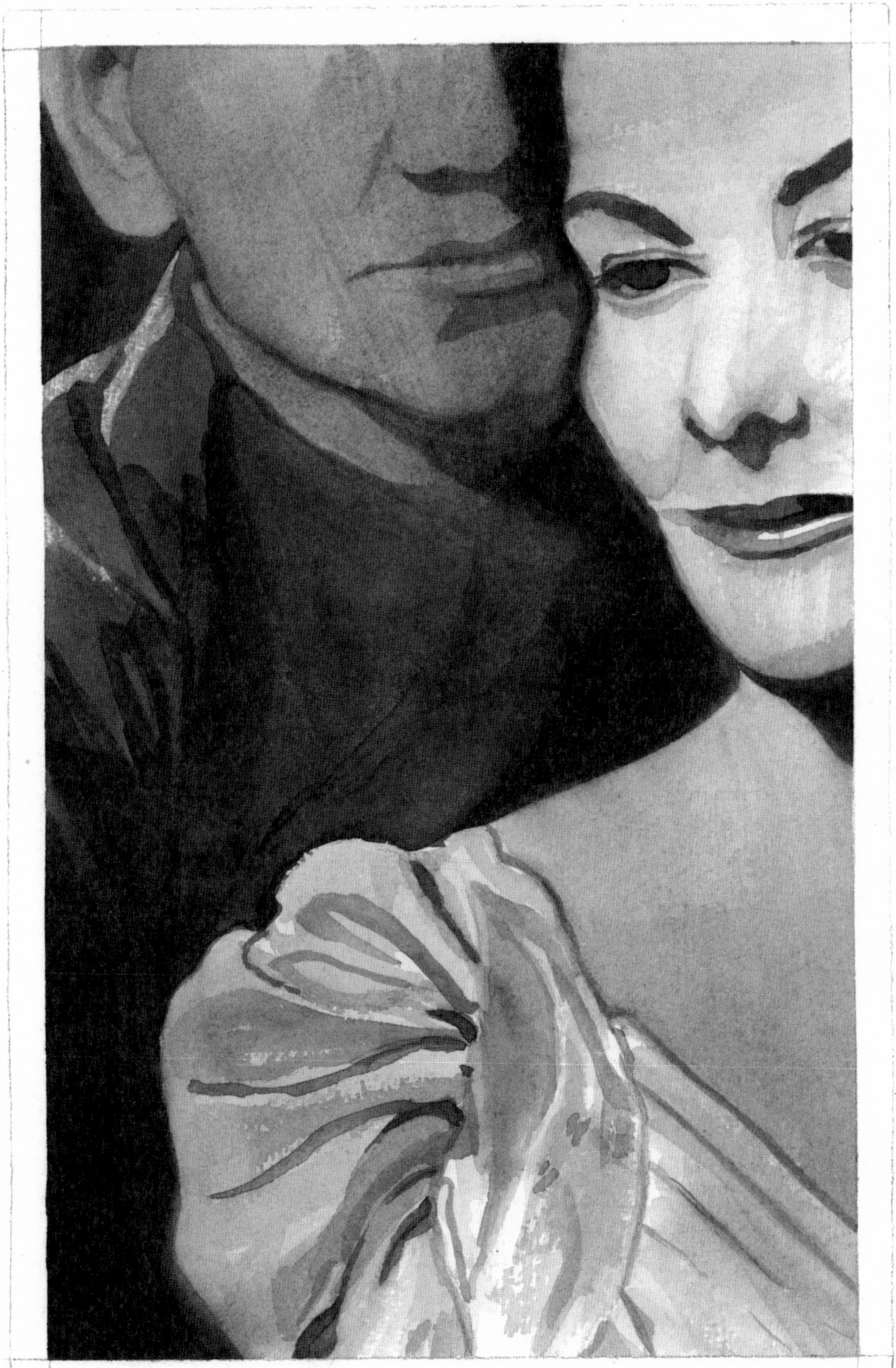

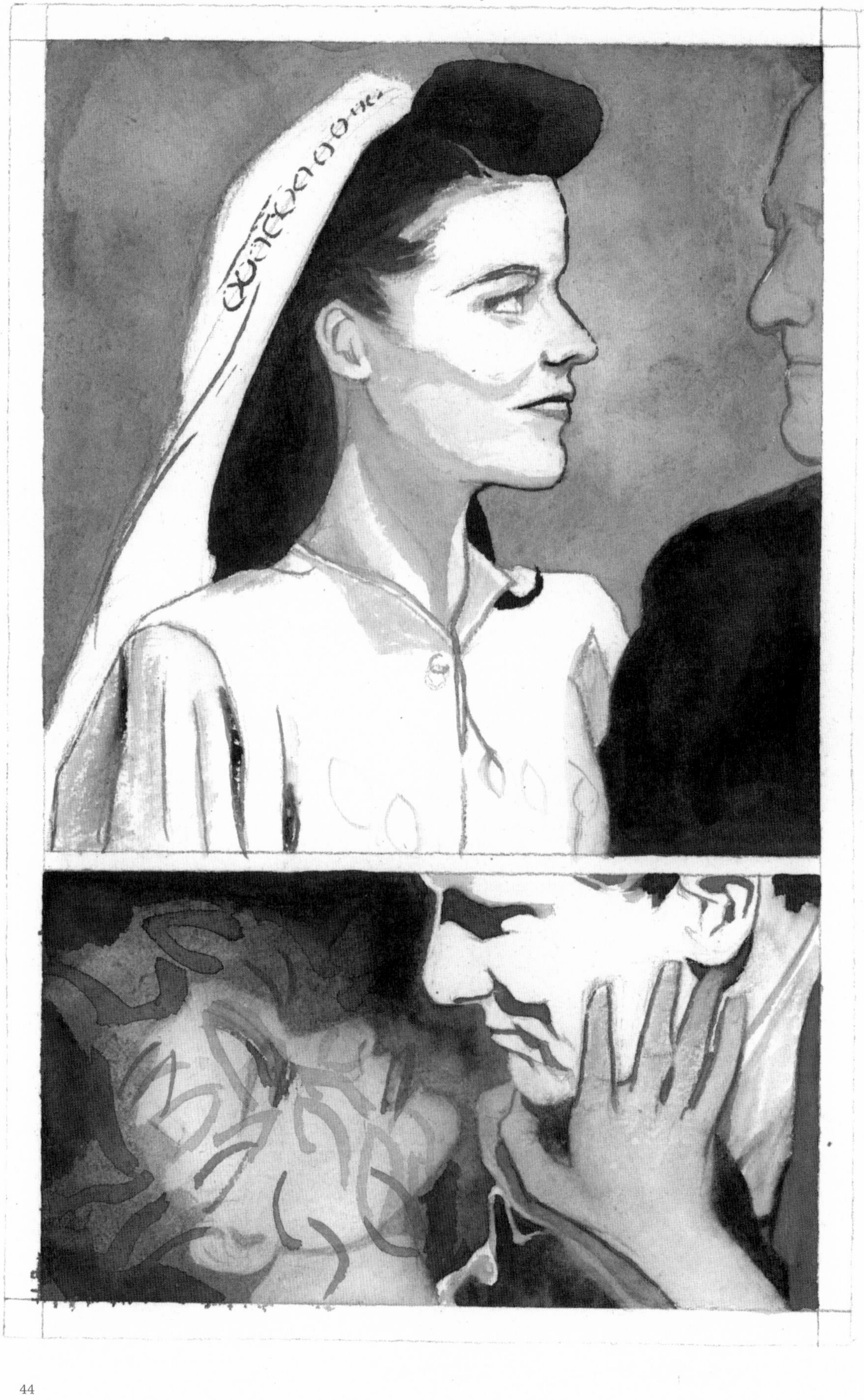

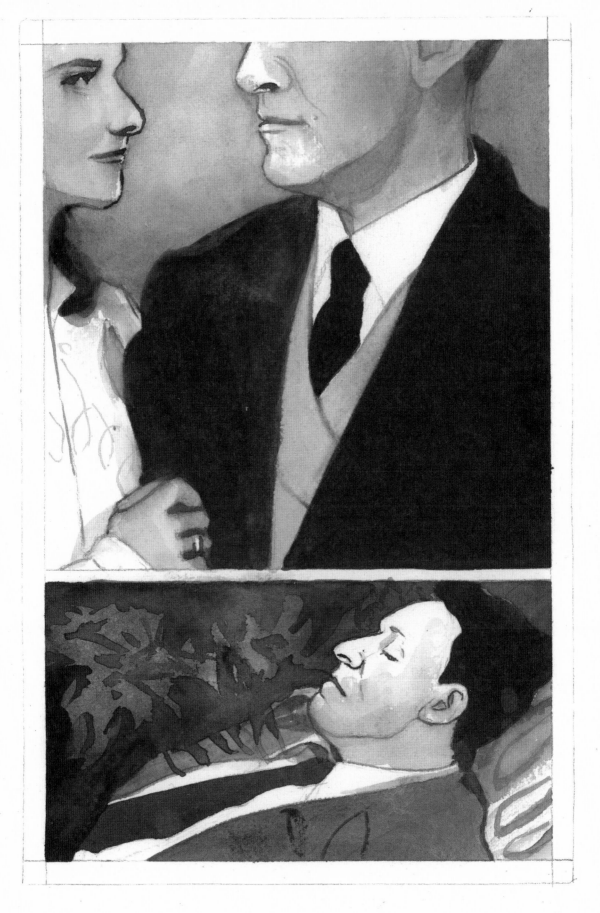

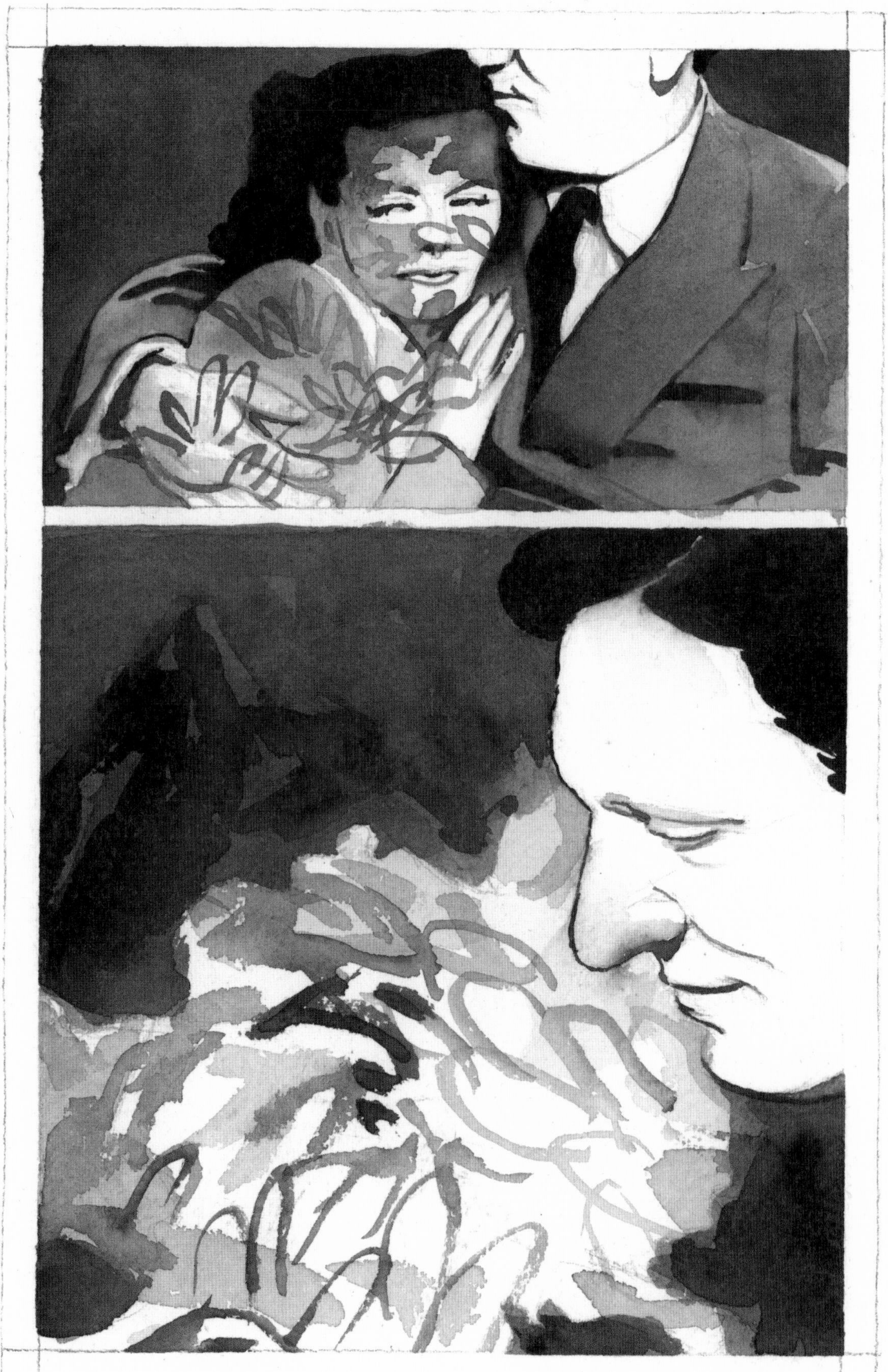

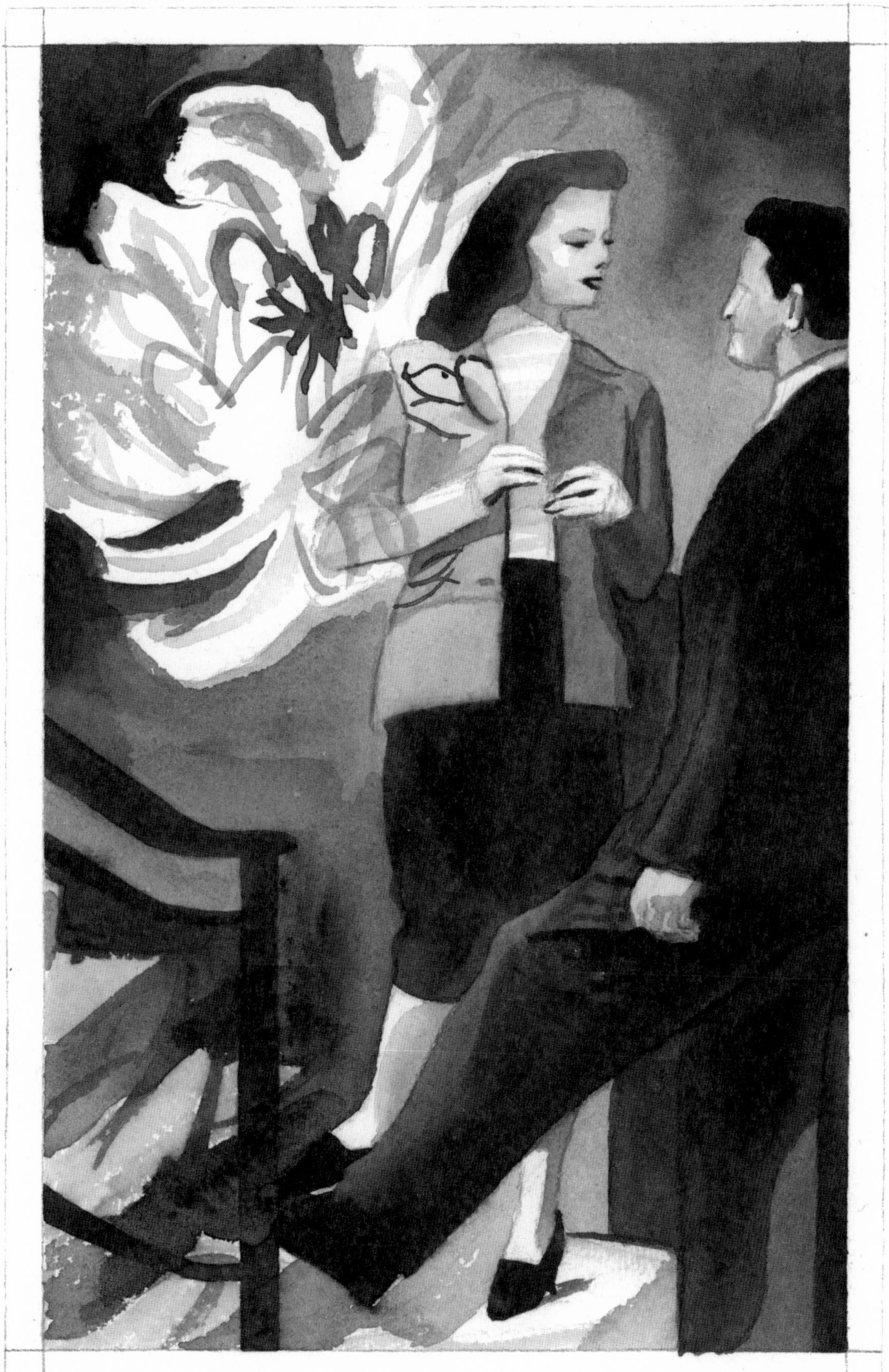

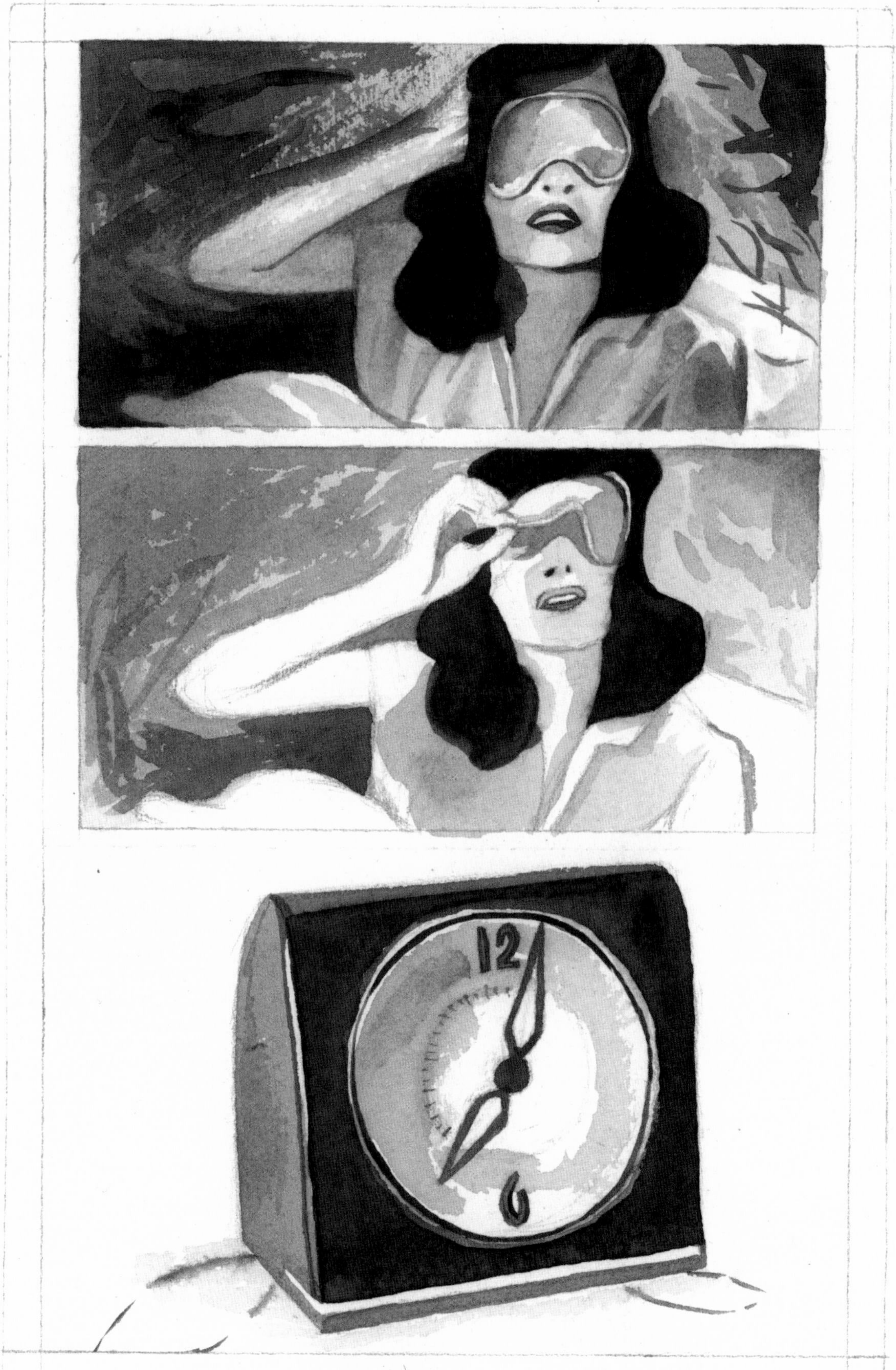

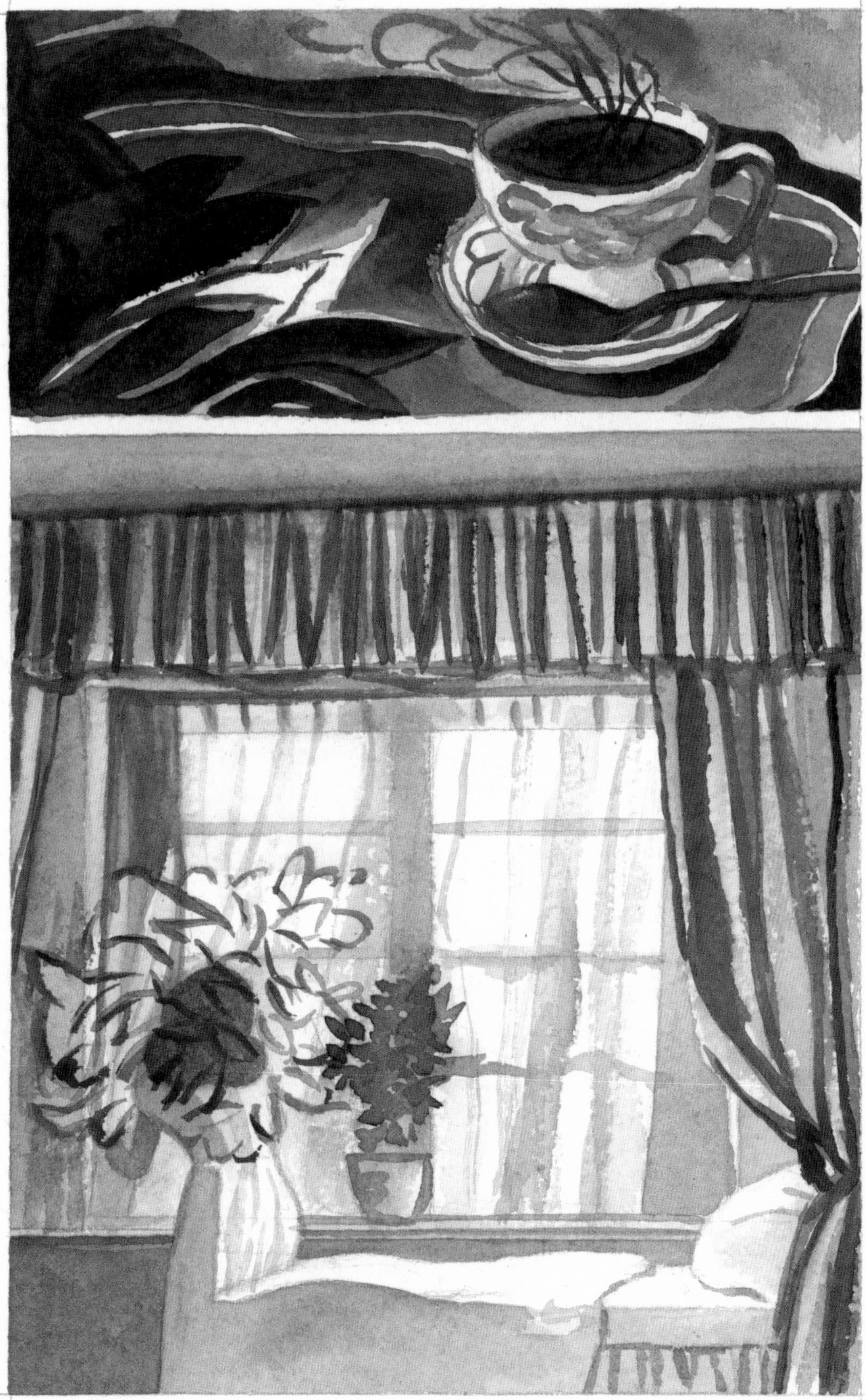

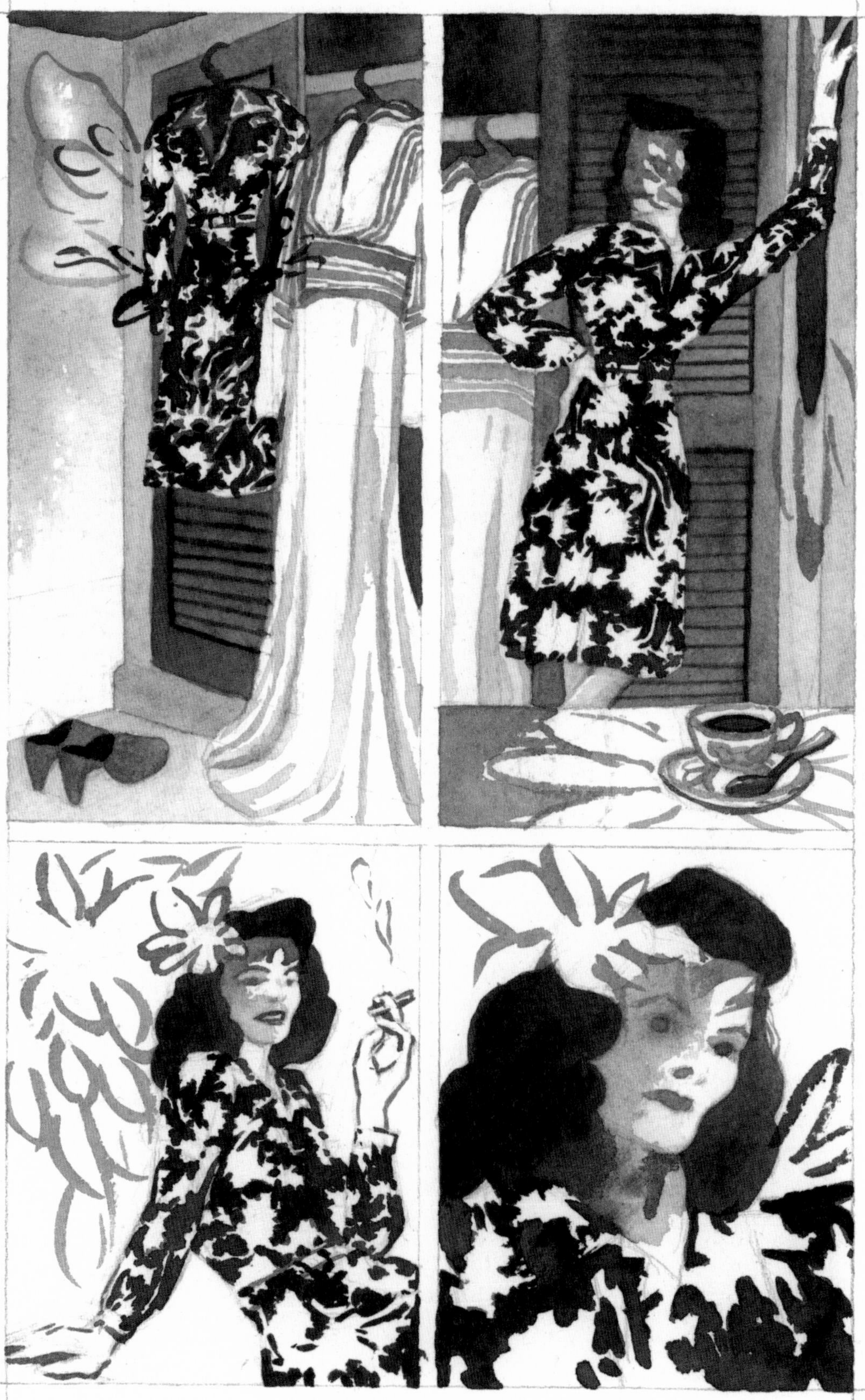

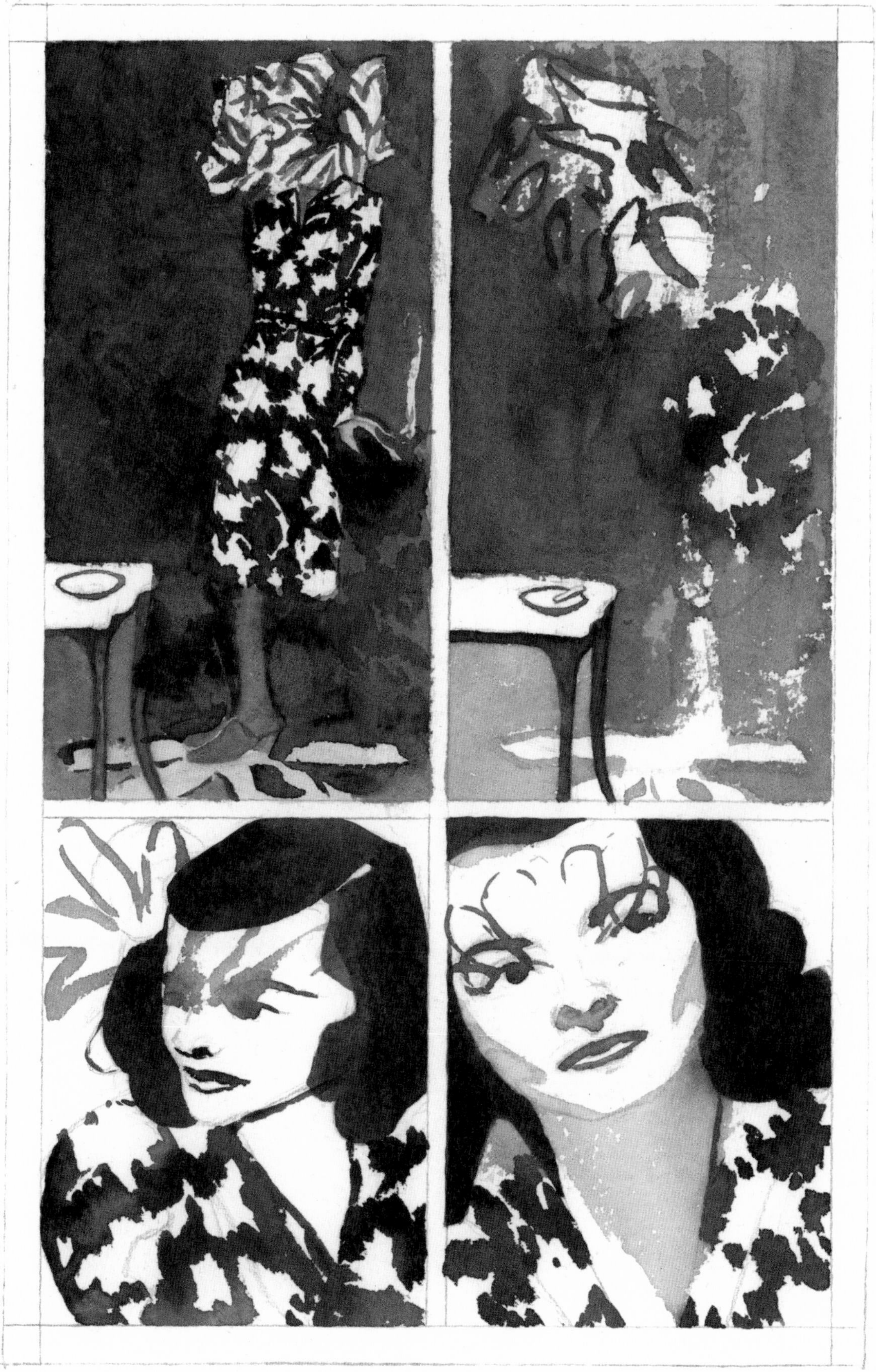

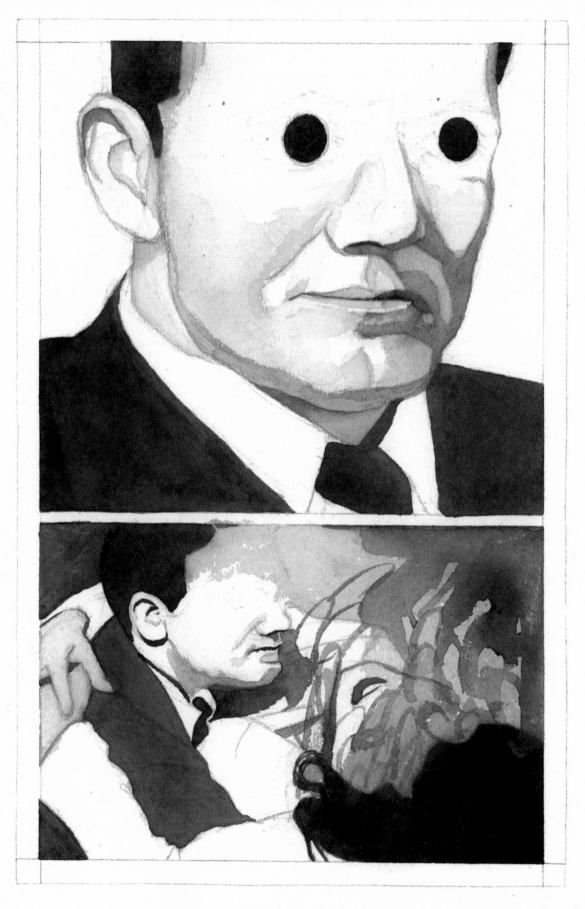

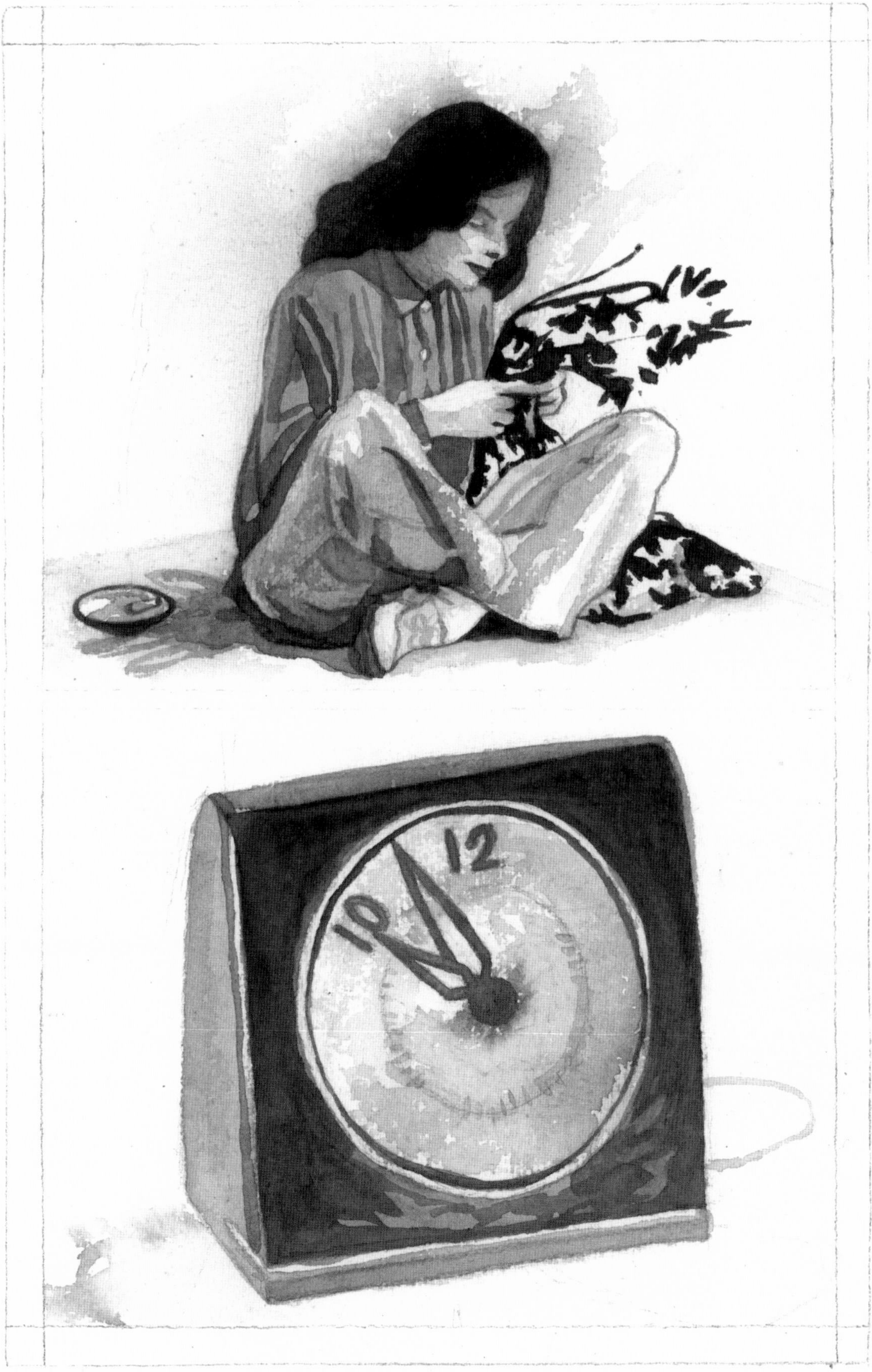

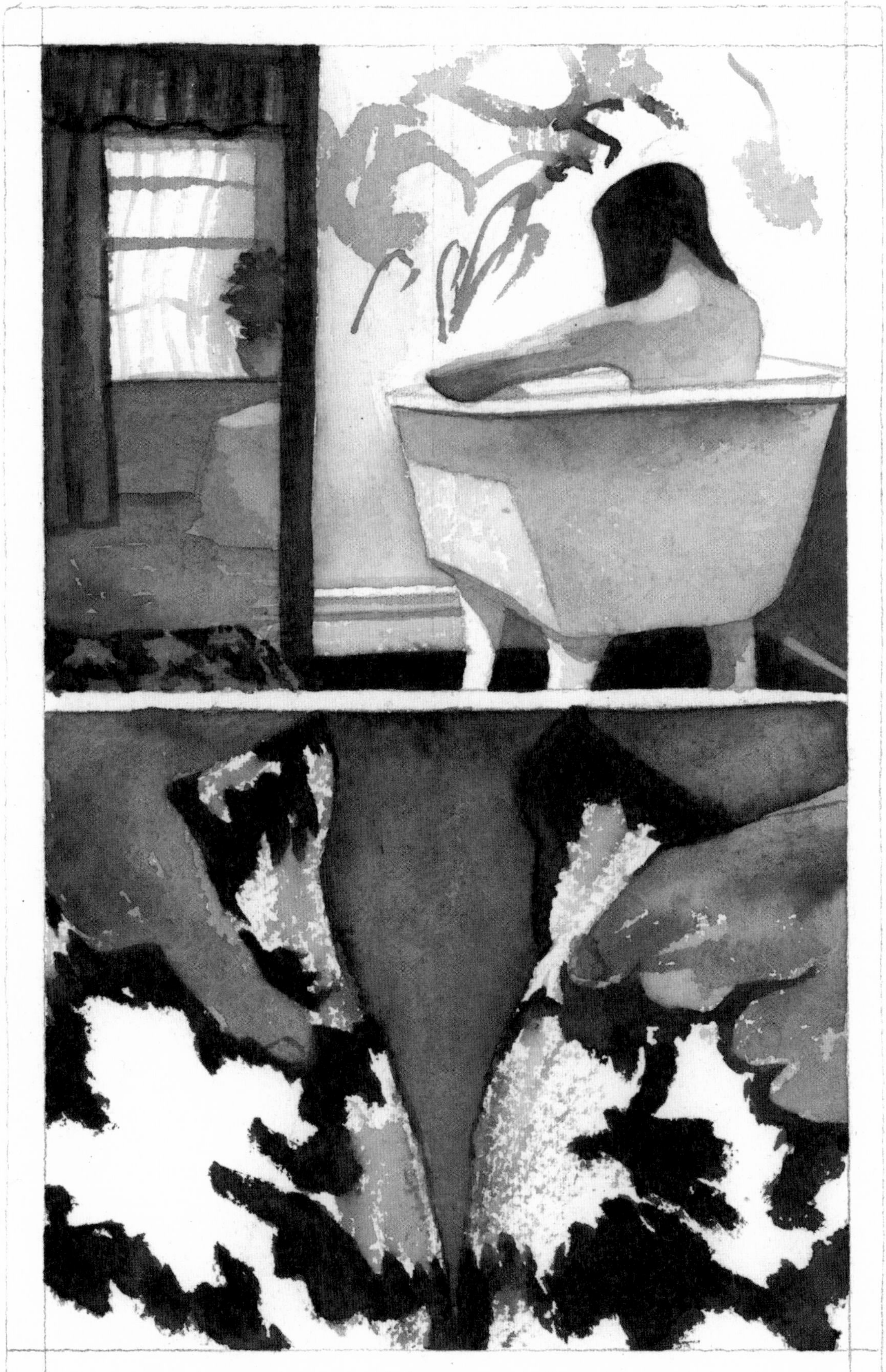

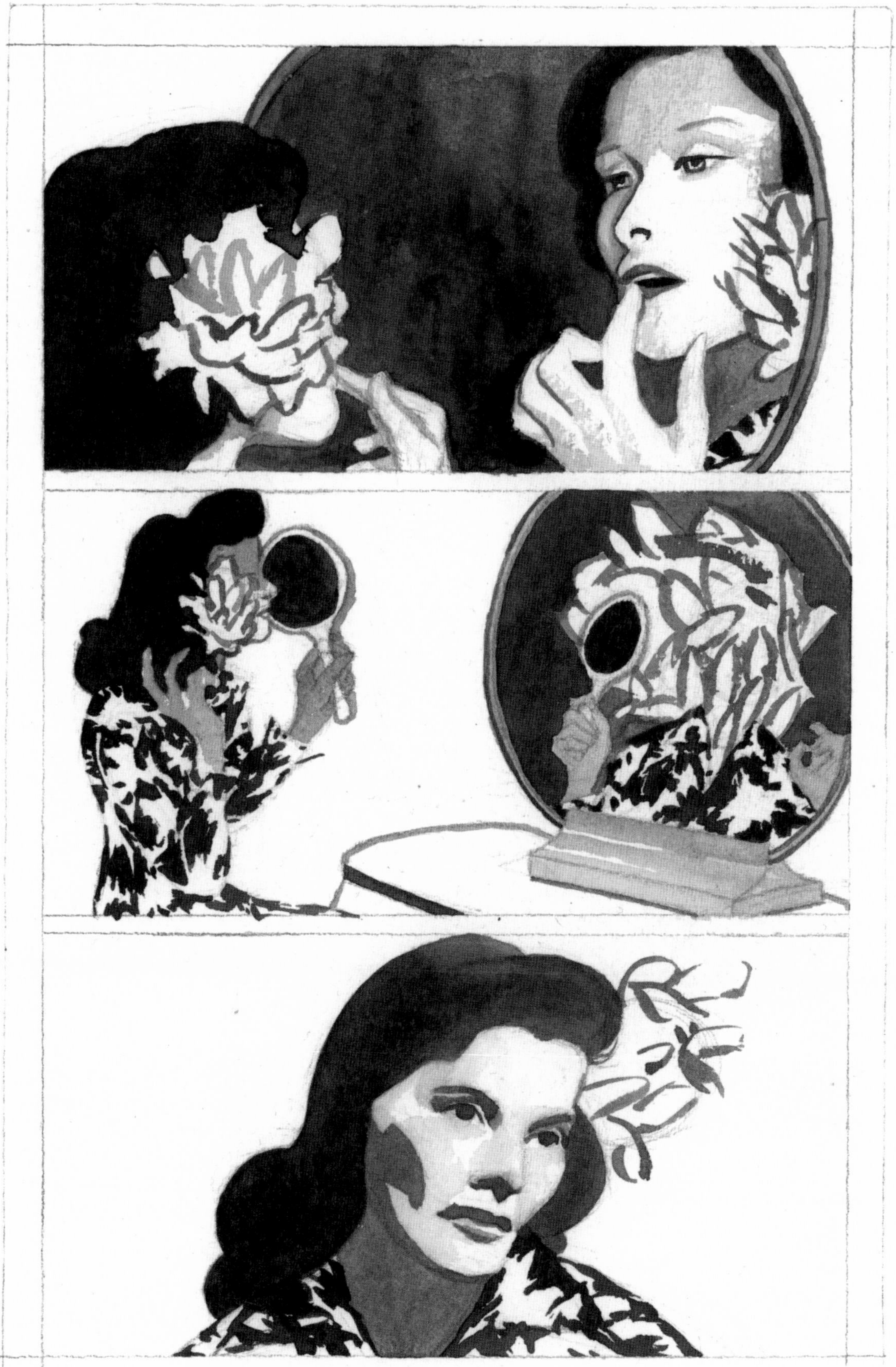

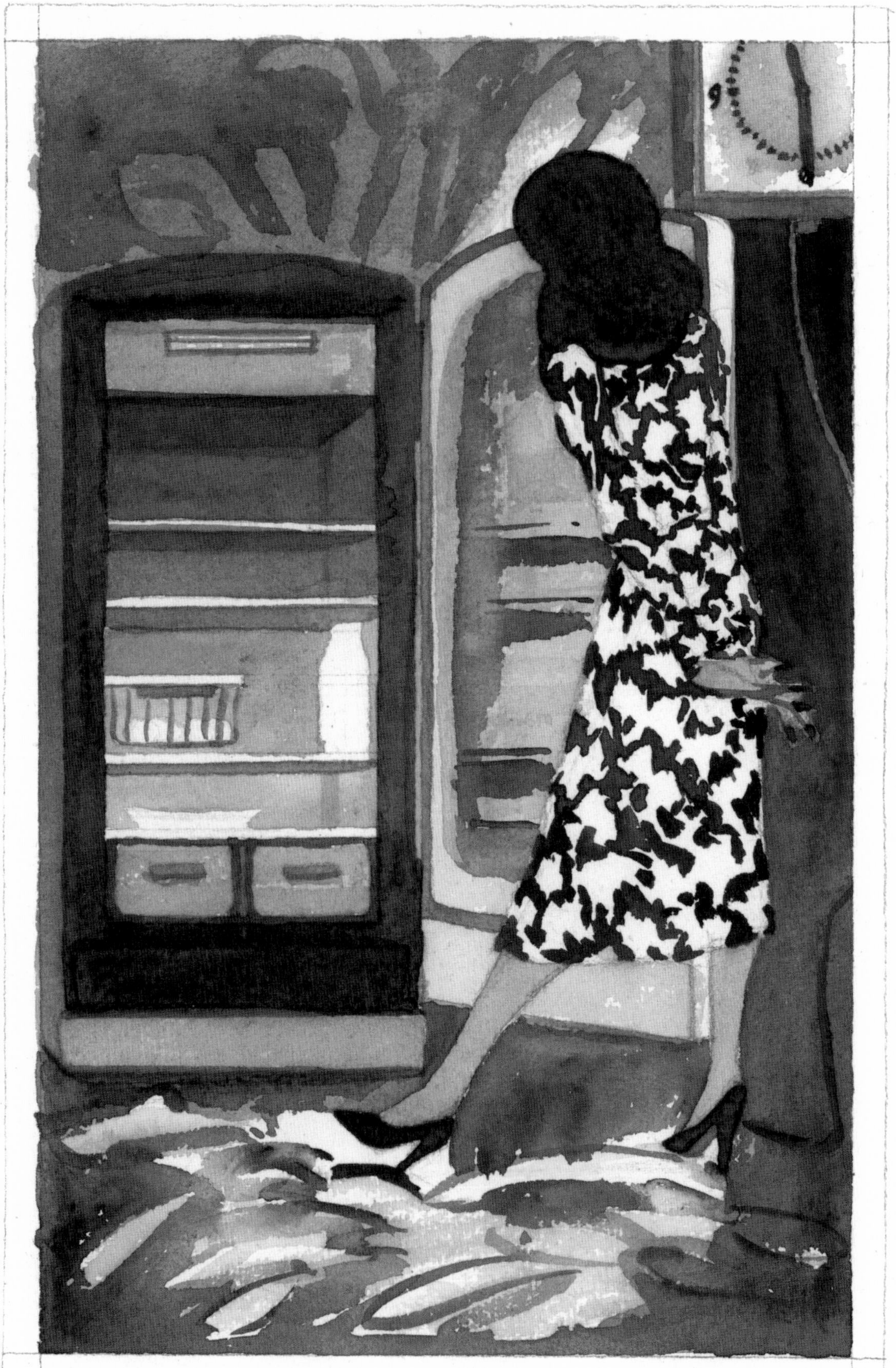

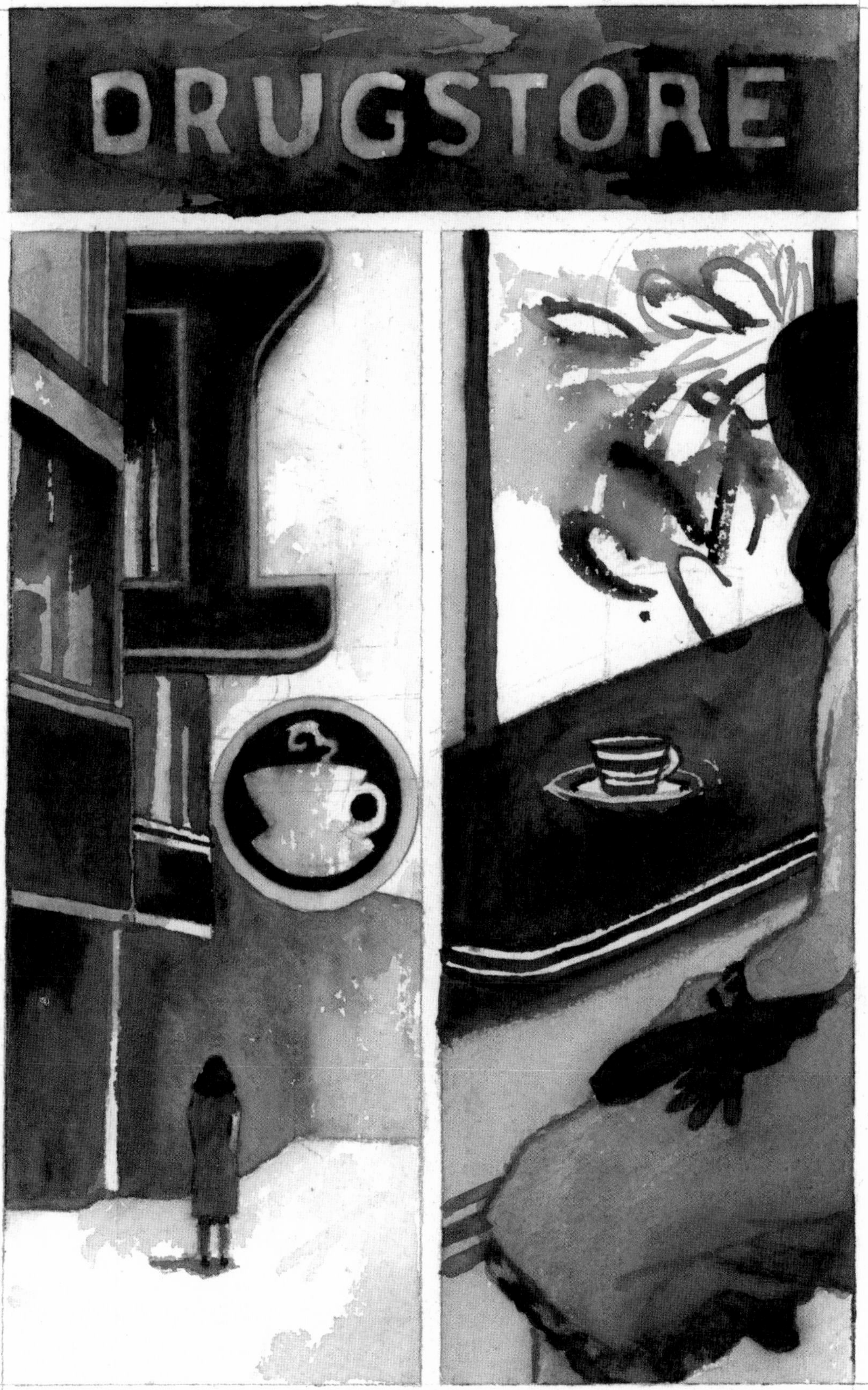
DRUGSTORE

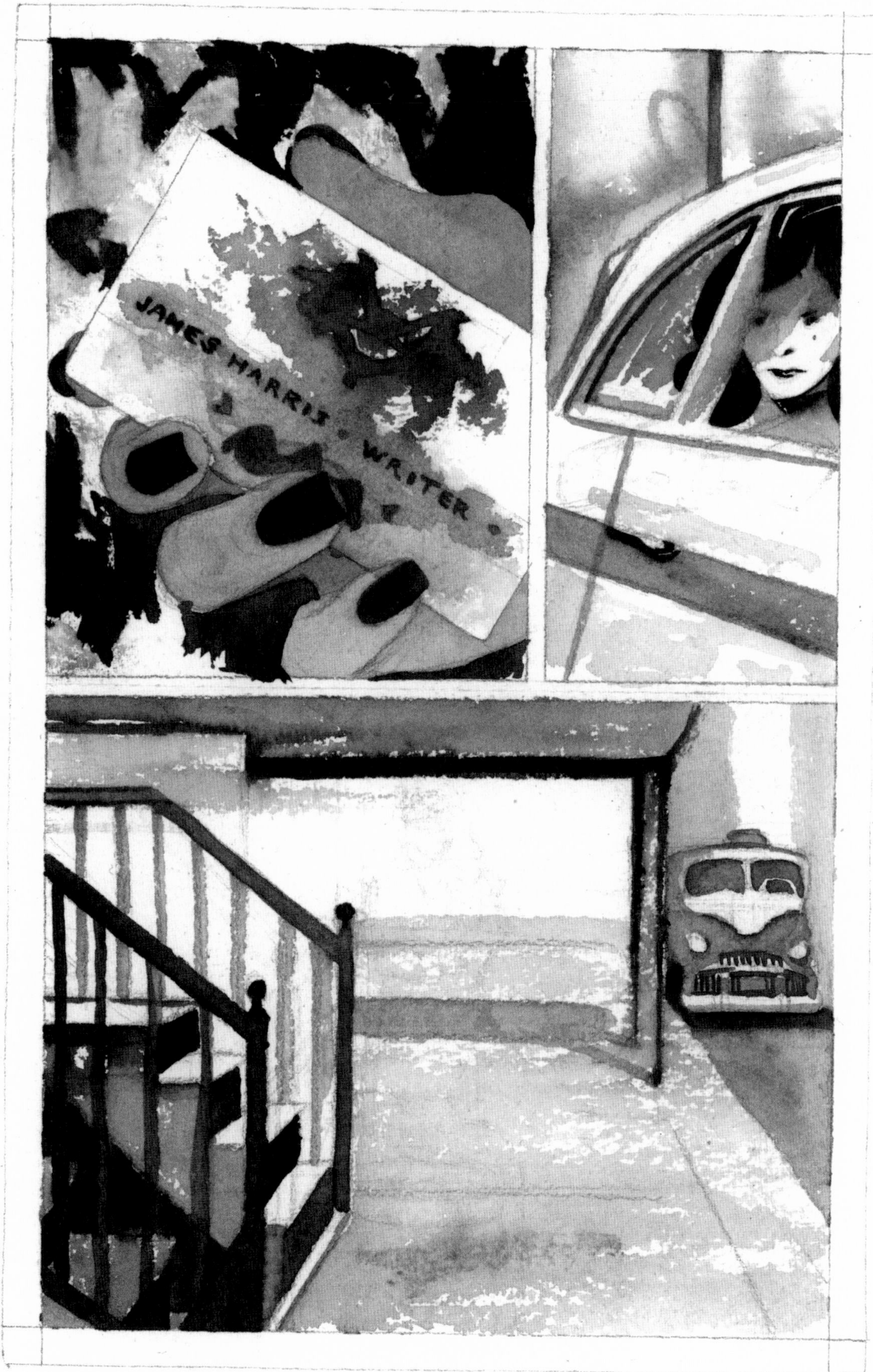
JAMES HARRIS • WRITER

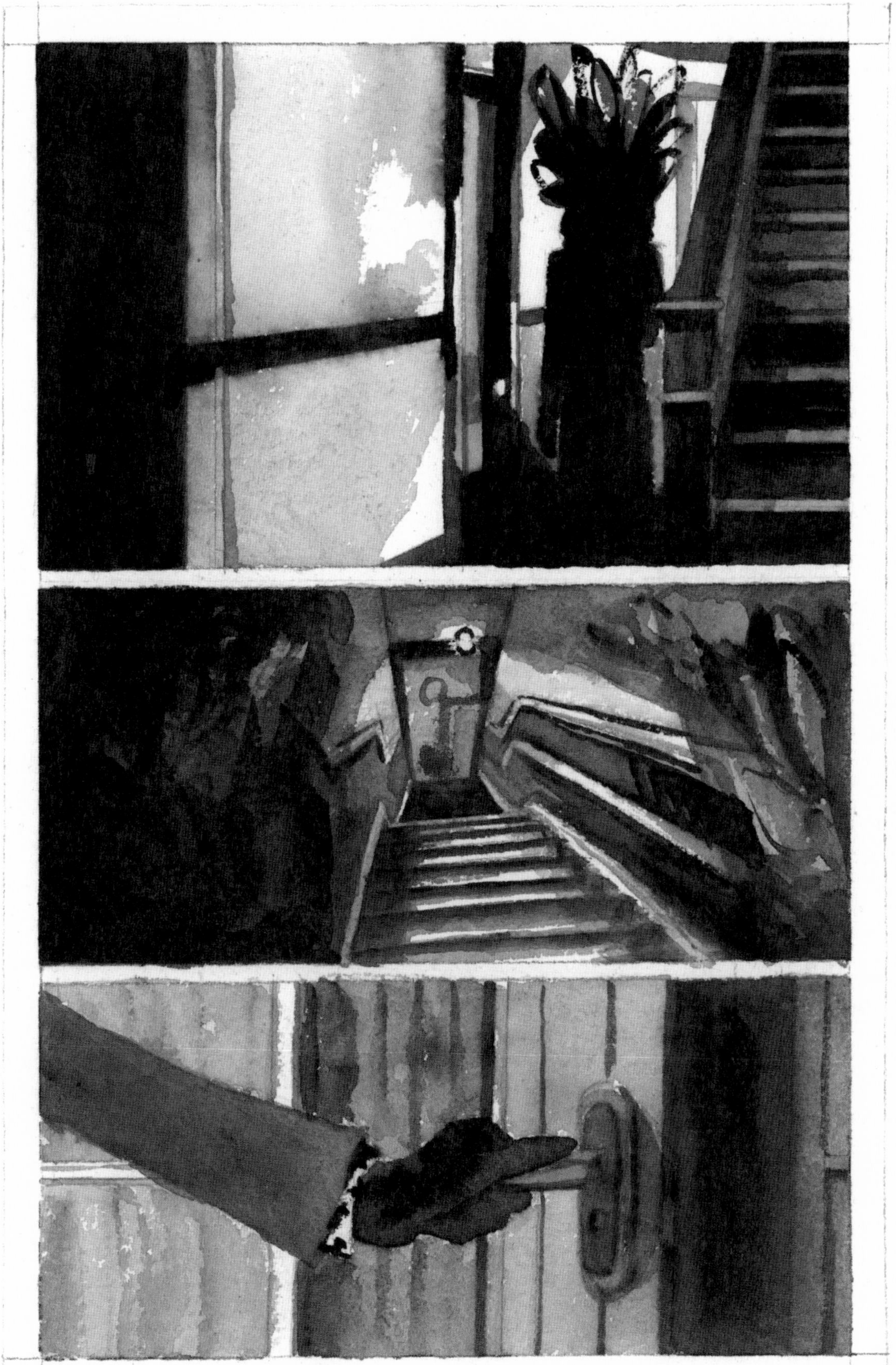

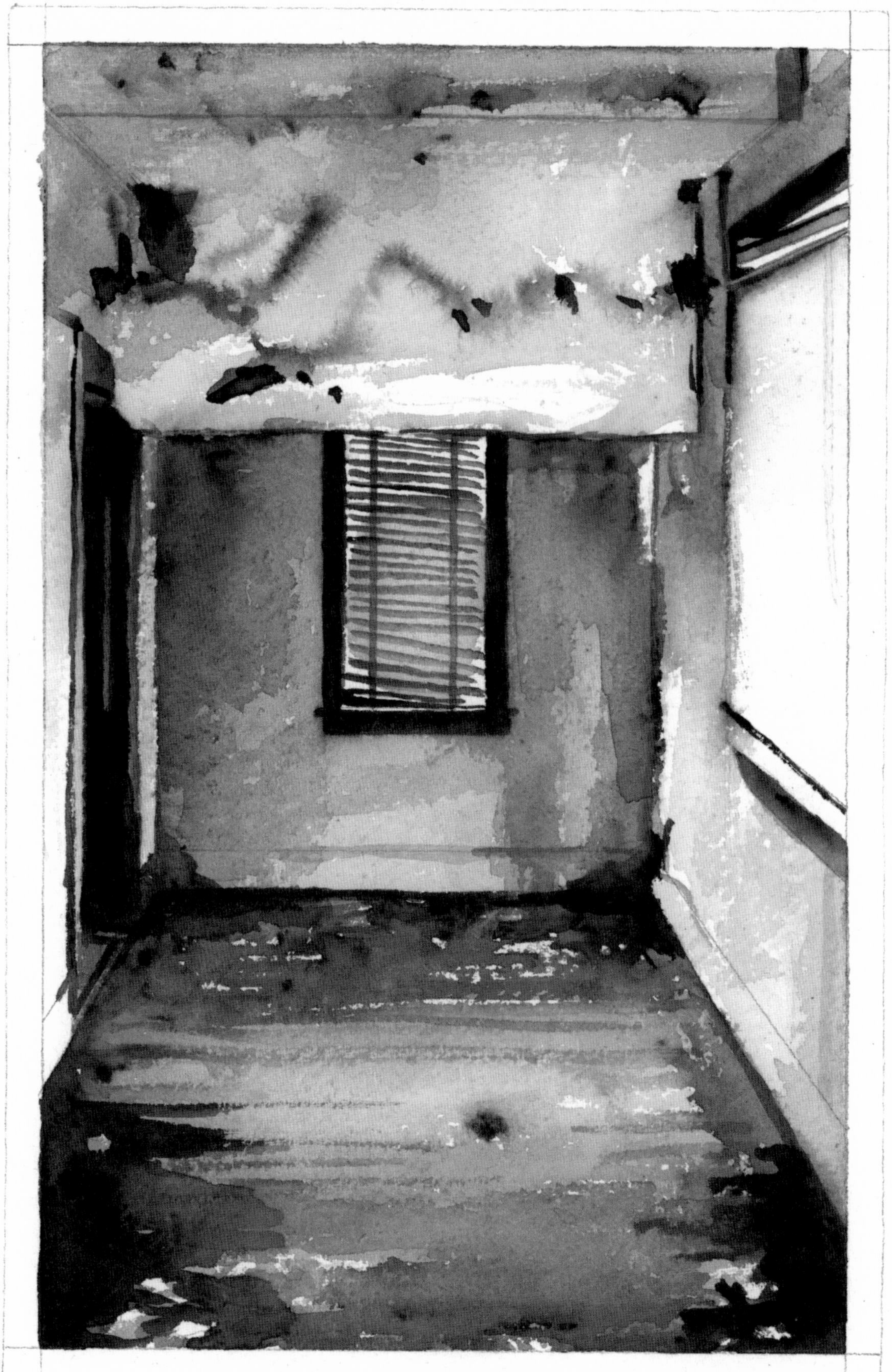

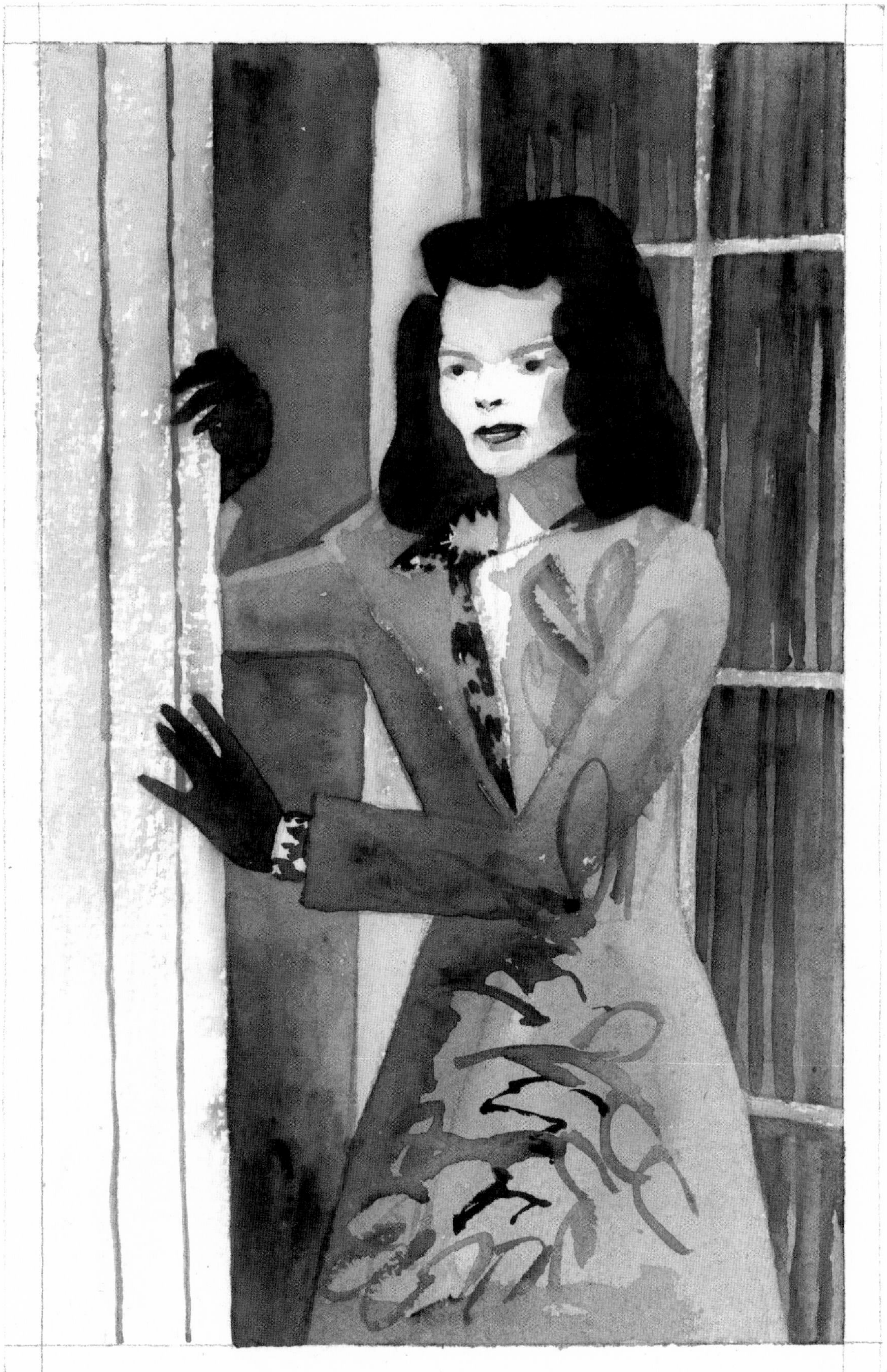

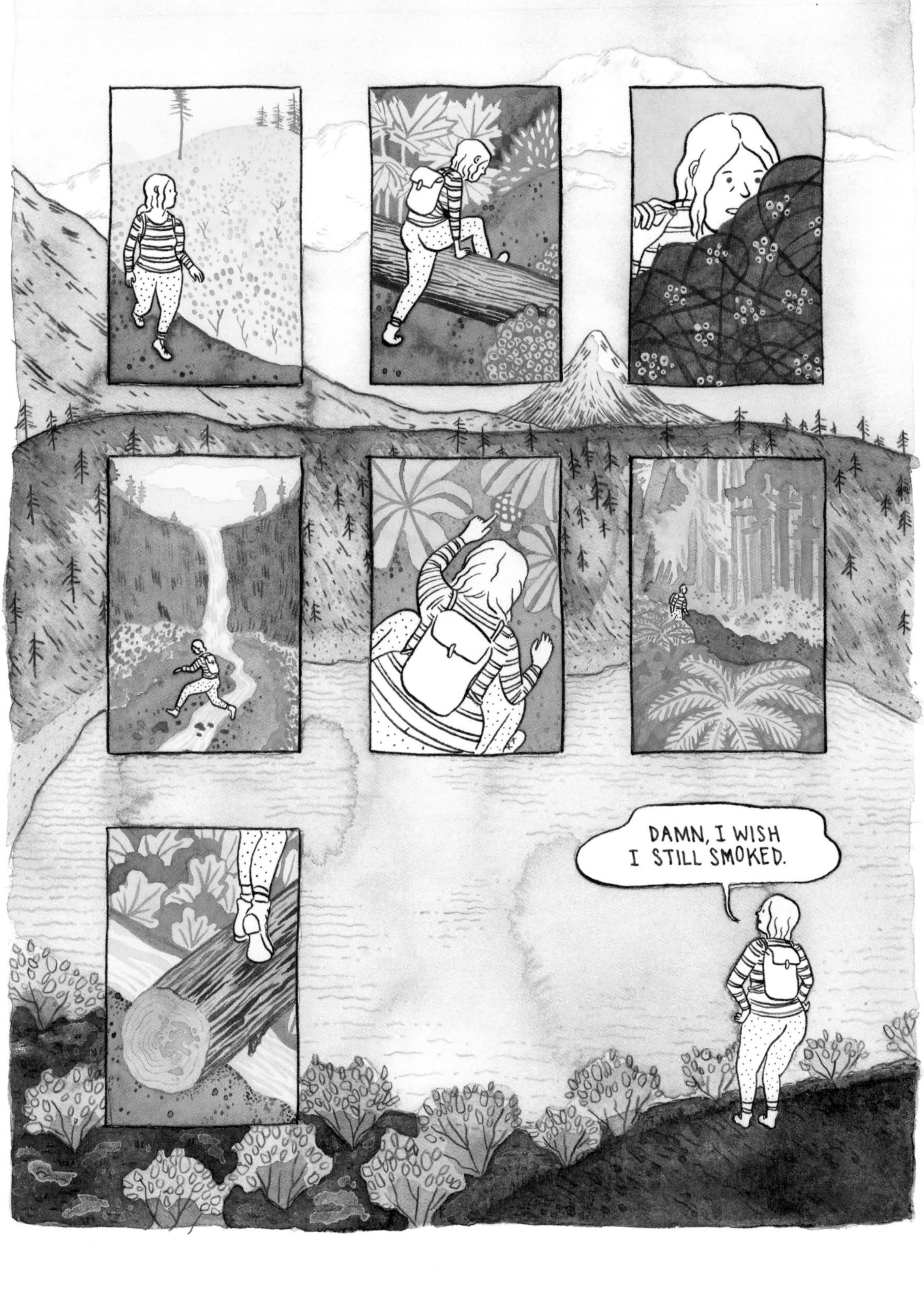
DAMN, I WISH
I STILL SMOKED.

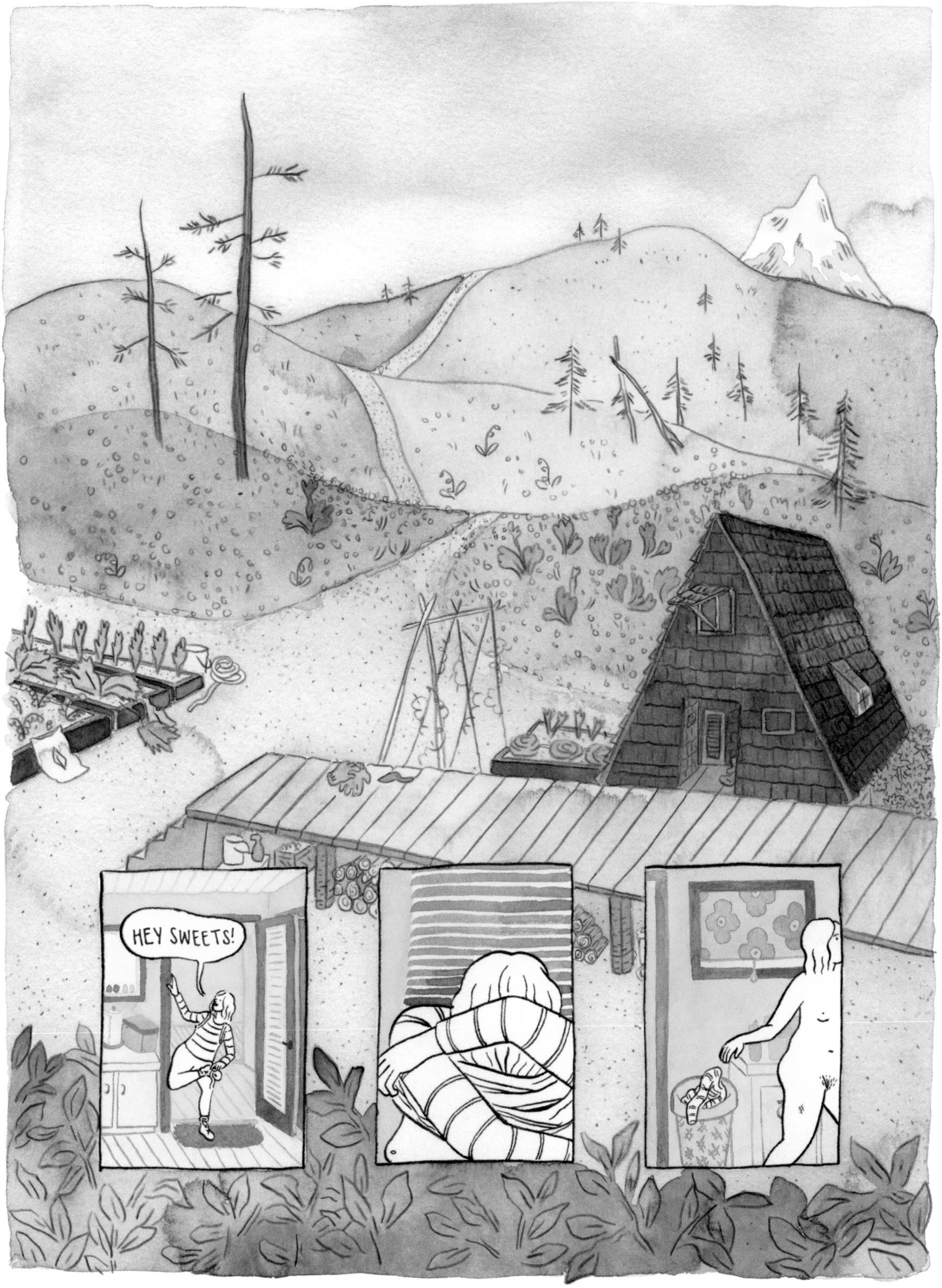
HEY SWEETS!

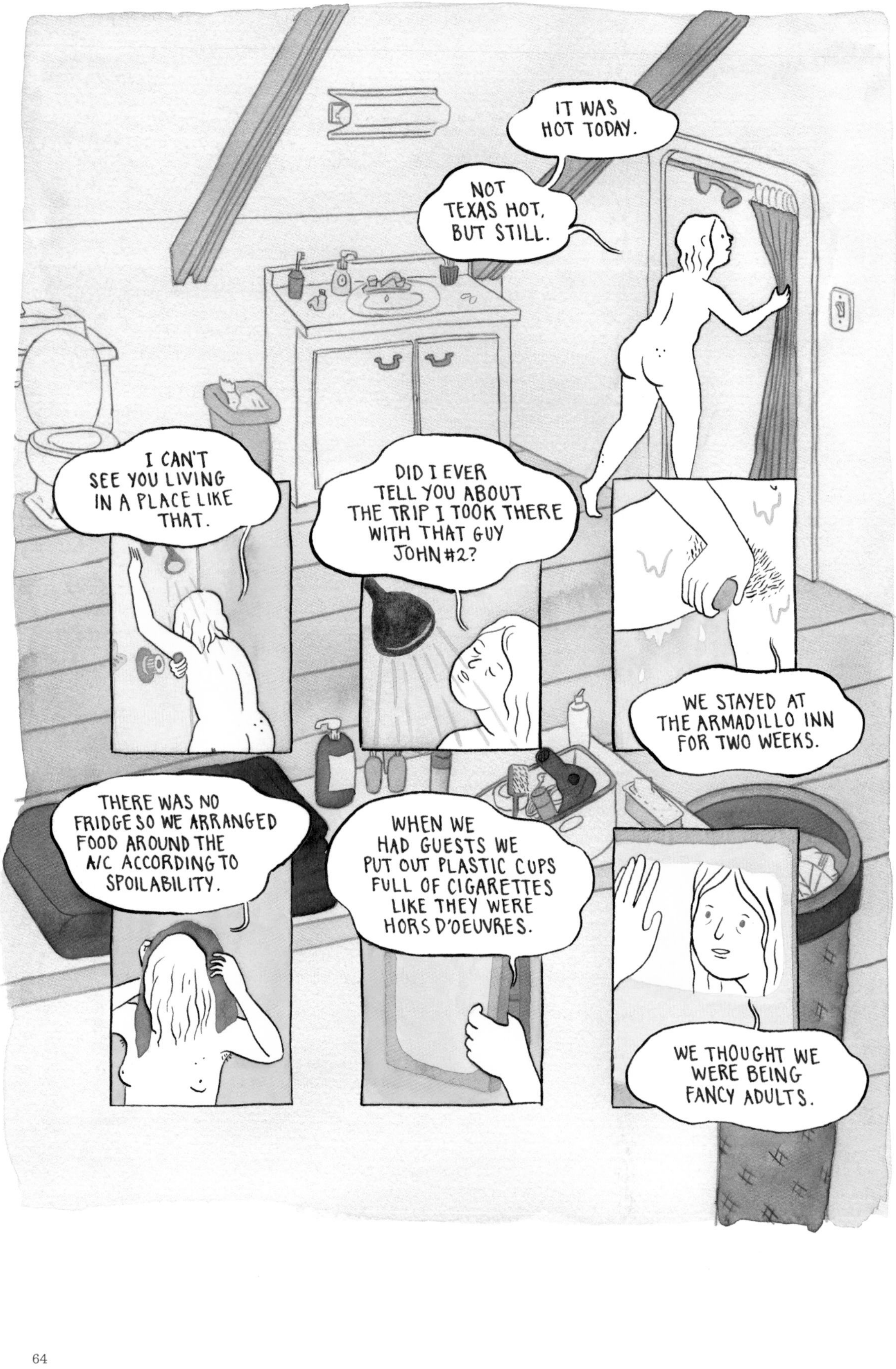
IT WAS HOT TODAY.
NOT TEXAS HOT, BUT STILL.
I CAN'T SEE YOU LIVING IN A PLACE LIKE THAT.
DID I EVER TELL YOU ABOUT THE TRIP I TOOK THERE WITH THAT GUY JOHN #2?
WE STAYED AT THE ARMADILLO INN FOR TWO WEEKS.
THERE WAS NO FRIDGE SO WE ARRANGED FOOD AROUND THE A/C ACCORDING TO SPOILABILITY.
WHEN WE HAD GUESTS WE PUT OUT PLASTIC CUPS FULL OF CIGARETTES LIKE THEY WERE HORS D'OEUVRES.
WE THOUGHT WE WERE BEING FANCY ADULTS.

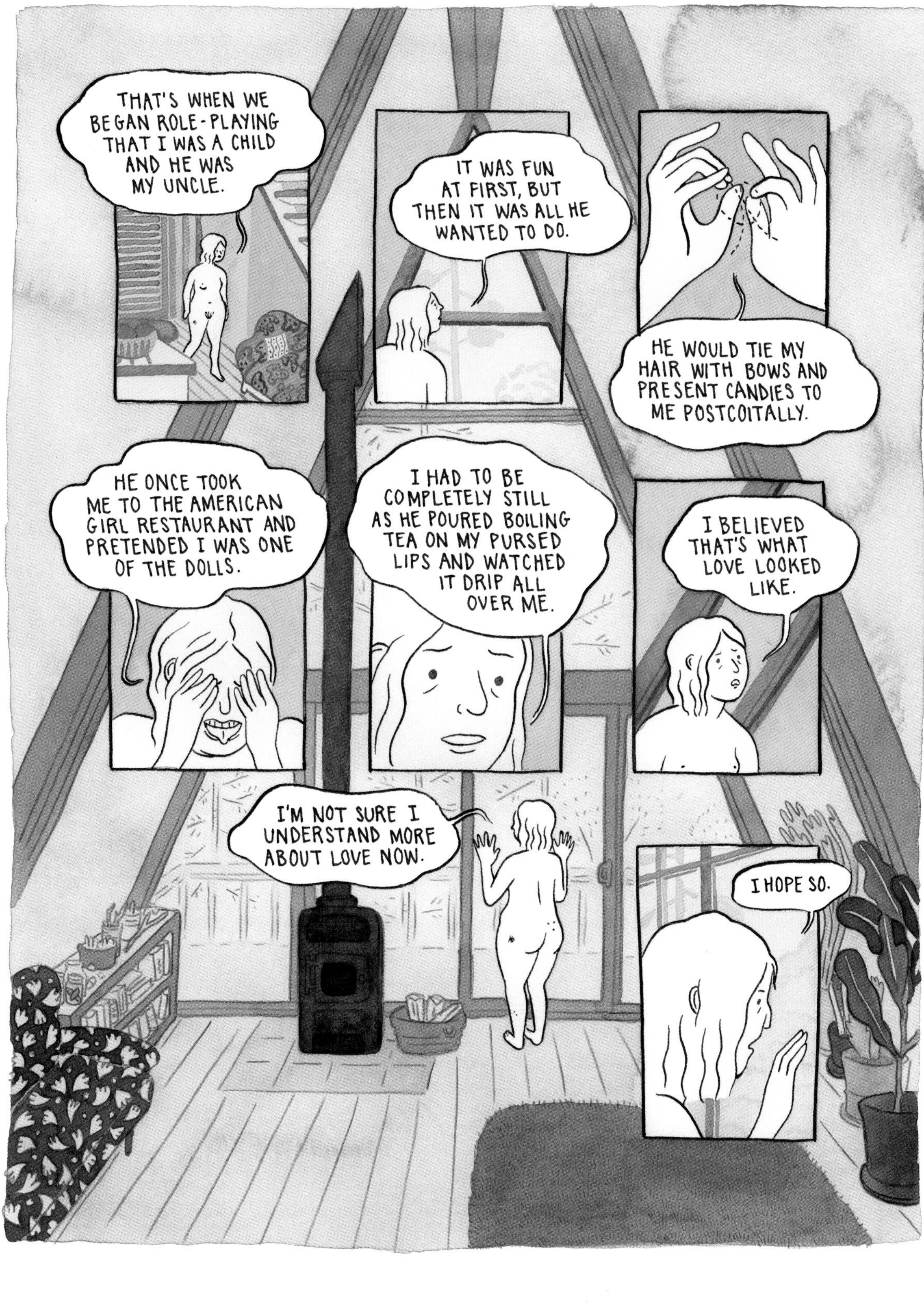
THAT'S WHEN WE BEGAN ROLE-PLAYING THAT I WAS A CHILD AND HE WAS MY UNCLE.
IT WAS FUN AT FIRST, BUT THEN IT WAS ALL HE WANTED TO DO.
HE WOULD TIE MY HAIR WITH BOWS AND PRESENT CANDIES TO ME POSTCOITALLY.
HE ONCE TOOK ME TO THE AMERICAN GIRL RESTAURANT AND PRETENDED I WAS ONE OF THE DOLLS.
I HAD TO BE COMPLETELY STILL AS HE POURED BOILING TEA ON MY PURSED LIPS AND WATCHED IT DRIP ALL OVER ME.
I BELIEVED THAT'S WHAT LOVE LOOKED LIKE.
I'M NOT SURE I UNDERSTAND MORE ABOUT LOVE NOW.
I HOPE SO.

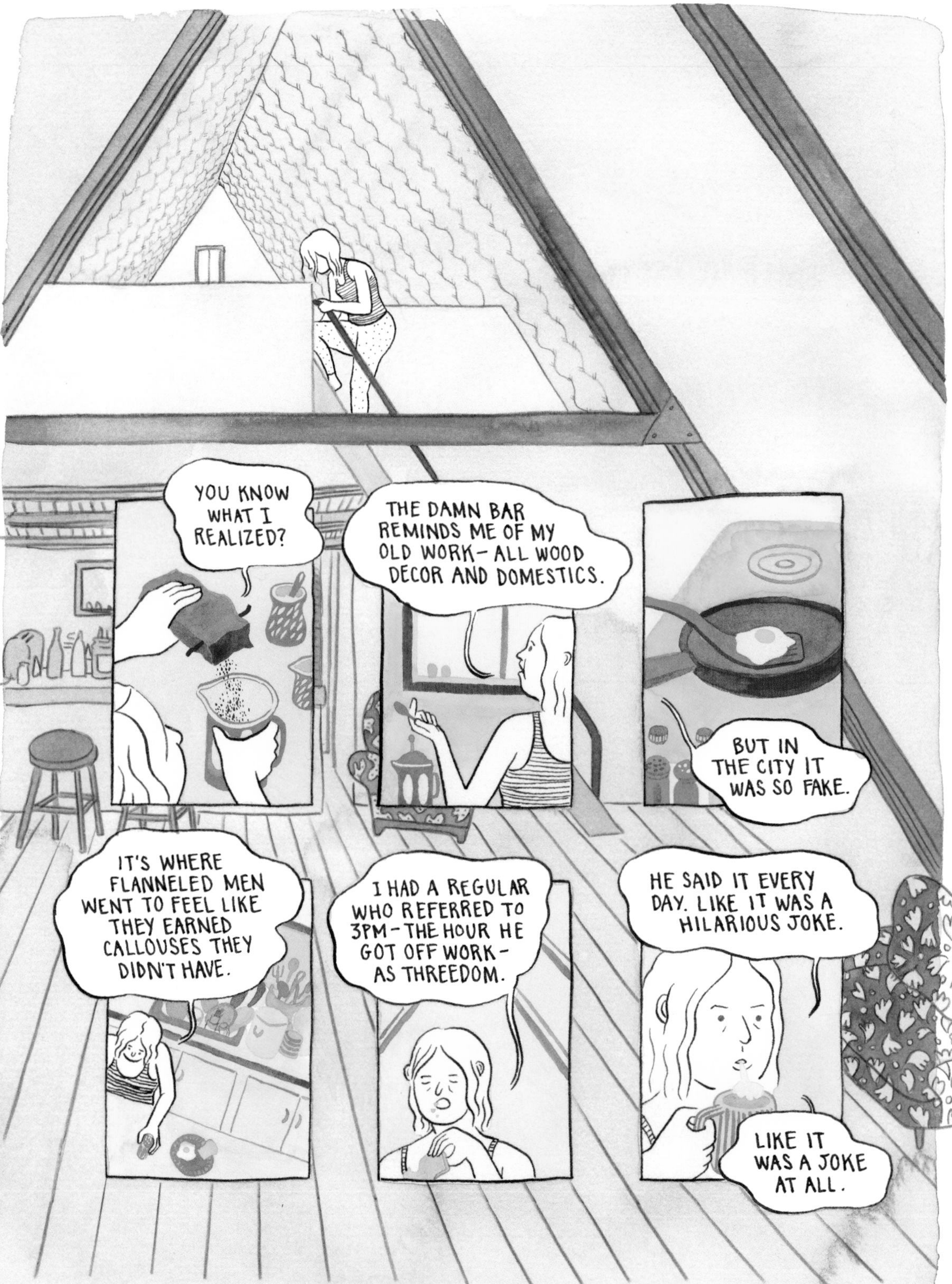
YOU KNOW WHAT I REALIZED?
THE DAMN BAR REMINDS ME OF MY OLD WORK- ALL WOOD DECOR AND DOMESTICS.
BUT IN THE CITY IT WAS SO FAKE.
IT'S WHERE FLANNELED MEN WENT TO FEEL LIKE THEY EARNED CALLOUSES THEY DIDN'T HAVE.
I HAD A REGULAR WHO REFERRED TO 3PM - THE HOUR HE GOT OFF WORK - AS THREEDOM.
HE SAID IT EVERY DAY. LIKE IT WAS A HILARIOUS JOKE.
LIKE IT WAS A JOKE AT ALL.

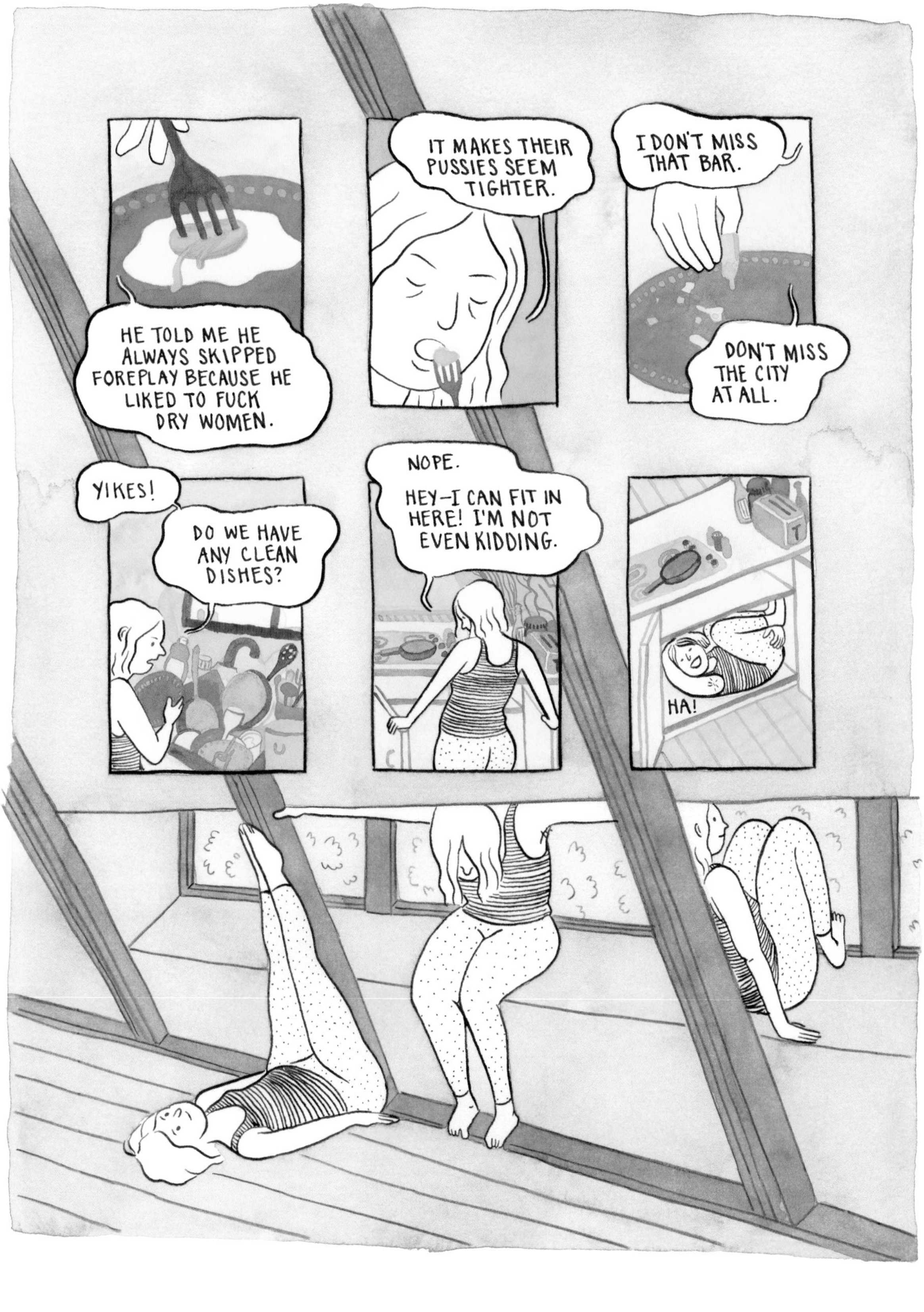
HE TOLD ME HE ALWAYS SKIPPED FOREPLAY BECAUSE HE LIKED TO FUCK DRY WOMEN.
IT MAKES THEIR PUSSIES SEEM TIGHTER.
I DON'T MISS THAT BAR.
DON'T MISS THE CITY AT ALL.
YIKES!
DO WE HAVE ANY CLEAN DISHES?
NOPE.
HEY—I CAN FIT IN HERE! I'M NOT EVEN KIDDING.
HA!

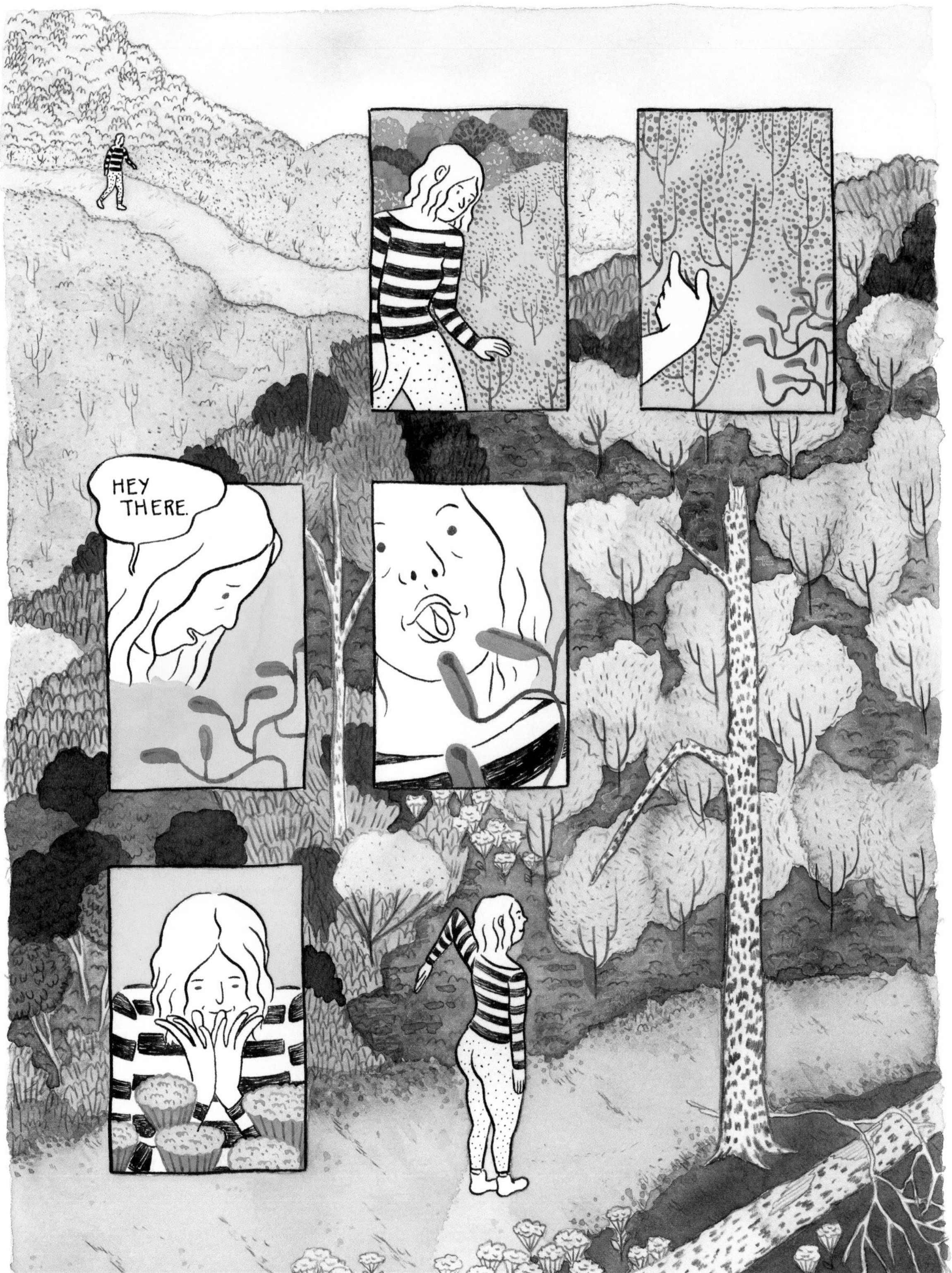
HEY THERE.

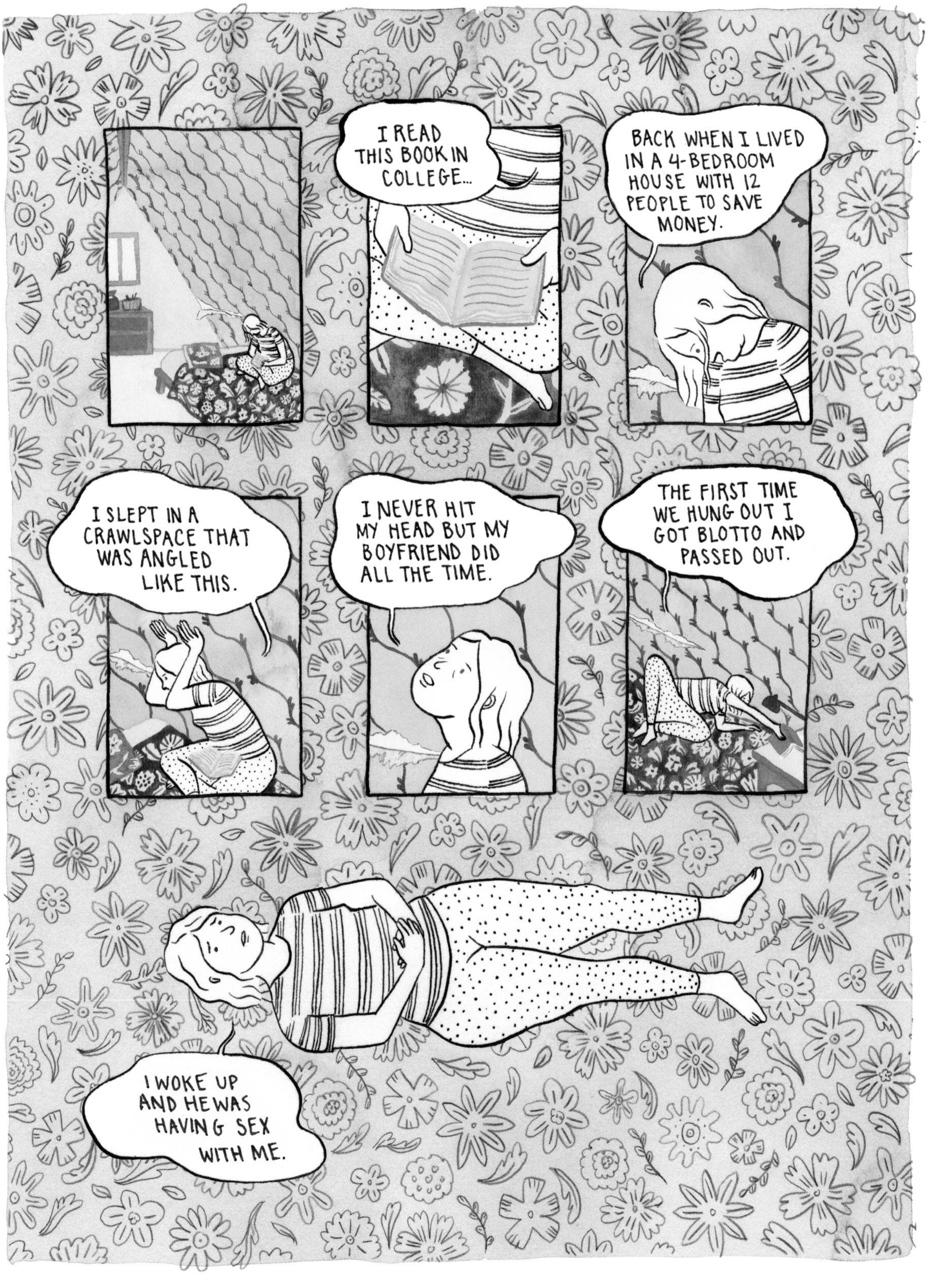
I READ THIS BOOK IN COLLEGE...
BACK WHEN I LIVED IN A 4-BEDROOM HOUSE WITH 12 PEOPLE TO SAVE MONEY.
I SLEPT IN A CRAWLSPACE THAT WAS ANGLED LIKE THIS.
I NEVER HIT MY HEAD BUT MY BOYFRIEND DID ALL THE TIME.
THE FIRST TIME WE HUNG OUT I GOT BLOTTO AND PASSED OUT.
I WOKE UP AND HE WAS HAVING SEX WITH ME.

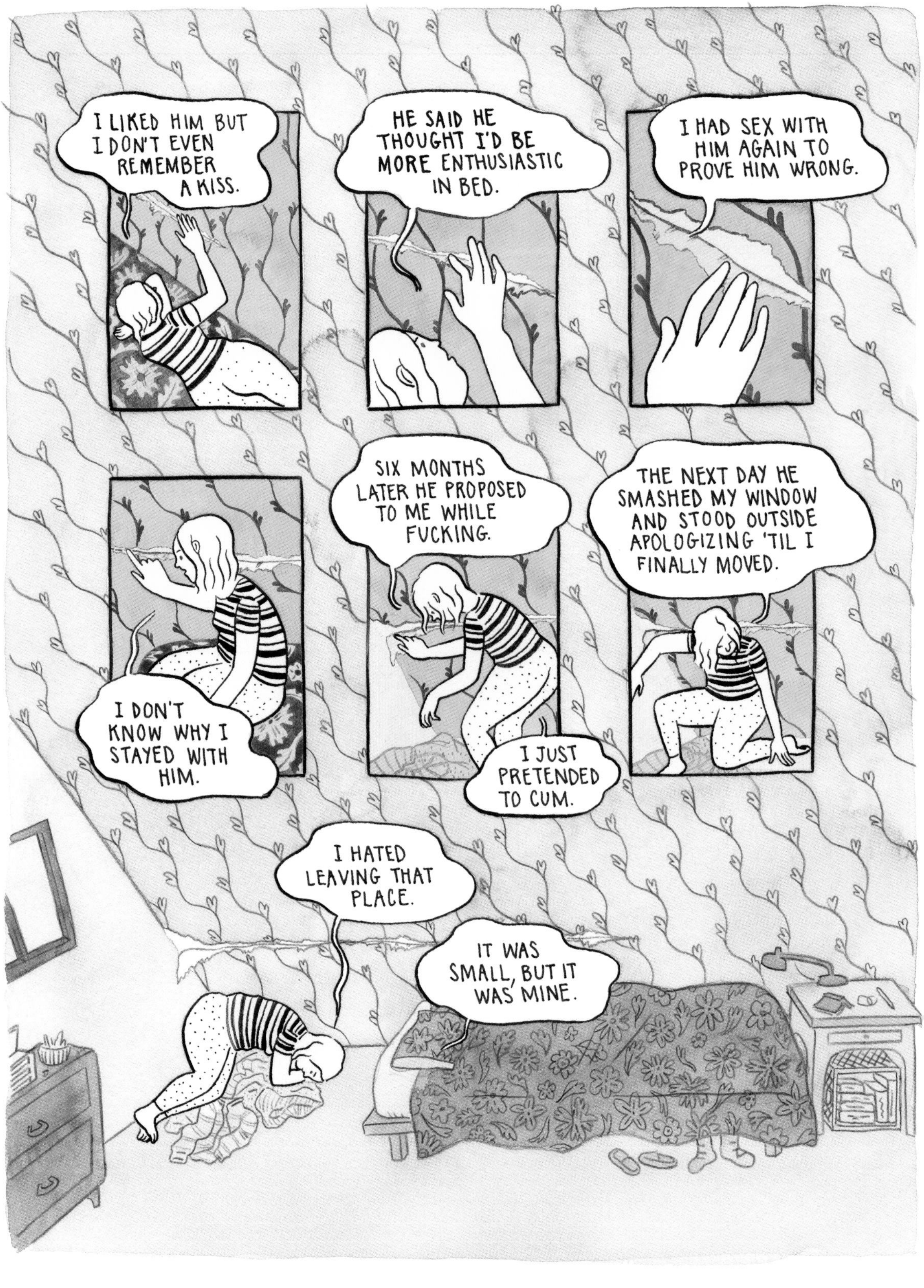
I LIKED HIM BUT I DON'T EVEN REMEMBER A KISS.
HE SAID HE THOUGHT I'D BE MORE ENTHUSIASTIC IN BED.
I HAD SEX WITH HIM AGAIN TO PROVE HIM WRONG.
I DON'T KNOW WHY I STAYED WITH HIM.
SIX MONTHS LATER HE PROPOSED TO ME WHILE FUCKING.
I JUST PRETENDED TO CUM.
THE NEXT DAY HE SMASHED MY WINDOW AND STOOD OUTSIDE APOLOGIZING 'TIL I FINALLY MOVED.
I HATED LEAVING THAT PLACE.
IT WAS SMALL, BUT IT WAS MINE.

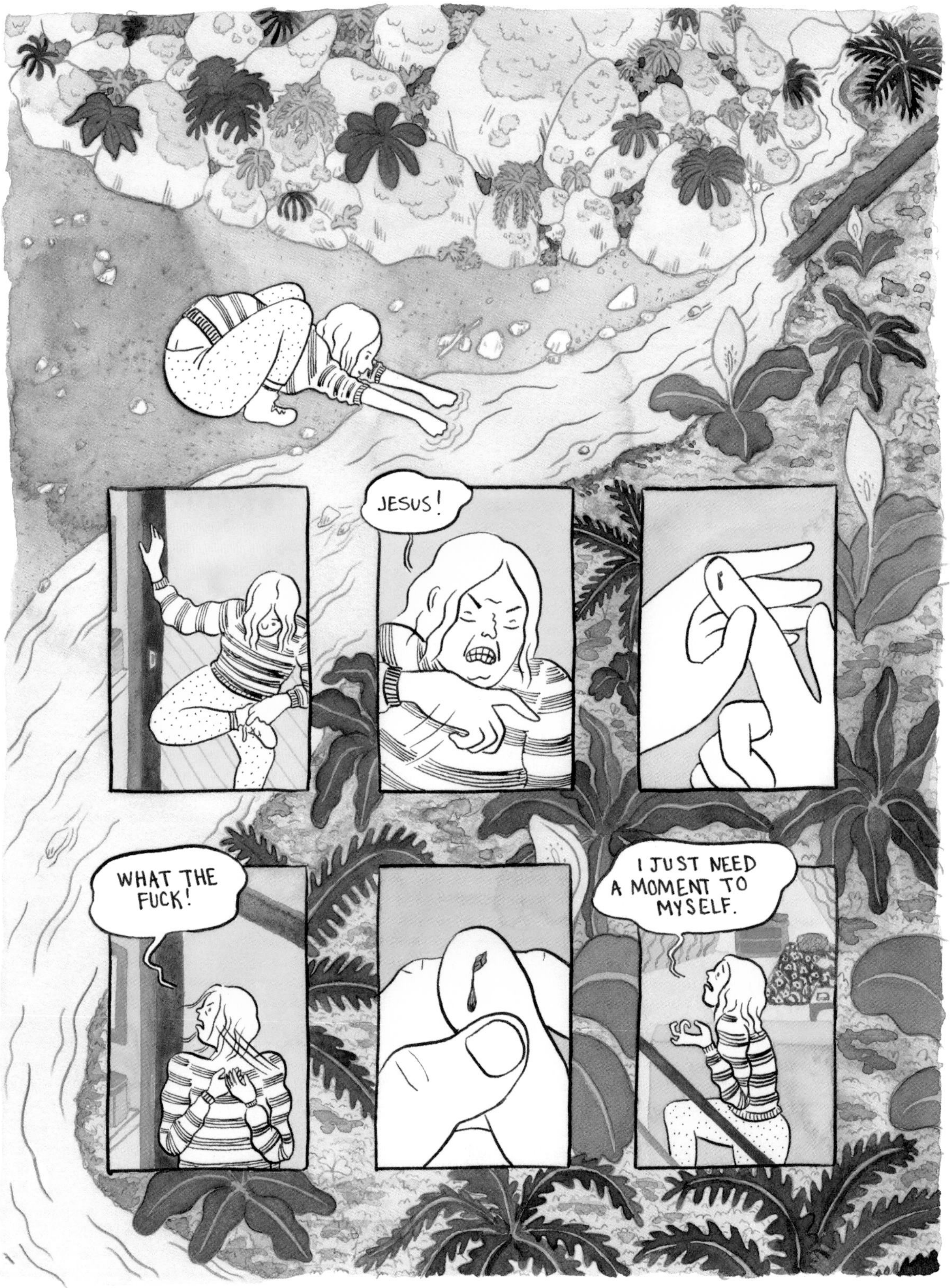
JESUS!
WHAT THE FUCK!
I JUST NEED A MOMENT TO MYSELF.

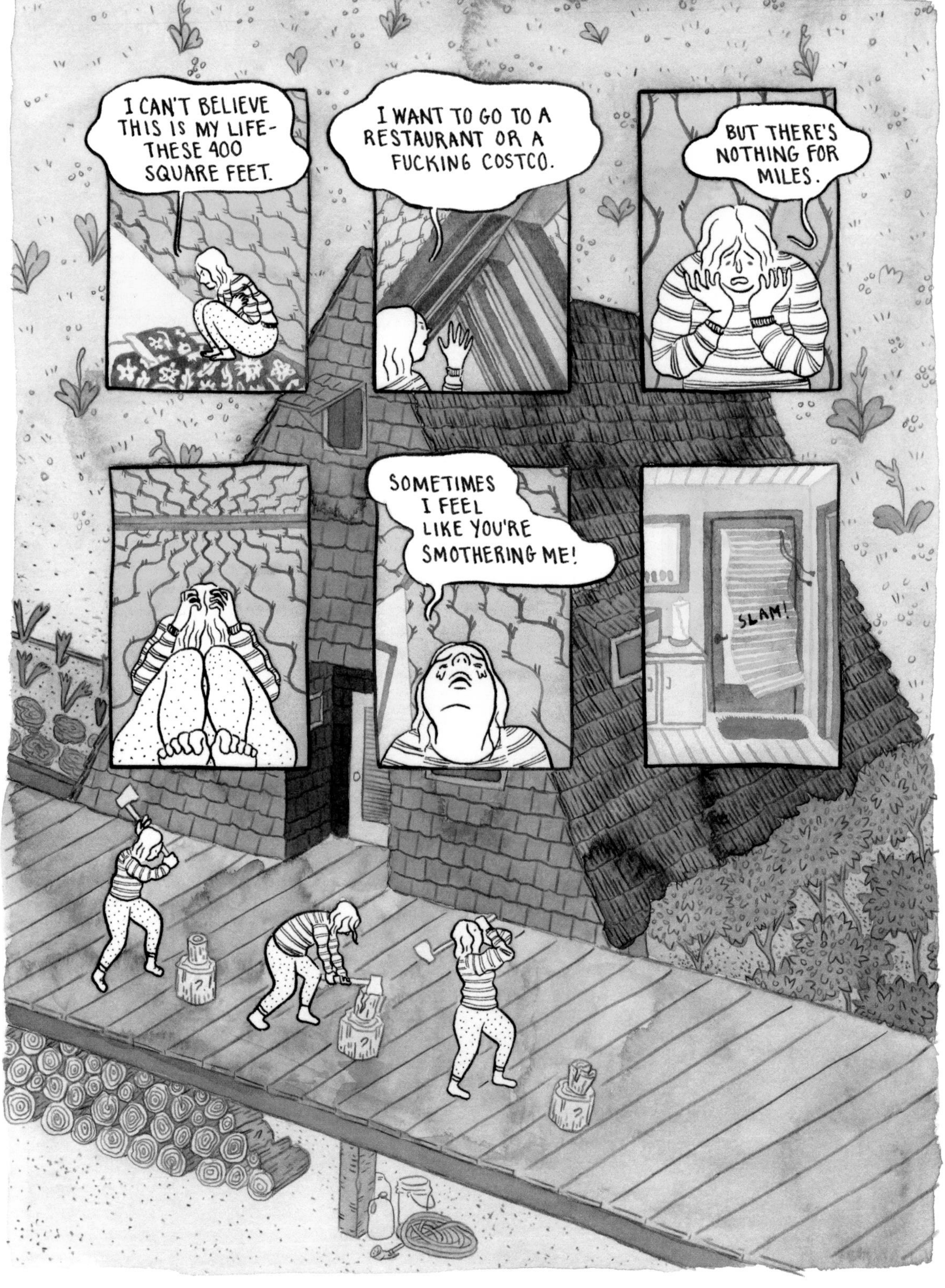
I CAN'T BELIEVE THIS IS MY LIFE- THESE 400 SQUARE FEET.
I WANT TO GO TO A RESTAURANT OR A FUCKING COSTCO.
BUT THERE'S NOTHING FOR MILES.
SOMETIMES I FEEL LIKE YOU'RE SMOTHERING ME!
SLAM!

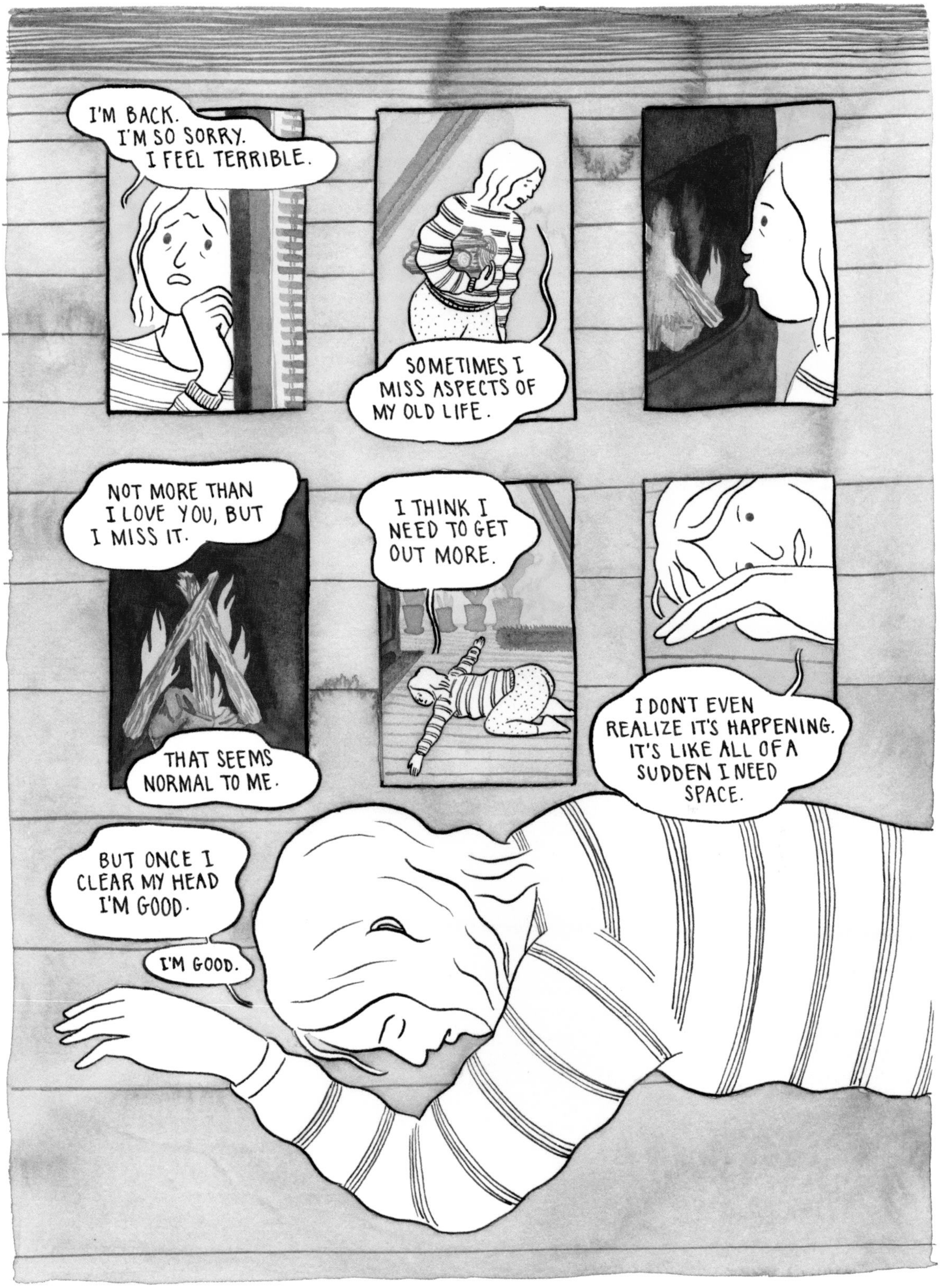
I'M BACK. I'M SO SORRY. I FEEL TERRIBLE.
SOMETIMES I MISS ASPECTS OF MY OLD LIFE.
NOT MORE THAN I LOVE YOU, BUT I MISS IT.
THAT SEEMS NORMAL TO ME.
I THINK I NEED TO GET OUT MORE.
I DON'T EVEN REALIZE IT'S HAPPENING. IT'S LIKE ALL OF A SUDDEN I NEED SPACE.
BUT ONCE I CLEAR MY HEAD I'M GOOD.
I'M GOOD.

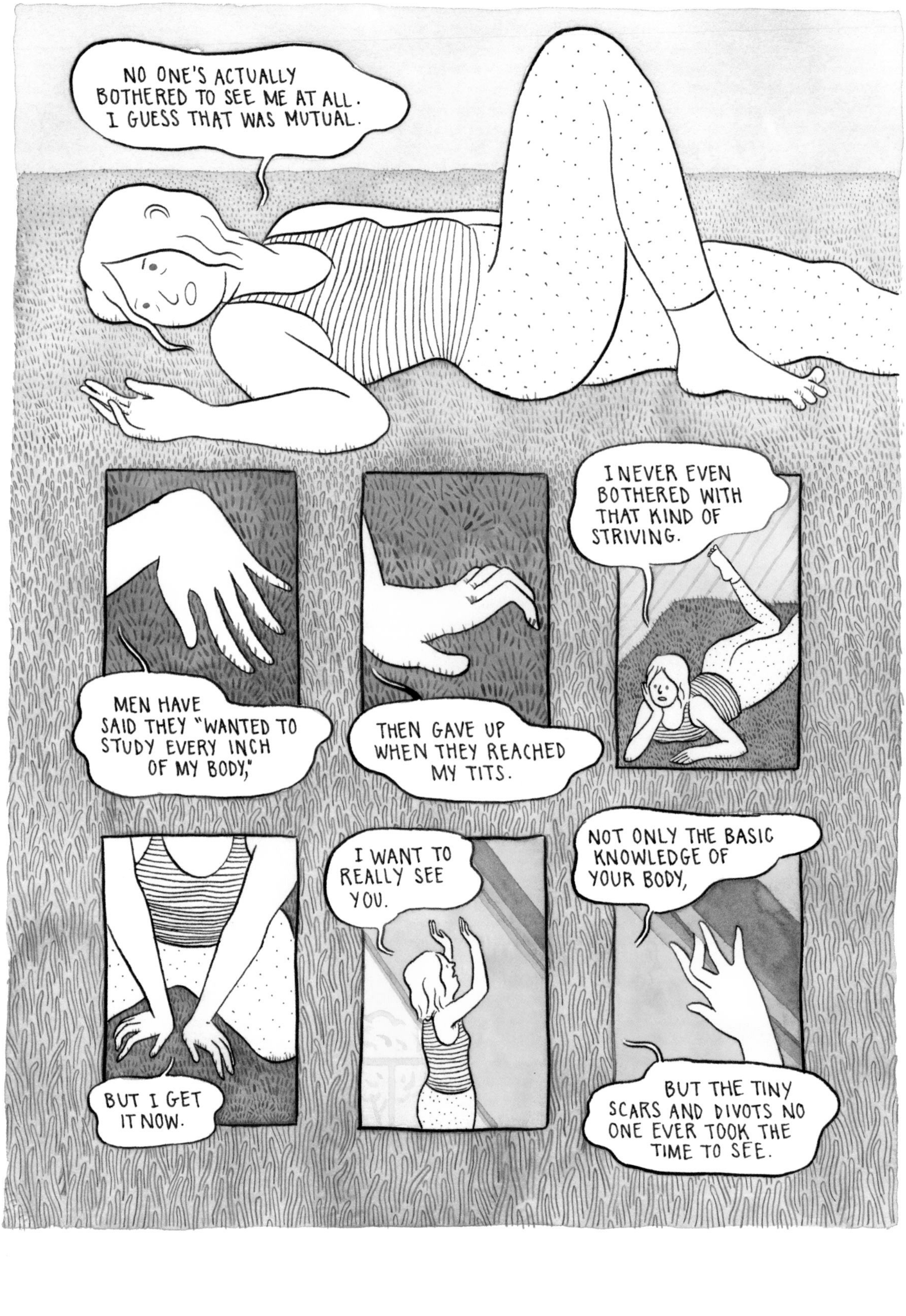
NO ONE'S ACTUALLY BOTHERED TO SEE ME AT ALL. I GUESS THAT WAS MUTUAL.
MEN HAVE SAID THEY "WANTED TO STUDY EVERY INCH OF MY BODY,"
THEN GAVE UP WHEN THEY REACHED MY TITS.
I NEVER EVEN BOTHERED WITH THAT KIND OF STRIVING.
BUT I GET IT NOW.
I WANT TO REALLY SEE YOU.
NOT ONLY THE BASIC KNOWLEDGE OF YOUR BODY,
BUT THE TINY SCARS AND DIVOTS NO ONE EVER TOOK THE TIME TO SEE.

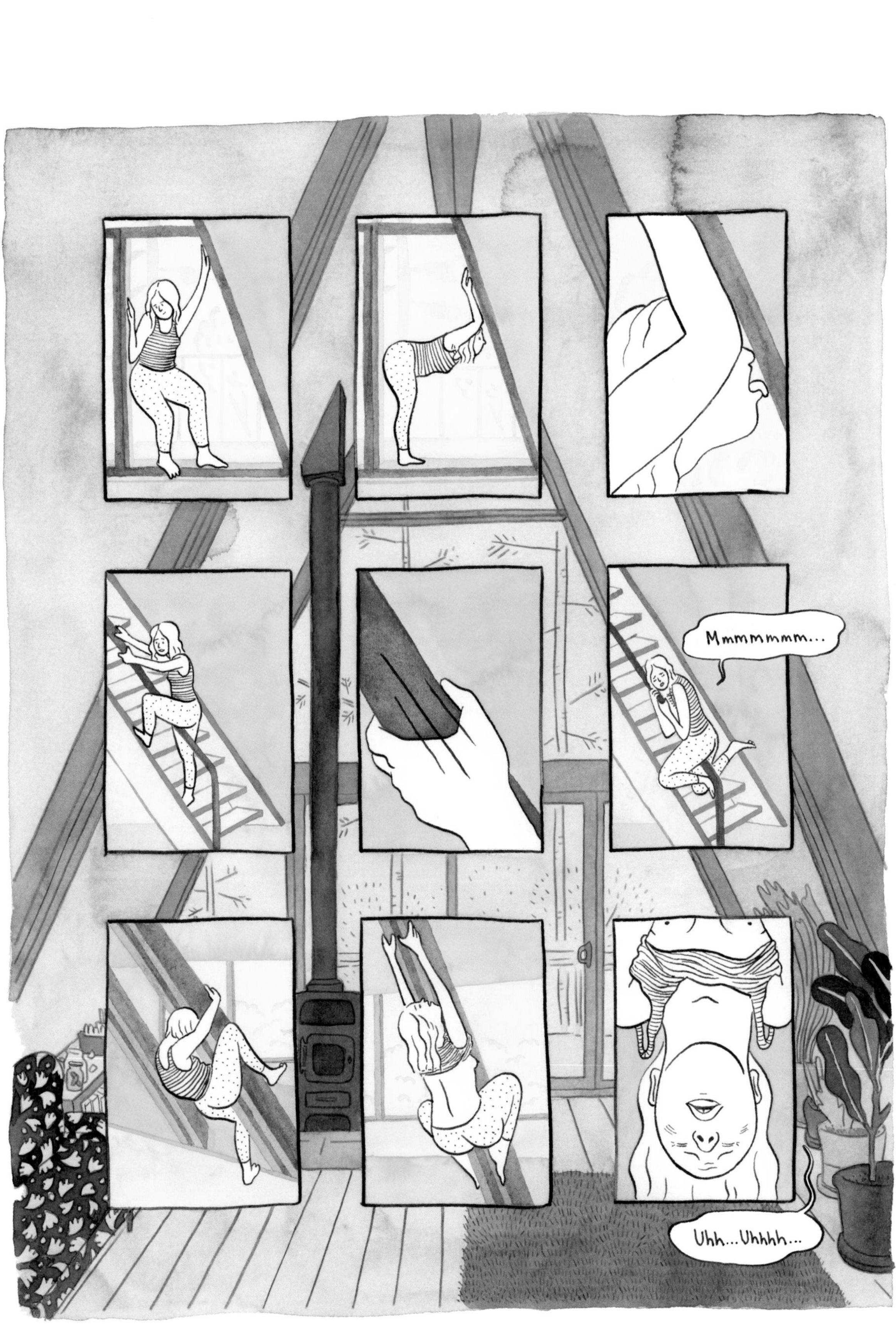
Mmmmmmm...
Uhh...Uhhhh...

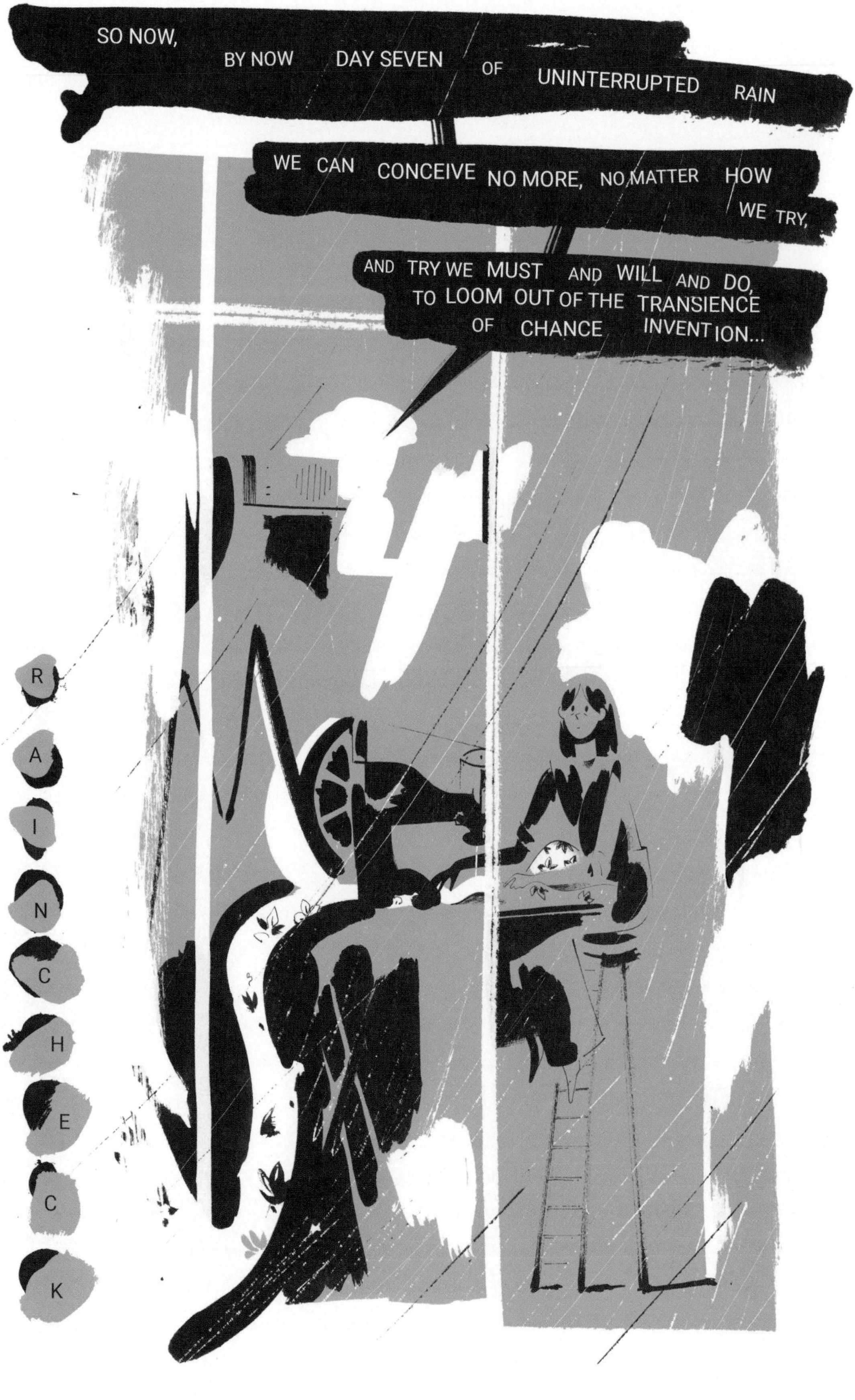
SO NOW, BY NOW DAY SEVEN OF UNINTERRUPTED RAIN
WE CAN CONCEIVE NO MORE, NO MATTER HOW WE TRY,
AND TRY WE MUST AND WILL AND DO, TO LOOM OUT OF THE TRANSIENCE OF CHANCE INVENTION...
R A I N C H E C K

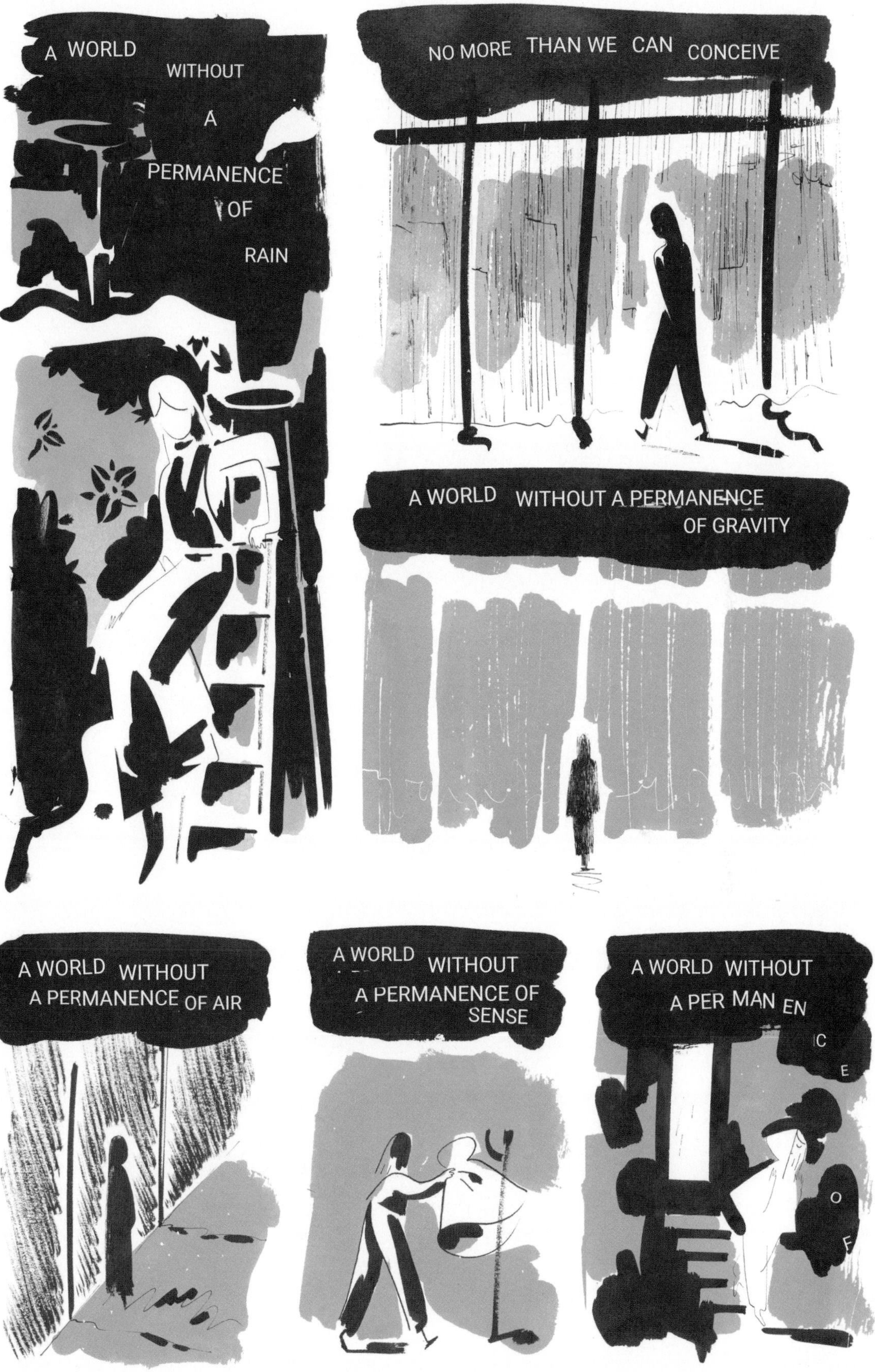
A WORLD WITHOUT A PERMANENCE OF RAIN
NO MORE THAN WE CAN CONCEIVE
A WORLD WITHOUT A PERMANENCE OF GRAVITY
A WORLD WITHOUT A PERMANENCE OF AIR
A WORLD WITHOUT A PERMANENCE OF SENSE
A WORLD WITHOUT A PER MAN EN
C
E
O
F

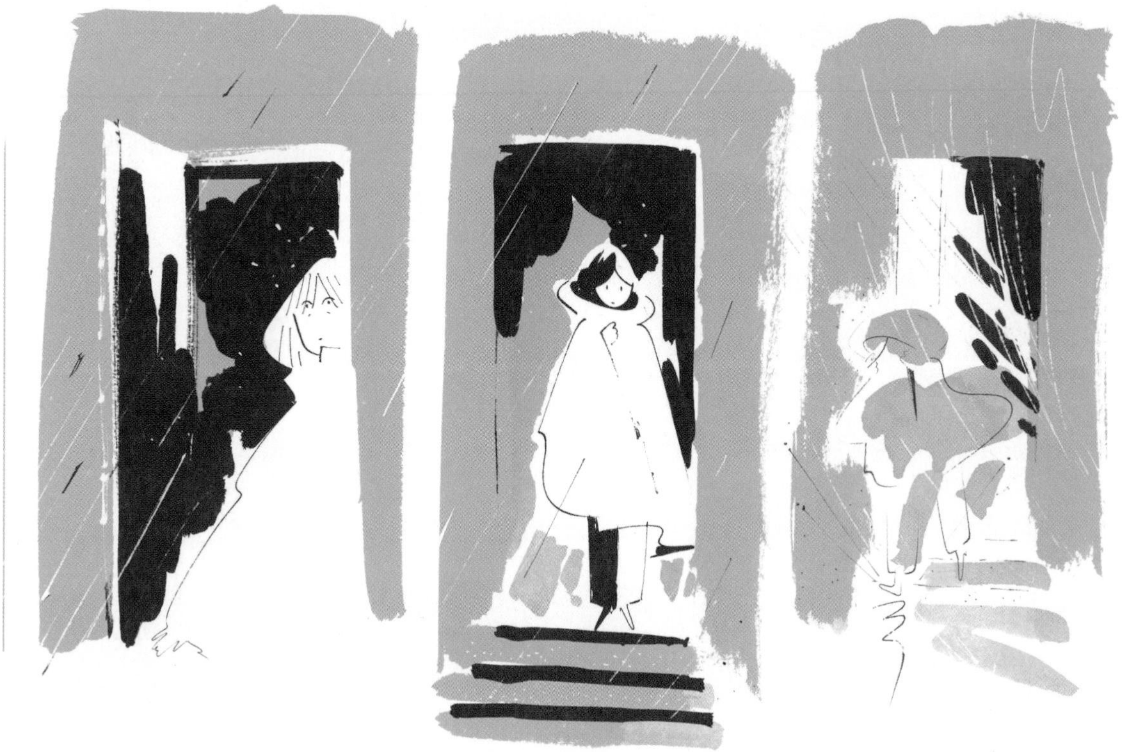

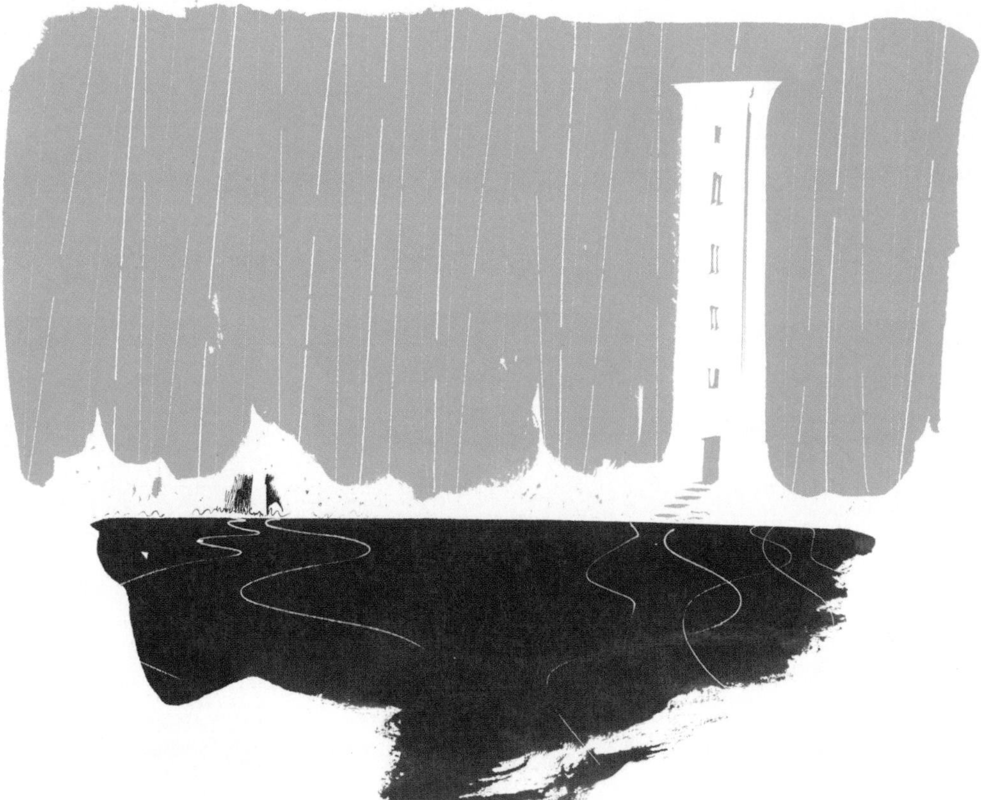

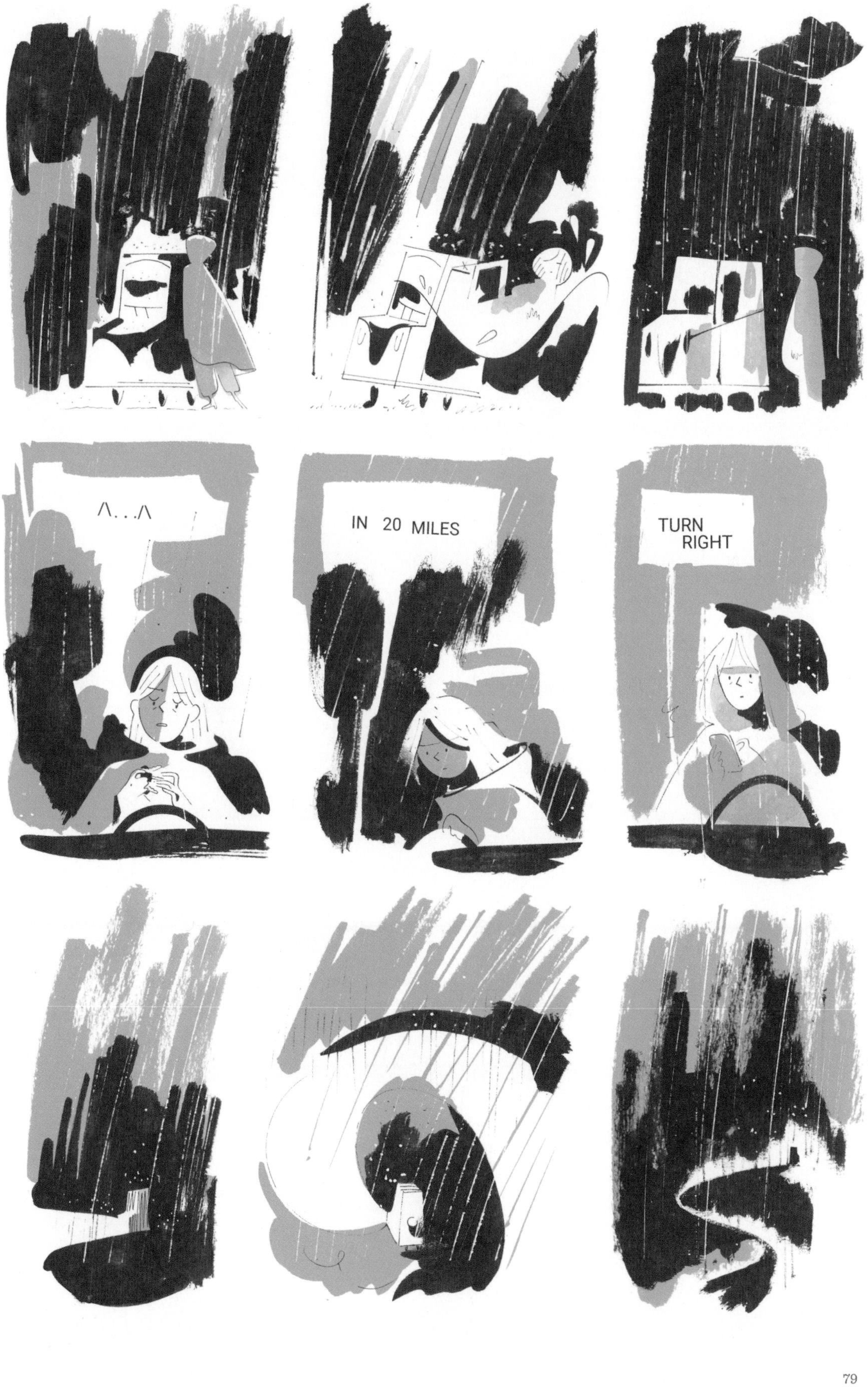
/\. . ./\
IN 20 MILES
TURN
RIGHT

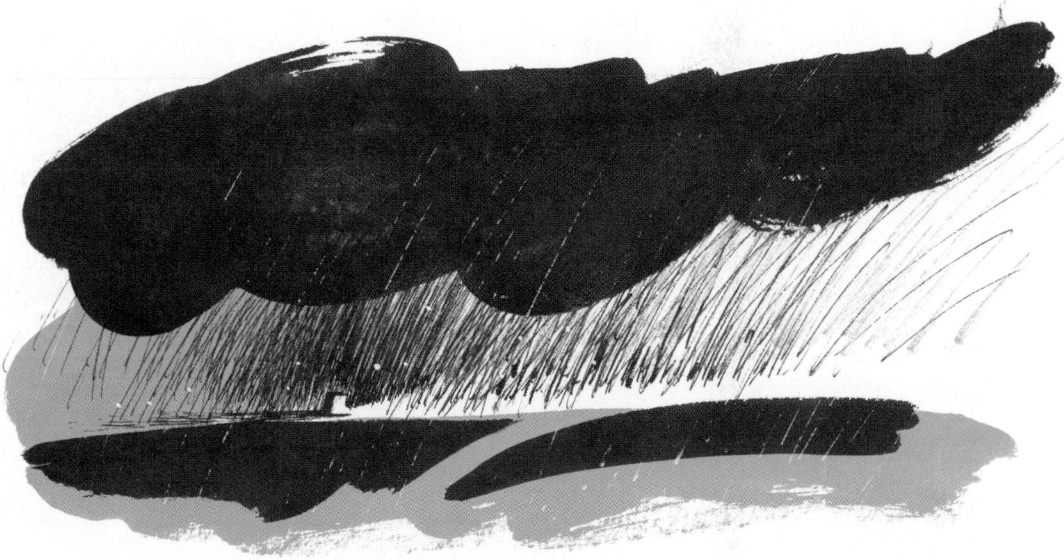

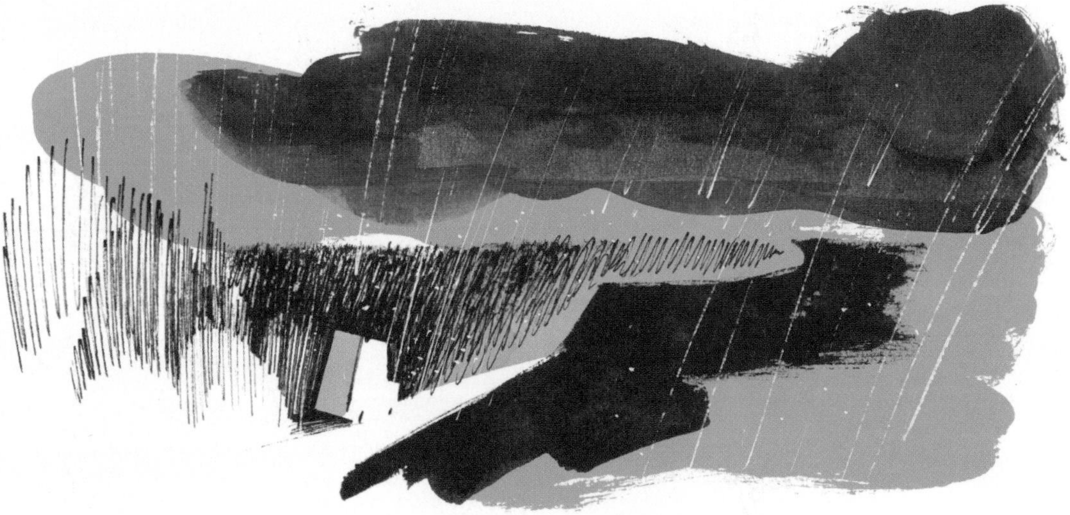

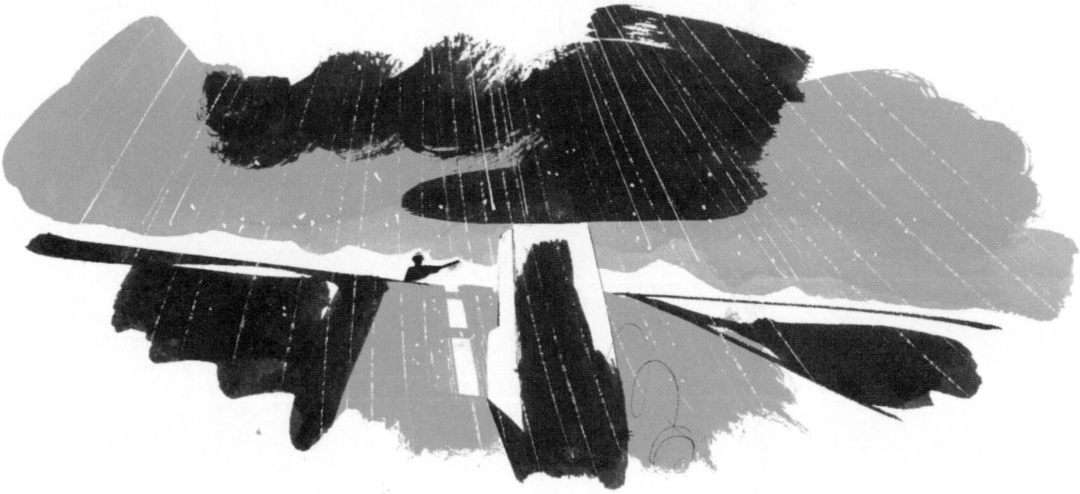

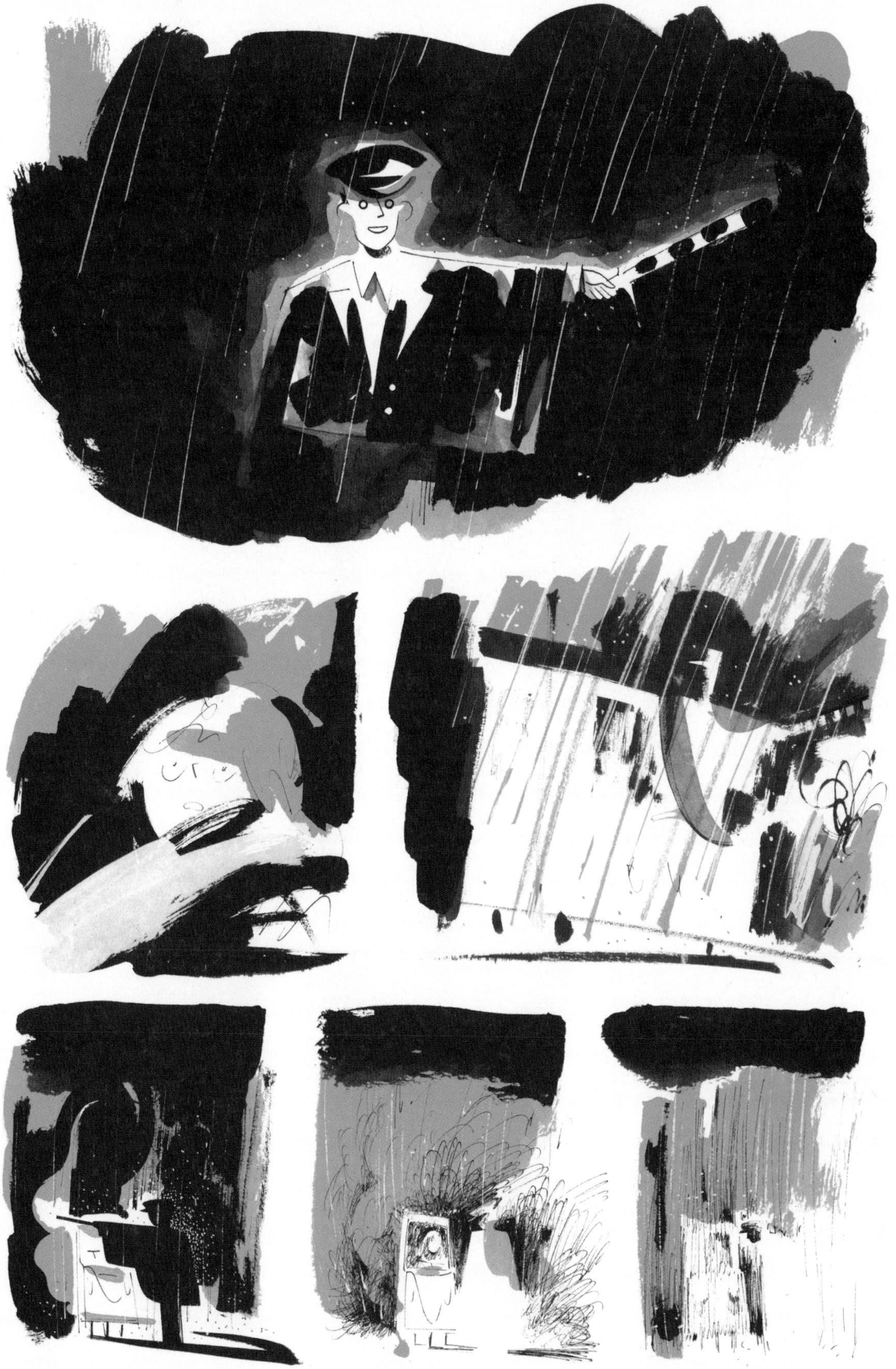

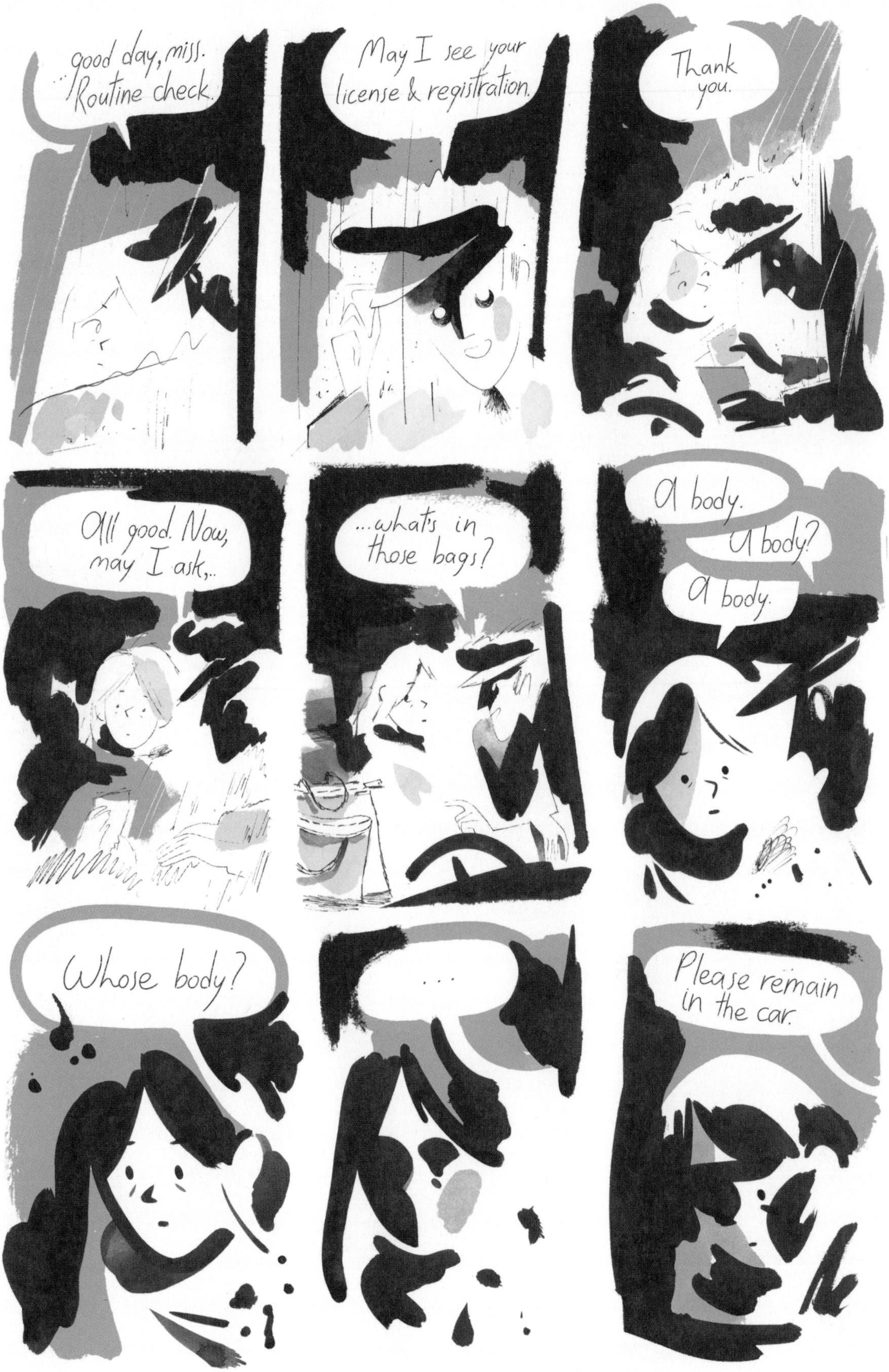
...good day, miss. Routine check.
May I see your license & registration.
Thank you.
All good. Now, may I ask,..
...what's in those bags?
A body.
A body?
A body.
Whose body?
...
Please remain in the car.

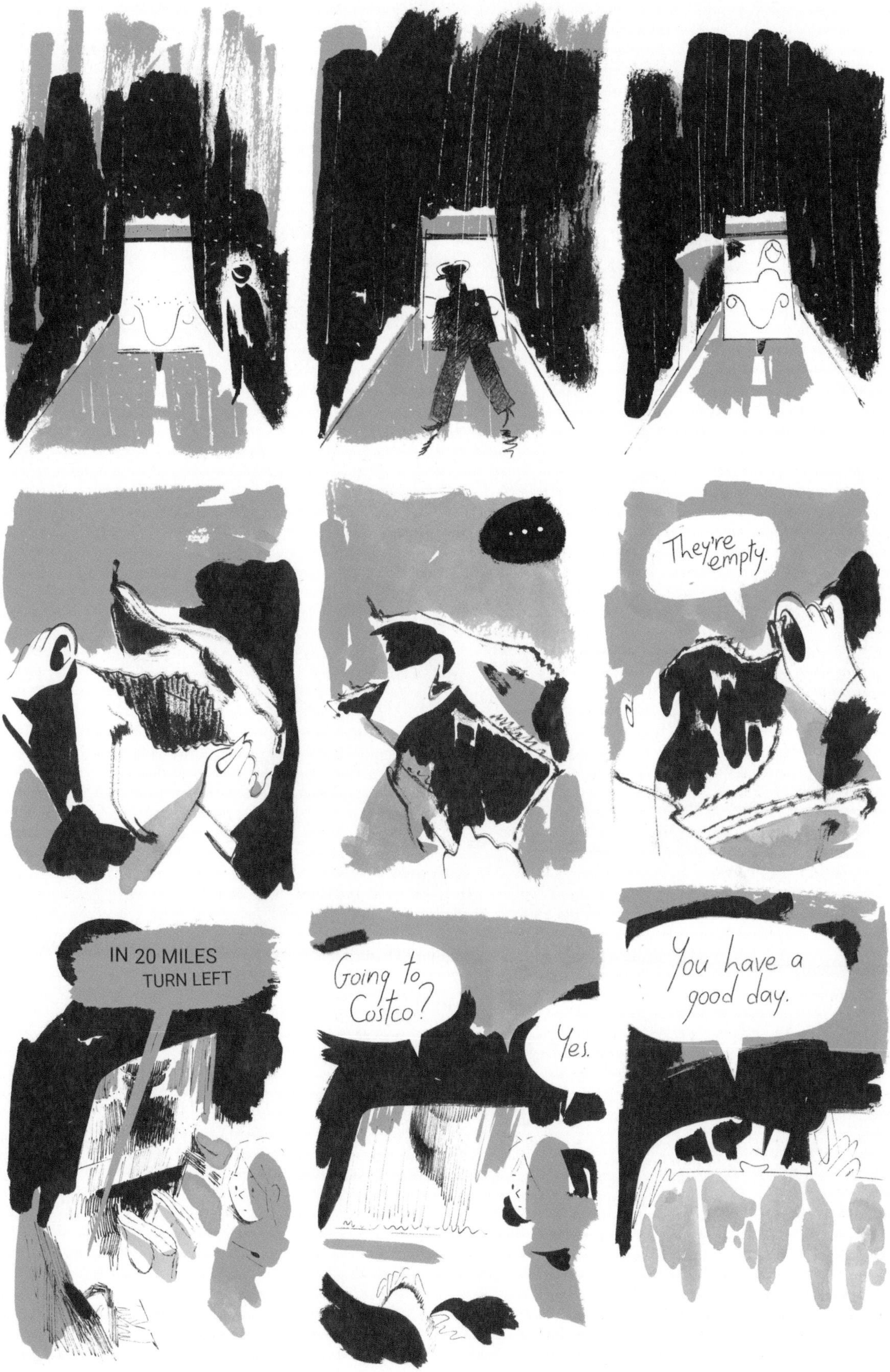
They're empty.
IN 20 MILES TURN LEFT
Going to Costco?
Yes.
You have a good day.

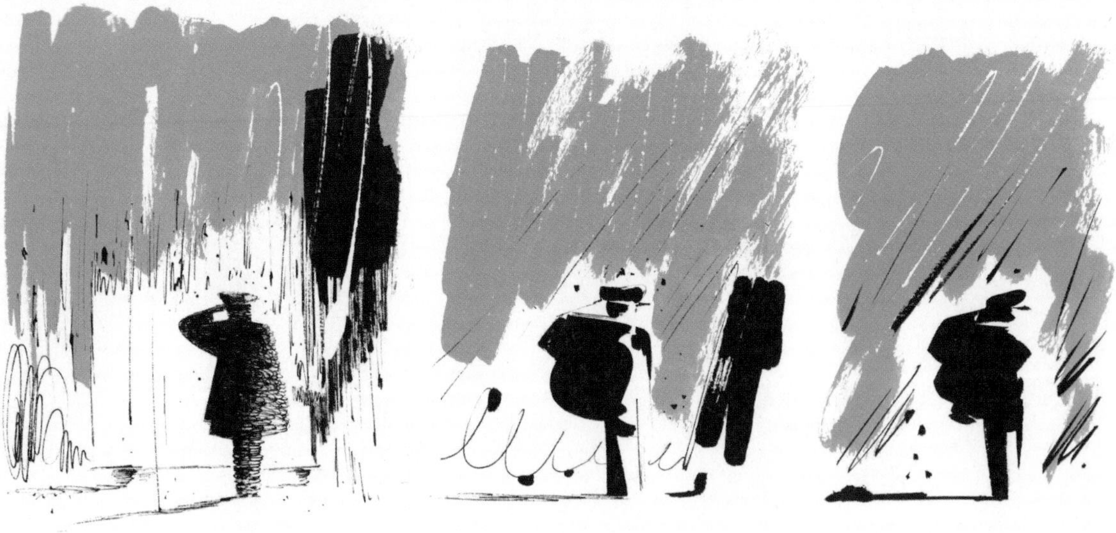

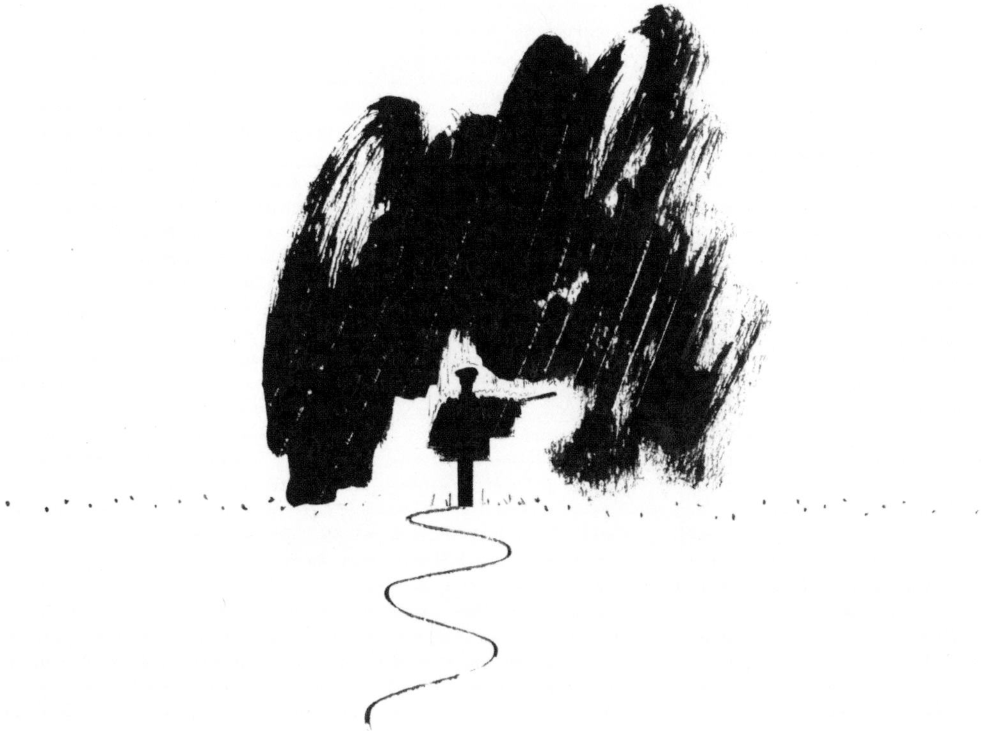

STRAWBERRY AND CHOCOLATE

JOSÉ QUINTANAR

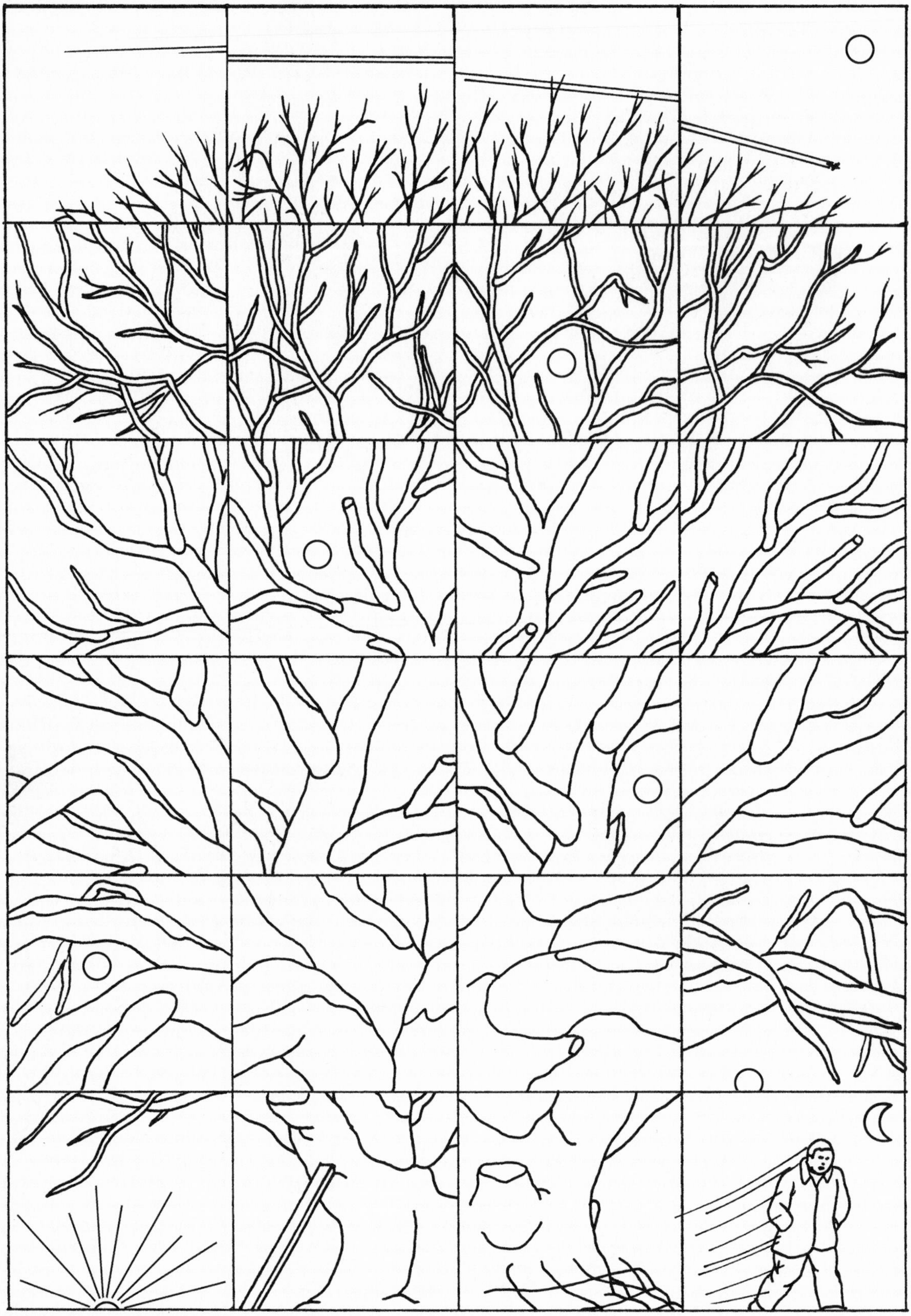

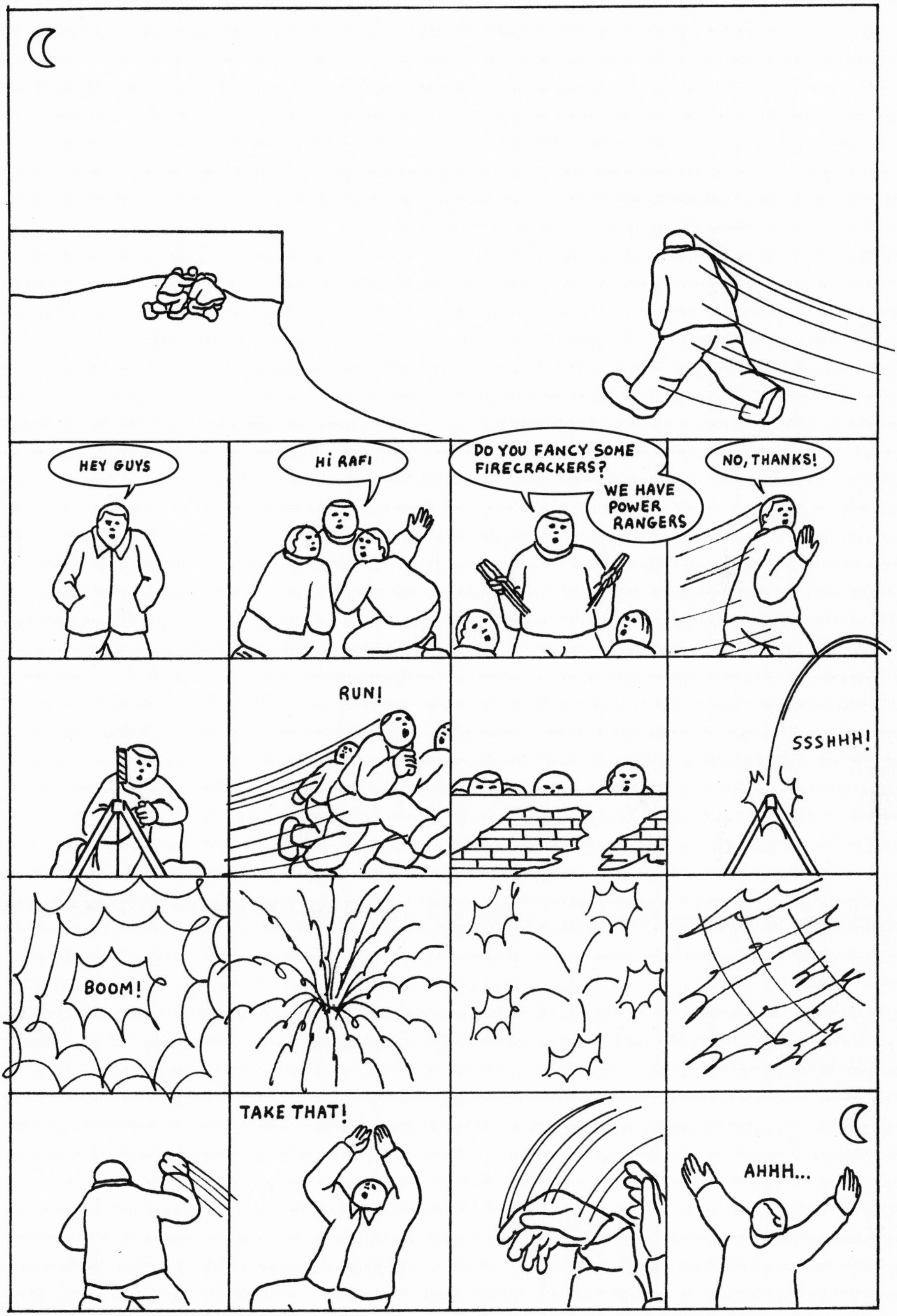
HEY GUYS
Hi RAFI
DO YOU FANCY SOME FIRECRACKERS?
WE HAVE POWER RANGERS
NO, THANKS!
RUN!
SSSHHH!
BOOM!
TAKE THAT!
AHHH...

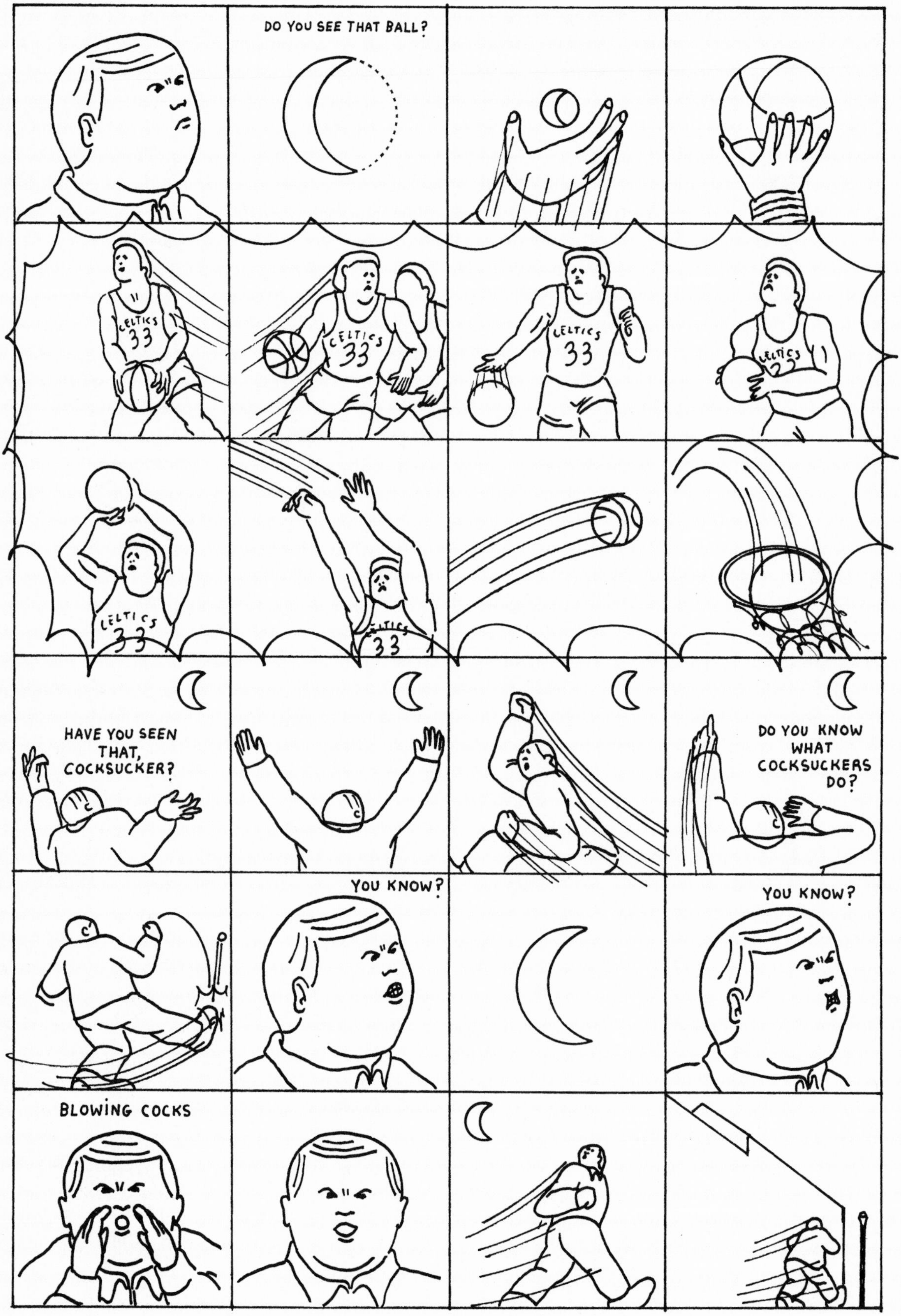
DO YOU SEE THAT BALL?
CELTICS 33
HAVE YOU SEEN THAT, COCKSUCKER?
DO YOU KNOW WHAT COCKSUCKERS DO?
YOU KNOW?
YOU KNOW?
BLOWING COCKS

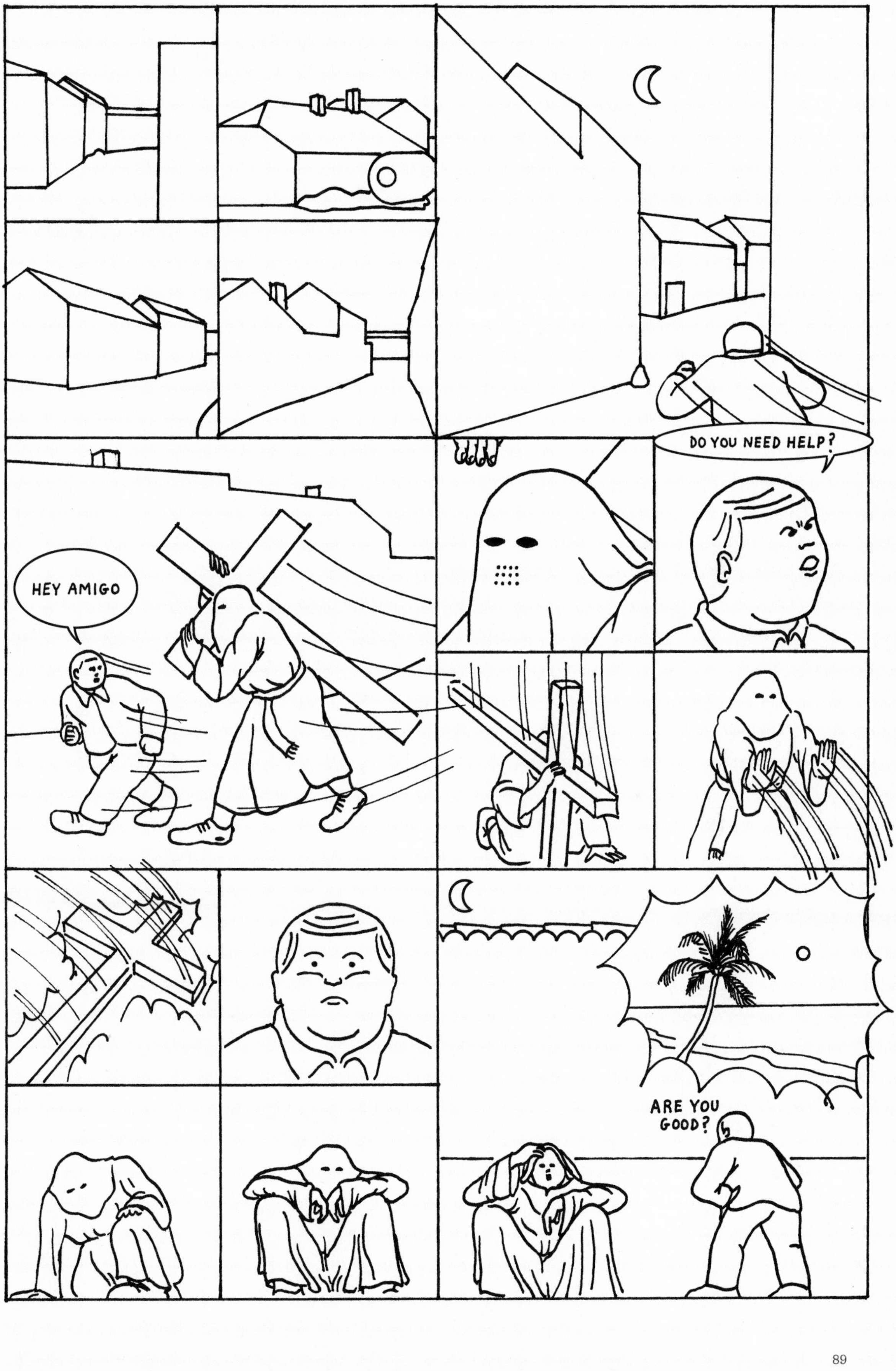
HEY AMIGO
DO YOU NEED HELP?
ARE YOU GOOD?

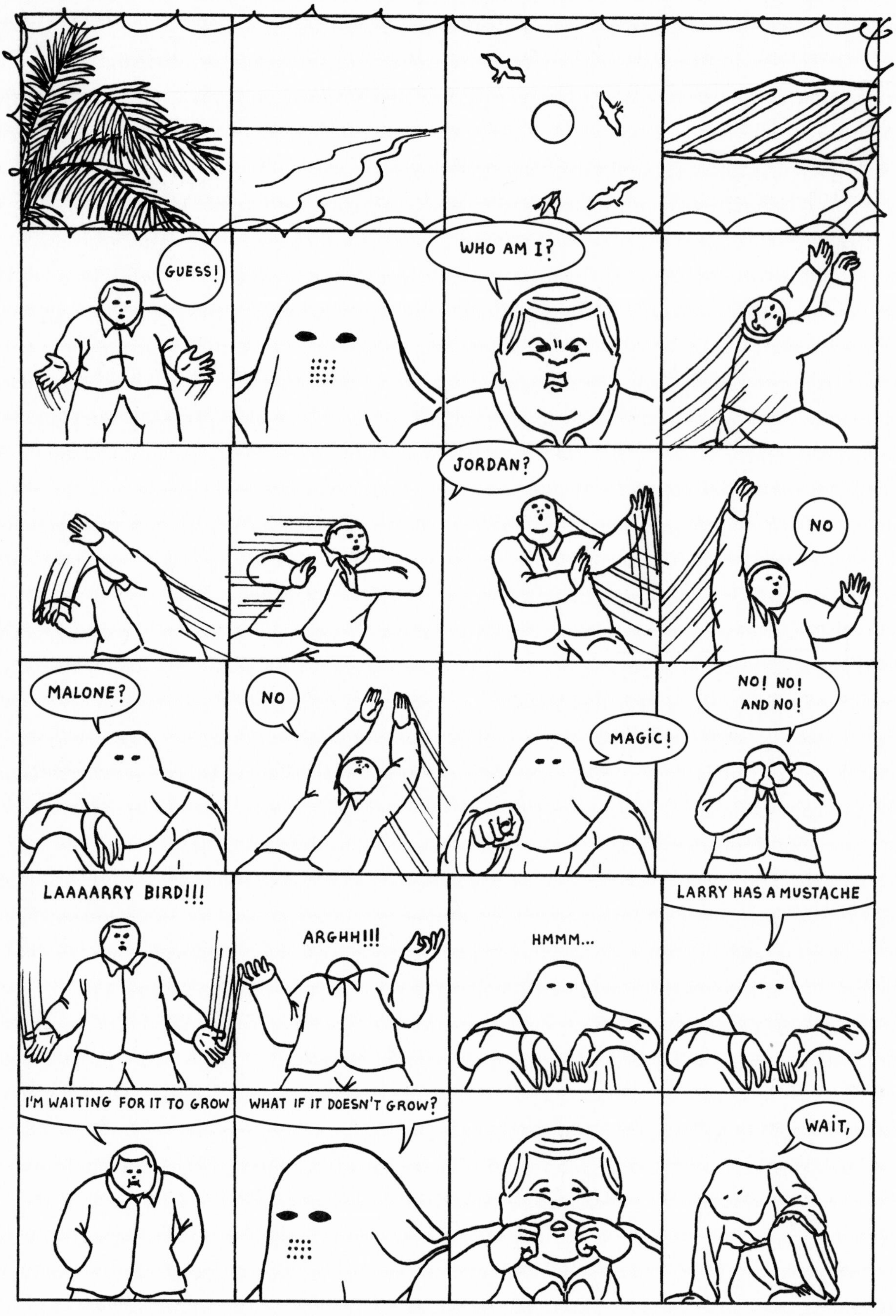

GUESS!
WHO AM I?
JORDAN?
NO
MALONE?
NO
MAGIC!
NO! NO! AND NO!
LAAAARRY BIRD!!!
ARGHH!!!
HMMM...
LARRY HAS A MUSTACHE
I'M WAITING FOR IT TO GROW
WHAT IF IT DOESN'T GROW?
WAIT,

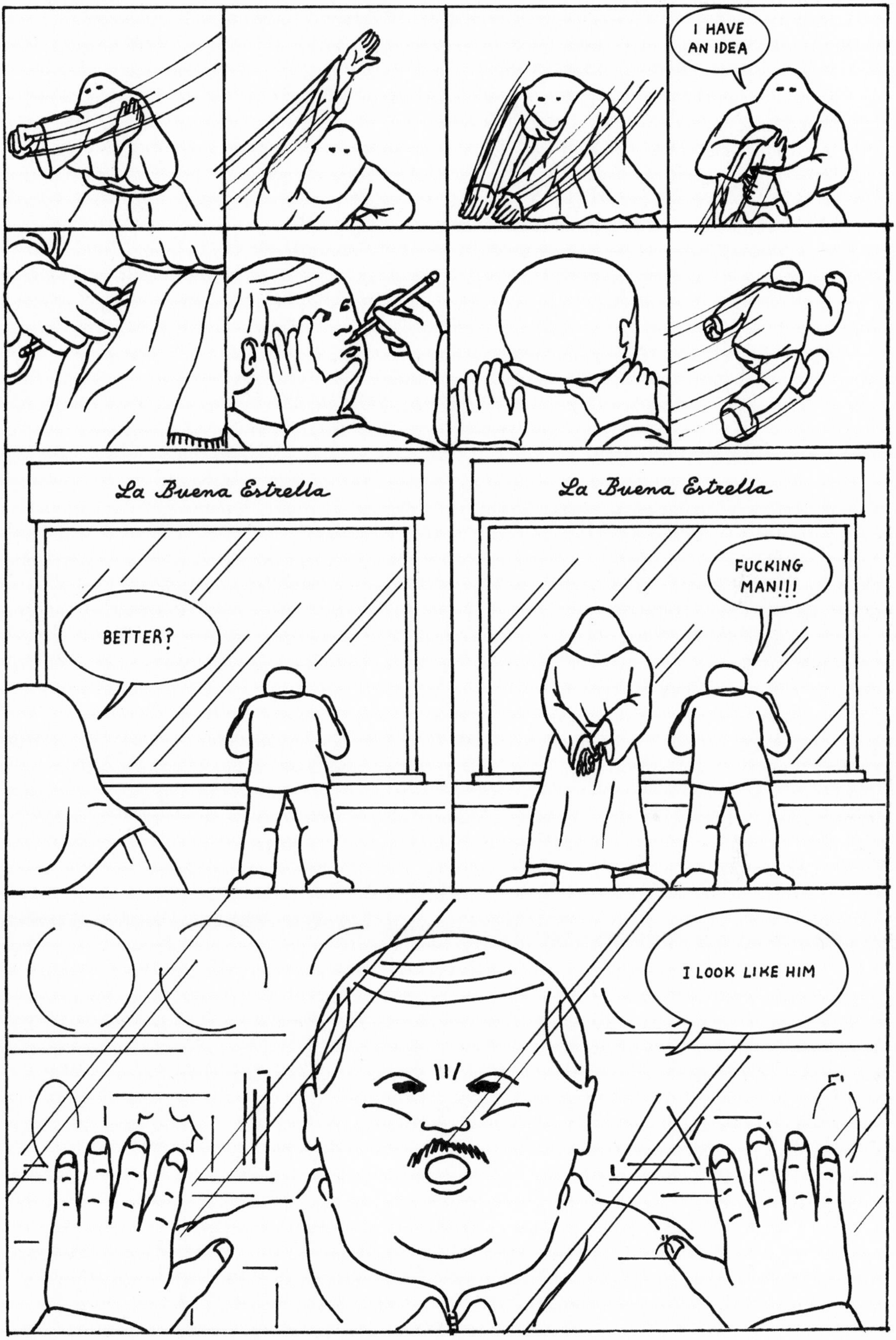
I HAVE AN IDEA
La Buena Estrella
BETTER?
La Buena Estrella
FUCKING MAN!!!
I LOOK LIKE HIM

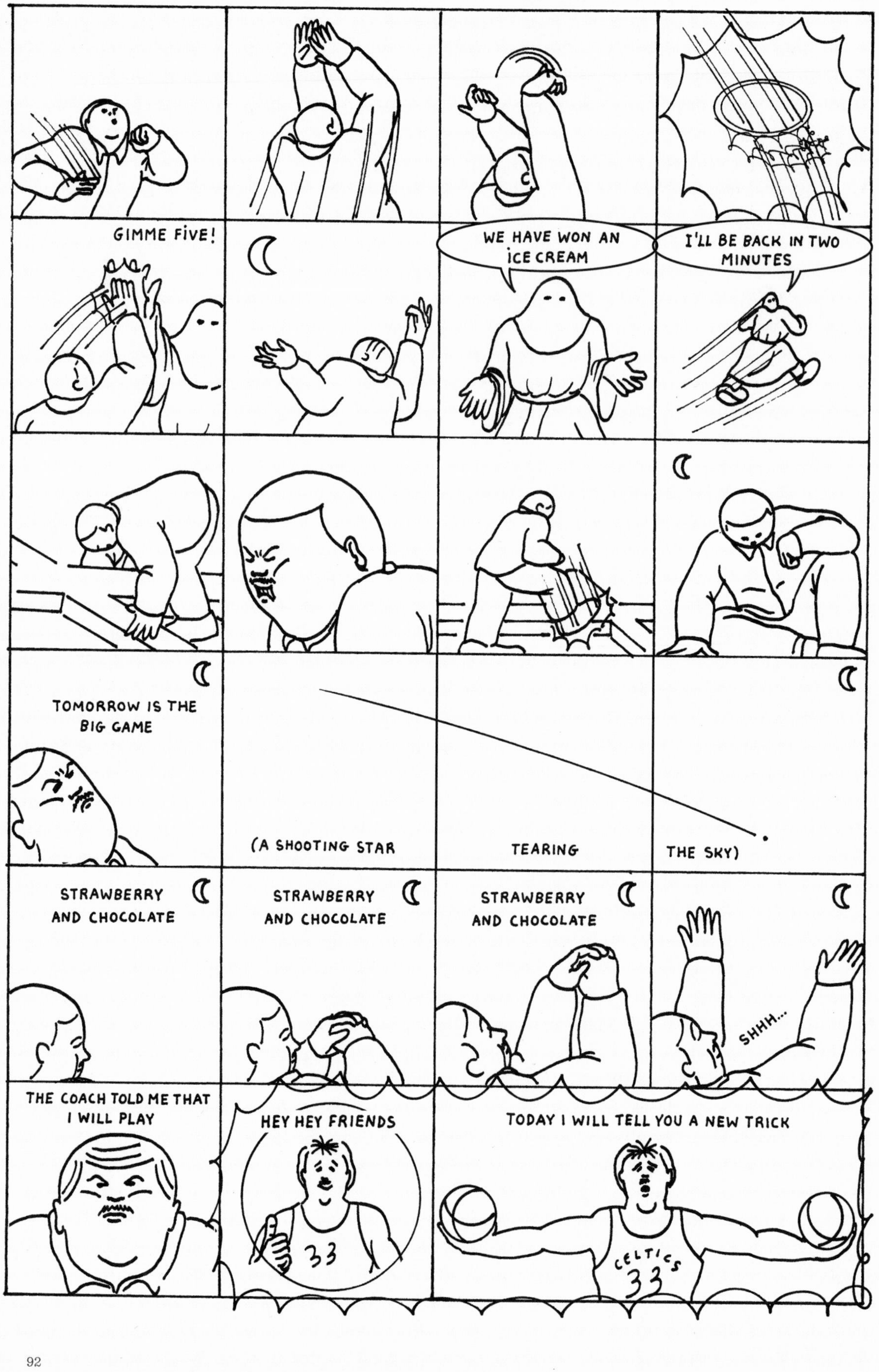
GIMME FIVE!
WE HAVE WON AN ICE CREAM
I'LL BE BACK IN TWO MINUTES
TOMORROW IS THE BIG GAME
(A SHOOTING STAR
TEARING
THE SKY)
STRAWBERRY AND CHOCOLATE
STRAWBERRY AND CHOCOLATE
STRAWBERRY AND CHOCOLATE
SHHH...
THE COACH TOLD ME THAT I WILL PLAY
HEY HEY FRIENDS
33
TODAY I WILL TELL YOU A NEW TRICK
CELTICS
33

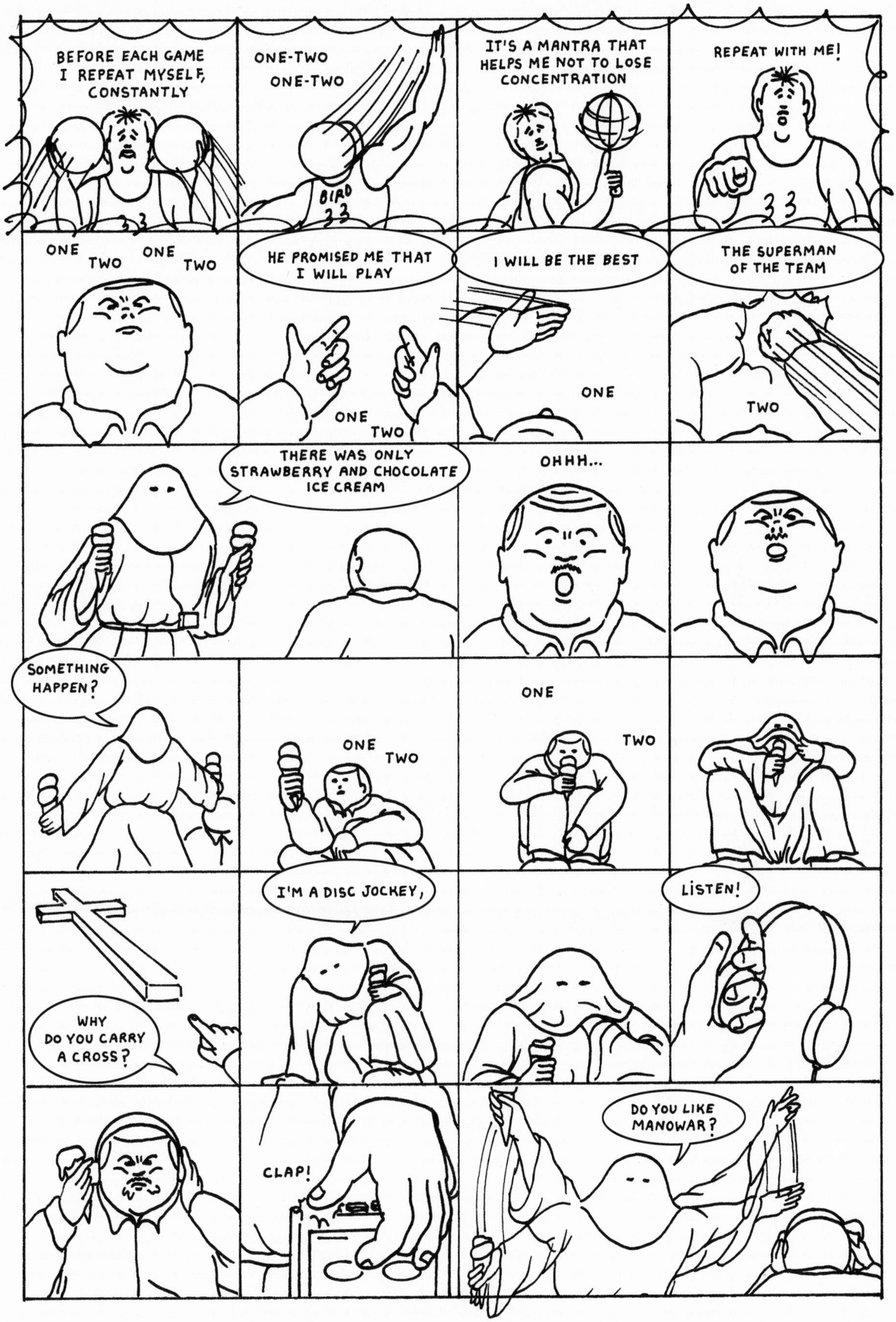
BEFORE EACH GAME I REPEAT MYSELF, CONSTANTLY
BIRD 33
ONE-TWO
ONE-TWO
IT'S A MANTRA THAT HELPS ME NOT TO LOSE CONCENTRATION
REPEAT WITH ME!
33
ONE
TWO
ONE
TWO
HE PROMISED ME THAT I WILL PLAY
ONE
TWO
I WILL BE THE BEST
ONE
THE SUPERMAN OF THE TEAM
TWO
THERE WAS ONLY STRAWBERRY AND CHOCOLATE ICE CREAM
OHHH...
SOMETHING HAPPEN?
ONE
TWO
ONE
TWO
WHY DO YOU CARRY A CROSS?
I'M A DISC JOCKEY,
LISTEN!
CLAP!
DO YOU LIKE MANOWAR?

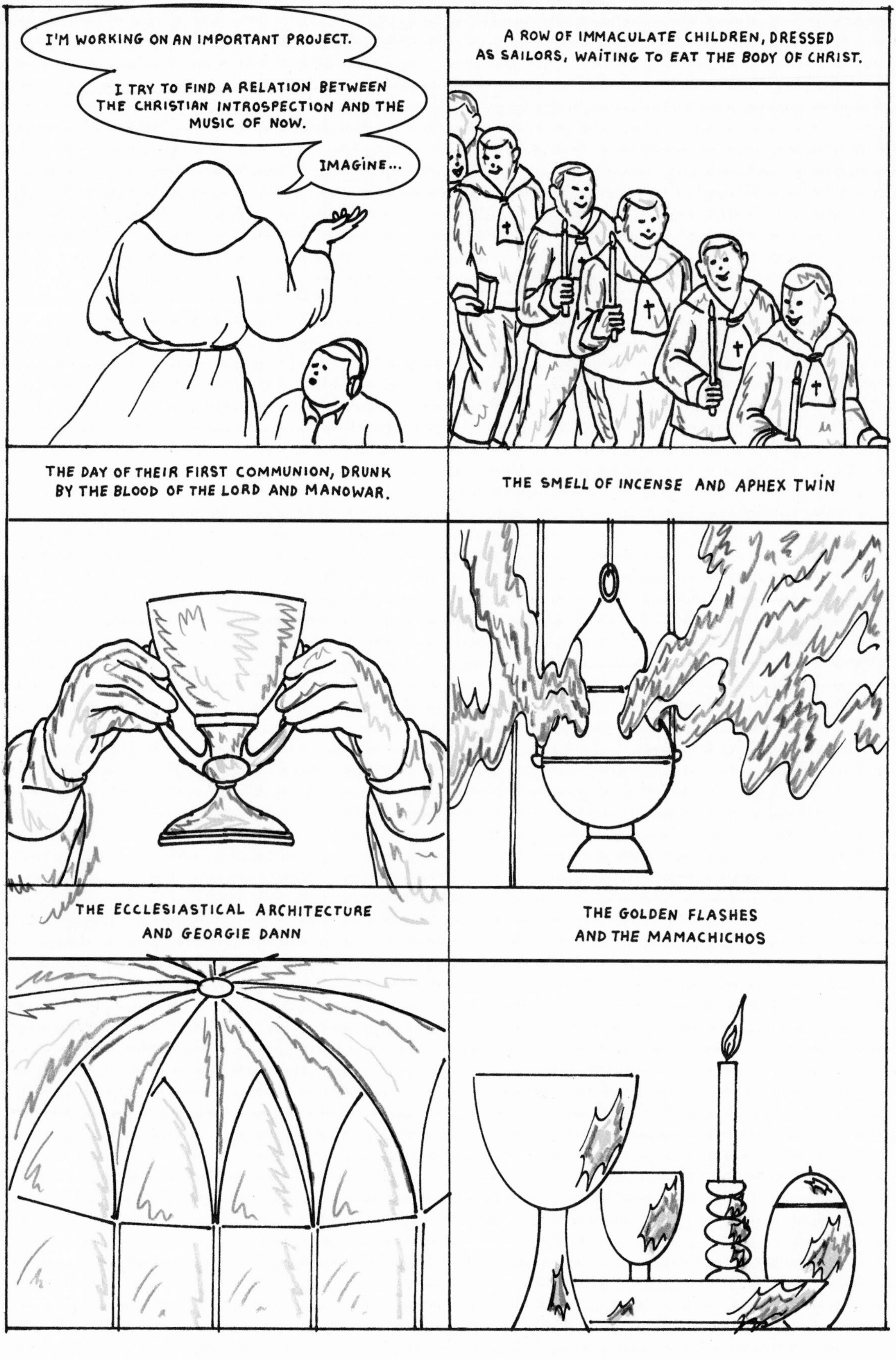
I'M WORKING ON AN IMPORTANT PROJECT.
I TRY TO FIND A RELATION BETWEEN THE CHRISTIAN INTROSPECTION AND THE MUSIC OF NOW.
IMAGINE...
A ROW OF IMMACULATE CHILDREN, DRESSED AS SAILORS, WAITING TO EAT THE BODY OF CHRIST.
THE DAY OF THEIR FIRST COMMUNION, DRUNK BY THE BLOOD OF THE LORD AND MANOWAR.
THE SMELL OF INCENSE AND APHEX TWIN
THE ECCLESIASTICAL ARCHITECTURE AND GEORGIE DANN
THE GOLDEN FLASHES AND THE MAMACHICHOS

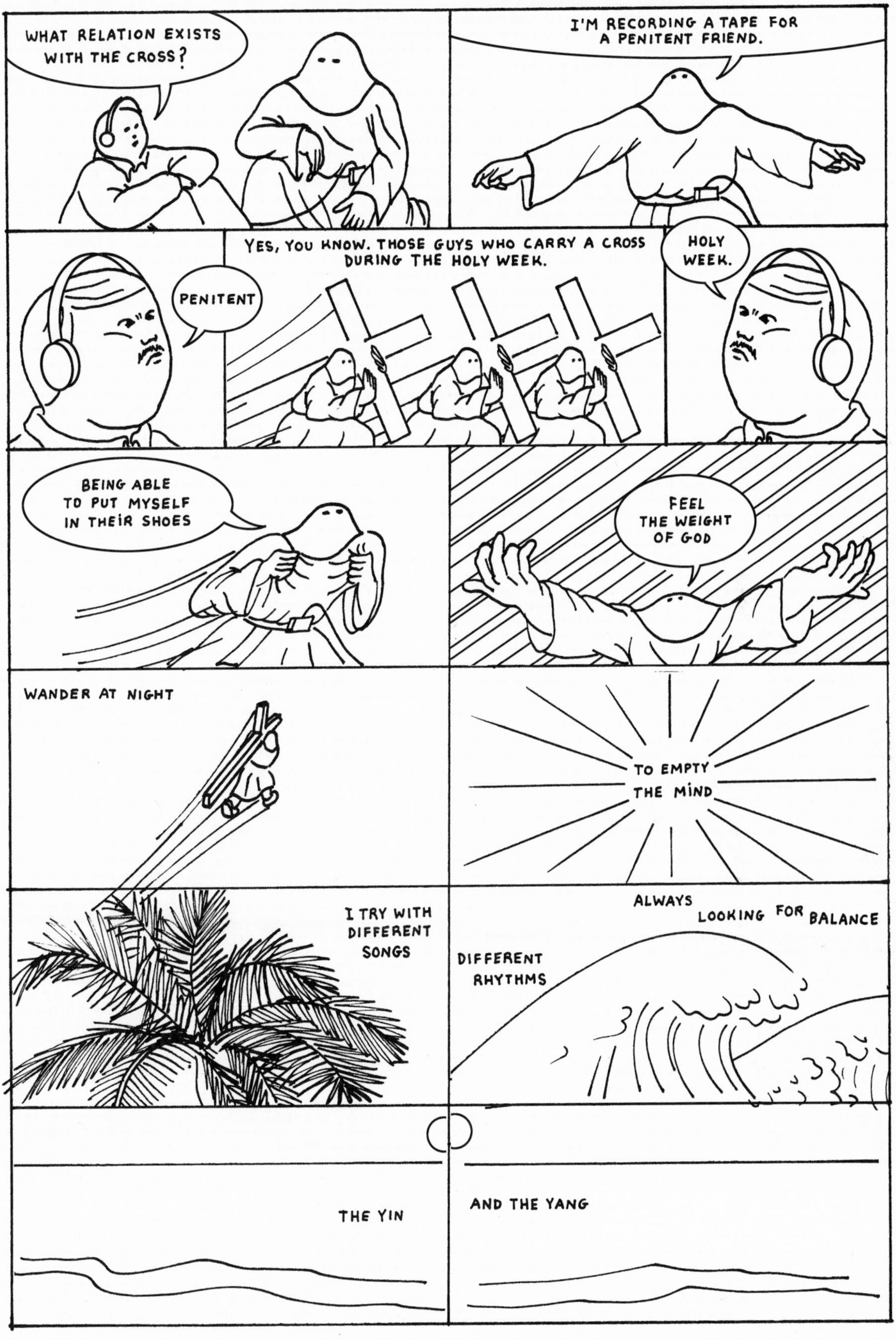
WHAT RELATION EXISTS WITH THE CROSS?
I'M RECORDING A TAPE FOR A PENITENT FRIEND.
PENITENT
YES, YOU KNOW. THOSE GUYS WHO CARRY A CROSS DURING THE HOLY WEEK.
HOLY WEEK.
BEING ABLE TO PUT MYSELF IN THEIR SHOES
FEEL THE WEIGHT OF GOD
WANDER AT NIGHT
TO EMPTY THE MIND
I TRY WITH DIFFERENT SONGS
ALWAYS LOOKING FOR BALANCE
DIFFERENT RHYTHMS
THE YIN
AND THE YANG

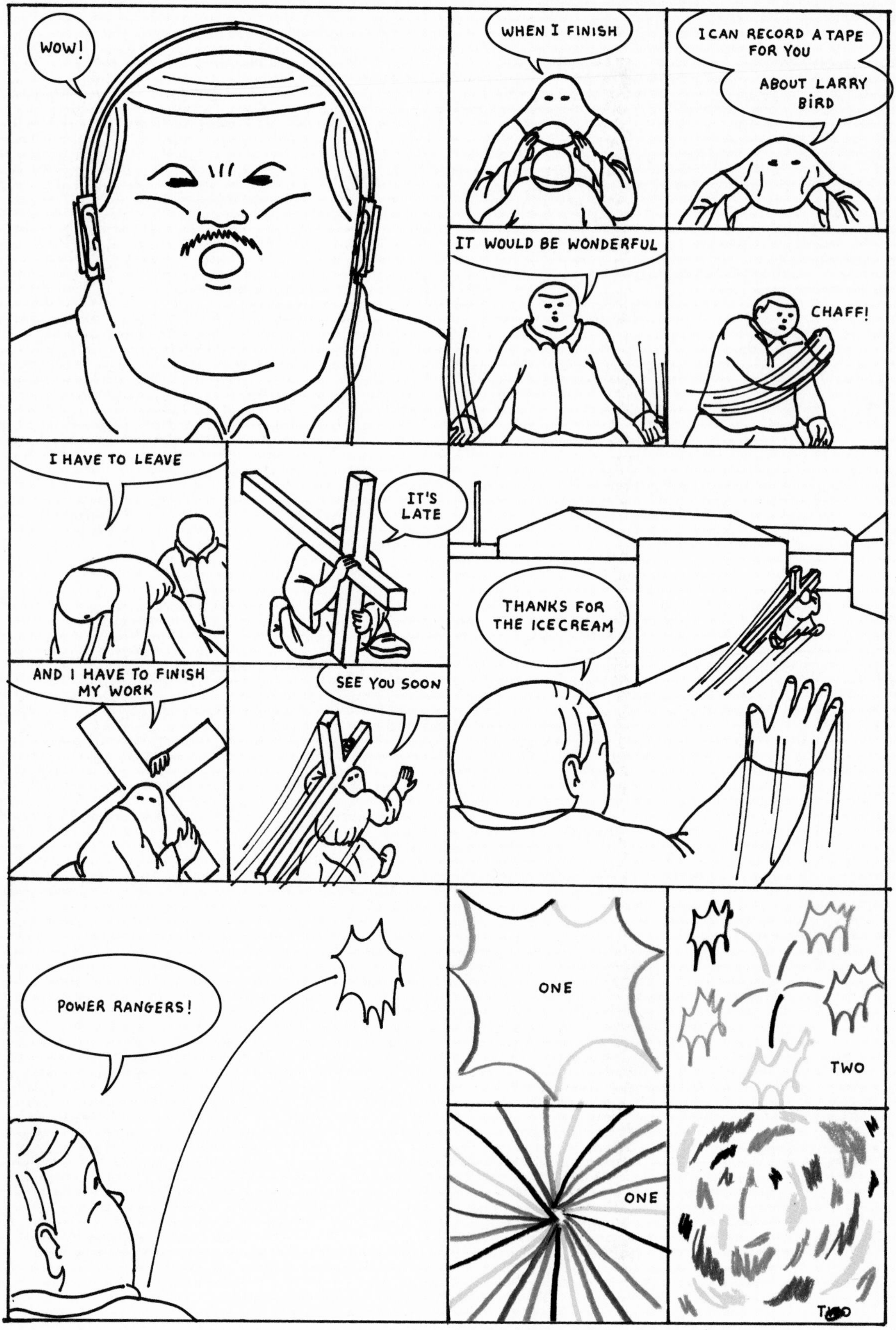
WOW!
WHEN I FINISH
I CAN RECORD A TAPE FOR YOU
ABOUT LARRY BIRD
IT WOULD BE WONDERFUL
CHAFF!
I HAVE TO LEAVE
IT'S LATE
AND I HAVE TO FINISH MY WORK
SEE YOU SOON
THANKS FOR THE ICECREAM
POWER RANGERS!
ONE
TWO
ONE
TWO

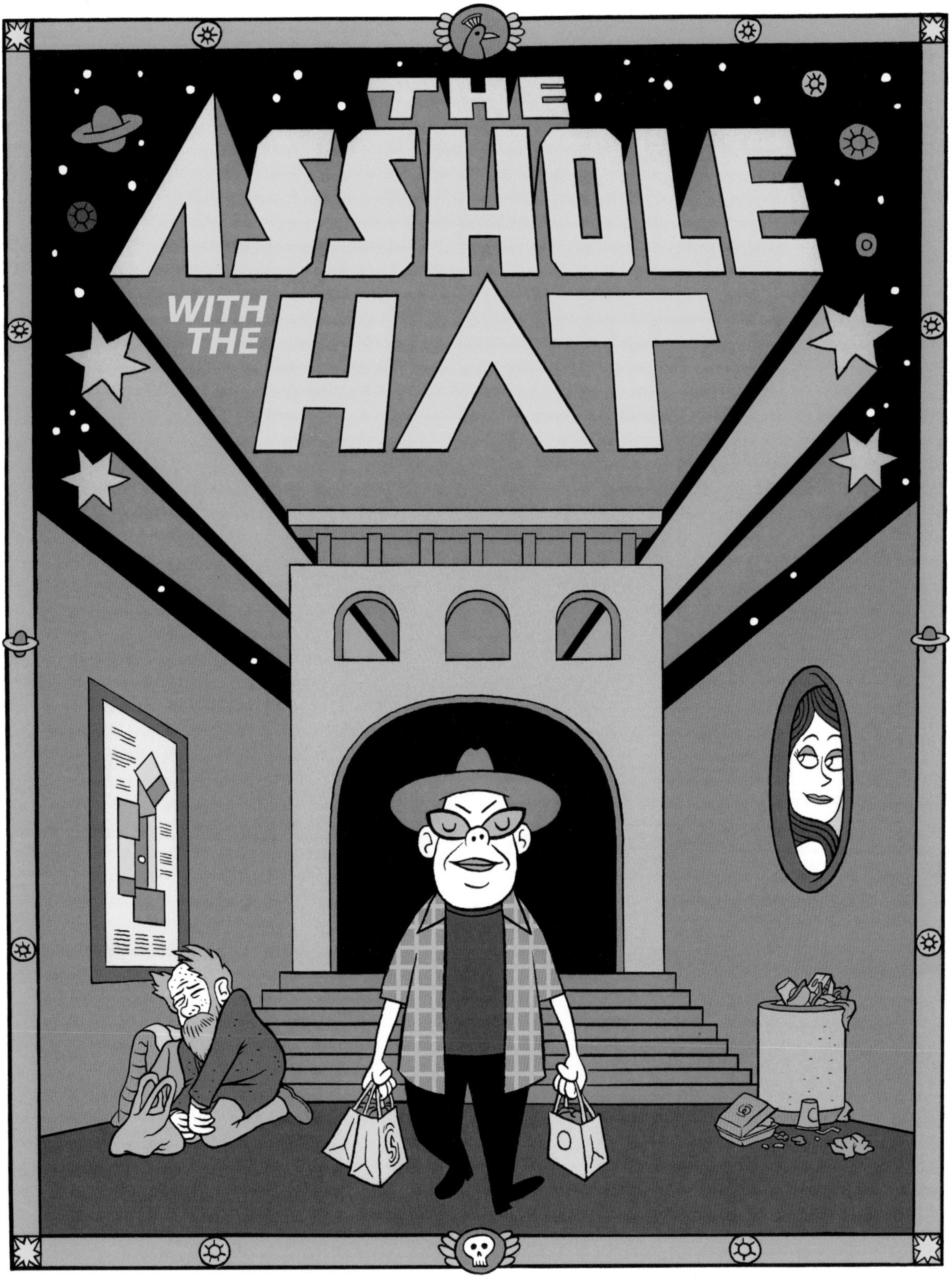
THE
ASSHOLE
WITH THE
HAT

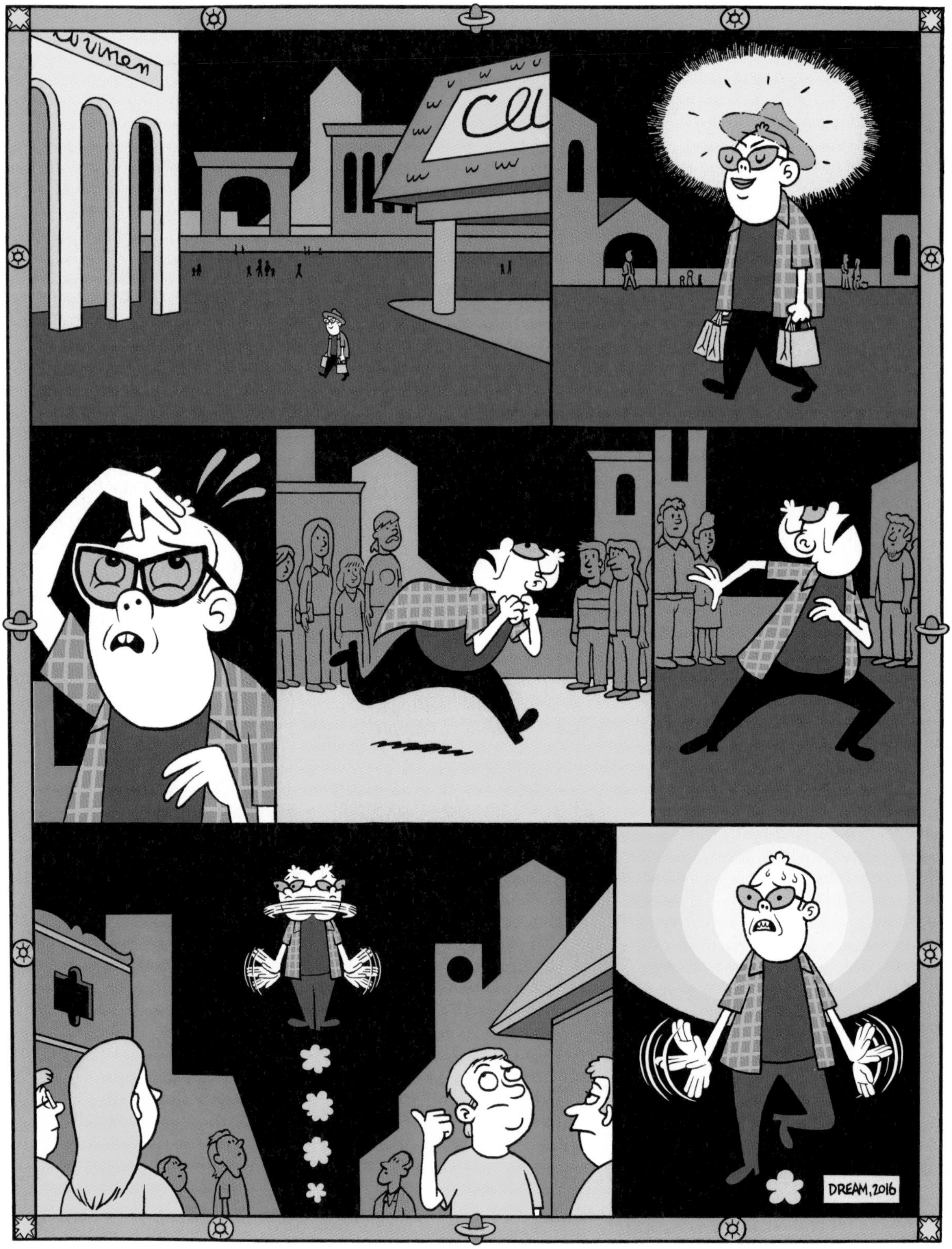
DREAM, 2016

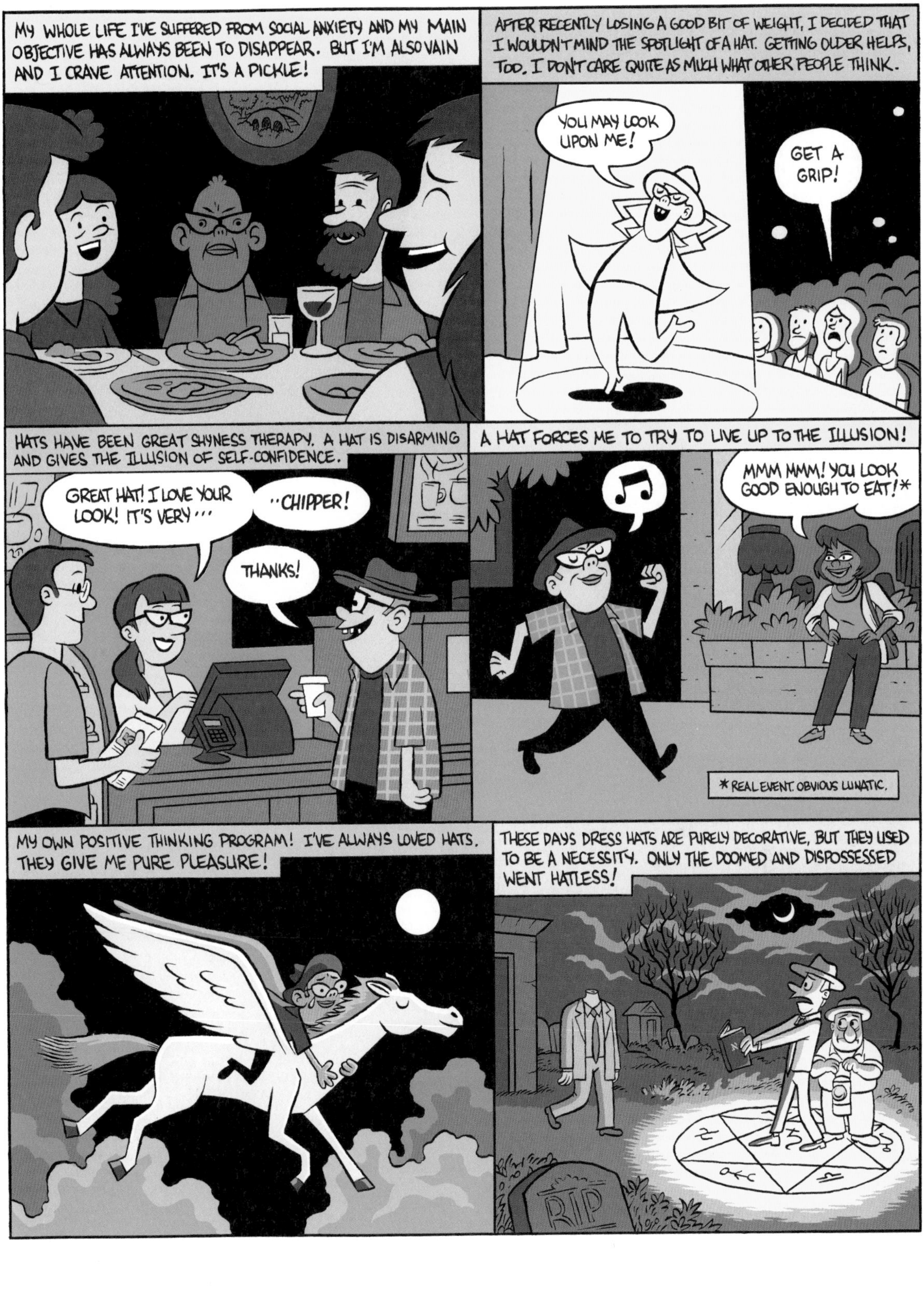

MY WHOLE LIFE I'VE SUFFERED FROM SOCIAL ANXIETY AND MY MAIN OBJECTIVE HAS ALWAYS BEEN TO DISAPPEAR. BUT I'M ALSO VAIN AND I CRAVE ATTENTION. IT'S A PICKLE!
AFTER RECENTLY LOSING A GOOD BIT OF WEIGHT, I DECIDED THAT I WOULDN'T MIND THE SPOTLIGHT OF A HAT. GETTING OLDER HELPS, TOO. I DON'T CARE QUITE AS MUCH WHAT OTHER PEOPLE THINK.
YOU MAY LOOK UPON ME!
GET A GRIP!
HATS HAVE BEEN GREAT SHYNESS THERAPY. A HAT IS DISARMING AND GIVES THE ILLUSION OF SELF-CONFIDENCE.
GREAT HAT! I LOVE YOUR LOOK! IT'S VERY...
...CHIPPER!
THANKS!
A HAT FORCES ME TO TRY TO LIVE UP TO THE ILLUSION!
MMM MMM! YOU LOOK GOOD ENOUGH TO EAT!*
*REAL EVENT. OBVIOUS LUNATIC.
MY OWN POSITIVE THINKING PROGRAM! I'VE ALWAYS LOVED HATS. THEY GIVE ME PURE PLEASURE!
THESE DAYS DRESS HATS ARE PURELY DECORATIVE, BUT THEY USED TO BE A NECESSITY. ONLY THE DOOMED AND DISPOSSESSED WENT HATLESS!
RIP

* A BRIEF HISTORY OF MEN'S HATS *

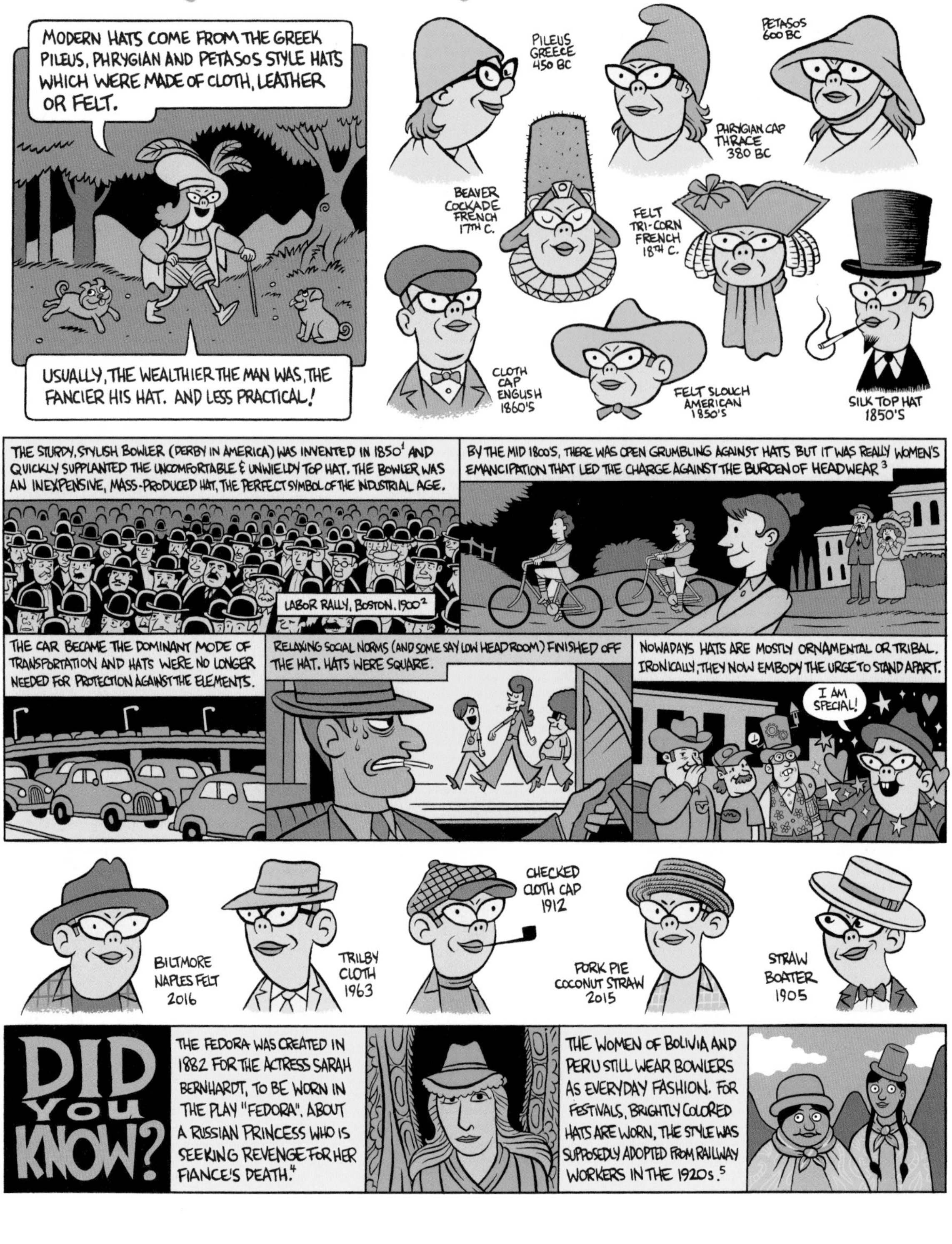
MODERN HATS COME FROM THE GREEK PILEUS, PHRYGIAN AND PETASOS STYLE HATS WHICH WERE MADE OF CLOTH, LEATHER OR FELT.
USUALLY, THE WEALTHIER THE MAN WAS, THE FANCIER HIS HAT. AND LESS PRACTICAL!
PILEUS GREECE 450 BC
PHRYGIAN CAP THRACE 380 BC
PETASOS 600 BC
BEAVER COCKADE FRENCH 17TH C.
FELT TRI-CORN FRENCH 18TH C.
CLOTH CAP ENGLISH 1860'S
FELT SLOUCH AMERICAN 1850'S
SILK TOP HAT 1850'S
THE STURDY, STYLISH BOWLER (DERBY IN AMERICA) WAS INVENTED IN 1850[1] AND QUICKLY SUPPLANTED THE UNCOMFORTABLE & UNWIELDY TOP HAT. THE BOWLER WAS AN INEXPENSIVE, MASS-PRODUCED HAT, THE PERFECT SYMBOL OF THE INDUSTRIAL AGE.
LABOR RALLY, BOSTON. 1900[2]
BY THE MID 1800'S, THERE WAS OPEN GRUMBLING AGAINST HATS BUT IT WAS REALLY WOMEN'S EMANCIPATION THAT LED THE CHARGE AGAINST THE BURDEN OF HEADWEAR[3]
THE CAR BECAME THE DOMINANT MODE OF TRANSPORTATION AND HATS WERE NO LONGER NEEDED FOR PROTECTION AGAINST THE ELEMENTS.
RELAXING SOCIAL NORMS (AND SOME SAY LOW HEADROOM) FINISHED OFF THE HAT. HATS WERE SQUARE.
NOWADAYS HATS ARE MOSTLY ORNAMENTAL OR TRIBAL. IRONICALLY, THEY NOW EMBODY THE URGE TO STAND APART.
I AM SPECIAL!
BILTMORE NAPLES FELT 2016
TRILBY CLOTH 1963
CHECKED CLOTH CAP 1912
PORK PIE COCONUT STRAW 2015
STRAW BOATER 1905
DID YOU KNOW?
THE FEDORA WAS CREATED IN 1882 FOR THE ACTRESS SARAH BERNHARDT, TO BE WORN IN THE PLAY "FEDORA", ABOUT A RUSSIAN PRINCESS WHO IS SEEKING REVENGE FOR HER FIANCE'S DEATH.[4]
THE WOMEN OF BOLIVIA AND PERU STILL WEAR BOWLERS AS EVERYDAY FASHION. FOR FESTIVALS, BRIGHTLY COLORED HATS ARE WORN. THE STYLE WAS SUPPOSEDLY ADOPTED FROM RAILWAY WORKERS IN THE 1920s.[5]

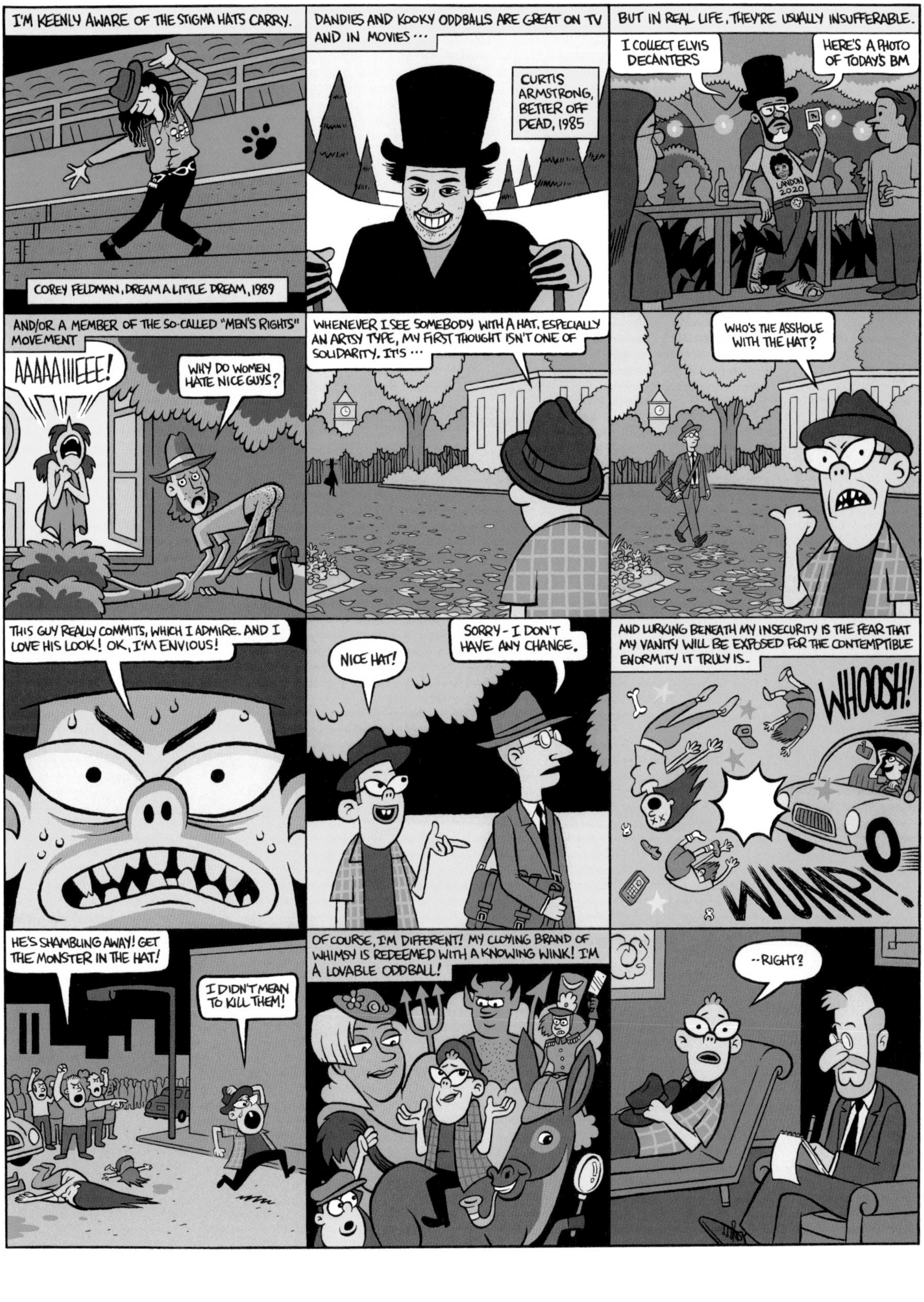
I'M KEENLY AWARE OF THE STIGMA HATS CARRY.
COREY FELDMAN, DREAM A LITTLE DREAM, 1989
DANDIES AND KOOKY ODDBALLS ARE GREAT ON TV AND IN MOVIES…
CURTIS ARMSTRONG, BETTER OFF DEAD, 1985
BUT IN REAL LIFE, THEY'RE USUALLY INSUFFERABLE.
I COLLECT ELVIS DECANTERS
HERE'S A PHOTO OF TODAY'S BM
LANDON 2020
AND/OR A MEMBER OF THE SO-CALLED "MEN'S RIGHTS" MOVEMENT
AAAAAIIIEEE!
WHY DO WOMEN HATE NICE GUYS?
WHENEVER I SEE SOMEBODY WITH A HAT, ESPECIALLY AN ARTSY TYPE, MY FIRST THOUGHT ISN'T ONE OF SOLIDARITY. IT'S…
WHO'S THE ASSHOLE WITH THE HAT?
THIS GUY REALLY COMMITS, WHICH I ADMIRE. AND I LOVE HIS LOOK! OK, I'M ENVIOUS!
NICE HAT!
SORRY - I DON'T HAVE ANY CHANGE.
AND LURKING BENEATH MY INSECURITY IS THE FEAR THAT MY VANITY WILL BE EXPOSED FOR THE CONTEMPTIBLE ENORMITY IT TRULY IS.
WHOOSH!
WUMP!
HE'S SHAMBLING AWAY! GET THE MONSTER IN THE HAT!
I DIDN'T MEAN TO KILL THEM!
OF COURSE, I'M DIFFERENT! MY CLOYING BRAND OF WHIMSY IS REDEEMED WITH A KNOWING WINK! I'M A LOVABLE ODDBALL!
--RIGHT?

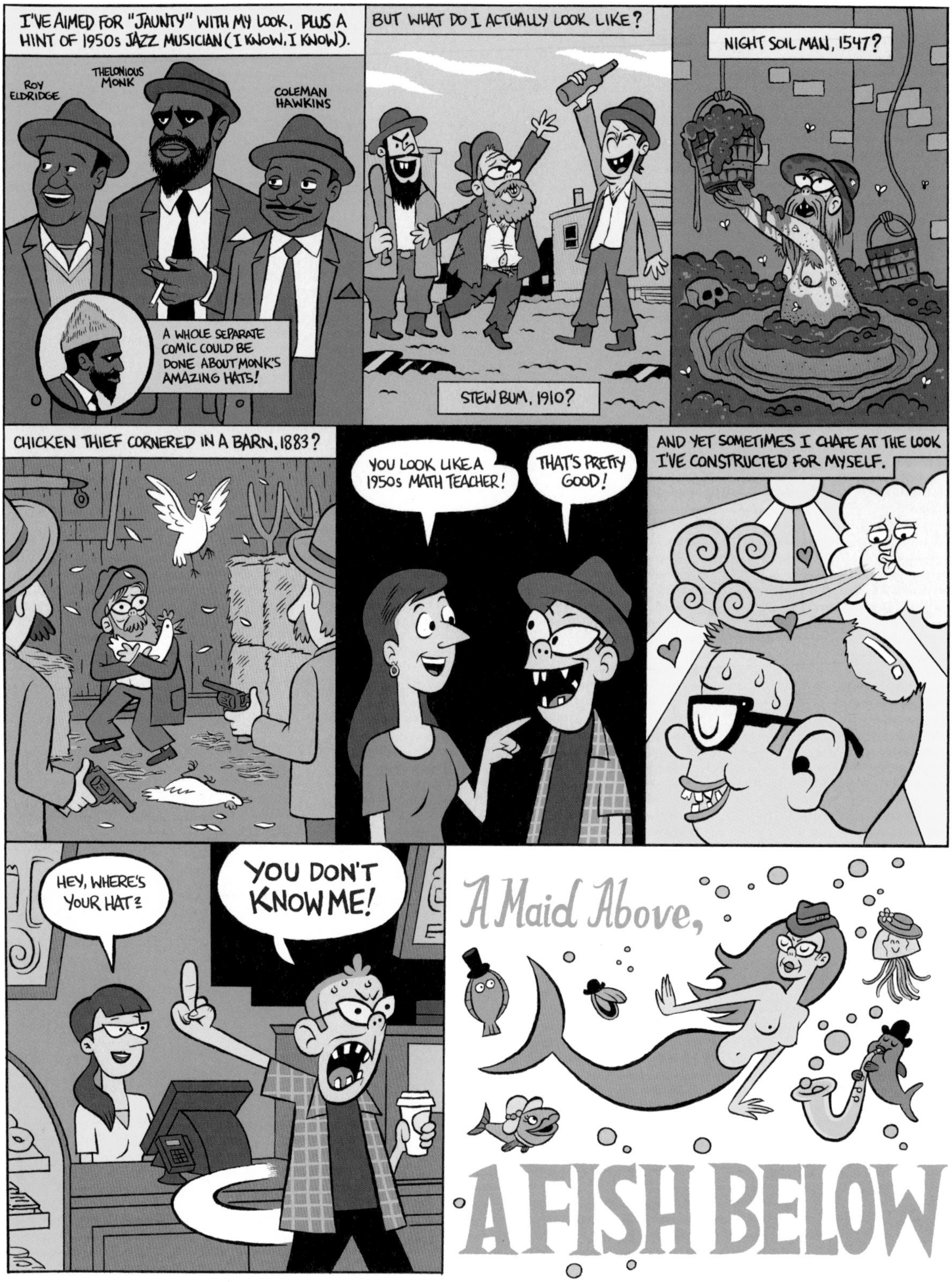
I'VE AIMED FOR "JAUNTY" WITH MY LOOK. PLUS A HINT OF 1950s JAZZ MUSICIAN (I KNOW, I KNOW).
ROY ELDRIDGE
THELONIOUS MONK
COLEMAN HAWKINS
A WHOLE SEPARATE COMIC COULD BE DONE ABOUT MONK'S AMAZING HATS!
BUT WHAT DO I ACTUALLY LOOK LIKE?
STEW BUM, 1910?
NIGHT SOIL MAN, 1547?
CHICKEN THIEF CORNERED IN A BARN, 1883?
YOU LOOK LIKE A 1950s MATH TEACHER!
THAT'S PRETTY GOOD!
AND YET SOMETIMES I CHAFE AT THE LOOK I'VE CONSTRUCTED FOR MYSELF.
HEY, WHERE'S YOUR HAT?
YOU DON'T KNOW ME!
A Maid Above,
A FISH BELOW

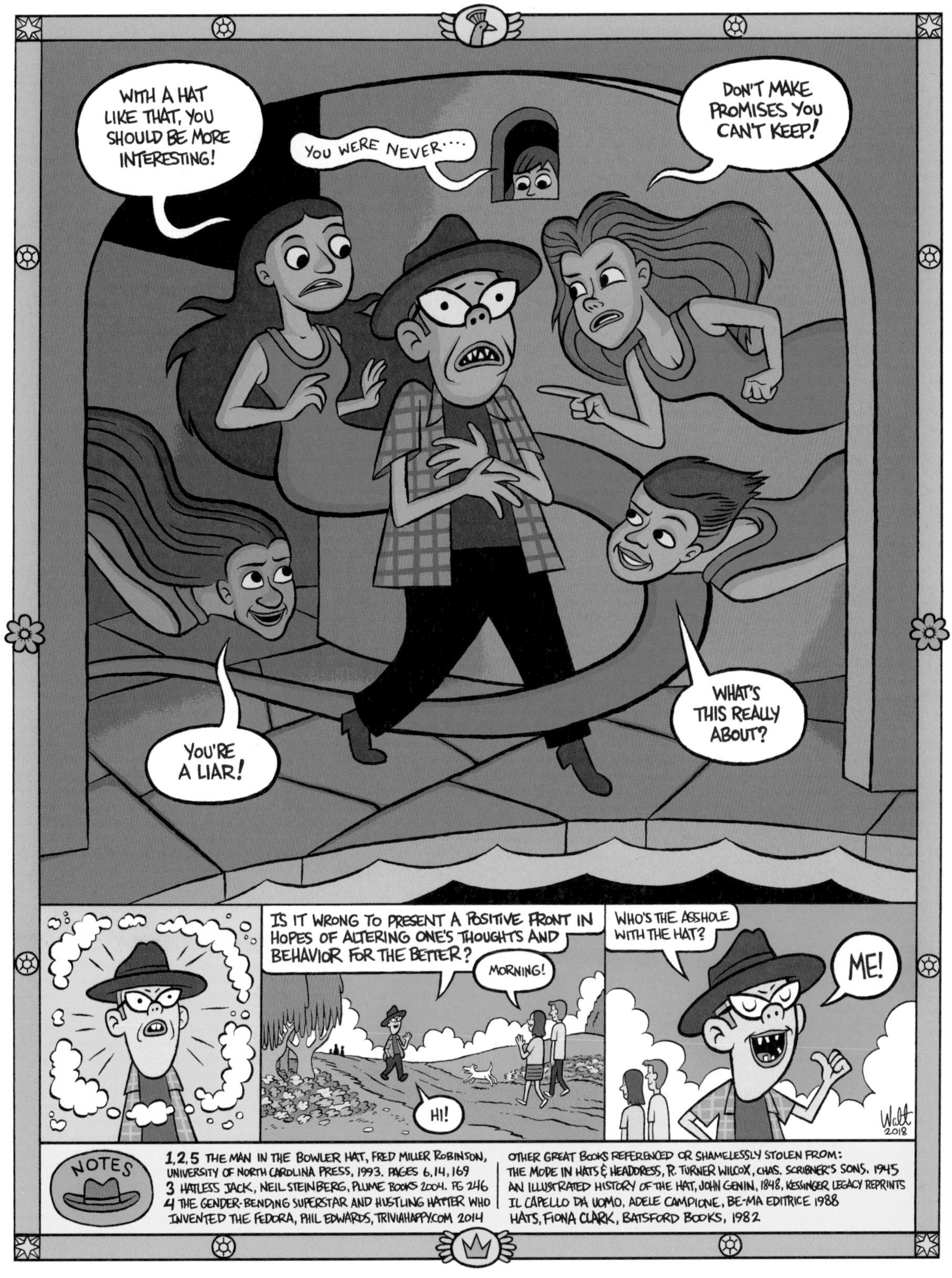

WITH A HAT LIKE THAT, YOU SHOULD BE MORE INTERESTING!
YOU WERE NEVER....
DON'T MAKE PROMISES YOU CAN'T KEEP!
YOU'RE A LIAR!
WHAT'S THIS REALLY ABOUT?
IS IT WRONG TO PRESENT A POSITIVE FRONT IN HOPES OF ALTERING ONE'S THOUGHTS AND BEHAVIOR FOR THE BETTER?
MORNING!
HI!
WHO'S THE ASSHOLE WITH THE HAT?
ME!
Walt 2018

NOTES

1,2,5 THE MAN IN THE BOWLER HAT, FRED MILLER ROBINSON, UNIVERSITY OF NORTH CAROLINA PRESS, 1993. PAGES 6,14,169
3 HATLESS JACK, NEIL STEINBERG, PLUME BOOKS 2004. PG 246
4 THE GENDER-BENDING SUPERSTAR AND HUSTLING HATTER WHO INVENTED THE FEDORA, PHIL EDWARDS, TRIVIAHAPPY.COM 2014

OTHER GREAT BOOKS REFERENCED OR SHAMELESSLY STOLEN FROM:
THE MODE IN HATS & HEADDRESS, R. TURNER WILCOX, CHAS. SCRIBNER'S SONS. 1945
AN ILLUSTRATED HISTORY OF THE HAT, JOHN GENIN, 1848, KESSINGER LEGACY REPRINTS
IL CAPELLO DA UOMO, ADELE CAMPIONE, BE-MA EDITRICE 1988
HATS, FIONA CLARK, BATSFORD BOOKS, 1982

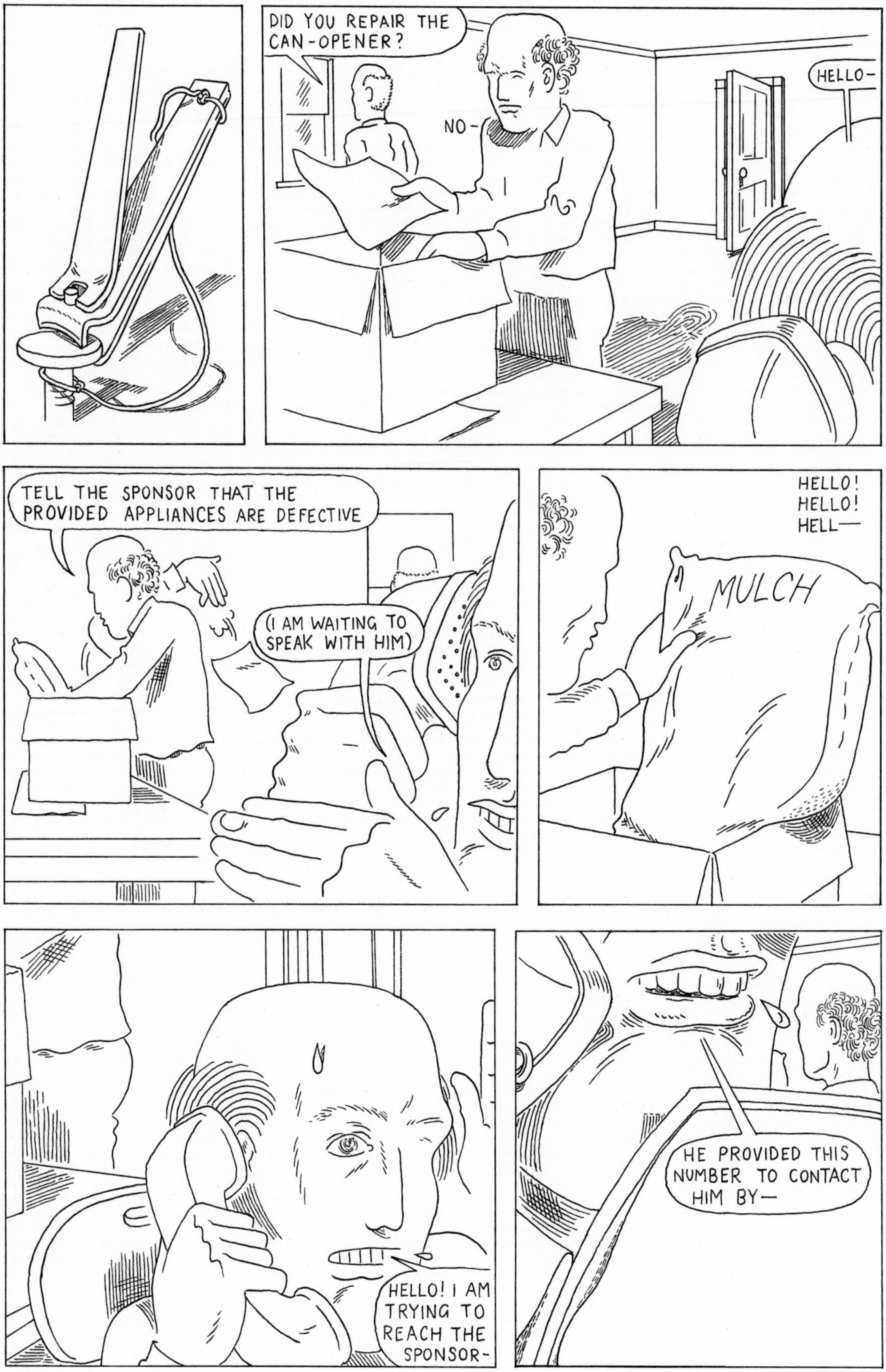
DID YOU REPAIR THE CAN-OPENER?
NO-
HELLO-
TELL THE SPONSOR THAT THE PROVIDED APPLIANCES ARE DEFECTIVE
(I AM WAITING TO SPEAK WITH HIM)
HELLO! HELLO! HELL—
MULCH
HELLO! I AM TRYING TO REACH THE SPONSOR-
HE PROVIDED THIS NUMBER TO CONTACT HIM BY—

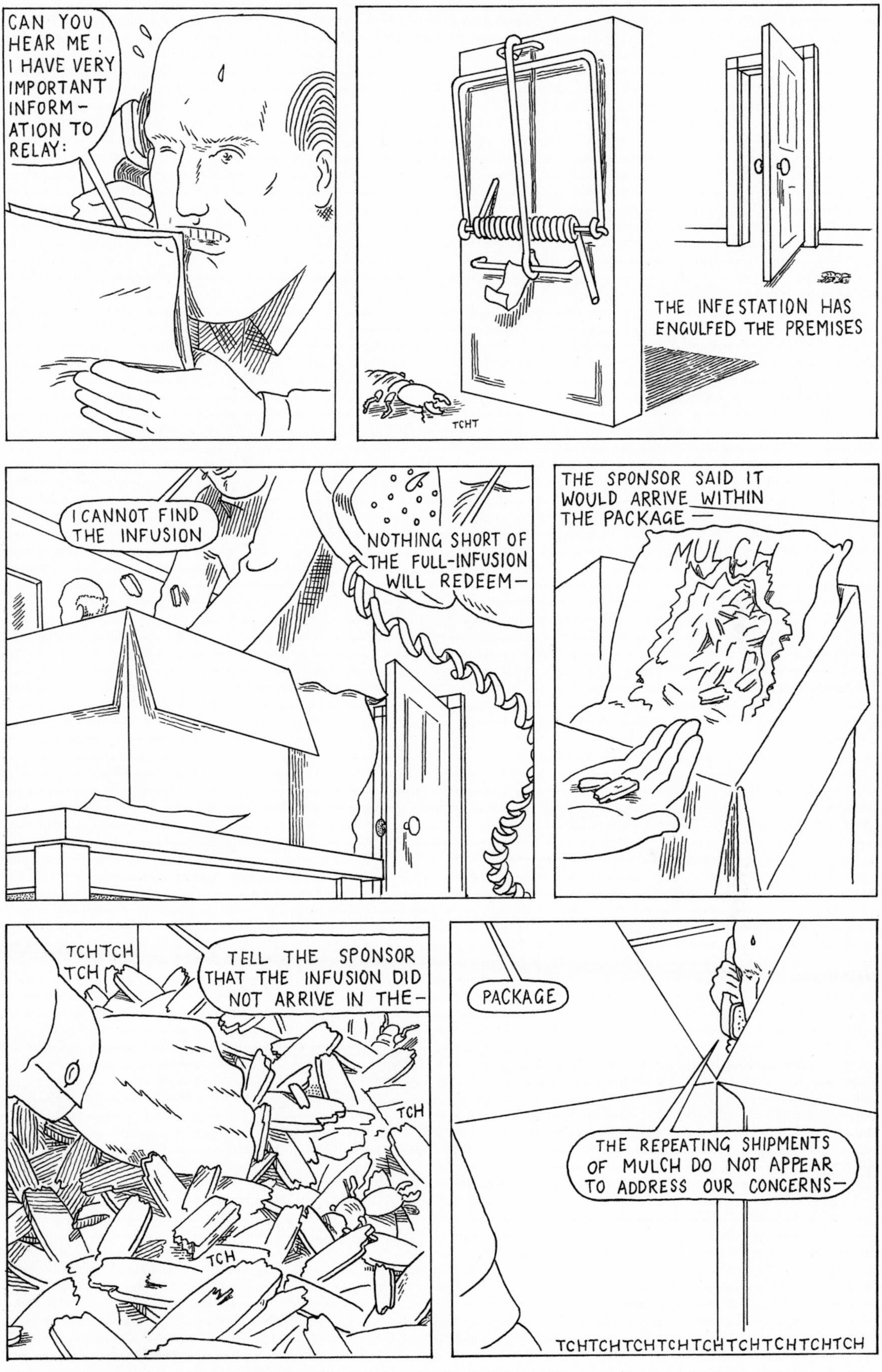
CAN YOU HEAR ME! I HAVE VERY IMPORTANT INFORM-ATION TO RELAY:
THE INFESTATION HAS ENGULFED THE PREMISES
TCHT
I CANNOT FIND THE INFUSION
NOTHING SHORT OF THE FULL-INFUSION WILL REDEEM-
THE SPONSOR SAID IT WOULD ARRIVE WITHIN THE PACKAGE—
MULCH
TCHTCH TCH
TELL THE SPONSOR THAT THE INFUSION DID NOT ARRIVE IN THE-
TCH
TCH
PACKAGE
THE REPEATING SHIPMENTS OF MULCH DO NOT APPEAR TO ADDRESS OUR CONCERNS-
TCHTCHTCHTCHTCHTCHTCHTCHTCH

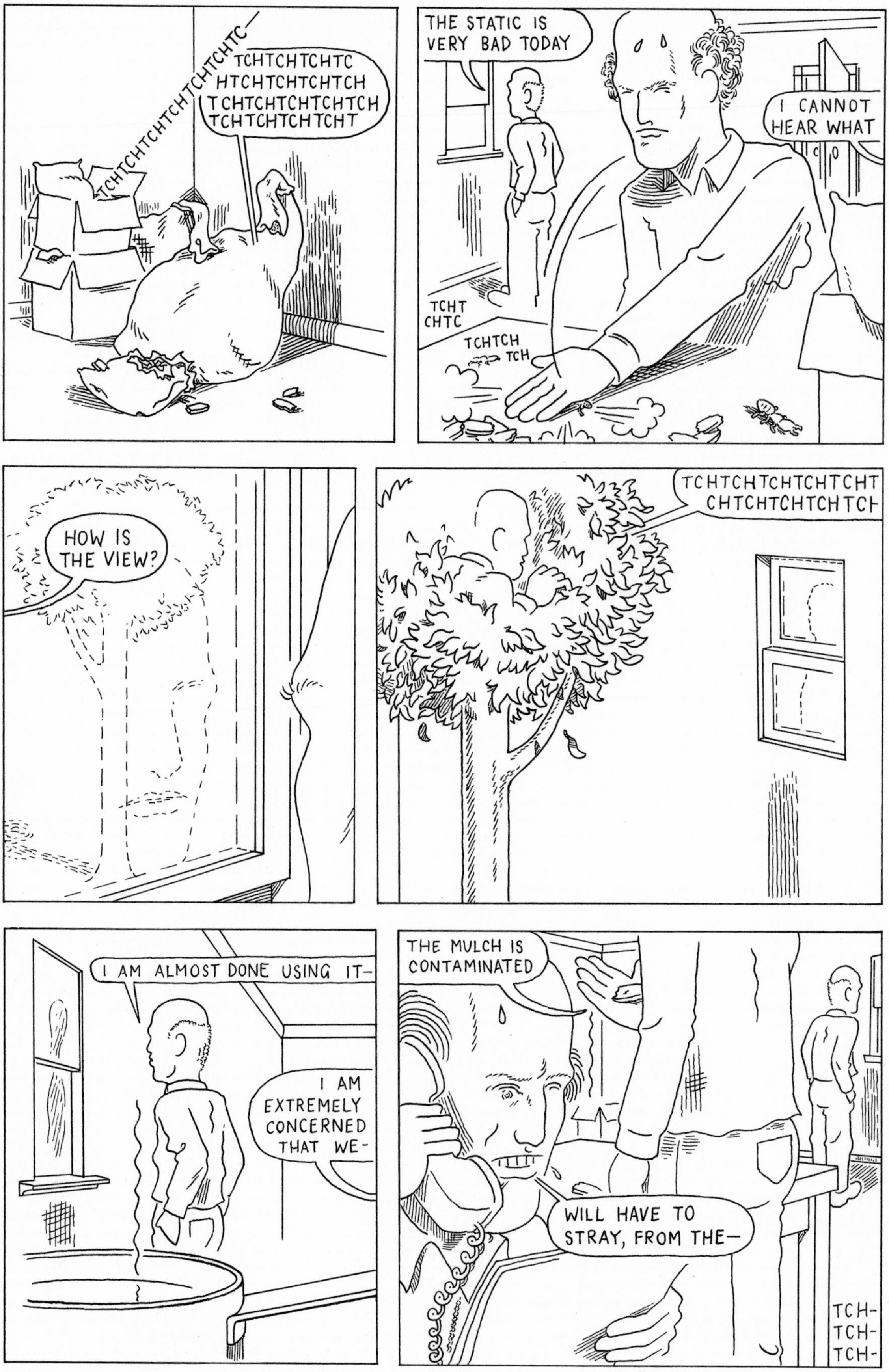
TCHTCHTCHTCHTCHTCHTC—
TCHTCHTCHTC HTCHTCHTCHTCH TCHTCHTCHTCHTCH TCHTCHTCHTCHT
THE STATIC IS VERY BAD TODAY
I CANNOT HEAR WHAT
TCHT CHTC
TCHTCH TCH
HOW IS THE VIEW?
TCHTCHTCHTCHTCHT CHTCHTCHTCHTCH
I AM ALMOST DONE USING IT—
I AM EXTREMELY CONCERNED THAT WE—
THE MULCH IS CONTAMINATED
WILL HAVE TO STRAY, FROM THE—
TCH- TCH- TCH-

PROVIDED-
INSTRUCTIONS:
I WILL DISPOSE OF THIS EXCESS-MULCH:
TCHTCHTCH TCHTCHTCH TCHTCHTCH TCHTCHTCH
THUB
TCHTCH
TCHTCH TCH
I AM SORRY WHAT DID YOU SAY I CANNOT HEAR YOU WELL—
PLEASE SPEAK UP THERE IS A HIGH VOLUME OF STATIC:
TCHTCHTCHTCHTCH-
TCH HTCHTCHTCHTCH
I CANNOT HEAR YOU OVER THE STATIC—
TCHTCH
TCHTCHTCH CHTCHTCHTCHT

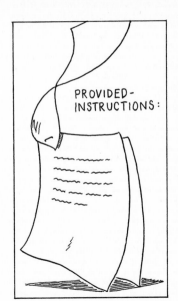

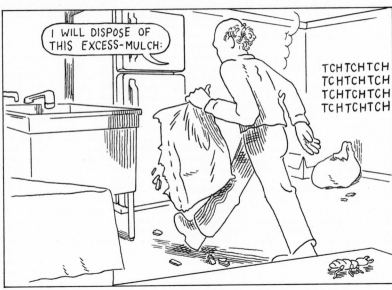

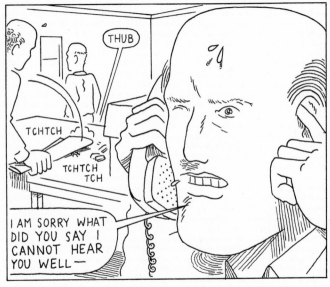

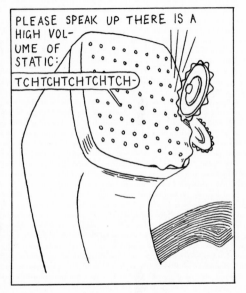

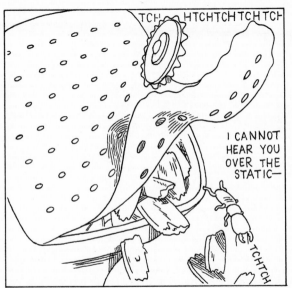

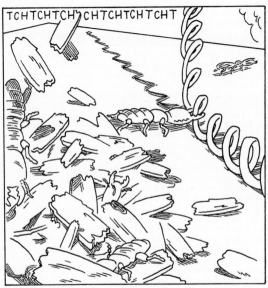

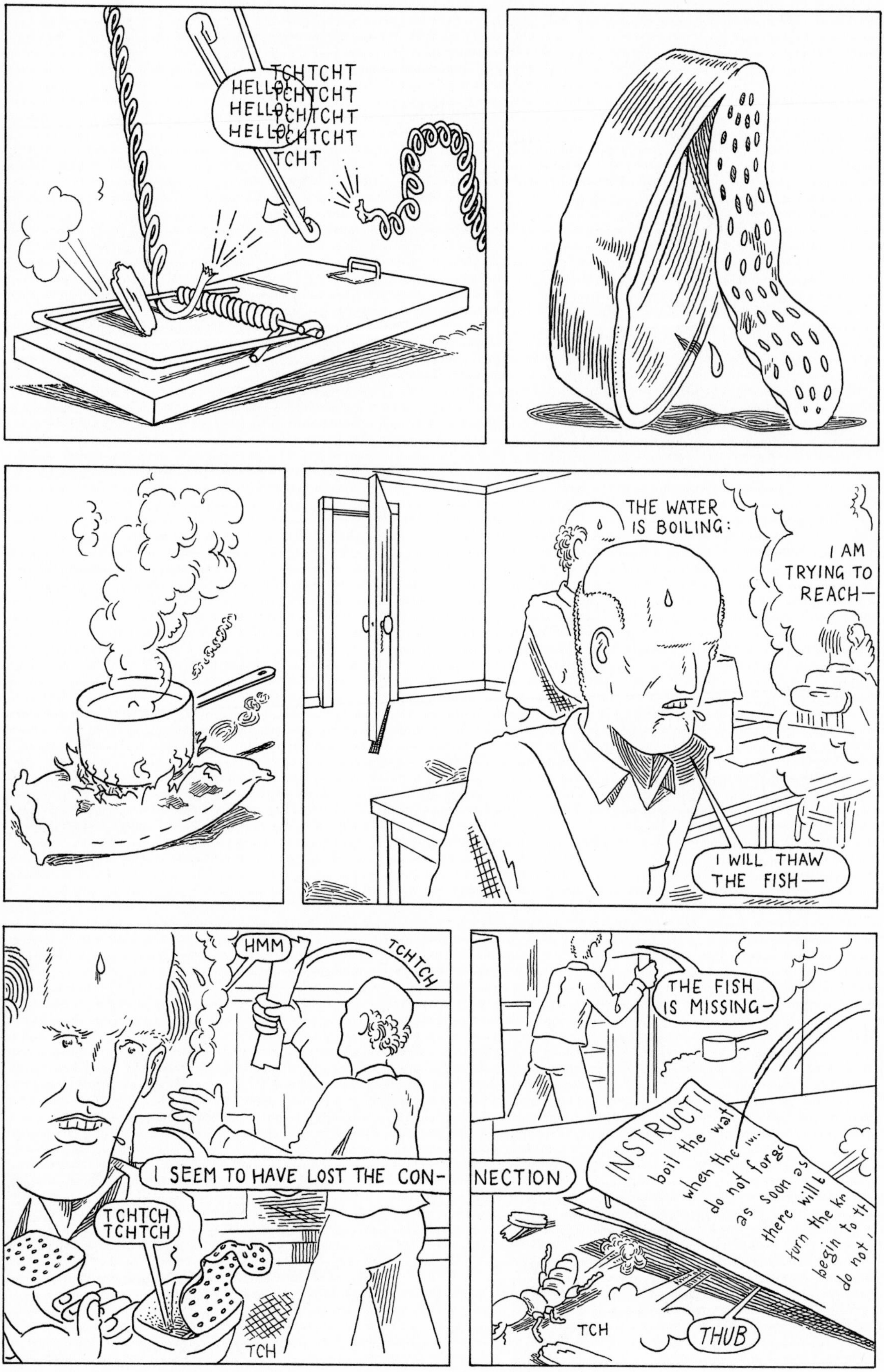
HELLO!
HELLO!
HELLO!
TCHTCHT
TCHTCHT
TCHTCHT
TCHTCHT
TCHT
THE WATER IS BOILING:
I AM TRYING TO REACH—
I WILL THAW THE FISH—
HMM
TCHTCH
I SEEM TO HAVE LOST THE CON-
TCHTCH TCHTCH
TCH
THE FISH IS MISSING—
NECTION
INSTRUCTI
boil the wat
when the
do not forg
as soon as
there will
turn the kn
begin to t
do not
TCH
THUB

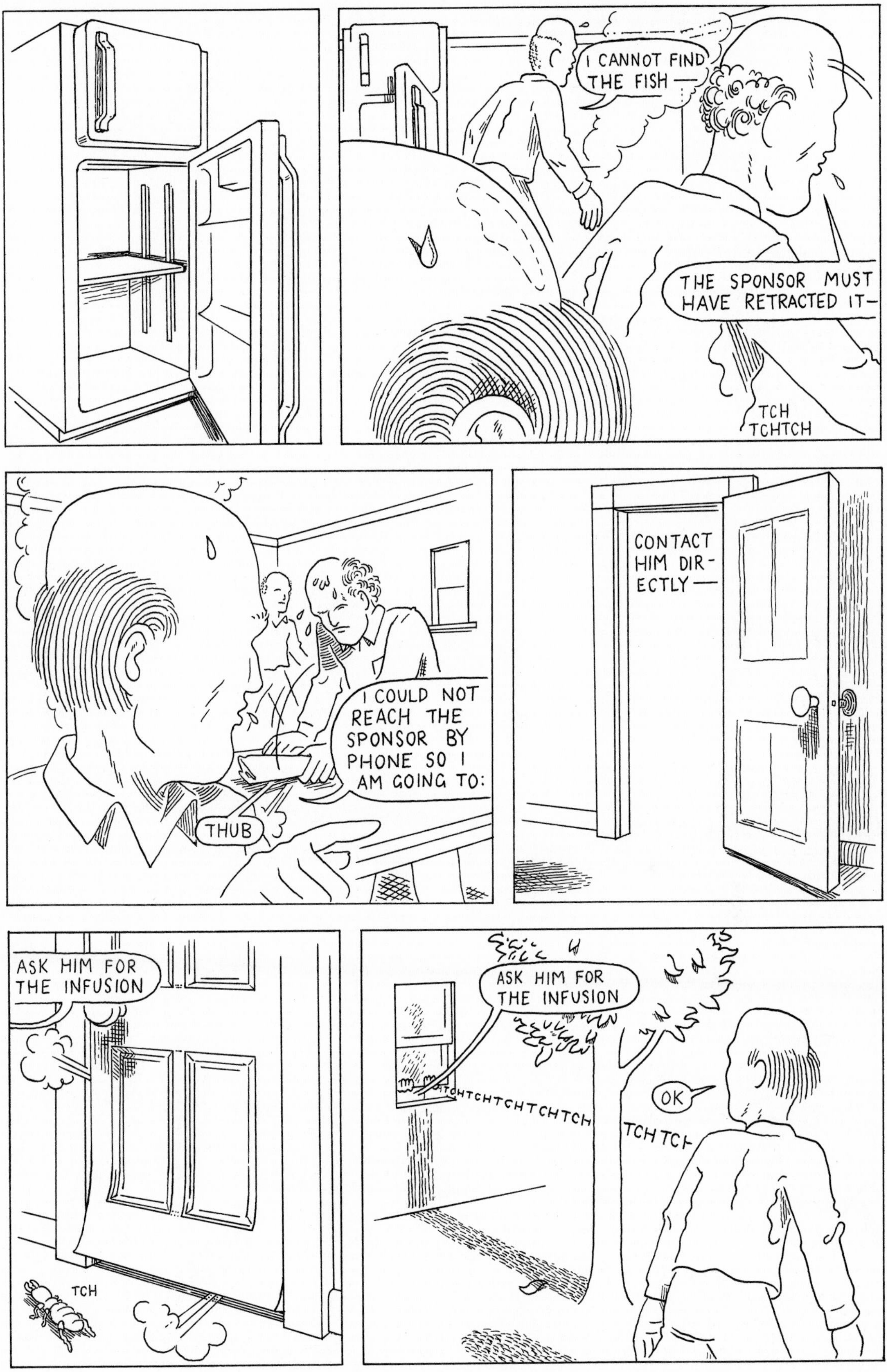
I CANNOT FIND THE FISH—
THE SPONSOR MUST HAVE RETRACTED IT—
TCH TCHTCH
I COULD NOT REACH THE SPONSOR BY PHONE SO I AM GOING TO:
THUB
CONTACT HIM DIR-ECTLY—
ASK HIM FOR THE INFUSION
TCH
ASK HIM FOR THE INFUSION
TCHTCHTCHTCHTCH
TCHTCH
OK

TCHTCHTCHTCHT
TCHTCHTCHTCHTCHT
TCHTCHTCHTCHTCHTCH
TCHTCHTCHTCHTCHTCH
TCHTCHTCHTCHTCHTCH
TCHTCHTCHTCHTCHTCH
TCHTCHTCHTCHTCHTCH
TCHTCHTCHTCHTCHTCH
TCHTCHTCHTCHTCHTCH
TCHTCHTCHTCHTCH
TCHTCHTCHTCHTC
TCHTCHTCHT
I HOPE HE IS NEARBY—
THE SINK HAS CLOGGED —

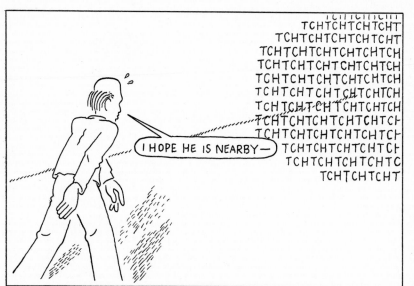

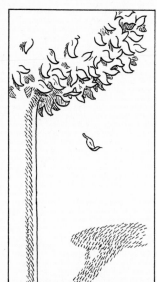

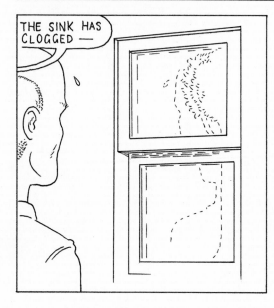

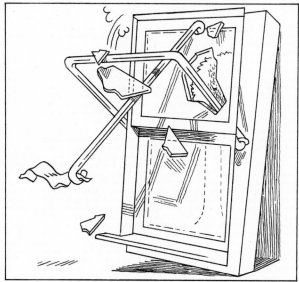

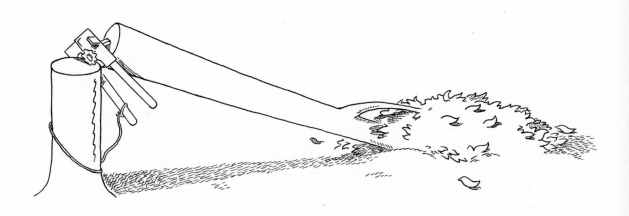

The Inspection of Shopping Carts

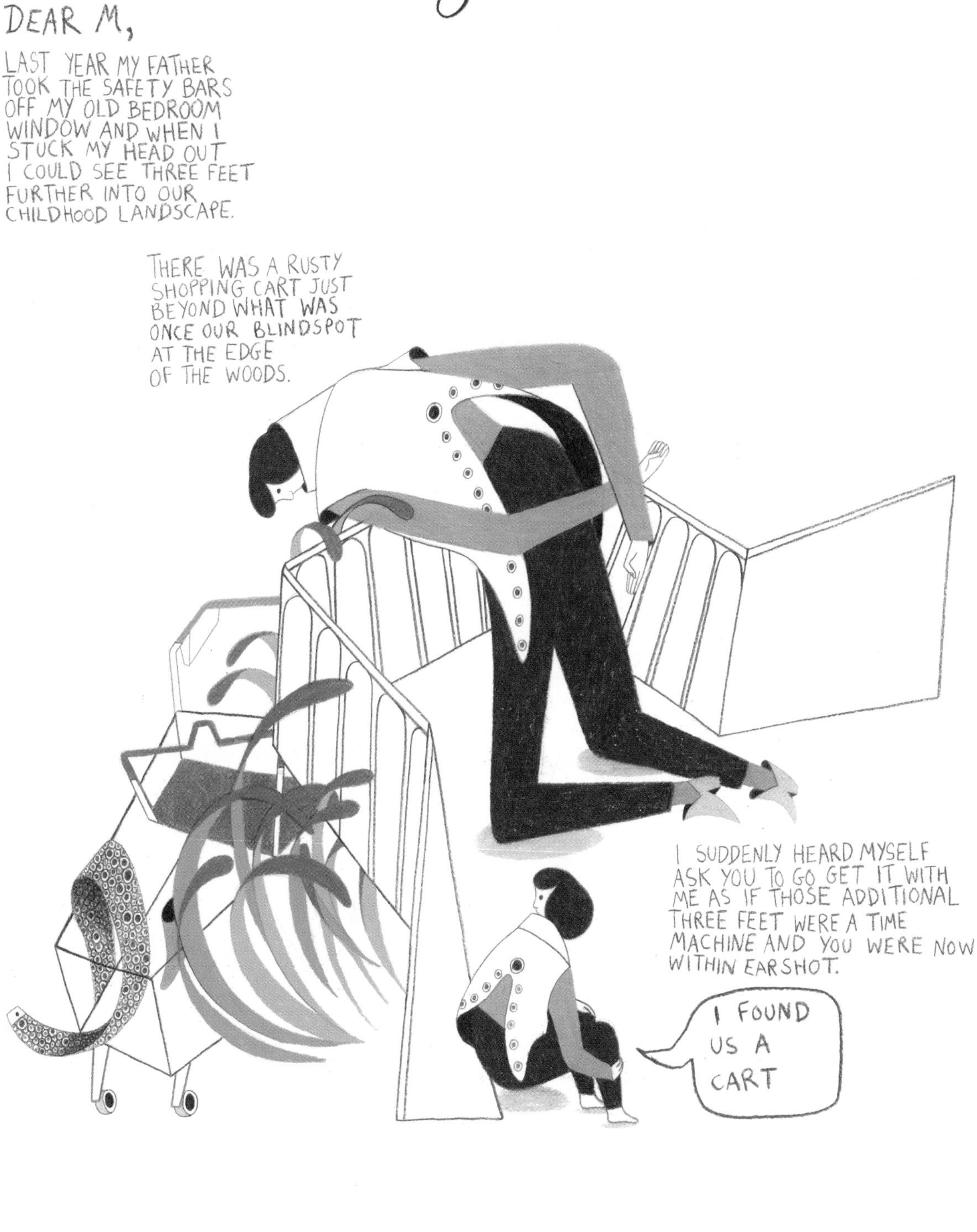
DEAR M,
LAST YEAR MY FATHER TOOK THE SAFETY BARS OFF MY OLD BEDROOM WINDOW AND WHEN I STUCK MY HEAD OUT I COULD SEE THREE FEET FURTHER INTO OUR CHILDHOOD LANDSCAPE.
THERE WAS A RUSTY SHOPPING CART JUST BEYOND WHAT WAS ONCE OUR BLINDSPOT AT THE EDGE OF THE WOODS.
I SUDDENLY HEARD MYSELF ASK YOU TO GO GET IT WITH ME AS IF THOSE ADDITIONAL THREE FEET WERE A TIME MACHINE AND YOU WERE NOW WITHIN EARSHOT.
I FOUND US A CART

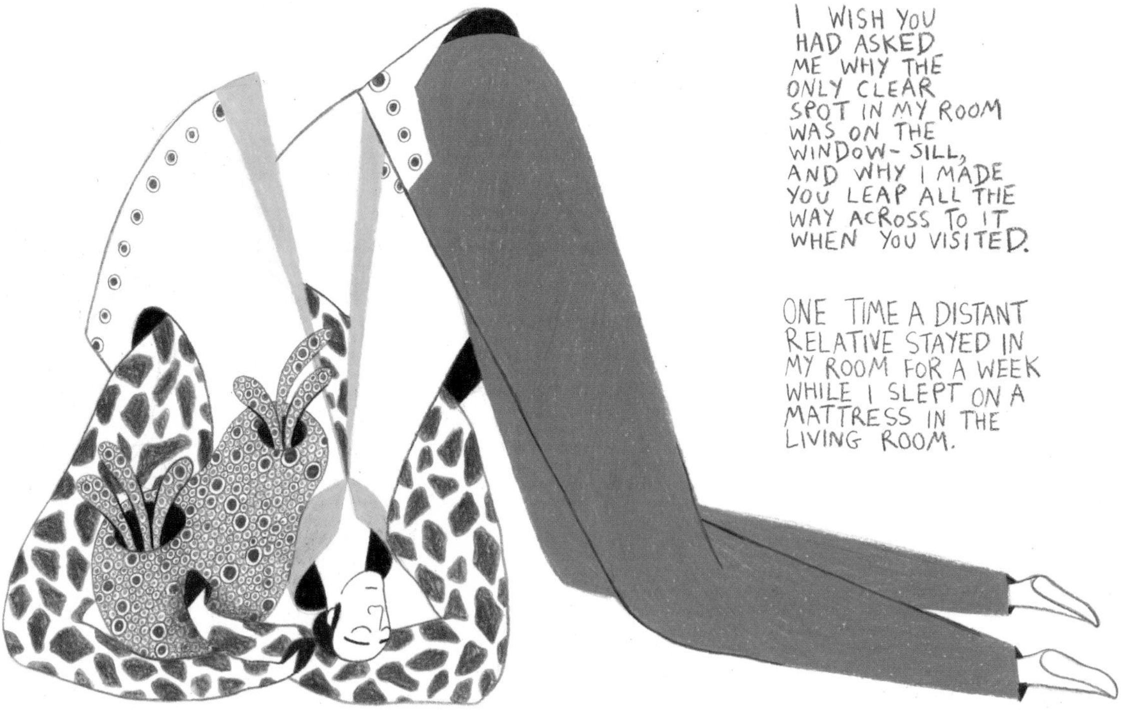
I WISH YOU HAD ASKED ME WHY THE ONLY CLEAR SPOT IN MY ROOM WAS ON THE WINDOW-SILL, AND WHY I MADE YOU LEAP ALL THE WAY ACROSS TO IT WHEN YOU VISITED.
ONE TIME A DISTANT RELATIVE STAYED IN MY ROOM FOR A WEEK WHILE I SLEPT ON A MATTRESS IN THE LIVING ROOM.

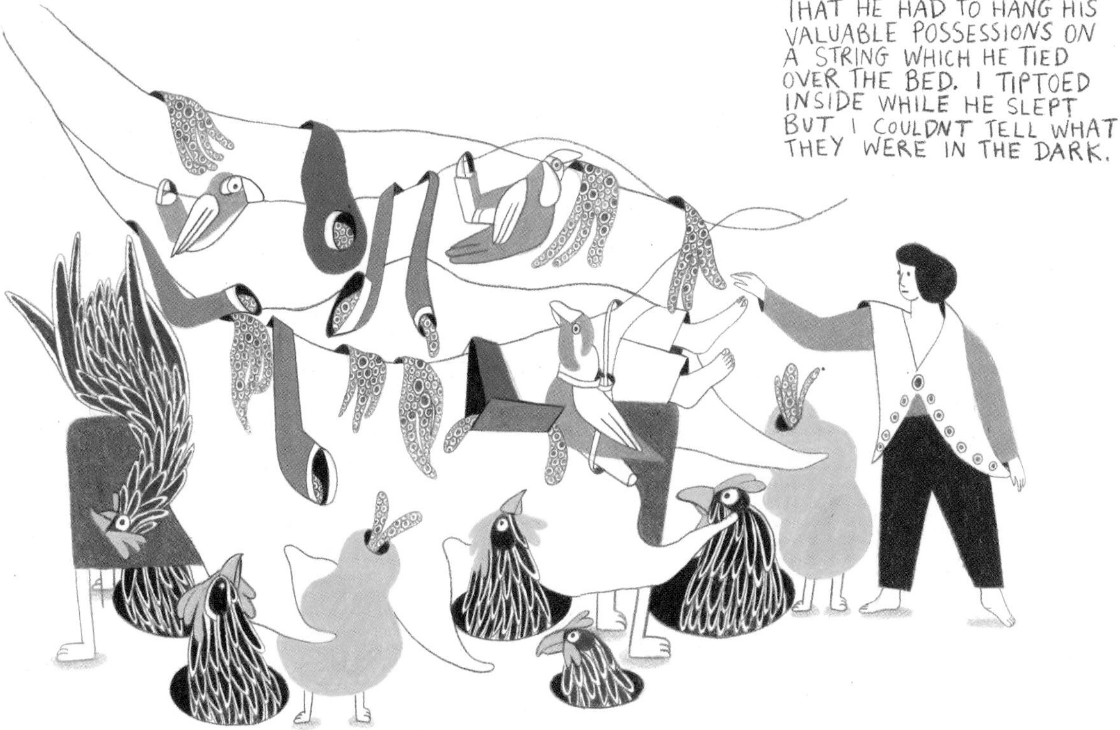
MY ROOM WAS SO CHAOTIC THAT HE HAD TO HANG HIS VALUABLE POSSESSIONS ON A STRING WHICH HE TIED OVER THE BED. I TIPTOED INSIDE WHILE HE SLEPT BUT I COULDN'T TELL WHAT THEY WERE IN THE DARK.

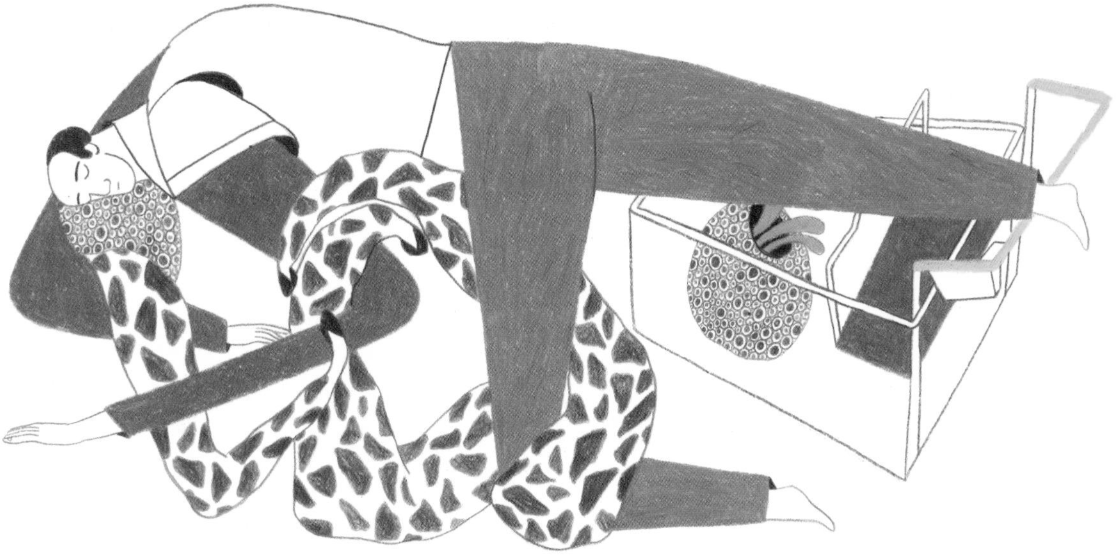
I OPENED THE WINDOW HOPING THAT ONE OF HIS TREASURES WOULD FALL AND DISAPPEAR INTO THE PILES OF MESS ON THE FLOOR.

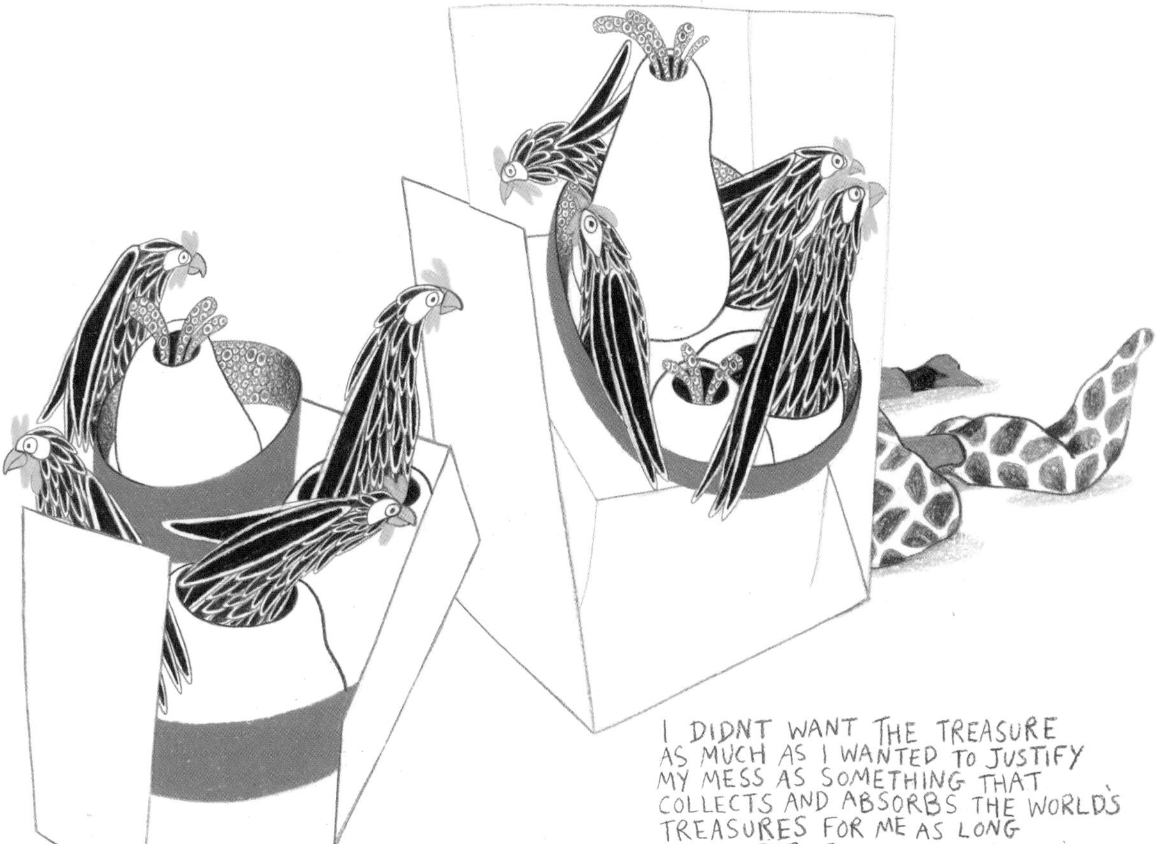
I DIDNT WANT THE TREASURE AS MUCH AS I WANTED TO JUSTIFY MY MESS AS SOMETHING THAT COLLECTS AND ABSORBS THE WORLD'S TREASURES FOR ME AS LONG AS I KEEP IT IN THE SAME CONFIGURATION SO THAT I COULD REMAIN AN INNOCENT THIEF.

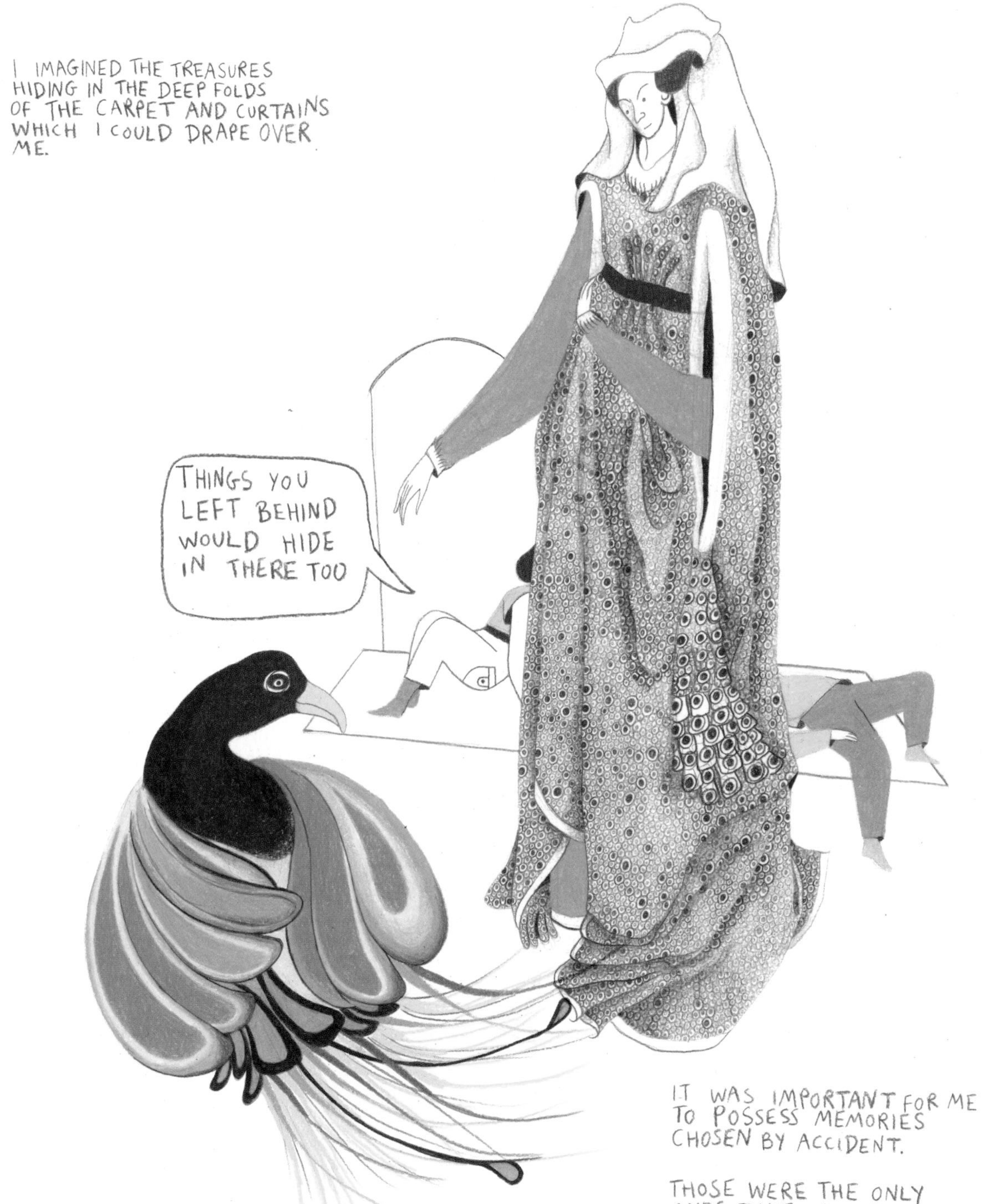
I IMAGINED THE TREASURES HIDING IN THE DEEP FOLDS OF THE CARPET AND CURTAINS WHICH I COULD DRAPE OVER ME.
THINGS YOU LEFT BEHIND WOULD HIDE IN THERE TOO
IT WAS IMPORTANT FOR ME TO POSSESS MEMORIES CHOSEN BY ACCIDENT.
THOSE WERE THE ONLY ONES THAT WOULD GROW CLEARER WITH TIME UNTIL ONE DAY YOU WILL EMERGE IN MY THOUGHTS LONG ENOUGH TO ANSWER.

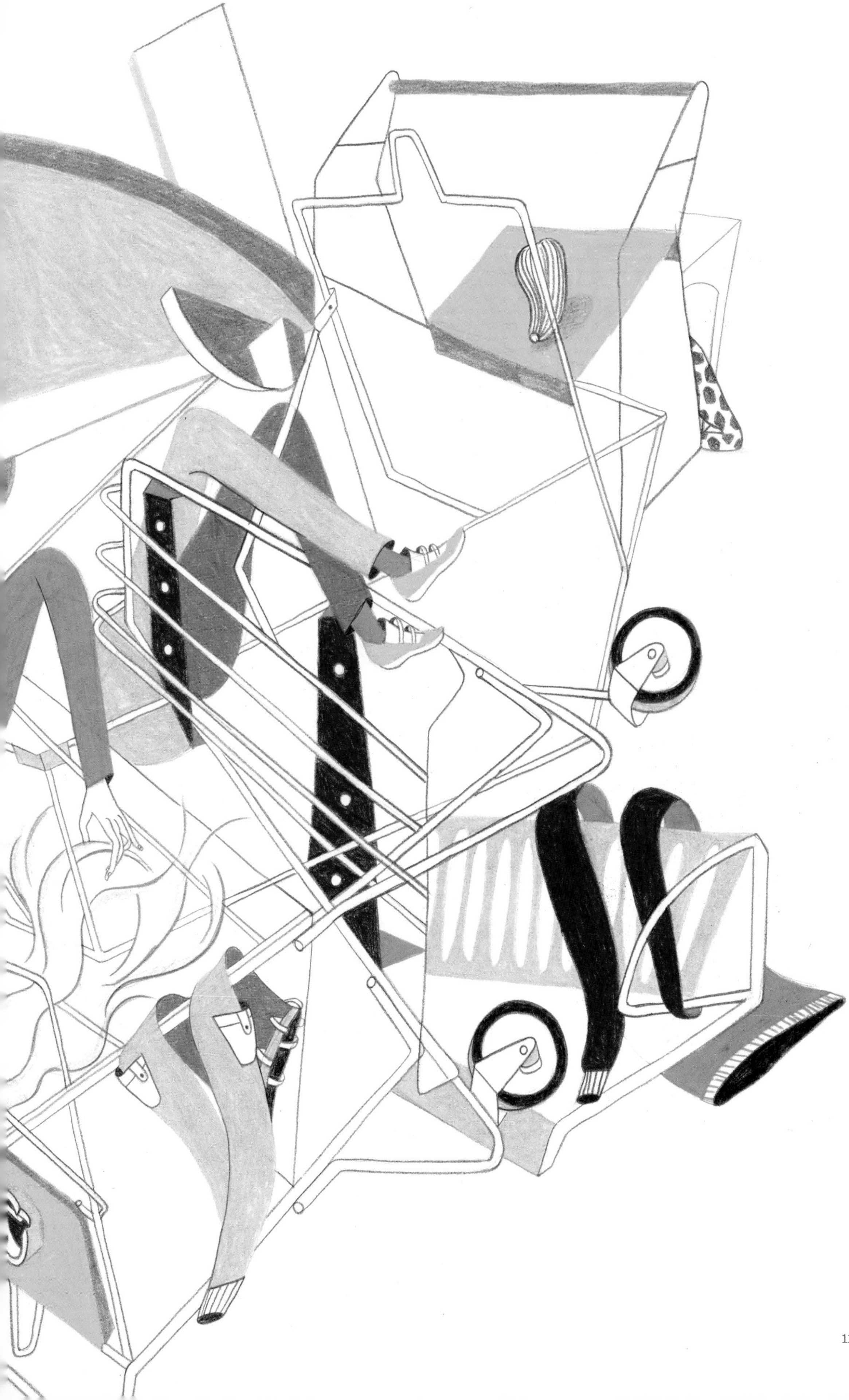

WHEN I MOVED TO COLLEGE
I PILED THE CONTENT OF
MY ROOM INTO THAT
SHOPPING CART.

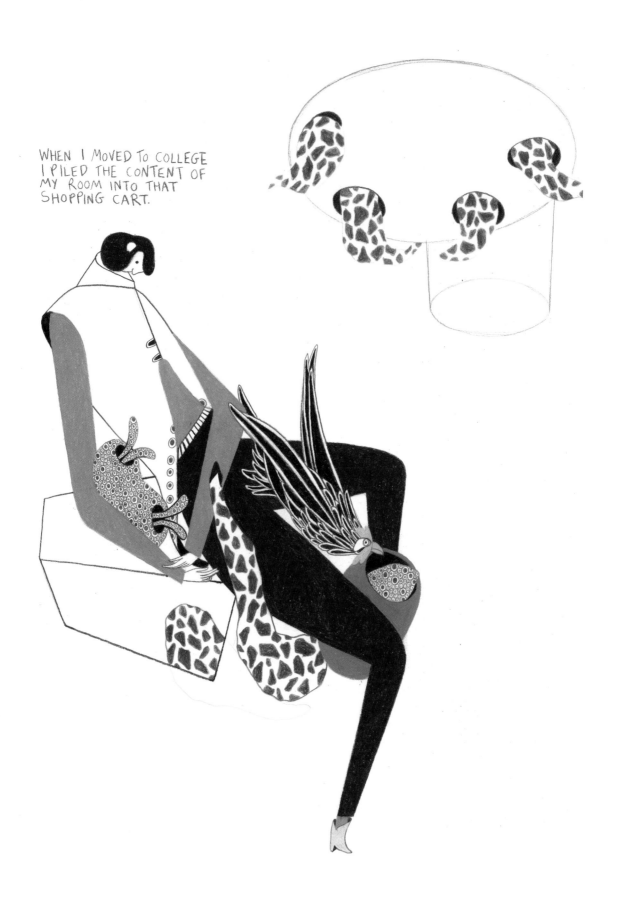

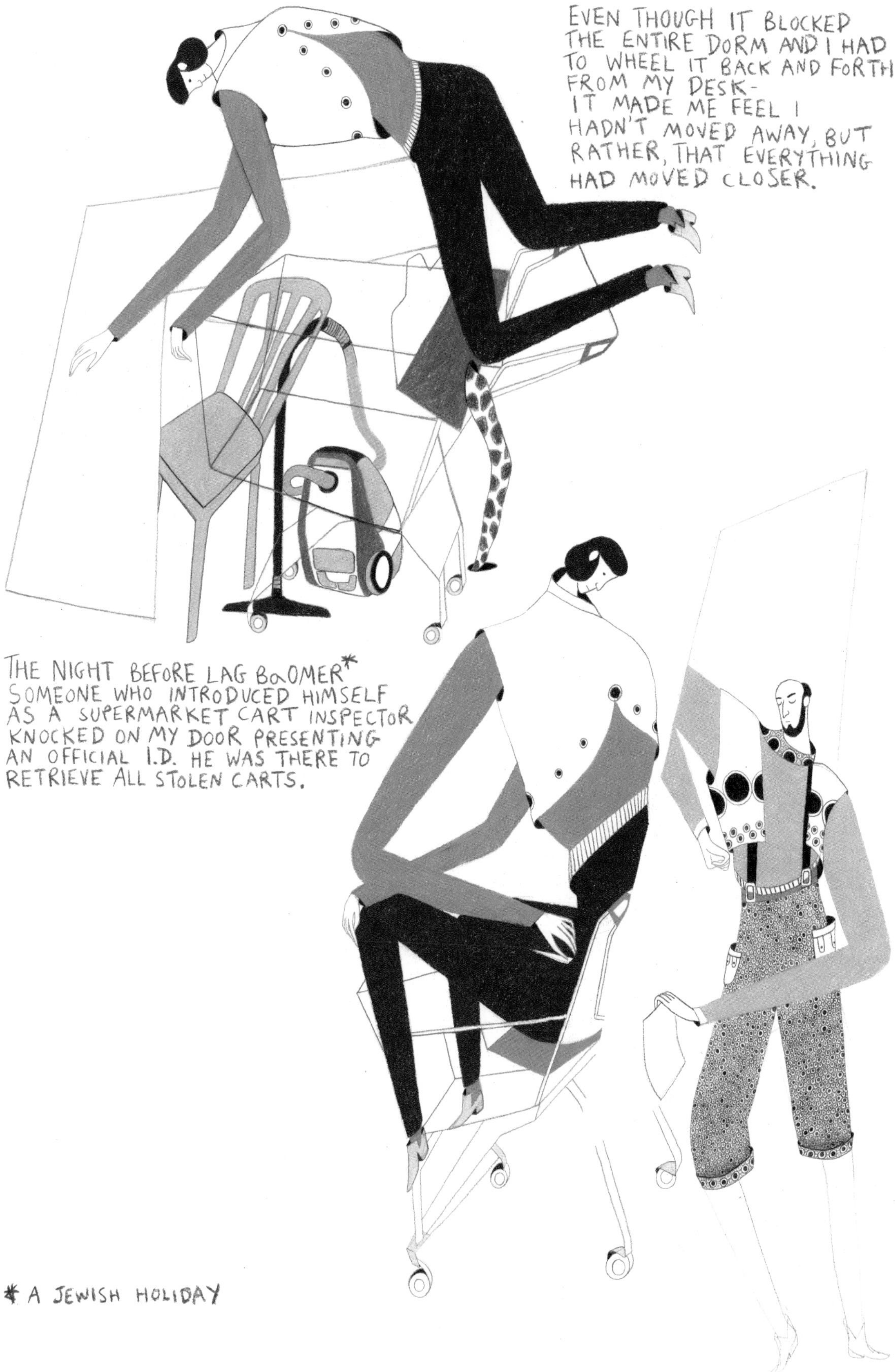
EVEN THOUGH IT BLOCKED THE ENTIRE DORM AND I HAD TO WHEEL IT BACK AND FORTH FROM MY DESK- IT MADE ME FEEL I HADN'T MOVED AWAY, BUT RATHER, THAT EVERYTHING HAD MOVED CLOSER.
THE NIGHT BEFORE LAG BaOMER* SOMEONE WHO INTRODUCED HIMSELF AS A SUPERMARKET CART INSPECTOR KNOCKED ON MY DOOR PRESENTING AN OFFICIAL I.D. HE WAS THERE TO RETRIEVE ALL STOLEN CARTS.
* A JEWISH HOLIDAY

LIKE EVERY YEAR AFTER LAG BaOMER,
THE STREETS WERE SCATTERED WITH
ROGUE SHOPPING CARTS WHICH HAD
BEEN STOLEN AND FILLED TO THE RIM
WITH SCRAPS OF WOOD AND FURNITURE
AND DRIVEN BY FEARLESS KIDS ON
THEIR WAY TO THE BONFIRES.

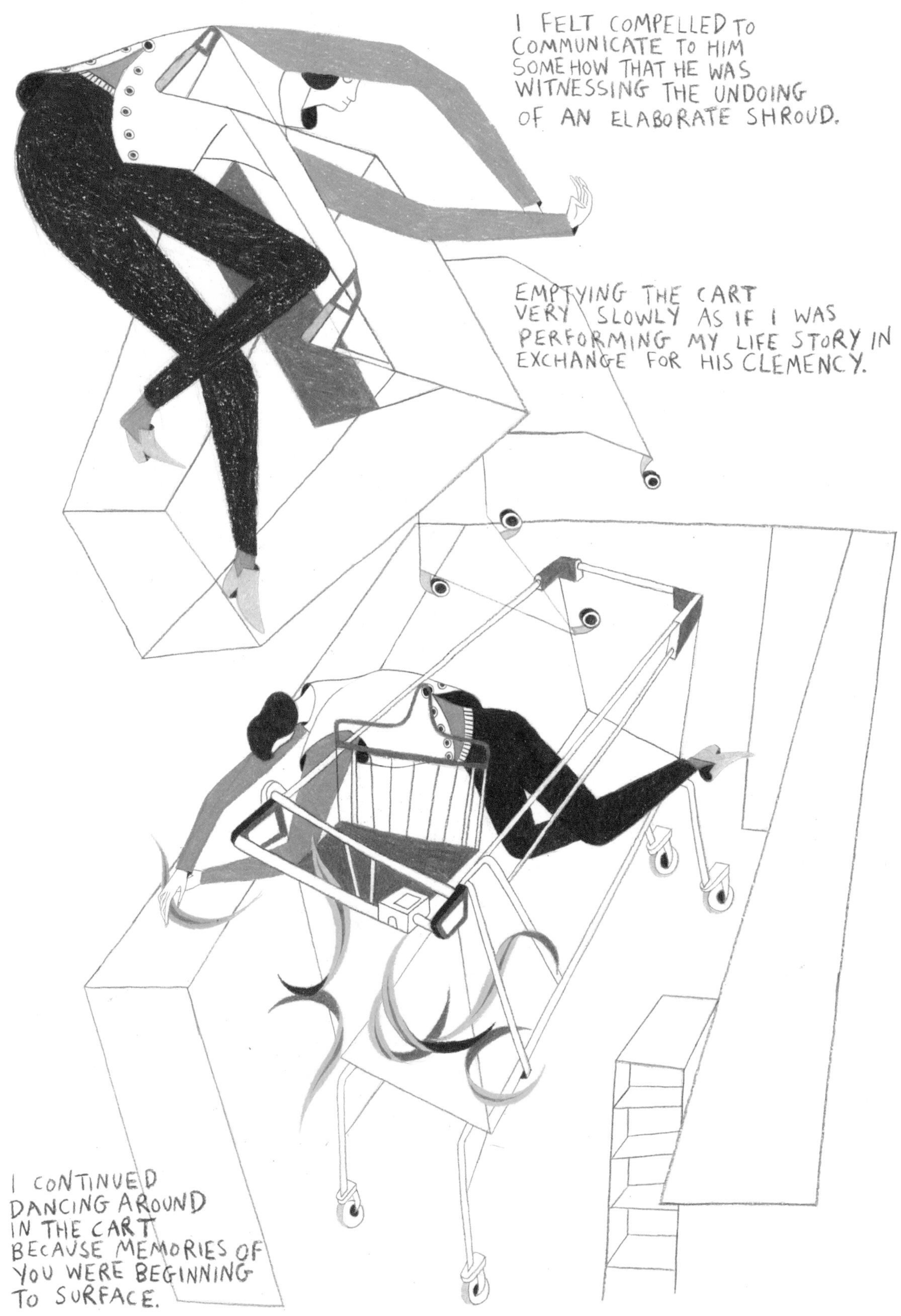
I FELT COMPELLED TO COMMUNICATE TO HIM SOMEHOW THAT HE WAS WITNESSING THE UNDOING OF AN ELABORATE SHROUD.
EMPTYING THE CART VERY SLOWLY AS IF I WAS PERFORMING MY LIFE STORY IN EXCHANGE FOR HIS CLEMENCY.
I CONTINUED DANCING AROUND IN THE CART BECAUSE MEMORIES OF YOU WERE BEGINNING TO SURFACE.

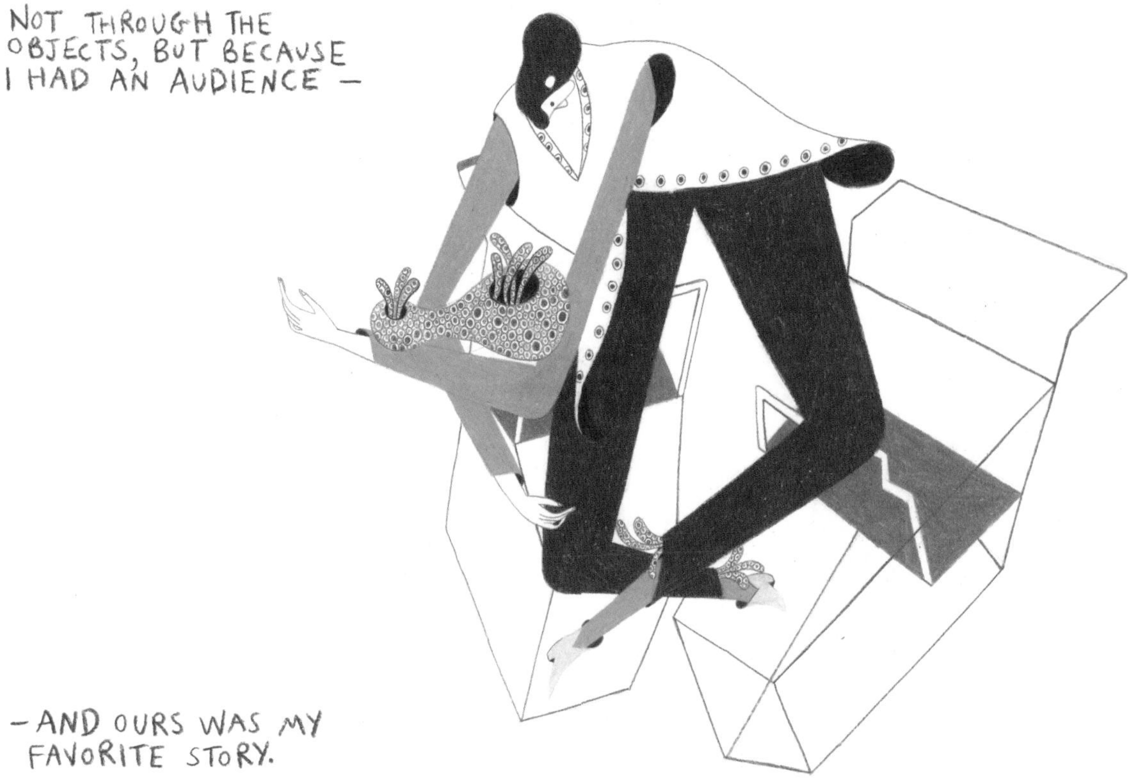
NOT THROUGH THE OBJECTS, BUT BECAUSE I HAD AN AUDIENCE —

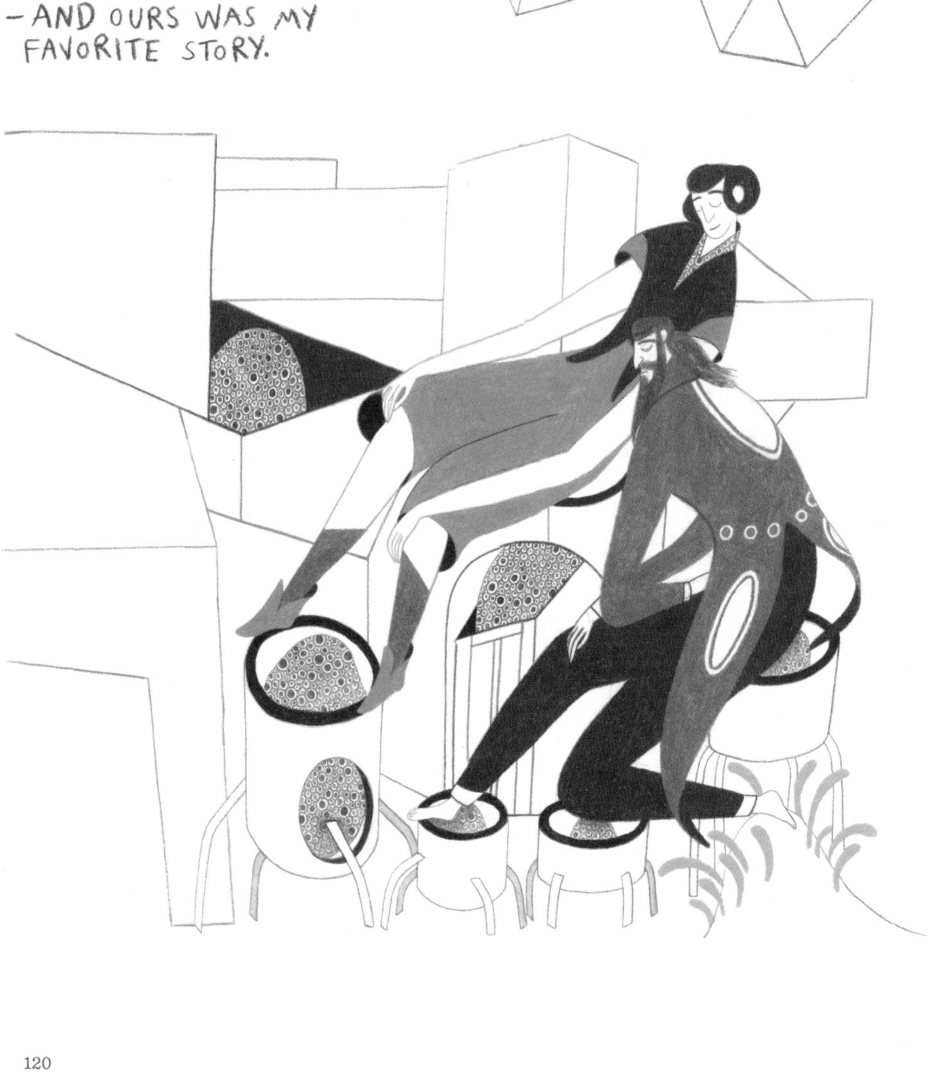
— AND OURS WAS MY FAVORITE STORY.

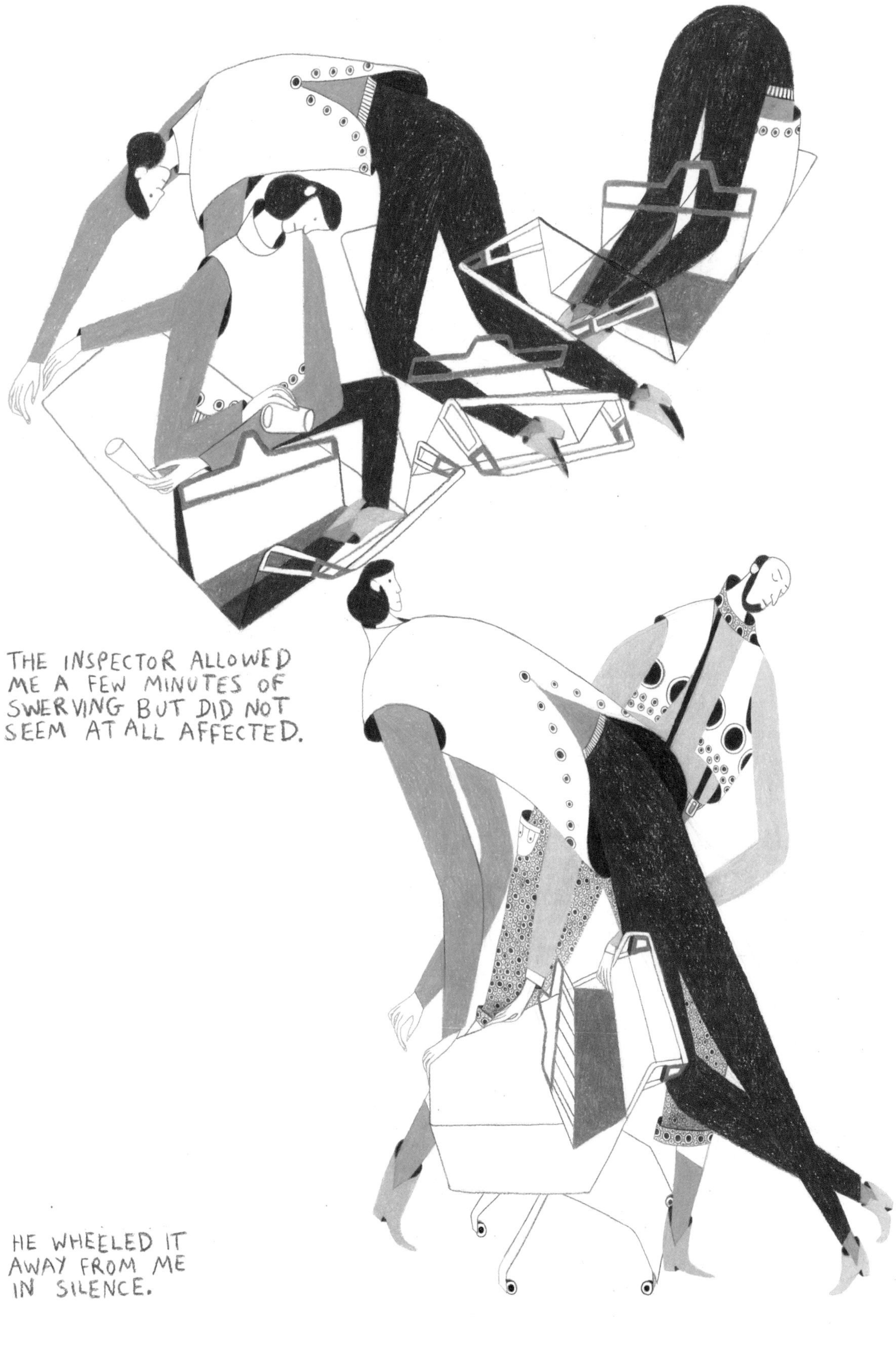
THE INSPECTOR ALLOWED ME A FEW MINUTES OF SWERVING BUT DID NOT SEEM AT ALL AFFECTED.
HE WHEELED IT AWAY FROM ME IN SILENCE.

THE NEXT DAY I WALKED
TO THE SUPERMARKET
ACROSS THE STREET AND
MIMICKED THE THINGS
I SAW BEING PLACED
IN THE CARTS BY
THE OTHER CUSTOMERS.

I WALKED HOME WITH
THE CART IN BROAD
DAYLIGHT, UNABLE TO
RELEASE IT FROM MY GRIP,
WISHING FOR THE WHEELS
TO BREAK OFF BEFORE I FIND
MYSELF DANCING AGAIN
IN FRONT OF AN AUDIENCE
WHICH ISN'T YOU.

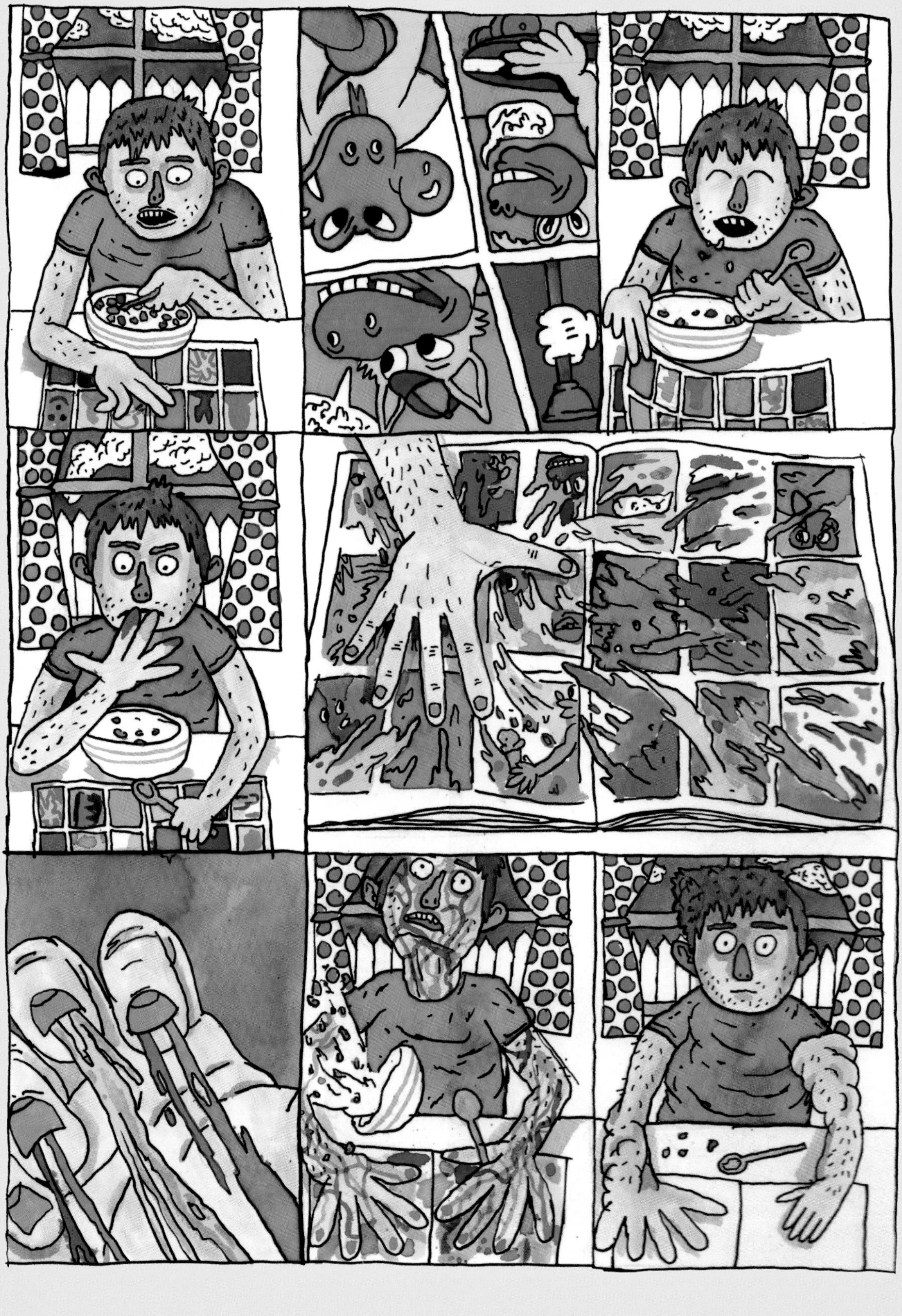

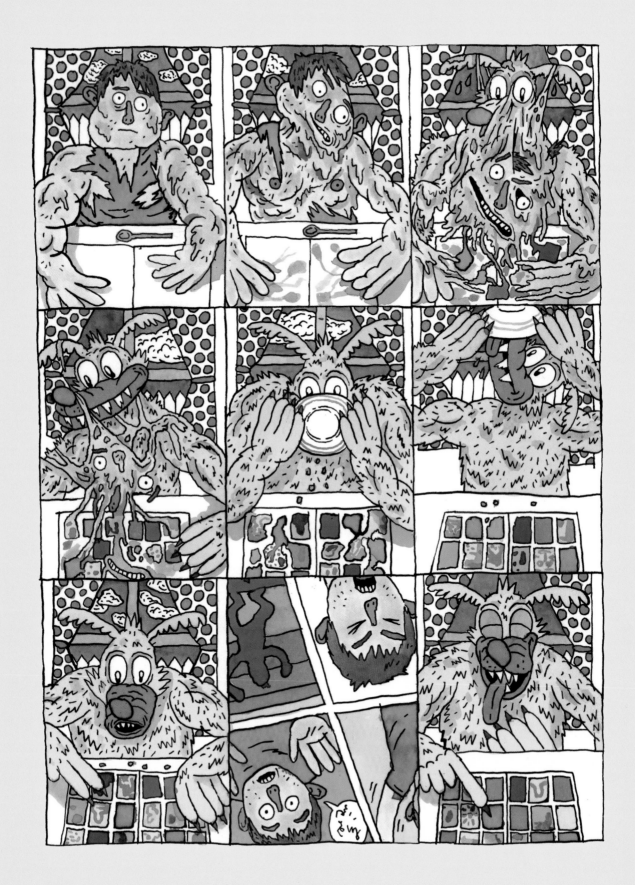

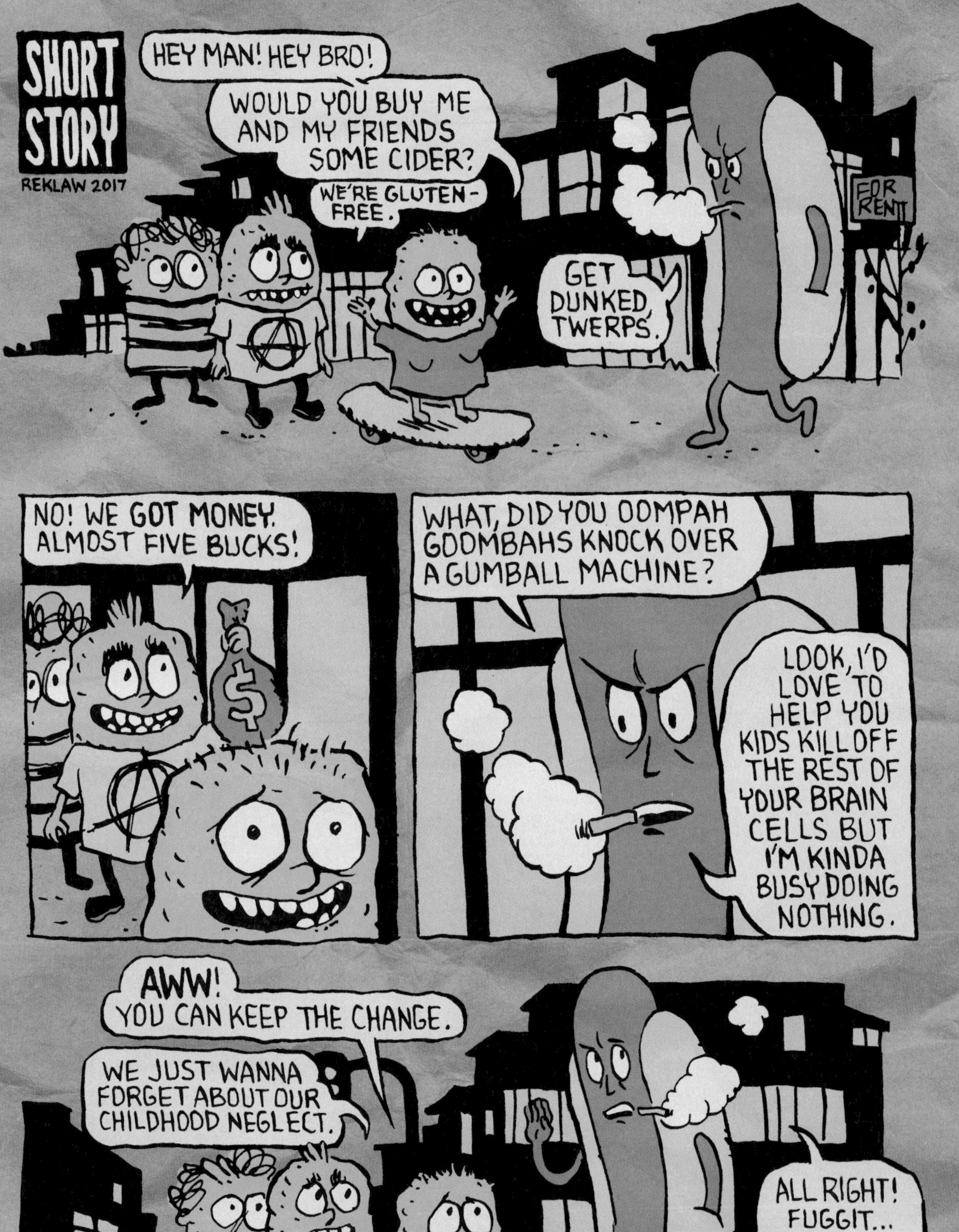
SHORT STORY
REKLAW 2017
HEY MAN! HEY BRO!
WOULD YOU BUY ME AND MY FRIENDS SOME CIDER?
WE'RE GLUTEN-FREE.
FOR RENT
GET DUNKED, TWERPS.
NO! WE GOT MONEY. ALMOST FIVE BUCKS!
WHAT, DID YOU OOMPAH GOOMBAHS KNOCK OVER A GUMBALL MACHINE?
LOOK, I'D LOVE TO HELP YOU KIDS KILL OFF THE REST OF YOUR BRAIN CELLS BUT I'M KINDA BUSY DOING NOTHING.
AWW! YOU CAN KEEP THE CHANGE.
WE JUST WANNA FORGET ABOUT OUR CHILDHOOD NEGLECT.
ALL RIGHT! FUGGIT... I GOTTA BUY CIGARETTES ANYWAY.

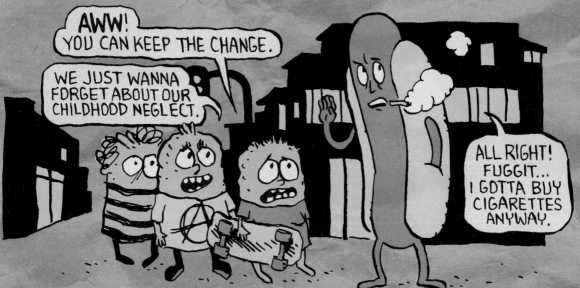

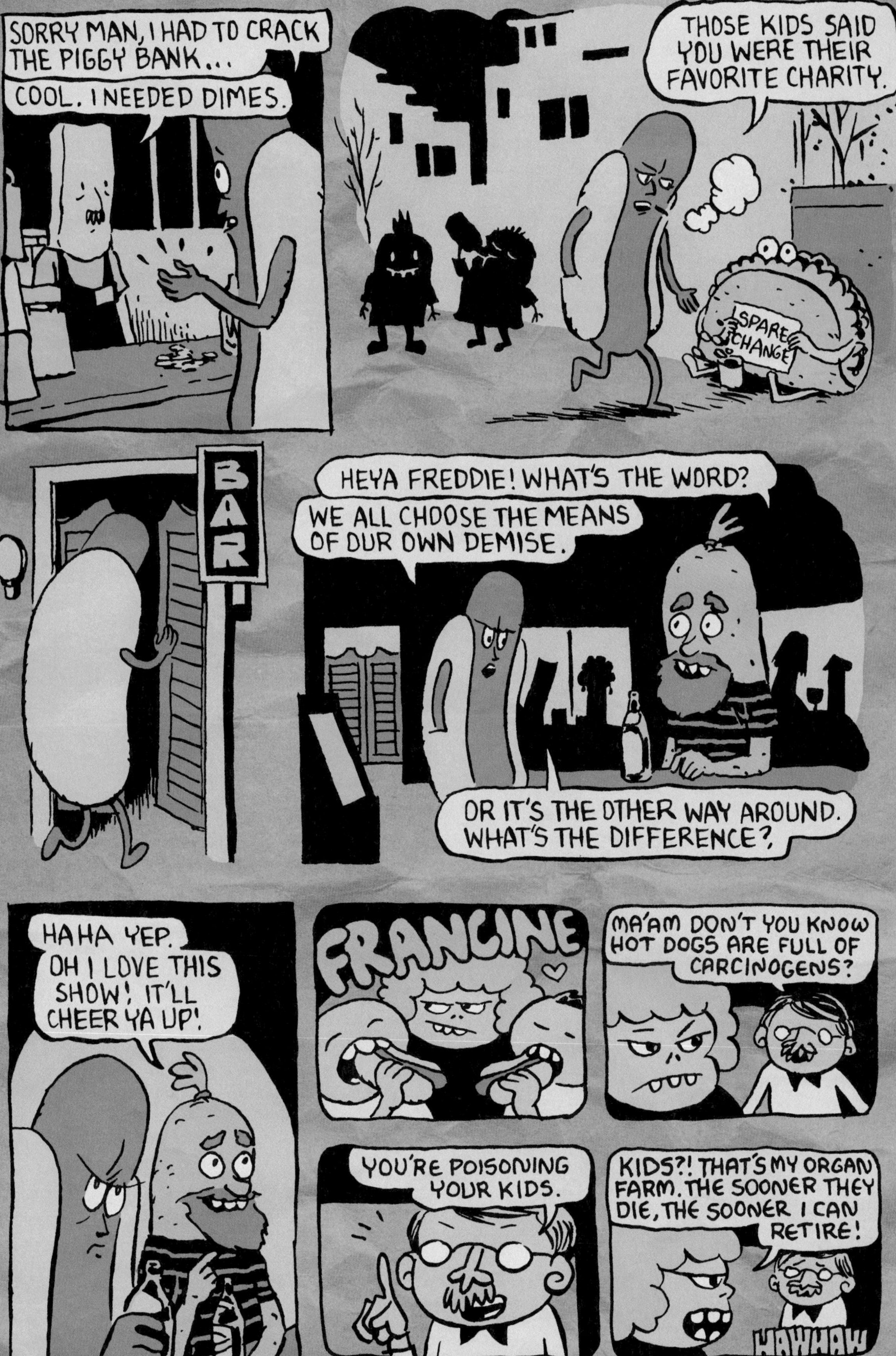
SORRY MAN, I HAD TO CRACK THE PIGGY BANK...
COOL. I NEEDED DIMES.
THOSE KIDS SAID YOU WERE THEIR FAVORITE CHARITY.
SPARE CHANGE
BAR
HEYA FREDDIE! WHAT'S THE WORD?
WE ALL CHOOSE THE MEANS OF OUR OWN DEMISE.
OR IT'S THE OTHER WAY AROUND. WHAT'S THE DIFFERENCE?
HAHA YEP. OH I LOVE THIS SHOW! IT'LL CHEER YA UP!
FRANCINE
MA'AM DON'T YOU KNOW HOT DOGS ARE FULL OF CARCINOGENS?
YOU'RE POISONING YOUR KIDS.
KIDS?! THAT'S MY ORGAN FARM. THE SOONER THEY DIE, THE SOONER I CAN RETIRE!
HAWHAW

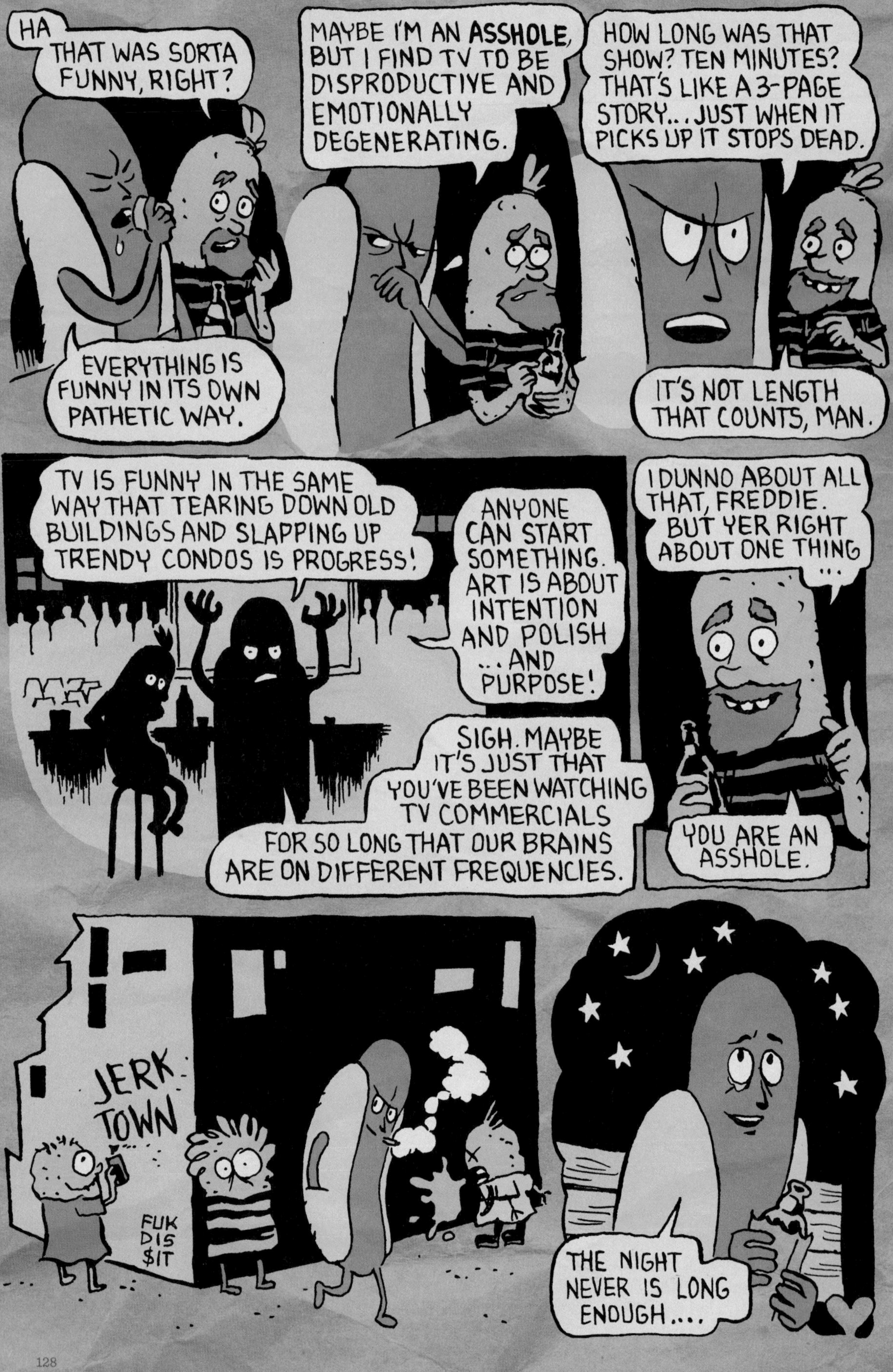
HA
THAT WAS SORTA FUNNY, RIGHT?
EVERYTHING IS FUNNY IN ITS OWN PATHETIC WAY.
MAYBE I'M AN ASSHOLE, BUT I FIND TV TO BE DISPRODUCTIVE AND EMOTIONALLY DEGENERATING.
HOW LONG WAS THAT SHOW? TEN MINUTES? THAT'S LIKE A 3-PAGE STORY... JUST WHEN IT PICKS UP IT STOPS DEAD.
IT'S NOT LENGTH THAT COUNTS, MAN.
TV IS FUNNY IN THE SAME WAY THAT TEARING DOWN OLD BUILDINGS AND SLAPPING UP TRENDY CONDOS IS PROGRESS!
ANYONE CAN START SOMETHING. ART IS ABOUT INTENTION AND POLISH ...AND PURPOSE!
SIGH. MAYBE IT'S JUST THAT YOU'VE BEEN WATCHING TV COMMERCIALS FOR SO LONG THAT OUR BRAINS ARE ON DIFFERENT FREQUENCIES.
I DUNNO ABOUT ALL THAT, FREDDIE. BUT YER RIGHT ABOUT ONE THING ...
YOU ARE AN ASSHOLE.
JERK TOWN
FUK DIS $IT
THE NIGHT NEVER IS LONG ENOUGH....